BOUNDLESS

BOOK SIX: AGE OF CONQUEST

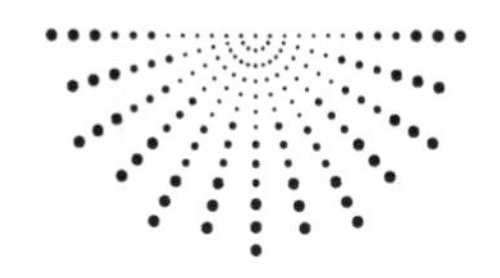

TAMARA LEIGH

TAMARA LEIGH

THE WULFRITHS. IT ALL BEGAN WITH A WOMAN.

A battle. A crown. The conqueror. The conquered. Medieval England—forever changed by the Battle of Hastings. And the rise of the formidable Wulfriths.

DECEIT WRAPPED IN SOMETHING SWEET

After aiding the English resistance who once more fail to reclaim their country from the invaders, Lady Marguerite returns home to Scotland in the aftermath of William the Conqueror's harrying of the North—and does not come alone. Accompanying the *Sparrow of King Malcolm's Court* is a warrior mistakenly believed her enemy, the price for which may be his irreparable loss of sight. Burdened by having laid the trap for a man she regrets not recognizing sooner, and strangely drawn to him, she determines she will be the one to tend this Norman. But that is possible only if he does not learn she is responsible for what could strip the warrior from him. When her deception is unveiled, will he reject what he has come to feel for her? When he leaves, will he take her heart with him?

A WARRIOR CAST IN SHADOWS DEEP

Gifted with a sense beyond the natural, which has made life seem more a sport than a battle, Sir Theriot D'Argent counts himself favored by God—until the night he aids villagers attacked by his fellow Normans and a good deed turns tragic. Stricken blind, his world reduced to shadows amid clouded light, he finds himself a prisoner of the King of Scotland and in the care of a lady whose voice and touch disturb as much as the belief her secrets are not hers alone. Will his sight be restored? Or is this divine punishment for aiding in England's conquest?

And what is he to do with feelings for the one whose trap ensnared him? Even were it possible to forgive her for a life cruelly altered, he would be a burden—and a danger for being unable to protect the lady from her murderous kin.

From Northern England to the Scotland of King Malcolm, the tale of Sir Theriot D'Argent and Lady Marguerite unfolds in the sixth book in the AGE OF CONQUEST series revealing the origins of the Wulfriths of the bestselling AGE OF FAITH series. Watch for LAWLESS: Book Seven releasing Spring 2021.

This novel is a work of fiction. Names, characters, places, incidents, and dialogues are either the product of the author's imagination or are used fictitiously. Any resemblance to actual events, locales, organizations, or persons, living or dead, is entirely coincidental and beyond the intent of the author.

Cover Design: Ravven

Ebook ISBN-13: 978-1-942326-50-2
Paperback ISBN-13: 978-1-942326-51-9

"For now we see through a glass, darkly; but then face to face: now I know in part; but then shall I know even as also I am known."
~ 1 Corinthians 13:12 KJV

PROLOGUE

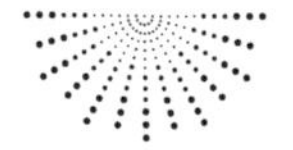

Northumbria, England
Late Summer, 1069

Her mother was dead. A year dead.

Dear Lord, the passing of four seasons! And no word sent nor warning given even this day.

Firming knees threatening to buckle, Marguerite stared at the weathered wood into which her own name was crudely carved and naught else—as if the woman beneath weed-infested earth had been no one's daughter, sister, wife, and mother.

She told herself it was wrong to hate the three standing with her, and yet it felt right, just as it had a year past when last she was here and the woman who had birthed her looked ten years older than she should.

A sudden chill making her wish for the plaid cloak she had not needed this warm day, silently she lamented, *I should have come sooner.*

"Dropped the firewood, clutched her chest, and landed on the hearth," her grandfather said. "Nothing for it but to dig a hole."

Marguerite gasped, and again when her uncle grunted agreement. "May you die without warning," he spoke the words cast at those one wished given no time to prepare for death, it believed in the absence of confession and absolution, ever the fallen were separated from God.

"Without warning," her cousin, Pepin, concurred.

As she struggled against screaming and setting herself at them, something in her head popped. Real or imagined, she did not know. What she knew was she had to leave. Hopefully, when Edgar the Aetheling, who had been granted sanctuary at the Scottish king's court, returned to England to battle the Normans, he would come through here and—

"Nay, even to think it is evil," she whispered.

"Do not speak that foul tongue," Uncle Gerald snapped.

She longed to continue in the language with which she was more familiar than her mother's, but it would delay her departure and might provoke a clash between her escort and kin.

Marguerite looked to the man who was her grandfather only for having sired her mother. In Norman-French with which he would find fault for an accent tempered by that of the Scots, she said, "We are leaving."

As she swung away, she sent heavenward, *Papa, I have no one now mama is with you and my brothers. I am alone.*

Or nearly so. The plump figure center of her escort hastened forward, skirts raised to sooner traverse the last of grass sucked dry of its green.

Cannie could not see the lone grave to which her mistress had been led, but likely she understood the elder Marguerite rested here beyond the fortress raised by her Norman family twenty-five years ago after crossing the channel by invitation of England's king—the childless Edward whose recent death had thrown wide the door to conquest of his kingdom by Duke William of Normandy.

Though this morn Marguerite had looked forward to sitting with her mother and filling an emptiness far different from this one, now hungry only for the comfort of Cannie's arms, she ran. Into a nightmare.

Beyond her escort, streaks of dark rain traveled horizontally, then the ten warriors handpicked by the King of Scots lurched forward.

"Nay!" she screamed.

They fell, and as Cannie looked around, she dropped, an arrow protruding from her back the same as her countrymen—eleven straight, feathered saplings refusing to bend in the breeze.

Marguerite landed on her knees beside the shuddering woman and reached to her, but grasped only air when she was yanked upright by the back of her gown.

"Those who fouled your blood are not your people," her uncle snarled.

She whipped around and, seeing her grandfather and cousin halt as if to observe something of interest, raked nails down Gerald's face. "Devils, all of you!"

Her uncle knocked her hand aside, gripped her neck, and thrust her distant.

Marguerite pried at the fingers denying her breath and kicked, but to no avail. Did something else inside her head pop?

Certes, the dimming of her sight was not imagined. Nor her grandfather's words. "Only enough to silence her, Gerald. I have plans for the half-breed."

What plans? she silently screamed, then all went black on this day of sunshine, sorrow, and horror.

~

AWAKENING on the floor of the gathering hall, Marguerite commanded herself to resume the breath of sleep. And attend to what was spoken beyond her.

"King Malcolm will retaliate," her uncle said. "You slew ten of his men, and he is fond of my niece."

Her grandfather gave a grunt of laughter. "Let him come. He will find no bodies to prove they arrived. And that half-breed…"

She shuddered. She had known she was not liked for her Scottish blood and the manner in which her sire took a Norman bride, but here was hatred. For this, which she had not fully understood when last she was here, her mother had been nearly cruel in ordering her to stay on her side of the border.

Had Marguerite known her namesake was dead, she would not have come. However, privy to Edgar the Aetheling's plans to lead an army out of Scotland to reclaim the English throne that was more his right than William the Conqueror's, she had feared for her mother. And King Malcolm, given to indulging the daughter of the man he had loved as a brother, had provided an escort who could not have known how emboldened her Norman kin by their countrymen's grip on England.

"Fear not, Gerald. We have only to keep her hidden until Patrick comes for her."

Here another reason her mother had not wished her to return. Her grandfather liked the Irish little more than the Scots, but his dealings with the man who had looked uncomfortably close upon his granddaughter were lucrative. And slavery was among the things in which the Irishman dealt.

Dear Lord, he intends to sell me to him, she sent heavenward.

"It could take weeks for the missive to find him and weeks longer before he arrives," her uncle said.

"Hence, we take her west on the morrow."

"What if one of our men talks?"

"Some are greedy enough to betray me for coin, but brave enough to venture forth if Malcolm comes? Brave enough to journey to Scotland and stand before that savage who might believe they were among those who put arrows in his men?"

"Still—"

"You worry like a woman!"

Scornful laughter ending on a cough alerted Marguerite another was here, and it was not her cousin, Pepin. "Heh, Gerald, our father regards you little better than he does me," creaked her younger uncle who was afflicted with a wasting sickness. More for him than their aging father, her mother had returned to her Norman family when her own mother passed. Marguerite liked Claude better than Gerald, but he was too sullen and demanding for her to feel kindly toward him beyond comparison to ones whom she now had cause to hate.

Almighty, forgive me, she sent heavenward, *but eleven are dead only for having served as my escort.*

"You are untouchable, wee brother," Gerald scorned. "That is nothing to be proud. Were you not—"

"Were I not infirm, we would resolve this with fists," Claude snarled. "And as I would be stronger of body than one who eats more than he moves, you would fall more heavily than I, *big* brother."

Boots pounded the floorboards, but her grandfather's shout halted his eldest son, then he barked, "Seek your brother's forgiveness, Claude!"

"You first told he behaved a woman, Father. Do you apologize, I will think on it."

"Claude!"

"I will not apologize!"

The silence of disbelief descended. Marguerite had not passed much time here while her mother tended her kin, but most of Claude's unpleasantness had been reserved for his sister and servants. When it spilled over, it had splashed the younger Marguerite, sprayed his brother, and misted his sire.

"Go, Gerald," her grandfather commanded. "Aid Pepin in concealing the bodies."

Her uncle cursed and slammed the door behind him.

"What is this, Claude? With what tongue do you speak?"

"An angry one."

"Why angry?"

"When last was I well-tended? While my sister lived. Though now my niece is here and can do for me what her mother did, you would give her to Patrick!"

"She would not stay!"

"She might."

"Non, and did we force her, the heathens would take her back."

"Possibly, but since you have slain Malcolm's men, we cannot test that, can we?"

"Their deaths were warranted. Diarmad the Mad abducted my daughter—twice!"

"Once!"

Marguerite's grandfather stepped nearer his son. "He took her and put babes in her belly. Now I have taken the one babe the Lord allowed to survive and the lives of her escort as payment. And they are not enough!"

"Then you can collect further payment when Malcolm sends his forces. *If* you and my brother survive."

"Silence!" Boots sounded again.

"Where do you go?" Claude called.

"I have a missive to write. Shout when she rouses."

His footsteps echoed down the passage, then the door of his private chamber closed.

Marguerite opened her eyes. Past a curtain of dark hair, she saw she was against the wall opposite the doors leading to the bailey and no servants were present. If she could silence Claude before he—

"There is not much time, Marguerite," he rasped. "Go out the rear window and stay low. When you are distant, run as never you have."

Lest he merely sought to discover the state of her consciousness, she floundered.

"Make haste, Marguerite!"

She rose to her hands and knees. The last time she was here, Claude had spent most of his days in a chair. Now he was on a narrow bed, propped up by pillows.

Finally, he dies, she thought as she peered into the gaunt face of one who looked nearer his father's age than his brother's.

Her widowed mother had answered her sire's summons six years ago, leaving her daughter behind so she could care for this brother who was expected to pass within a year. He had not, but soon now.

"Oui, I depart the world." His eyes moistened. "As I wish to join my sister above, I shall please God by aiding her daughter."

Recalling the pitiful grave that was more fitting for a hunting dog than beloved kin who had spent her final years on those who did her no honor, Marguerite said, "Above? No holy ground does she rest in—and likely no box holds her body."

Claude eased his head back. "Though I protested that, I could do naught. But I must be well with it the same as you."

"Well with my mother buried like a dog? With no word sent me of her passing?"

His half-hooded eyes unhooded. "Quiet! He will hear you."

She thrust to her feet. "How am I to be well with that?"

He gripped her hand, and when she wrenched free, hurt spasmed across his face. "Much I have pondered God this past year, Marguerite. As if He ponders me, oft He appears in my dreams and eases the pain of losing one who loved the unlovable by assuring me my sister is with Him—and her beloved husband."

Swept with memories of the big Scots who had carried his little girl on his shoulders and many years later held her hand one side and her mother's the other as an unbreakable fever broke upon death, Marguerite caught back a sob.

"I hated that barbarian for taking her from us," Claude bit. "I hated him for all the tears our mother wept and for which my father cursed her for making my sister believe a marriage of love possible."

He sounded sincere, but the loss of urgency that she depart roused greater suspicion. However, when she stepped near, she saw he was not fully present.

"Uncle?"

He blinked. "Marguerite, daughter of Marguerite, run."

"But if they—"

"I will go to the floor so they think you overpowered this weak excuse for a man. I do not believe they will pursue you any more vigorously than they shall for fear you will reach Malcolm, but more you will suffer if caught."

She hesitated, then bent and kissed his perspiring brow. "The Lord be with you."

"More, with you."

Marguerite bundled up her skirts and climbed out the window. Standing amid withered herbs, she looked back and saw her uncle's shoulders and head go from sight as he eased off the bed.

Then she ran.

~

THEY WERE the shepherd to her sheep—ever turning her from Scotland. If they could corner her, they would become the wolf to her sheep.

There being no means of securing a horse without drawing the attention of one who defended that border demesne, the only homeward progress Marguerite had made was during the first hour, and it was too little. On foot, skirts knotted up to free her legs, she struggled to stay ahead of pursuers who had numbered a dozen at the outset. Had she not turned opposite the direction they knew she would flee, they would have taken her to ground before now.

When they picked up her trail again as she moved south, only four of her grandfather's men tracked her, the remainder likely continuing their search near the border. Now those who carried torches through the night had surely caught sight of her amid the trees. How else could they draw so near that their Norman-French accents were clear as they shouted words of which she could make no sense above the pound of her heart?

Lord, let me not have come this far only to fall, she prayed and, bending low, traded one cover for another.

She listened to their advance, and when the light of torches bent around the tree against which she pressed herself, hastened to the opposite side and drew from her hose the dagger her sire had insisted she conceal lest the one on her belt was taken.

But of what use against four warriors? fear asked of her.

Faced with defeat, do not make it easy for the enemy to seal their victory, her sire answered from years past when he taught her the swipe and throw of a blade. *If no opening can be made nor miracle granted, defend your dignity.*

The dignity of the Scots ahead of the venom of these Normans, she told herself.

"She is here!" her uncle shouted. "You—left. You—right. You—watch our backs." Deftly, he made a noose of his men of which he would be the knot, and this time he might do more than mark her throat.

"Lord help me," she whispered.

"Show yourself!" he commanded, this time in the language of the Saxons that was near enough that of Lowland Scots she understood perfectly. "My patience wanes, and you will like me even less when I am at my meanest."

No place to run outside of torchlight, she thrust off the tree. One reach of the legs, two…

Shouts and hooves sounded behind and both sides—and, unexpectedly, ahead. How had four riders become seven? How had these three gotten in front of her?

By eschewing torches, she realized.

There being no opening that could not be closed quickly, she was tempted to go to her knees in supplication that might spare her life, but she heard her sire say, *Fight, wee sparrow!*

She would have tried had not the three before her spurred past and, in the Saxon language, answered the curses and threats shouted in Norman-French. And did one of those voices belong to a woman?

Marguerite swung around. Seeing Gerald and his men attacked by those lacking torches, she told herself, *Here your opening. Here your miracle. Run!*

But what the Lord provided was thwarted by the twist of an ankle, and too soon the clash ended. Though she had managed to remain upright and limp opposite, once more riders came for her. Exposed by moonlight penetrating the trees, she turned.

The three slowed, and the giant of a man whose red hair and thick beard were in the Saxon style, said in the words and accent of the conquered, "Peace be with you."

She shifted her gaze to another sizable man whose stout frame sat lower in the saddle and appearance was also distant from the conquerors. And the warrior far left…

The woman Marguerite had heard, a single braid draping her shoulder.

"I am Vitalis," said the red-headed warrior as he reined in. "Here, Zedekiah…" He jutted his chin. "…and here, Em. Those miscreants will trouble you no more."

Her uncle and his men were dead?

"Three felled, and the fourth who fled was injured severely

enough that come the morrow, he may be more dead than alive," he added.

"Norman swine," growled Zedekiah.

"What are you called?" Vitalis asked.

Noting blood on his tunic, she closed her mouth. These Saxons—doubtless, rebels—had reason to hate Normans, and a Norman she was on the side of her mother. If she spoke, they might hear the enemy about her before they heard her father's people. Too, many English disliked the Scots as much as they did Normans.

"Your name?" he repeated.

She considered again the man and woman on either side of him and saw the latter scrutinized the one whose knotted skirts showed her hosed legs. "Be not afeared," said the one called Em. "We are Saxons the same as you."

Of course they believed that of her. She had been pursued by Normans, Gerald had called to her in Saxon, and these untamed Northern lands were still of England though Malcolm wished to make them his.

"Tell us your name," Em prompted.

Marguerite touched the bruised flesh of her throat, moved fingers to her lips, shook her head.

The stout one grunted. "Mayhap a mute."

"Likely a vow of silence," Em said.

Vitalis urged his mount forward, and when Marguerite jumped back and stumbled, drew rein. "We cannot know what you have suffered, but as you are injured—thus, greater prey to the invaders—you will have to trust your fellow Saxons. Come."

She shook her head.

"You may keep your dagger to hand."

Another shake.

Now Em advanced on her. "You can share my saddle."

More than Marguerite wanted to refuse, she longed to accept. Others of her grandfather's men could be en route—

perhaps all were it believed she had abandoned the hope of Scotland. Having been on the verge of being captured, she had even less chance of escape now she was injured.

She looked from the woman who appeared a few years younger than she to the men. *Lord, do not forsake me as you forsook Cannie and my escort,* she silently beseeched, then slid the dagger beneath her belt.

When Em drew alongside, Marguerite fit her uninjured foot in the stirrup and the rebel gripped her arm to aid in swinging her up behind.

Though the ride that followed was rigorous, she was grateful lest fatigue, sorrow, and the pain of a day without end render her senseless and dump her from the saddle.

Upon reaching camp, Marguerite was assured she was among friends, but she did not believe it, most of the Rebels of the Pale regarding her with suspicion as they set cooking fires ahead of the dawn. Not that she thought Em insincere. Simply, the woman believed her one of their own.

Previous to Malcolm granting sanctuary to Edgar the Aetheling, whom Saxons wished to reclaim England's throne, the King of Scots was disliked by the English for his raids across the border. Though they must think better of him now Edgar and his family were guests at his court, they could not yet know how great the support to be given the young man in asserting his right to the throne.

In a month—two at most—Edgar would bring forces south to join with the Saxon resistance and Danes come across the sea. By the sword, the city of York would be emptied of its three thousand Normans and made the eastern base from which to begin ousting the conquerors. Until then…

Hold your tongue and remain the mute, Marguerite counseled as she exercised restraint in satisfying hunger that made her long to tear at the dried meat with her teeth.

"More ale?" Em asked.

Marguerite looked from the warming fire before which they sat, accepted the cup, and drained it.

Hearing a sharp breath, she saw the woman's eyes were on her throat. Then just as Em expressed shock over the bruises, Marguerite reacted to eyes only now she noticed were of different colors—one blue, one brown.

"I was born this way," the woman said and jutted her chin. "You were not born that way."

Marguerite shook her head.

"Did the Normans...?" Em swallowed loudly. "Ever they take what does not belong to them."

Realizing it was believed she had been ravished, Marguerite shook her head vigorously.

"Then you are fortunate—or blessed as you would say if you are a holy woman. Are you of the Church?"

Another shake.

"Does a vow of silence—repentance for sin—seal your lips?"

Unable to decide whether it was best to deny or acknowledge that, and embracing the comfort silence would afford while she mourned her dead, Marguerite did not respond.

"It matters not, but we shall need a name. Though I do not read well, I can make sense of bits and pieces. Can you write it?"

Marguerite could write and read in three languages, but—

"There is another way," Em said as if to save her the embarrassment of being illiterate. "Is your name's first sound the same as Aelfled?"

Certain there was no harm in this, Marguerite shook her head.

"What of Beatrice?" When that was rejected, Em continued through the letters until a name beginning with *M* made Marguerite nod. Half a dozen names were submitted that began the same, and when Em landed on *Margaret,* she was rewarded with a nod. Not only was it the Saxon equivalent of

Marguerite's Norman name, but it was that of the Aetheling's sister with whom King Malcolm was entranced.

"Margaret is a pretty name, but I expected something softer."

Was *Marguerite* softer? She supposed so, its ending more musical and of higher pitch than the one by which these rebels would call her.

"Now we must determine how to return you to your family, Margaret. Your home is here in the North?"

Much farther north, Marguerite thought and shook her head.

"The Midlands?" When that was rejected, Em said, "The South? That was my home until—" Now she shook *her* head as if her thoughts were unwelcome. "You have family, have you not?"

That hurt. All those of her blood were dead, as well as Cannie not of her blood. As for the Scots who called her their own, she dare not venture there. She shook her head again.

"I am sorry for what those Normans made you suffer. Mayhap Vitalis will allow you to join us. Would you like that?"

Lady Marguerite of the Scots among Saxon rebels? It seemed wrong, but for now it was her only option. She bobbed her chin.

"What skills have you besides giving threat with a dagger?"

She could do more than threaten, though little beyond defense of her person. Better she was known as Marguerite of fine needlework, ink and quill, and knowledge of herbs.

"Have you an interest in learning weapons?" Marguerite's wide-eyed surprise made her grimace. "Worry not. There are other ways to support the resistance."

After all that had happened since learning her mother had died, it was tempting to seek instruction in arms, but she was a lady and would not be among these people long.

"You can cook?" Em asked.

Marguerite had aided her mother and Cannie in preparing and serving meals, but not for any of great number. Another shake of the head.

Em considered Marguerite's fouled gown. "Are you a lady?"

That would be more obvious were she at court, but her traveling garments were simple, albeit of quality material.

When she did not respond, annoyance flitted across Em's face. "Do you know the healing arts?"

Marguerite nodded.

"A useful skill, and one we will need in great measure if the Aetheling decides to be a man and come out of the North to rally his supporters."

Em had good cause to question Edgar. Not only was he young but, from Marguerite's observations, more given to sitting a throne others placed him on than fighting to win it for himself. For that, when his great-uncle, King Edward, died, it was not a Saxon of royal blood who next wore the crown but the powerful, renowned warrior, Earl Harold Godwinson. And even he could not keep hold of England when the Duke of Normandy brought war to these shores.

Oh Malcolm, I fear the aid you give Edgar will be squandered, she thought. Though she suspected her king believed it himself, if he had set his mind on wedding the sister, aiding the brother would seal the bargain.

Em stood. "Whilst you gain your rest, I shall speak with Vitalis."

There being nothing Marguerite wanted more than to be alone, she nodded.

A short while later, having made her bed distant from the rebels, she huddled beneath her blanket and yielded to grief over the loss of her mother, Cannie, and Malcolm's men. For hours she wept, and when finally she grew numb, turned her thoughts to Scotland to which she would return once her ankle healed.

"Within a fortnight," she whispered, "Nay, a sennight."

She could not know that seven days would become six months, during which the Aetheling-led resistance and his Danish allies took the city of York by slaying thousands of

Normans while Marguerite watched from afar.

An extraordinary victory.

An inspiring victory.

A temporary victory.

Within days, the Danes' betrayal saw the city once more in Norman hands. Then came the harrying of the North, thousands of innocents destroyed by William the Conqueror who ordered the land wasted to ensure those who continued to resist his rule were denied support and resources.

Six long months playing a mute Saxon in England, then Marguerite known as Margaret determined to go home before she tore the heart of a man that did not deserve to be torn twice in a lifetime.

CHAPTER ONE

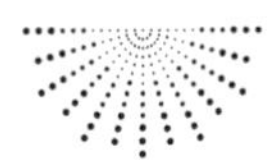

Northumbria, England
Late Winter, 1070

"Accursed Edgar!" Marguerite muttered.

His bid for the crown lost when King William's bribery of the Danes overturned the Aetheling's victory at York, once more he had crossed from Scotland into England.

Not with Malcolm's blessing, she was certain, though possibly his indulgence were he aware of the undertaking of the one whose sister was to become Queen of Scots—an indulgence that could devastate innocent Saxons, just as William's harrying had done, the sight of which her escort had tried to spare her by going wide around fire-ravaged homes, the carcasses of animals, and the bodies of men, women, and children who should have fled sooner.

Now the Norman contingent—King William's solution to the rebellion—that had not reached this village where Marguerite and her escort paused for the night, approached. And Edgar who had ridden hard down its center with a score and ten men had led them here.

In the midst of panicking villagers, the Aetheling leapt from the saddle. "Take cover! We do battle!"

Having donned her mantle and shoved her feet into slippers removed in preparation for bed, Marguerite pushed past her escort outside the inn. "What have you done, Edgar?" she demanded in a voice coarse from disuse.

The young man who had begun issuing orders to his men came around. "Who are you to—?" His eyes widened and color drained.

She supposed she must seem a ghost. A sennight before the Saxon resistance led by the Aetheling took York, tale had reached the Rebels of the Pale that Scotland's king had laid waste to a border demesne held by a Norman family. None of the rebels had known the identity of that family nor the reason for the attack, but Marguerite had—and that her king held her grandfather responsible for his missing ward and her escort.

Guilt had gripped her for not trying harder to return home. Not that it would have significantly altered Malcolm's vengeance, but proof she lived might have spared Claude as she was certain her grandfather was not spared—nor Gerald were he the one who escaped the Saxon rebels who defended her.

If Claude yet lived when they came, she reminded herself as ever she did to assuage guilt.

Still, remorse aplenty for others lost to the blade and fire, especially if among them were servants who had nothing to do with the massacre of Malcolm's men and Cannie.

"You are supposed to be dead, Lady," Edgar said in a voice deeper than remembered.

She stepped over ground moistened by light snow that had fallen earlier. As the four warriors tasked with returning her to Malcolm's court drew alongside, she said, "Perhaps now that you bring Normans down upon this village, it shall be so. And you dead with me."

The white sheet made of his face darkened. "'Tis treason to wish a king dead!"

She nearly berated him further for having no care for those who, were they truly his subjects, would be deserving of his protection, but her gaze was drawn to a man with a slight hitch, greying hair bound back, plaid cloak aslant.

"Ye are alive, Sparrow!" he called.

Sparrow... In that moment, more than ever she missed her sire's endearment and that which earned it—whistled melodies that accompanied songs she had either learned or composed. Though whistling had been acceptable when she was young, it became less so as she grew into a woman, but despite those who frowned on a lady making music with pursed lips, she had not abandoned the joyous amusement until she fled her grandfather. Not only had it been necessary to go silent, but since then she had little cause and desire to whistle.

Seeing her escort form a barrier between her and the one who approached, she said, "All is well. Hendrie is King Malcolm's man and was a friend to my sire."

They eased back, then she was in the Scot's arms, his whiskered kiss on her brow, the warmth of his body making her more aware of how chill the night.

"I am glad to see you, Hendrie!"

"And I you. We thought you dead, the same as your escort and Cannie though no body was found."

Before her grandfather and his people were slain, how much had they suffered over ignorance of her whereabouts? she wondered.

"We have no time for this," the Aetheling bit. "We must prepare to fight."

Marguerite pulled free of Hendrie. "You endanger these people! Pray, take your men and lead the Normans away."

Edgar's jaw shifted. "As our horses are exhausted, we fight here. But fear not, we have a dozen more men than they."

She had not looked close at those who accompanied him. Now she saw they were mostly Saxons, the handful of Scots surely token assistance granted by Malcolm. Though warriors, many were of a good age and all appeared nearly as exhausted and in need of refreshment as their mounts. Even if the approaching Normans numbered fewer, likely Edgar's party was doomed—worse, the common folk fleeing to the wood.

"If you give the Normans no cause to pause here, God willing they will pass through without harming the villagers and their homes," Marguerite said. "Now go!"

In the light of torches set on either side of the inn's door, his upper teeth showed, then he raised a hand.

She jumped back from the slap she should have known Hendrie would not allow to land.

Holding to the Aetheling's arm, the Scotsman growled, "She is my king's ward. Behave, boy!" He shoved him back.

Edgar's resentful eyes moved from Hendrie to Marguerite. "You are right, Lady. Best to draw the Normans away." But rather than gain the saddle, he ordered a score of his men to ride west, all those named appearing the least of his warriors—and Saxons rather than Scots.

Because the former were more likely to do as bid? Because he dared not risk Malcolm's men? Regardless, those twenty would be sacrificed in the hope Normans did not pause where Edgar hid.

However, from Marguerite's time with the rebels and all that was told of the harrying, she feared his solution would benefit him no more than the villagers. If the Normans did not search the village, once they overtook their weary prey and discovered their numbers were reduced, they would return—and wreak destruction even were the Aetheling gone.

Marguerite looked beyond the warriors to the men, women, and children kicking up cold earth as they fled, then lunged at the prince.

Hendrie caught her back. "The little man is decided. We can but ensure ye are safely delivered home."

Home. Still she had one, but these people... "Edgar!" she called. "You must—"

He swung around. "I must stay alive! *That* is what England's rightful king must do."

Despite misgivings in the short time she had known him at Malcolm's court, she had hoped he would prove worthy to wear the crown, but from what she had distantly witnessed when the Rebels of the Pale joined his forces to take York and now this, that to which he aspired seemed impossible. Perhaps he was too young and inexperienced. Perhaps given much time he would grow into a leader. But who would be sacrificed in the *in between?*

After ordering the mounted men to ride, Edgar said, "If you truly wish to protect these people and yourself, Lady, give aid in finding a place to hunker until danger is past."

She wanted to refuse, but soon riders yet black upon the night would appear, then would come the silver of sweeping swords, the red of blood, the bright of fire.

She looked to Stephen on her right who held close his words as once she had done and who had scouted the village before they secured lodgings. "I believe already you know where we will be safest."

The Norman who only appeared a Saxon inclined his head. Then Edgar and what remained of his men gave themselves into his hands.

~

FIRE IN THE NIGHT. Again.

He could not put them out, so great the raging and rapid the spread, but that did not stop him from drawing near nor doing what his fellow Normans would deem witless.

Sir Theriot of the family D'Argent knew he had risked his standing with the king—or worse—when he declined William's order to lead a contingent in destroying the homes, food, and livestock of innocent Saxons. Though preventing those resources from falling into rebel hands would sooner hobble the resistance, his conscience would not permit him to be the cause of more suffering by people who had accepted Norman rule with assurances their lives would be better than when they were ruled by one of their own.

King William had been angered, but as if anticipating the youngest D'Argent brother would insist on serving in a manner that might singe his soul but not consume it, he had yielded. Thus, the same as once his brother had done, Theriot used his tracking skills to disrupt pockets of resistance lest their efforts lead to the loss of more lives and homes.

The flames in the distance rose higher, the same as all fires he happened upon in the wake of the harrying. But this one set by Normans was unlike others. *Those* Theriot had not been responsible for.

"You should have stayed gone, Edgar," he growled. "This battle you cannot win. That crown your narrow head cannot support. These people do not deserve one who thoughtlessly endangers them."

As the last of the Normans who had fallen back to torch the village set after those in pursuit of the Aetheling, Theriot patted his restless horse. "Now we go, my friend," he said and spurred across the night whose smoke thickened as they neared the village which, hopefully, Edgar's arrival and departure had emptied of its residents. As that had not been true of several burning communities from which Theriot had plucked old people, children, and animals, here he must go as well—and more imperative since he shared the blame for this.

Albeit confident he had the favor of God who kept a hedge of protection around him, he must do his part by proceeding with caution. Though he eschewed the gnashing of scissors and scraping of blades to allow his hair to lengthen and face to whisker, he knew it only looked possible he was Saxon.

Blessedly, the desperation of those he aided and that he spoke no word had allowed him to preserve the lives of dozens caught between the rebels and a Norman king who had lost patience with those he claimed had forced him to do the unimaginable that was now far more than imagined.

Had Theriot a say in it, he would lock King William in a room with Edgar and King Malcolm and toss in swords. Whoever emerged would rule.

He nearly laughed at that. Though he knew little about Edgar beyond his age and that his sword skill was unremarkable, and he understood Malcolm's reputation as a warrior was well earned, he was certain if William fought both at once, the duke who became a king would triumph.

The way of mankind, he thought. *In matters of power and money —and when do the two not clasp hands?—the biggest, meanest, and most cunning prevails.*

He reined in near enough the village to quickly get in and out, but not so near to be seen providing he kept watch on clouds moonlight occasionally penetrated.

Dismounting, he wrapped around his lower face the cloth he had carried on his person since surviving the Battle of Hastings. Before the harrying, it had been a reminder of how untouchable the Lord had made him compared to his kin. Of late, it also served to filter smoke.

Theriot touched the D'Argent dagger on his hip, then sent up a prayer for the sharpening of senses whose edges had been somewhat dulled by the tracking of Edgar that left little time for restorative sleep.

"Amen," he said and took a handful of grain from one of his packs. His horse gazed at him out of eyes so pale their blue was seen even in the night, then nudged his rider's shoulder.

Theriot opened his hand. When it was emptied, he drew his sword. "Be still, Ciel. I shall not be long."

Not all the village was alight. The Normans who torched the inn, smithy's shop, and a dozen thatch houses had been too eager to rejoin the hunt to ensure complete devastation. Too, since recent snowfall dampened all, fire would not easily jump from one building to another.

He happened on no bodies along the main road and side streets, and it could only be hoped none were in the blazing buildings. Certes, many of the inhabitants had made it to the wood ahead of the Normans' arrival. Not only did Theriot sense the fear of those who huddled there watching their village burn, but anger that caused fine hairs to prickle. And there could be eyes and anger here, too.

Cautiously, he advanced lest his shifting chain mail reveal him, reaching out with his senses for any who sought to harm him while he searched for Saxons left behind like the elderly man and woman recently pulled from a burning hovel.

After passing between two buildings untouched by fire, he slipped around the back of one across from the inn and heard a sound so shrill it rose above that of a roof collapsing farther down the road. Was it of a child?

It came again, and he was inclined to believe it a cat, but the rumble, crackle, and hissing of fire feasting on timber could be responsible for the distortion.

Not a child, he beseeched. Then staying low and close to the cover of buildings not yet aflame, he began making his way toward the cry that came again and again.

CHAPTER TWO

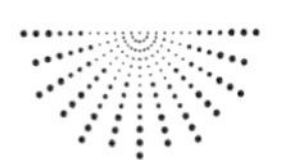

"A child is out there! Do you not hear it?"

"I believe so, Lady," Hendrie said where he sat beside Marguerite in the long-abandoned stable.

As Stephen anticipated, the building had escaped fire, either because it went unnoticed, else the Normans saw no reason to waste time on something so dilapidated it could be of no use to anyone.

Albeit dangerous, its timbers creaking though there was barely a breeze, it was safer for the mounted riders crowded inside than outside, too little time having passed since Edgar's pursuers spurred away and it being possible one or more Normans would turn back to confirm no one of interest appeared.

"We must give aid!" Marguerite turned in the saddle.

The Scotsman groaned, and when she dropped to the ground, he and the escort who had brought her North did the same, including the Saxon injured during an encounter with Normans shortly after they began the journey to Scotland.

"Remain here," Hendrie said. "We will go—"

"If 'tis a child, more easily I can coax it out."

"Very well, though only because it appears the Normans are gone."

"What do you, Lady Marguerite?" Edgar demanded.

"I heard a child."

"As did we all. Now accept it is doomed and get astride."

"Nay!"

"I will not have you risk revealing us!"

She stepped alongside his mount. "That we might do were we to ride from here, but we go on foot."

"Get astride!"

She turned away.

"Hendrie, take that woman in hand!"

"We shall protect her," the Scotsman said and accompanied her outside.

Marguerite was grateful that past the hard of Hendrie was a soft heart and, like her sire and their king, he indulged her.

As they ventured from the stable cast in the shadows of ancient trees, the cry came again, and they veered toward three outlying homes, the center of which was aflame.

"That may not have been a child," Hendrie said.

She recalled its last cry. It had not sounded entirely human, but terror made animals of men, women, and children, just as it had done her when she fled her grandfather's men, running farther and faster than believed possible.

"But it may have been," she said, and continued forward until he yanked her down amid winter grass.

"See there," he rasped as the others went to ground. "At least one doubled back."

"I see naught."

"'Twas fleeting. To reach those homes, he had to travel amid fire light."

"Those homes?" she asked warily.

"Likely, he heard the cry as well."

Now more she feared for the child. Still, lest the man merely sought to aid one of his own, she said, "You are certain he was Norman? His hair cut close and—"

"That I could not determine, but he carried a sword. Even if a villager possessed such a blade, I warrant none moves like a warrior trained for stealth—indeed, I wager much 'tis a Norman come to finish what was begun."

"The child," she whispered and heard it cry again before timbers snapped and the house began to collapse.

She scrambled to her knees.

The cry sounded again with less volume, and momentarily a figure appeared amid the flare of flames. His silhouette revealed though his hair was not long like that of most Saxon men, neither was it cropped close. And he did carry a sword, meaning more likely a murderous Norman than a villager.

Marguerite did not believe her wit was quick, but in that moment she knew how to turn him opposite. After what she had witnessed of the harrying during her journey, tempered as it was by her escort going the long way around, if this Norman fell to her efforts to keep his bloody blade from a child, so be it.

She looked to the men who had paused at the inn with her, directed three to retrieve the child, and before they could question her, thrust upright and said, "Hendrie and Stephen, we shall draw the Norman away. Now give chase."

Feeling Hendrie's hand on her skirt, she wrenched free of one whose reflexes in his younger years would not have allowed her to escape, and ran toward the enemy.

A CAT. Seeing a lithe body leap from the window of the house nearest the one consumed by fire, Theriot exhaled relief that it was no child and the animal was safe.

But then a scream split the air.

Two figures ran from the direction of a deeply shadowed

building on the outskirts of the village, and one wore a gown. There was a lope in the stride of the man coming behind the woman as if he was injured, but he gained on her.

Though fatigued senses sounded a warning to which Theriot ought to attend, knowing hesitation could be the difference between saving and losing the woman to injury or death, he raised his sword high and reached his legs long.

She screamed again and veered toward the dark that would improve her chance of escaping one of Theriot's countrymen—non, two, another Norman appearing behind the first of those who had surely turned back from pursuing Edgar.

To sooner be recognized as the scout who set them after the Aetheling, he yanked the cloth down around his neck. "Leave the woman be!"

He could not be certain they understood, but hopefully his accent would give them pause, allowing their prey to further distance herself.

Immediately, they ceased their pursuit. Then they were running at him.

Not his countrymen, he saw now, and those who sought to harm a woman of their own people were not of the class who worked nor prayed. They were of the class who fought, and this D'Argent had revealed a Norman in their midst.

He veered away. Though it would appear he fled, it was strategy for this warrior who knew the dark better than most. Amid the ring of chain mail whose weight burdened in the moment but would prove invaluable, he widened the distance between himself and the enemy, trading the fire's glow for the shadows just as the woman had done.

Then he halted, pivoted, and looked from the silhouetted Saxon with the hitch to the other who followed. As the former drew nearer, Theriot shifted right to gain the full breadth of both opponents' shadows which the fires cast long across the winter field.

Their faces were unseen, but he knew the Saxons intended him great ill. If he remained concealed in their shadows, the light behind them would reveal their swings and maneuverings far better than they would his own.

Unfortunately, the clouds were beyond his control, but not the Lord's. Providing his great protector prevented the moon from shining full upon the land, Theriot could come out of this whole as he had every seemingly hopeless clash—above all, that of Hastings when each Saxon blade that sought to end his life was deflected.

Now in this northernmost English village, another clash. The Saxon of hitched stride was muscled, as told by his silhouette and slam of his blade.

Theriot's strength was beyond equal to his opponent's who he guessed nearly twice his age, though it required much effort to hold to the dark as he drove the man back. Now with the second Saxon nearly upon him, he swung his sword harder, causing the first Saxon to lurch to the side.

Theriot turned his attention to the new arrival. This warrior was of lean build and fast, requiring a half dozen meetings of the sword before Theriot spilled first blood.

The man cursed in Saxon, but it was not his native language, his accent so diluted it had to have been many years since he crossed from Normandy.

Continuing to keep his back to the dark and move inside his opponents' shadows, Theriot confirmed he had bled the second one's sword arm when the fire's glow revealed the man clasped the upper portion with the opposite hand to keep his blade before him.

Theriot could have finished him, but the gap between that blow and the one the older Saxon now sought to land was too narrow. Trading one shadow for another, Theriot swept up his sword to meet the one swinging toward his head.

"Valiant, lad!" the man mocked in a graveled voice that went beyond confirming his years. Just like Theriot's other opponent, neither was he Saxon, his accent that of the Scots, which made more sense than that the woman was attacked by one of her own—at least in this circumstance since often the fairer sex had to protect themselves from supposed friends as much as foes.

A prey for all seasons, his sire had once described women as being vulnerable in this world whose minutes, hours, and days were measured out by men. For that, Theriot had done as Godfroi D'Argent would approve, providing distraction that permitted the woman to escape.

Now as he and his opponent pushed off each other, realization struck. After locating the Aetheling, Theriot had stayed near until he could overtake a Norman contingent to set after Edgar. During that time, he had seen Scots amid the Saxons, and among them an older one who rode at the Aetheling's side and walked with a hitch—this man, meaning those who fled ahead of the Normans had left some behind, possibly the prince himself. Had these men sought to capture the woman for fear she would reveal them if Normans returned?

As the Scotsman once more came at him, distant movement drew Theriot's gaze to where he had found a cat. Three sword-wielding figures appeared amid firelight, and they came this direction.

God willing, they were Normans, but since they would be nearly upon him before he could confirm it, he must eliminate these two.

He bellowed, and his backhanded swing caught the Scot's blade near the hilt, twisting the man around and sending his sword flying. But once more the killing blow would have to wait, the one injured earlier approaching from the left.

Staying the shadow of the Scotsman who sought to recover his weapon, Theriot arced his blade down and up to protect his sword arm. As the meeting of metal staggered both men,

Theriot drove an elbow into his opponent's nose. It dropped the warrior, and this time there was space to land a killing blow. And that he did.

Though he heard the dying man's Norman-accented words, there was no time to make sense of them. As he turned toward the Scotsman, the clouds thinned, casting more light on Theriot, his enemy, and the three who neared. Unfortunately, it was not enough to determine whether the latter were friend or foe.

"Almighty!" he called on the Lord and ran at the Scotsman who had retrieved his sword but had yet to assume a defensive stance.

A scream sounded, sending Theriot's gaze to the woman who should be far gone—she of slim figure whose mantle flew off her shoulders and loosening braid appeared dark of color.

The distraction of her allowed the Scotsman to escape the blade that should have caught him across the neck. Worse, Theriot's momentum betrayed him. Before he could come around, his enemy was at his back.

Instinct his only defense in the moment, he dropped to the chill ground, and the wind of the sword that could have sliced off his head passed over it—or so he thought ahead of shattering pain.

Had the edge or flat of the blade landed? If the former, had it cleaved open his skull and begun spilling out all he was beyond a soul that needed no earthly shell to survive? Likely the flat of the blade, for he remained conscious enough not only to deny his opponent his rest but give the accursed woman another chance to escape.

Hand no longer one with his sword hilt, he flipped onto his back. Pain doubling behind his eyes, he knocked aside the Scotsman's next stroke with his mail-covered arm, and with the other closed fingers around the cross guard of his enemy's sword.

As the warrior tried to wrench free, Theriot thrust the blade to the ground, forcing the man to his knees beside him. Though he attempted to roll to the side to wrest the sword from him, pain radiating from the back of his head and waning consciousness incapacitated him. And greater the threat of senselessness when the clouds parted and the moon shone so bright it felt as if he stared into the sun.

Feeling his hand on the enemy's sword loosen, silently he appealed to his protector, *Aid me, Lord!*

A great weight thumped down on his chest, then a hand gripped his throat.

Not this, he sent heavenward, *not after all You have brought me through.* And yet here was death wearing the face of the Scotsman whose bound hair had loosened, its grey revealing Theriot D'Argent would die at the hands of one older than believed.

Receding consciousness moving him down a dimming tunnel, he heard his departed uncle who had trained him at arms shout, *You cannot be well with such a death, son of Godfroi, nephew of Hugh! A D'Argent gives no quarter! Fight to the end!*

Theriot strained the muscles of his throat and managed wheezes of breath aided by the bunched cloth around his neck that provided a thin barrier between his airway and the Scotsman's hand.

Even if this is your end, take with you one who harms innocents, he told himself, then reached to his hip and turned his hand around his dagger.

"Pray, cease!" the woman cried, over and again in an accent Theriot thought of the Scots one moment, the Normans the next, then Saxon.

As he pulled the dagger from its scabbard and turned its point to drive it into his assailant, the Scotsman spoke words that escaped the one who intended to slay him. When the man turned his head to the side, Theriot looked that direction.

There the woman he had sought to aid. Despite her blurred edges, something was familiar about she whose mouth moved, arms reached, and hands splayed as if someone held her back. Someone did—a long-haired warrior, and he was no Norman, nor the other two who would surely arrive soon had they not already.

Theriot tightened his grip on the dagger and drove it into the Scotsman's side.

Breath was returned to him when the older man released his throat, reared back, and loosed the sword rendered useless by the one who had somehow kept hold of the cross guard.

Determined if he could not escape death, neither would the one responsible for it, Theriot drew out the dagger's blade to drive it in again. And missed when the man lurched forward and reached with open hands to his enemy's eyes.

Theriot jerked his head opposite, and as he once more sought to drive the blade into the man's side, the woman repeated, "Cease! Pray, cease!"

Feeling the give of flesh though it did not go as deep as before, he saw she was on her knees clawing at the earth as if to free herself. And she, for whom he gave all, was the last thing he looked upon before everything went black and the pressure on his eyes became agony that crashed into pain at the back of his skull.

CHAPTER THREE

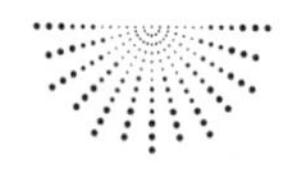

Central Lowlands
Scotland

One dead, two nearly so, and either because of a child who could not be saved or one who did not exist.

The latter, the villagers had assured Marguerite when they ventured out of the wood—rather, the few who would speak to her. And surely those had done so only because they hoped to sooner see the back of one associated with the Aetheling who brought the harrying to their village.

While their physician tended the two fallen warriors to allow them to travel beyond the reach of vengeful villagers, as well as murderous Normans who might return were it discovered Edgar was not among the pursued, Marguerite had sat amid shadows and wept as done too many times since departing Scotland.

So many deaths. And now one for which she was responsible—that of the Norman added to her escort to ensure their safe passage should they encounter King William's forces. And ensure it Stephen had done, ending an attack a sennight past by identifying himself to his countrymen. Now that warrior was buried in winter earth far from home. What would prove even more tragic was if the two warriors who survived what Stephen had not were also lost. And for what?

Just as it was likely no child had been in danger, the one who first answered that cry was of no danger to any until he was set upon.

After Hendrie and the unconscious Theriot D'Argent she had too late recognized were loaded into a wagon, what remained of the Aetheling's men and Marguerite's escort had departed the village.

That was two days ago, and providing the morrow was as uneventful, by next eve they would be in Dunfermline where Hendrie could be properly tended by the king's physician. And Sir Theriot...

Breathing in cold air, Marguerite turned on the bench whose lack of springs made her long for the saddle. First she looked upon Hendrie who slept away his pain and the wagon's jostling. Pleased his color continued to improve, she shifted her regard to the brother of Sir Dougray and Lady Nicola of the family D'Argent with whom she had become familiar while in England.

What could be seen of his face showed the grey cast continued to deepen. Unlike Hendrie who awakened often, the Norman had yet to rouse. However, he breathed better than the man into whom twice he had thrust a dagger. To sooner heal, did his body cling to the dark behind the cloth covering his lids and the lids covering his eyes?

Would those eyes heal? What of his mind? Though there was only swelling at the back of his head caused by the unintentional turning of Hendrie's blade that landed the flat, the injury could prove as deadly as fractured bone.

She shuddered. "I am to blame. Pray, forgive me, Sir Theriot." Likely futile beseeching, whether because he did not survive to test the strength of his ability to forgive, else he lived and deemed her unforgivable.

A groan sounded.

Seeing Hendrie's eyes were open, she swung her legs over the backless bench and dropped into the space between the men who had nearly slain each other.

"Is he dead?" Hendrie rumbled.

During his last awakening, she had revealed the identity of Theriot D'Argent that had caused her to plead for an end to their contest, which Hendrie had done only after damaging the Norman's eyes. The revelation had settled the Scotsman sufficiently that his demands for the return of his dagger had subsided. Still, were it possible to slay the enemy with whom he was forced to share a sick bed, he might.

"He yet lives," she said.

His nostrils flared. "Show me."

She slid an arm beneath his shoulders and narrowly avoided his forehead clipping her chin when the wagon lurched over deep ruts.

"He lives," he muttered, and she followed his gaze to the face at the rear of the wagon, it having been deemed safer the enemies lie at opposite ends.

"I care not what ye believe of the D'Argents, this one is foe," Hendrie said.

She eased his head back onto the blanket folded into a pillow and started to withdraw.

"Foe, not friend, Marguerite. Best left beside the road to fill the bellies of other beasts."

She had deigned not to argue that when last they spoke, but seeing he was more alert and certain vengeful imaginings would keep him awake, she settled beside him. "As told, I cannot know why he was there, but even were he among those who pursued Edgar, if he is the same as other D'Argents, he did not seek to harm what likely he also believed a child."

"*If* he is the same as those Normans you hold in high regard."

As done often these past days, she recalled the first time she met the youngest D'Argent brother. Four months past, after the rebels gained and lost the city of York, the Battle of Stafford was fought with no better result for the resistance. That night, she had been among the defeated rebels Vitalis took to the D'Argent camp raised distant from fellow Normans who celebrated their victory with such exuberance one would not guess they also suffered losses.

Sir Theriot had stood apart, moonlight running the silver in his hair, stance that of a warrior prepared to wield his sword. But the same as his kin, he had maintained the truce that allowed the seriously injured Em to be given into the keeping of Dougray D'Argent who had a care for the rebel.

Vitalis having determined Marguerite would stay with the woman she had come to regard as a friend, caring for her until a physician was found distant from the battlefield, Sir Theriot had called her name and strode forward to assist in getting her astride.

She was not easily given to attraction and certainly not by physical appearance alone. However, the chevalier's gaze that seemed to see beyond the shadow cast by her hood, confident swing of his arms, and reach of his stride had made something move through her at a speed and intensity never before felt.

And more it was felt when he gripped her waist, boosted her into the saddle, and slid one hand to the small of her back. As she had peered down at him, suppressing words of gratitude that would reveal she was not mute, moonlight intimate with his face showed a mischievous glint in eyes of an indeterminate color and a smile more comely for what it conveyed with so slight a curve.

It had occurred what she felt could be similar to that experienced by her formidable sire. Marguerite had thought sweet his insistence his heart had known her mother's when first he set eyes on her, but she had believed it exaggeration.

That night it had seemed possible for how aware she was of Theriot D'Argent and his hand on her. When he removed it and wished her Godspeed, she had dismissed those feelings by naming them fanciful.

Still, as was habit when leaving behind something to which she wished to return, she had looked back as they departed the camp and saw he stared after them—of no great note since the others did as well, but then he raised a hand as if he knew that of all those in the camp, she looked back at him.

During the journey that delivered her and Em to the barony of Michel Roche, often she had thought on that and his smile. And afterward... Less so, though months after Sir Dougray and Em wed and Baron Roche provided Marguerite an escort to Scotland, Sir Theriot was wont to come to mind and make her heart feel lonely.

"Methinks you place too much value on that one's kinship, Marguerite," Hendrie said.

She cleared her throat. "I am fair certain this chevalier is the same as his brothers. You heard him when he believed I was pursued by Normans. He commanded them to desist. It surprised until you had him to ground and I saw he was young with the silver of the aged in his hair. It was then I recognized him as a D'Argent whom I briefly met while in England. And understood."

"What ye *wished* to understand. It was no coincidence he appeared in the village after his countrymen set it afire. He must have been among them and turned back to see if the flames flushed out Edgar."

It was hard to accept that, but were it true, surely it was because he served the usurper and must do as bid. "Even so, I do not believe he would have harmed the child had there been one nor made sport of me had my pursuers been his countrymen."

Hendrie gave a grunt of disapproval, then a groan of discomfort.

Fearing for his stitches, Marguerite turned back the blankets.

"Ere we went for the one lurking amid the fires, I wagered he was a Norman," he slurred. "I won that wager, just as I believe I win the wager he was there to finish what was begun."

Pressing her lips, Marguerite raised his tunic and peeled back the bandage. The stitches held and discolored flesh appeared no worse than before—a good sign Theriot D'Argent's blade had struck nothing vital with the deep thrust nor the shallow one.

Grateful to find Hendrie had returned to sleep, she tucked the blankets around him and crawled to the man at the rear of the wagon who she hoped would become a prisoner of the King of Scots rather than Edgar the Aetheling.

Before unbinding his eyes to once more assess damage which included swelling, burst blood vessels, and abrasions, she looked to those who rode ahead.

Thankfully, Edgar remained at the fore. Each time he brought his mount alongside the wagon and spoke aloud his hatred of the Norman, it turned her belly, as did that which he wore on his belt alongside his own weapons—the jeweled dagger that nearly ended Hendrie's life.

Since surely he wished to thrust that blade into one who had aided in denying him the throne, likely the only reason he had not acted on that impulse was because Marguerite had claimed the D'Argent's life as Hendrie's privilege and asserted King Malcolm would look ill on any who challenged his man.

Next, Marguerite considered those riding behind the wagon. Though she had tried to persuade the three Saxons to return to their liege in Derbyshire, assuring them the Aetheling and his men would deliver her home, they had refused. Even in the absence of the fallen Stephen, they would see that with which they were entrusted to its end. When they were rested and their injured companion sufficiently recovered, they would return to England with tidings their Norman friend had been lost to a D'Argent.

"'Tis upon me," Marguerite whispered to the man she crouched alongside, then began unbinding eyes whose color she could not see past the thick of clouds bordered by bleeding whites. And might never see.

Though she tried to set her mind on the task before her, continually her thoughts and emotions drifted. Still this attraction, as if she knew him beyond that first meeting, the second fateful one, and now this. Still she named herself fanciful—now pitifully so for what she had wrought. But were there a cure for these feelings, surely it would be Theriot D'Argent's hatred when he learned who was responsible for his injury.

"Lord, help me," she whispered.

~

WAS THIS DEATH? This darkness the place of those denied heaven? He did not believe it, and yet what else might such misery be?

He tried to shift his eyes in search of light, but that slight movement was so painful he nearly voiced it, and it was a struggle not to raise hands to his face to determine if this dark was beyond or upon him.

Feel! he told himself. *What do you feel?*

Something across his cold brow whose lower edge coursed the tops of his cheeks and nose. The pressure was minimal, but he was fairly certain this darkness was of a binding cloth. If so, he was yet of the world. But where in this world, and how was it he came to be here?

It hurt to search backward, and when the effort caused

consciousness to recede, he returned to unraveling the moment by engaging senses that had ever been his greatest strength.

Cold air on his upper and lower face and around and in his ears revealed he was out of doors. Beneath a sore neck, warmth lent by garments and blankets weighted him in the absence of chain mail.

The muscles of unbound feet and legs engaged when tensed, as well as those of hands and arms.

Still I am whole, he assured himself. *I have only to allow time for my head to come right and remove the covering from my eyes, and I shall escape whatever ill is intended me.*

Awareness of his body mostly restored, he lowered lids that felt as if they raked claws down his eyes. The grit of dirt, he thought, but rather than search backward to recall who cast it in his face, he focused on feeling beyond himself and questioned why everything was so still.

It was as if, long in motion, he had come to an abrupt halt. When his attempt to make sense of that sharpened the pain in his head, once more he turned from the past and commanded himself to listen.

A buzz became a drone, then just as one's eyes slowly focus after sleep opens them upon a new day, he began to hear night sounds, which meant the dark above accounted for his inability to see through the cloth.

Next, he sought sounds not of creatures and foliage but of men. They were here, one so close his breathing told he slept alongside Theriot in the opposite direction. More distant were the sounds of others—snores, restless shifting, the night patrol's quiet steps.

Concluding there were fewer than a score of men in the immediate area, Theriot attempted to determine which side of night they were on. Deeply, he pulled breath through nostrils and across a dry tongue. The first recognizable scents were of rich soil and trees ever green, next the mildewed straw beneath him, then that which drifted on the air. Though the sound of crackling fires was absent, he smelled and tasted the smoke and sweet sap of moist wood that must have required much persistence to light it.

During winter, warming fires were built large providing they posed little threat to their travelers. Now only embers remained, meaning he was on the side of night nearest day.

For some minutes, he rested senses weakened by whatever had been done him, then called on another sense as natural to him as it was unnatural to others. And found it closed to him, and no matter how much he pried, he could not open it.

Loathing this helplessness, once more he tried to delve the past. Though the pressure in his head increased, silently he commanded, *Go back...back...*

Was that fire in the night? Burning buildings? Smoke wending toward clouds obscuring the moon?

Consciousness wavering, he recalled assuring his horse he would not be long, the cry of what sounded a child, the scream of a woman, and a clash with warriors, one a Scotsman and the other one of his own countrymen.

What words had the latter spoken as he bled out? They eluded, though there had been something familiar about them.

Next, he recalled the slam to the back of his head, the Scotsman's grip on his throat, the dagger in his hand, the woman's pleading, her partially shadowed face he had thought familiar, and—

Sudden shattering pain determining utter darkness was a better place for Theriot D'Argent, his last thoughts were, *I failed her. If she lives, ever she will suffer what was done her. Unforgivable.*

CHAPTER FOUR

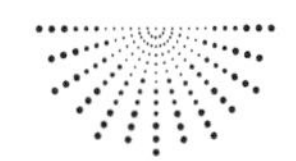

Dunfermline, Scotland

"Home," Marguerite breathed where she had reined in atop one of many hills that held at the center of their outstretched palms her beloved Dunfermline situated inland of the sparkling Firth of Forth that emptied into the North Sea. The last of winter lingered, but soon an abundance of green would make the eyes ache.

"It looks a cold place," muttered one of her three escorts who had accompanied her to savor the sight free of the wagon's bump and rattle.

She looked from him to the others and paused on the Saxon who had been injured early in their journey from Derbyshire. He was pale, and more evident that with cheeks brightly spotted by cold. When she had tended his shoulder this morn, she had seen signs of infection. Blessedly, soon the king's physician would tend him.

"Aye, a cold place, but not much longer." She jutted her chin. "You see the tower on the ridge above the glen?"

"Impressive," one said.

She nodded. "King Malcolm has other palaces, but though this one is of no grand size, it is his jewel."

"It does not look well fortified."

"It is, albeit more by God who made the place on which it stands than by man who set cut stone upon it." She sighed. "Now I am home, your duty is done."

"Nay, Lady," the long-bearded one said. "Baron Roche commanded us to deliver you into King Malcolm's hands."

She longed to argue the weather was good and might not hold, but there was stubborn about their faces.

Peering over her shoulder, she saw Edgar's entourage moved along the road gently curving down from the first hill that permitted a glimpse of Dunfermline. After confirming the Aetheling remained at the fore, she turned back and considered the hill that rose up after the descent of this one.

"Do we go a bit farther, better we shall see the glen below the tower of Malcolm Canmore," she said.

The three agreed, and soon she glimpsed movement of those who lived in the town near the palace. Happiness in that, and yet sorrow stung her eyes.

She was not returning with her mother as intended when last she was here peering back at what she left behind. Never again would Cannie nor Malcolm's men slain by her kin look upon this. And after trying to do some good in an England crippled by the conquering, she had been given a heinous parting gift beyond that of the harrying—the burning of the village, the death of Stephen, and the clash of Hendrie and Theriot D'Argent that could put one or both in the grave.

"Though I ache to give this horse my heels," she said, "I have strayed too far."

Without further word, they walked their mounts back up the hill toward Edgar and his men.

~

HAD the sense closed to Theriot opened? Or had something other than the feeling of being watched with great enmity snatched him out of darkness?

Eyes yet pained by grit, he raised his lids halfway. Still he could see no light though the sun was warm upon his face. Either the cloth was very dense or several layers thick. And the scent…

He breathed deep.

"Will you ever awaken?" asked one whose voice Theriot had only before heard at a distance—most recently while tracking the Aetheling camp to camp while awaiting an opportunity to set a Norman contingent after he who had left Scotland to test the waters of rebellion amid the harrying.

"I would have you conscious just long enough to know the wrath of one whose blood is of the royal line unlike that of your liege whose nobility was halved by a common woman free with her favors." Edgar gave a grunt of satisfaction. "Soon I shall be king."

As Theriot confirmed the movement beneath him was that of a wagon and he continued to share the straw bedding with one whose head was opposite, the Aetheling continued, "I am most interested in knowing what you think of the trap I laid for you."

Trap? Theriot searched backward and found himself in the village, memories and sensations of that night more clearly flashing through him than when first he returned to consciousness. But he could make no sense of Edgar's boasting.

Idle boasting, he determined and wondered how much longer the fearsome King of Scots would suffer this one to whom he granted sanctuary. Not much longer if it was only rumor Malcolm was to wed the young man's sister. But even if the princess did become his queen, reins would have to be drawn on the Aetheling before he endangered Scotland beyond saving.

I am thinking better, Theriot congratulated himself on the speed and depth of thought which had been plodding and shallow.

"Ah, the Norman dog awakens!"

Theriot checked his body to discover what had revealed him. He did not smile, but the muscles of his mouth were engaged, satisfaction tautening what should have remained slack.

"I wager you are in much pain."

He was, though less so than when last he was conscious.

"Alas, it is only the beginning of what you shall suffer. When we reach the palace, Malcolm will recognize my claim upon you."

Scotland, Theriot silently named the land over which he was conveyed. As for the palace, was not the one nearest the border a league distant from the great estuary? As for Edgar's claim on this Norman, why did he not already have first right?

"When he weds my sister—with my permission—Malcolm shall be my brother-in-law," Edgar confirmed the rumor. "Then his forces and mine will kick your William back across the sea."

Theriot let his mouth curve.

"You think it funny?" Edgar snapped. "What is funny is how easily a warrior with your family's reputation put both feet in my trap."

Doubtless, his silvered dark hair was responsible for him being identified as a D'Argent, but still the question of the trap of which he spoke...

"I know you Normans. Give you a woman to chase and you will put her to ground, use up the good of her, and swell her belly with a babe best left to the wolves."

The whelp had cause to believe that of many Normans, but not this one, Theriot reflected a moment before he made sense of the trap. If Edgar had set one, then he and some of his men had remained in the village, sending the majority ahead to draw the Normans away—and quite possibly those were sacrificed the same as much of the village the Aetheling should have gone around.

Theriot must have been seen when he was forced to leave the cover of dark to save what proved a cat. Hence, a screaming woman had drawn him out and onto the swords of men Theriot had believed fellow Normans.

"You would have made a misbegotten child on her, eh, Theriot D'Argent?"

It surprised his Christian name was known, there being D'Argents aplenty with claim to the surname. The only explanation his fatigued mind could root out was that one or more of the Normans in pursuit of the Aetheling had been captured and forced to reveal how the contingent learned of Edgar's movements.

"You fear me," the young man said, "and you should, as evidenced by the fine dagger ever I shall carry to attest to having bested a D'Argent."

Just as Theriot was aware he lacked sword and armor, so too the dagger earned alongside spurs upon the attainment of knighthood. But knowing that fine weapon was on the belt of one so unworthy...

Though he would reveal more of his state of consciousness, he said, "*You* bested me, pup?"

He heard the Aetheling's sharp breath and his mount grunt in response to tension.

"You merely threaded a trap, little Edgar, sending a woman to risk her life as you dared not yourself—just as you sacrificed the men sent from the village to lead the Normans away whilst you shook in the shadows. And I have enough wits about me to recall it was a Scots who put me to ground, not one who will never be king no matter how much he dreams, schemes, and prays—even if he makes his sister a purse of gold good for the trading."

Above the sound of the entourage's ascending progress that

caused the blood in Theriot's lower extremities to move toward his head, he felt the wrathful words the Aetheling longed to pour out.

As he waited, he assessed his circumstances. Since his life had been spared, possibly he would be ransomed—if his family did not come for him before then. And they would when they learned he was missing and where he was held.

Unfortunately, since he had very little contact with his own these past months beyond alerting contingents to pockets of resistance, it could be many weeks before any questioned his whereabouts. And even then, how would they know he had been taken to Scotland?

Ciel, he thought. Providing the horse left outside the village had not been discovered by the Aetheling, it might lead his family to him. Not only was the steed of fine markings—its body the color of pewter, mane black, and face white—its unusual blue eyes marked it as belonging to Theriot. Eventually a villager would find it, and if it was seen when the D'Argents came looking for the king's scout, they would learn what had happened there when he who wished to be king endangered his people.

"Aye, the Scotsman did my bidding," Edgar finally spoke. "Poor Hendrie."

Then that one was dead? Those thrusts of the dagger ended his life?

"You are a fool to underestimate me," the Aetheling said, then came the scrape of a blade exiting a scabbard. "A fine weapon this, but more than the lovely sapphire, I am impressed with how sharp the blade and precise the point—good for scooping out eyes."

Theriot grunted. "Certes, in that I do not underestimate you—that you, whole of body, could succeed in putting out the eyes of an injured, weaponless man."

The silence seethed, then Edgar said, "Were I to finish what Hendrie began, many would consider it merciful."

Theriot's first thought was he meant to use the D'Argent dagger to end his enemy's life, but a memory unfolded and more intensely he felt the grit in his eyes as he saw again the Scotsman's hands ahead of feeling thumbs press against his eyes.

Almighty! Not grit but damage. But so greatly he was blinded? For that he could not see light through the cloth?

"Aye, merciful," Edgar drawled. "Methinks even my pious sister would agree 'tis best to put a blind dog out of its misery."

Theriot's breath came hard and fast, but though he commanded the warrior to think before acting, panic with which he was unfamiliar caused his control to snap. He cast aside the blanket, wrenched off the eye covering, and saw light. At first that was all, as if he peered through watered milk, but as he began to rise and move toward the Aetheling, dark smudges appeared.

Then the pain in his head exploded, all went black, and a Scottish voice snarled, "Fool, Edgar! Fool!"

WHEN MARGUERITE REACHED the top of the hill and saw Edgar was no longer at the fore of those ascending that side, she spurred her mount forward. But she could not reach Theriot D'Argent soon enough to prevent further injury being done him.

"What have you wrought?" she demanded as Edgar sidled his horse away from the wagon whose driver had reined in only when she and her escort neared.

"Not what was due him!" The Aetheling returned the D'Argent dagger to its scabbard, jutted his chin at Hendrie. "Worse I would have done had he not gotten to him first."

Marguerite looked to the Scotsman whose face was contorted with pain where he lay half covered beneath blankets, then to the prisoner whose upper body draped the wagon's rear gate. Though she had been unable to see all that transpired, doubtless it began with Edgar.

"Leave us, knave!" she snarled.

"Know you to whom you speak?" the prince demanded.

"Aye, one who is so courageous he works ill on the injured!"

With a jab of spurs, he urged his mount toward her, but her escort inserted themselves between them. Cursing her, Edgar reined around and sped away.

As the entourage resumed its advance, Marguerite stepped off her mount's stirrup into the wagon. The wheels once more in motion, it was no easy thing to ease the muscular weight of Theriot D'Argent off the edge without further injuring him, but at last she settled him on the straw.

When his head rolled to the side and she saw his injured eyes were exposed and jaw reddened, she looked to Hendrie who pressed a hand to his side. "Should I tend you first?"

"Nay, lass. This old Scots has less bend in his steel than that young Norman."

Marguerite retrieved her medicinals from behind the bench, settled alongside the chevalier, and shrugged back her mantle. "Tell what happened, Hendrie."

"D'Argent turned violent—not that Edgar did not give him cause. Thus, I landed a kick ere the Aetheling could use the dagger on him. And see, the Norman is quiet again and yet breathes."

She knew Hendrie was hurting, but as she tended the chevalier's new injury, she pressed, "What passed between them?"

"Taunting, at which Edgar is adept."

"What words, Hendrie?"

"When I came right, he was boasting of taking the dagger

from D'Argent—though he did not reveal the manner in which it came to him."

Marguerite remembered, having nearly slapped Edgar when he dismounted alongside the fallen men and, without asking after Hendrie, snatched up the weapon drawn from the Scotsman's side.

"What set the Norman to raging was when he learned the reason his eyes are covered—of the trap that may permanently blind him."

Once again stabbed with guilt over what she had wrought, Marguerite smoothed salve over a jaw beginning to swell.

"A trap Edgar claimed was of his own devising," Hendrie added.

She faltered. These past days she had worried over revealing to the chevalier what could prove a terrible fate and claiming responsibility, but now that Edgar had...

Having also salved the chevalier's abraded lids, she folded the binding cloth and worked her mind over what could be done with this day's ill. Shortly, she had her answer.

Relieved Hendrie's face reflected an easing of discomfort, she said, "I will be the one to restore the chevalier to health. And easier that shall be if he does not know I am responsible for what was done him."

Disapproval bent his mouth. "How do you plan to hide that? He saw you—" He broke off. "Ah, I know yer thinking."

She inclined her head. "If night did not deny him the ability to recognize me, providing his eyes are as damaged as they appear, he will be unable to look near upon me until he recovers his sight."

"*If* he recovers it."

"As for my voice..." She searched backward to recall what Theriot D'Argent might have heard. "Since I spoke very little and it was in Saxon, my voice should be unknown to him."

Too, though this long unused throat softens, she thought, *there is yet the rough about the words come off my tongue.*

"As added precaution, I shall address him in his language, and if I must speak in my own in his presence, I shall be mindful."

"Malcolm will not like it."

He was protective of her, and more he would be after her ordeal over the border. However, there was hope he would yield when he learned of the D'Argents—had he not heard of them already.

She considered the chevalier's face that greatly resembled his oldest brother's, then finished binding his eyes, tucked the blankets around him, and crawled the planks to Hendrie.

"Will you not give aid in persuading our king to allow me to tend D'Argent?" she asked.

He snorted. "As you speak of one who twice stuck me with a dagger, I will not."

Heart sinking, she eased the bandage off his injury. "With or without your aid, that is how it must unfold, Hendrie."

"Ah, wee sparrow, do you not see that Norman is kindling for the fire, his nicked edges keen for the sharpening?"

Relieved Hendrie's stitches had not torn through, she reached for salve. "I see it, but not only am I responsible for that kindling and those edges, I am knit to his family by kindnesses shown me and the rebel, Em, who has wed into them. I understand why you wish him dead, but by way of the D'Argents, I see the good of him." She pressed the bandage in place, lowered his tunic, and turned the covers over him. "Hence, best he is commended to my care than that of others who will regard him as the enemy."

"He is the enemy."

She drew her mantle around her and flipped the hood over her head. "Only because he answers to a liege different from ours."

He peered at the one he had kicked unconscious. "You said he was the only Norman found in the village. Do you not think that strange?"

"As told, I believe he sought to give aid to what sounded a child."

"Be that so, still the question of why he alone turned back. As all know, Normans run in packs for the wolves they are."

A thought struck. "Mayhap he did not turn back. Perhaps he merely happened on the fire."

Hendrie frowned. "Still, where is the rest of his pack? Unless…"

Hoping whatever occurred would render Theriot D'Argent blameless, she leaned in. "What?"

"Unless he served as a scout and set those Normans after the Aetheling."

Knowing Sir Theriot was a warrior of the battlefield rather than the shadows, she nearly rejected that. However, had not his brother, Dougray, been a scout?

"Lord," she breathed.

"Lord, indeed. We were mindful of the contingents, but of a single Norman versed in stealth?" He shook his head. "Our own scouts mapped the Normans' movements, ensuring they remained distant, then a great force came at us. If your D'Argent sent them, he is as responsible for the fires as Edgar."

Her resolve threatening to wither, she raised her chin. "Still I will tend him. That is how it must unfold."

CHAPTER FIVE

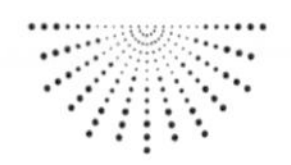

"You live!" It was not the first time the King of Scots said it, the second, nor third. And still he held to her. When he eased back, it was just enough to kiss her brow. "Almighty, you live, Marguerite!"

She tried not to cry, but tears flowed over his rejoicing of her return that had coincided with his own from the North where he had put down an uprising.

Mostly, the people of Scotland were united under one king, unlike England with Saxons aplenty rejecting Norman rule, but this country had its disagreements which must be resolved by the blade when negotiations failed. Though Malcolm was feared, far more he was respected by the Scots than ever King William would be respected by the English.

Sadly, sometimes even a good king must rule by fear those who will not be ruled any other way, Marguerite's sire had explained the need to bear arms against one's own. *But those who first seek the good of their countrymen, requiring only wise guidance beneath a firm hand... Aye, Daughter, they have earned the right to be ruled by respect.*

As she believed Malcolm did, though ever she was troubled

by his raids into England. Albeit on a far lesser scale than William's harrying, her king harassed those same people who offended or stood in his way. Hopefully, if he wed Princess Margaret and she was as devout as told, her influence would make him a better neighbor to the English.

He pulled back, and she thought the man who neared his fortieth year more handsome than ever. Having ignored all save she who bounded from the wagon when she saw he rode before his army, he studied her tear-streaked face.

"What is this, Sparrow?" he said in the Gaelic spoken at court somewhat more than the Saxon and Norman-French of those who had served him long before the conquering of England. Then giving her no time to answer, he said, "Ye have suffered badly these months."

She swallowed. "Other than what happened on my grandfather's lands, not badly."

His brow furrowed. "You are not going to take me to task for slaying that old man, are ye—not after what he did to my men and your Cannie?" At her hesitation, he said, "Before we slew all, we had them dig up those they murdered so we could bring them home with your mother for burial."

Marguerite gasped. "She is at my sire's side?"

"She shares with her husband hallowed ground I denied those who put arrows in the backs of my men." His brow lowered further. "Aye, we made good use of that foul, mass grave, and to ensure your grandfather suffer longest, he went in last."

Imagining that, she closed her eyes.

He gave her a shake. "Task me not, Sparrow."

She considered asking after Claude who had saved her, Gerald who may have been the one to escape the Rebels of the Pale, and her cousin, Pepin, but it could wait.

"I task you not." she said softly.

He grunted. "Be assured, I hear enough from my Margaret and dance to *her* disapproval."

My Margaret. She liked that for the happiness and reverence with which he spoke it. "Then it is certain you shall wed the Aetheling's sister?"

"Indeed, though 'twas difficult to persuade her, so set was she on becoming a bride of Christ. Fortunately, Edgar understood the advantage of our union. As he is head of the family and the princess was moving toward love for me, he came to my side and she agreed."

Hopefully, it was true Edgar had not forced her to abandon her vocation.

"I see you worry over she who is a pearl to me," Malcolm said. "Fear not. She has set her heart and mind on serving God by furthering my knowledge of His word so better I honor and grow His Church in Scotland. Once you are further acquainted, I believe my Margaret and Marguerite shall become great friends." He frowned. "Your name and hers are so close, there will be confusion." He chuckled. "Ah, here my excuse to more often name her *Meg*—better yet, *My Pearl* over which she blushes so prettily."

By his glances, stares, and how near he had drawn to her when first she arrived, Marguerite had known he was attracted to the woman of twenty and five years, but he had not spoken of it as he did now—as if the formidable King Malcolm, whose only love was Scotland, were half his age and the Aetheling's sister his first love.

"Dubh will be glad to see you."

He spoke of the hound gifted her three months before she departed to bring her mother home. Averse to dogs for making her nose itch, she had tried to return Dubh, but the king did not like her and Cannie living alone in the cottage and had given much thought to which of his hounds best suited her.

The relatively small three-year-old female, who could no

longer pup for having taken a boar's tusk to the belly, had seemed as indifferent to Marguerite as she was to the hound, and as determined to return to the palace as her mistress wished she would—until that last month when both began to accept what could not be changed.

"Dubh may not remember me," Marguerite said.

"Aye, she will." The king glanced past her. "We are chilled and travel weary. Let us settle before a fire with refreshments, and *My Pearl* and I shall listen to the tale I am more eager to hear for how you came to be in the company of my betrothed's brother."

Marguerite followed his gaze to the wagon beyond her three escort. "I am eager to tell it, though I would do so in the privacy of your apartment once—"

"Who are those men?" he asked after the Saxons who peered at them over their shoulders.

"My escort from Derbyshire, which I shall explain after your physician tends Hendrie and one of the Saxons who—"

"Hendrie is injured?" That Scots nearly as dear to Malcolm as her sire had been, he thrust back the plaid cloak draping one shoulder and with long-reaching strides moved his muscular bulk up the incline. Marguerite nearly had to run to stay his side, and moments later groaned when Edgar urged his mount toward his future brother-in-law.

When she and the king reached the wagon, Hendrie rumbled, "Your Grace."

"Who harmed ye, man?"

Hendrie jutted his chin. "He whom I blinded—a Norman."

Malcolm stepped nearer and looked down at the unconscious D'Argent. "For what is he here? For what does he live?"

Marguerite set a hand on his arm. "I shall explain when we speak."

"Much danger Lady Marguerite has escaped," Hendrie said.

"Pray, do not further indulge her lest this Norman proves her undoing."

The king grunted. "Aye, best we speak in private, Sparrow."

"Brother!" Edgar called.

Marguerite was glad her gaze was on Malcolm. Though the emotion shifting across his eyes was fleeting, it was annoyance. But whereas he did not long suffer that dealt by others, likely his tolerance was greater for the brother of his pearl.

"We must speak," the Aetheling said as he neared.

Malcolm placed a hand on Marguerite's arm. "This long lost lady has first claim on me, but we shall talk—if not this eve, the morrow."

The Aetheling's mouth tightened. "Best soon, Malcolm," he said and reined around.

"The morrow 'tis!" the sovereign of Scotland corrected he who was a dispossessed prince to a king no longer dispossessed.

Though the Aetheling's back stiffened, he continued forward.

"He has become more difficult and demanding now I am to wed his sister," Malcolm said. "As once my birthright was denied me—and for it the foul Macbeth and his stepson are dead—I sympathize with him, but my forbearance nears its end."

She raised her eyebrows.

He smiled crookedly. "An end which lies beyond the day I make his sister my queen." He turned her aside. "Ye shall ride the remainder of the way with me so I may begin knowing your tale."

When she was seated before him on his destrier, she began to relate all that had happened, beginning with her arrival on her grandfather's lands and the grave to which she had been led.

ALL WAS AGREED, though likely only because the princess who had sat silent throughout finally spoke.

Holding to the crucifix around her neck, setting her other hand atop Malcolm's which impatience had made into a fist, Edgar's sister had vouched for the D'Argents. Though she admitted to having met none of that family, she had heard enough of their character and deeds to believe that were there any good Normans, they were among them.

The King of Scots had mulled that nearly as long as Marguerite's testimony that covered most of her experiences with the D'Argents, then slid his fingers between his beloved's.

Marguerite having remaining standing, he had told her to sit. Perched on the edge of a chair, relief had nearly slumped her when he agreed to claim rights to the prisoner by way of Hendrie. Regarding her request to be given care of the Norman, his *nay* had become *aye*. With conditions.

No apartment within the tower would be afforded Theriot D'Argent—instead, this hut inside the stone walls surrounding the palace. The prisoner would be bound to the bed, and under no circumstance was she to release him unless the watch outside were inside. She would sleep at the door, and her hound who was less than overjoyed by her return was to remain at her side.

Marguerite had accepted the conditions. Though this Norman was a D'Argent, she did not truly know him beyond the feeling she knew him. And even were he of the same cloth as the others, under these circumstances his weave could prove snagged—or irreparably torn.

Leaning against the door she had closed behind the physician, she raised her moist gaze to the rafters. He who had first tended Hendrie in the tower and assured her the Scotsman would live had said the same of Theriot D'Argent. That had been welcome. As for the chevalier's eyes...

She had not asked for Colban's diagnosis, but as he of good

face and figure examined them, she had heard his sighs and seen the shakes of his head as of one who believes a task insurmountable.

Throughout, the chevalier had moved only to breathe and groan over probings, the kick to his jaw surely having further rattled him.

He will live, she reminded herself. *But how?*

Lowering her gaze from the smoke wending through the hole in the roof that also served as a giver of light in day and a window on the stars at night, she considered the pit at the center of the open room. The warming fire was a good one, its consumption of well-cured wood creating as little smoke as possible.

Next she looked to the corner opposite her pallet laid alongside the door and through the light haze considered the warrior. He was rendered helpless, and not only because his wrists were roped to the bed posts.

Herself bound, albeit by guilt, silently she pleaded with the Lord to restore his sight, for what was a warrior who could not see? Though being of the family D'Argent he would not be reduced to begging for coins and scraps from passersby, likely he would suffer lifelong care by loved ones or those of the cloister.

She pushed off the door and, trailed by her hound, crossed to the chevalier who was propped on pillows to allow her to slide drink between his lips.

All the D'Argents she had seen were fit with good faces, raised to good heights and, excepting their fair-haired half-brother, had dark hair shot through with silver as if God had marked them as special. This D'Argent was no exception. Indeed, even more—

"Be not fanciful, Marguerite," she rebuked and started to turn away.

"Marguerite," he rasped, sweeping her back to when first he had spoken a name not quite her own and she had marveled over feelings not due one who but assisted in getting her astride. Now she searched the chevalier's face, but unable to look beyond the cloth covering his eyes, could not know if he had awakened or merely questioned what he heard her speak across his dreams.

"Marguerite?" he repeated harshly, causing Dubh to rumble and draw near.

She lowered to her knees. "Oui, Lady Marguerite," she said in his language, repressing her Scots lilt as much as possible. "You are in Scotland at the court of King Malcolm."

His head jerked, nostrils flared.

"Can you hear me, Sir Theriot?"

"A dog is here," he slurred. "I smell it. More, I smell you. And not…for the first time."

Recalling when she led him distant from what she believed a child, she wondered how he had caught her scent—had she even one in particular—since she had been unable to draw near when Hendrie dropped him.

The wagon, she realized. Though he had been unconscious while she tended him, she had been near enough that were his sense of smell keen, her scent might have gone behind the veil between them. What of her voice when she conversed with Hendrie in their own language? Was it well enough heard he had known a woman tended him during their northward journey?

She prayed not since she must distance this lady of Scotland from the village woman who was both bait and trap.

If only I had accepted the princess's offer to bathe in her apartment! she silently rued having made do with a basin of water and towel.

"You do not like I know your scent," he said.

What had revealed her? She might yet carry a recognizable

scent, but what had delivered her disquiet unto one lacking sight?

"Why does it bother?" he asked thickly.

She shrugged, then remembering he could not see, said, "It seems an intimate observation. I can hardly be comfortable with it though that knowledge was surely gained while I aided the physician in tending you."

"Am I ill?"

Then he did not remember what was learned before Hendrie's kick? Because of further injury to his head? "You are, but you will be well again in time." It was not a lie. It *was* possible he would recover fully, but if he did not, he would live.

If in spite of what is lost to him, he considers it living, her conscience stabbed.

"It is dark," he rasped and tugged at one hand then the other as if to explore his eyes.

Fearing when he realized he was bound he would remember the reason for the darkness, she held her breath.

But he groaned and said, "Soon the dawn, Marguerite?"

Tears stung her eyes. "Oui, soon." Though she knew that for a lie in one way, night having only descended, God willing it would not be in the way that mattered most to this warrior.

Hearing his dry swallow, she retrieved a cup and set its rim to his lips. "Drink, Theriot."

As he sipped, she was glad only she was here to question what possessed her to be familiar with his name.

He eased his head back and, as she returned the cup to the table, once more tugged at his wrists. "What—?"

Marguerite covered his right hand with her own. She meant only to give it a reassuring squeeze, but he turned his palm up and gripped her hand hard.

"Soon the dawn?" he said with such desperation tears flooded her eyes. "You are certain it comes?"

Swallowing a sob, she nodded, then forced words he could hear. "It comes. Now sleep."

He exhaled long, his head rolled to the side, and his breathing deepened.

His hand did not immediately go lax, and when it did, she firmed her hold on it. "Lord, Lord," she whispered, emotions threatening to spill, "heal him. Make him whole. Pray, undo what I did."

Once more stifling a sob, she released his hand. As she drew back, she swept her gaze over his relaxed face, then his hair. And reached. Gently, she pulled through her fingers strands darker and silver brighter for the sheen of oil accumulated these past days, and might have lingered longer over them had not the hound thrust her snout near.

"Dubh!" she gasped and dropped back on her heels.

When the dog was satisfied with what could be learned of the Norman's scent, she trotted to the fire pit.

To keep her hands from once more touching what they ought not, Marguerite clasped them in her lap. *Beyond this tearing guilt, too much I am drawn to you, Chevalier,* she silently lamented. *Though I knew Michel's kisses, never did I feel this much pull for him, and here we are only at the beginning.*

"Of what is also the end," she said and retreated to her pallet where, over and again she reminded herself of why she was here and what she must do to ensure the chevalier did not reject her care—beginning with a thorough bath to wash away whatever reminded him of the woman who Edgar told was part of the trap.

It was wrong, she knew, the same as her prayers for the Lord's forgiveness in advance of lies and half-truths, but she saw no other way to gain the trust necessary to aid in this man's recovery.

Moving her thoughts elsewhere, she recalled her meeting with Malcolm in which she had learned the barest bones of the vengeance he had worked on her kin. "Oh, Claude," she breathed. "I am sorry for your death, but much grace shown that you passed ere my king's coming."

As for Gerald, Malcolm had told he was not present when vengeance fell upon her grandfather and his people. Thus, likely that uncle had died at the hands of the Rebels of the Pale.

But he may be out there, perhaps even his son, fear whispered. *Beware of the unseen more than the seen, Marguerite, daughter of Diarmad the Mad. Beware.*

CHAPTER SIX

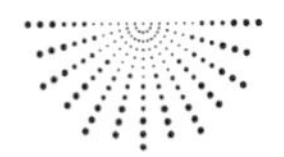

He raged. And how!

Praying the men given watch over Theriot did not harm him, Marguerite snatched up her skirts, descended the tower steps, and ran across the bailey beneath the regard of those patrolling the walls.

Damp hair swinging across her face, she rounded the hut she had departed at sunrise accompanied by the hound she had forgotten to collect from the hall. Finding the door open, she sprang inside.

Norman-accented shouts sounding all around, she saw past the men lunging left and right—attempting to advance and avoid kicks—the bed lay on its side. When she was past the fire pit, she noted the posts to which the chevalier remained bound bent as if to snap, and his eye covering was down around his neck.

"Enough!" she commanded in Norman-French with which the Scotsmen were passing proficient. "Give him space!"

Malcolm's men retreated, and as she drew level with them, she saw the lower face of one was bloodied, likely from a kick to the teeth. Of greater concern was Theriot, as much because he seemed savage enough to tear his arm from its socket, as the thrusts of his body caused his head to come close to striking a post. Already he had taken two such blows. One more could finish him.

"Lady!" a guard barked in Gaelic when she stepped forward.

She flung up a staying hand that would be honored only if she remained out of reach of those kicks. "Hear me, Theriot!" she cried.

He did, as told by the jerk of his body, a curse of less volume, and blood-red eyes whose clouded centers landed on her face. Then he stilled and stared—sightlessly, she was fairly certain though his eyes were on hers as if he knew where to find them.

"It is Lady Marguerite of the night past," she said. "Do you remember when we talked?"

He narrowed his lids as if to better see what could not be seen. "Oui, we spoke of the dawn that comes soon. It did not, Lady. Still it is as dark as a blizzard gone grey, and this one who cannot see through the snow is fettered like a man given unto the torturer."

Once more observing the reach of his legs, she took another step forward, causing the Scots who advanced with her to grumble. Seeing the swelling of Theriot's abraded and bruised lids had lessened like that on his jaw whose thickening whiskers would cover the injury before it fully healed, she said, "I am sorry for it. Be assured, no harm is intended. It is precaution, as are these men set to watch over you in my absence."

"Precaution?"

"As told on the night past, you are at the court of King Malcolm in Dunfermline."

"Edgar," he growled.

"Oui, he and his men—"

"For what did they bring me here?"

Why are you not prepared for that question? she rebuked herself. "I wish I had an answer—"

"Who are you to me, Lady who speaks my language as if it is her own and yet has the Scots dancing all about her tongue?"

If it danced now, what would he say if she made no effort to hide it? "As I am fairly skilled at healing, you have been given into my care to do as the physician directs, and since you are Norman and…"

"A prisoner," he said with a jut of his chin that caused perspiration-dampened hair to shift across his brow.

There being no way to make pretty of his circumstances, she said, "Oui, for that my king orders precautions taken to ensure my well-being."

"I am not of the stamp of men who harm women."

"I do not believe you would, but King Mal—"

"Why do you not believe it? Do you know me?"

She swallowed. "Princess Margaret has told though the D'Argents answer to the usurper, they are well regarded by many of the English."

"So well regarded much I shall suffer when your king recognizes her brother's claim on me?"

"I believe it was the princess who persuaded her betrothed otherwise. Thus, King Malcolm claims rights to you by way of his man, Hendrie, who…"

"Who sought to blind me!" he spoke what she could not. "And for it is dead."

Before Marguerite could think how to respond, one of the Scots grunted with amusement, causing those unseeing eyes to move his direction.

"He is not dead," Theriot said with such certainty and resentment she was both relieved she did not have to make a lie of it and dismayed she could not since it might settle him.

"Your dagger struck nothing vital," she said.

He growled, and she wondered if it was as much for confirmation Hendrie lived as memory of Edgar's taunting over that weapon now on the Aetheling's belt.

His eyes shifted as if he searched his memory. "That accursed Scotsman was in the wagon with me." His brow furrowed. "It was he who kicked me."

"Only to quiet you lest Edgar do great harm."

"Then I am to be grateful to this Hendrie?"

"He was a good friend to my sire, is a good friend to my king, and your enemy only because of what was done the village by Normans and his belief you intended further ill."

She hoped he would defend himself, confirming he was not among those who set fires and that he had only sought to aid a child, but he eased back against the slumped mattress.

"We must set you aright, Theriot. Will you allow me—?"

"Does this Scots lady believe herself my friend?"

Because she had not titled him, she realized. "Certes, I am not that to you, *Sir* Theriot. Not yet."

"And never shall be!"

"Will you allow us to set you aright?" she repeated.

He narrowed his eyes. "I shall control my anger—for the moment."

"Aid me," she instructed the guards and started forward.

"Leave, Lady!" the chevalier demanded.

She faltered. "I will help settle you and tend your injuries."

"I must relieve myself! Though I do not doubt I have suffered intolerable indignity having bodily needs tended by another, I will suffer no more." As if interpreting her hesitation as consideration rather than discomfort, he added, "If your Scotsmen are as fierce as I have been told, they will have no trouble ensuring this sightless man behaves."

"Of course," Marguerite said and instructed the men to unbind him and provide whatever he required.

As she turned away, the older one gripped her arm. "You saw what he is capable of," he said in their language and nodded at his companion who wiped blood from his lower face.

Remembering to answer in Norman-French, speaking

slowly to ensure he fully understood, she said, "Oui, but forget not our king told he may be unbound providing two guards are within. The same as our sovereign, I trust you can subdue him without doing harm should he lose control again." She pulled free, crossed the hut, and closed the door behind her.

Listening for further struggle, she recalled what she had witnessed upon entering. Such ferocity she had only seen from afar whilst tucked away during clashes between rebels and Normans.

Not true, she corrected. She had been very near when his brother met at swords with another Norman who believed the rebel, Em, his property. However, there had been control to Sir Dougray's ferocity and anger, unlike Theriot's.

Because we have made an animal of him, she thought. *A wounded, cornered animal who believes he has naught to lose.*

Hearing sounds at her back, she held her breath. They were only voices of little volume and emotion, then came the thump of the bed returned to its legs.

Marguerite closed her eyes. "Lord, heal this D'Argent so he not dwell in the dark the remainder of his life. And if you will not restore his sight..." Remembering Diarmad the Mad whose identity was derived as much from being a man of the sword as a husband, father, and friend, she shook her head. "What then, Lord? How am I to persuade a warrior no longer a warrior that life is worth living?"

And how are you to ease this guilt? her conscience submitted. *Because of you, Stephen is dead and Hendrie and this Norman injured nearly unto death.*

"Prayer," she whispered. "More prayer."

ALONE, just as he needed to be until he vanquished the anxiety that so strained his chest it felt as if his ribs would crack. But soon Lady Marguerite of an accent neither purely Scots nor Norman-French, of freshly washed hair and clean, hearth-dried garments, would enter.

Turning his face toward his left wrist bound to a post, the movement causing ache to spear the back of his skull, Theriot tried to make sense of what the woman and the guard spoke on the other side of the door. Frustratingly, their voices were too low and he could not even determine which language they used though his hearing was keen.

Seeing smudges of dark through a milky haze, he opened the hand toward which he directed his gaze, splayed his fingers and closed them. The smudge moved as had those of the men who had not mistreated him while setting the room aright—though he had sensed the one who smelled of blood longed to drive a fist into this Norman's face.

It had been difficult to contain anger of a capacity he had not known he possessed, especially when they released his wrists to allow him some dignity, but he had provided no excuse to do to him half what this unrecognizable vengeful self wished to do to them. Instead, he had perseverated on a lesson taught him by his uncle who had trained him into a warrior and his sire who had striven to shape him into a man pleasing to God.

Patience, Theriot! one had bellowed and the other had said firmly with a hand atop his son's shoulder. *When time allows, in all things patience.*

Certes, much time he would have to await an opportunity to escape. The great unknown was whether he would be prepared for it.

Ribs further strained, he assured himself that in accord with God's favor shown him all his life, his vision would be restored, then moved his thoughts to Lady Marguerite from whom there were things to be learned.

Win her to your side, he told himself. *You know what moves women—how to make them look once and again, put pink in cheeks, open mouths to laughter, and close lips to receive kisses.*

When finally she entered, this D'Argent given to flirtation felt a predator. He would have hated it were he the Theriot he better knew than this one whose emotions dwelt in the dark the same as his sight, but for now there were things he needed from her.

Proceed cautiously, he counseled. *From the rough of her voice and that her king permits her to tend you, she may be of an age of much experience.*

Feeling her gaze, he said, "As you see, I behaved, Lady."

"I thank you."

Attending to her footfalls over the dirt floor, he found they numbered only two less than those of the Scotsmen outside. From her voice, already he knew she was of good height for a woman, and now something else. She did not shorten her stride to appear more feminine. And another thing learned—rather, confirmed—was the length of this dwelling, which he was fairly certain was half its breadth.

The lady halted. "Until drink and viands arrive, will you allow me to tend your injuries?"

He tugged on his wrists. "I cannot harm you."

"I saw what your kick did to the man whose front teeth are loose. As your legs remain unbound..."

He shifted them atop the blanket. "Many the weapons made of one's head, legs, feet, hands..." *And thumbs,* he silently added. "What I should have said is I *will not* harm you. Unfortunately, all I have to give is the word of a D'Argent."

"That is enough." It was said with certainty, and further he was surprised when she lowered to the mattress, allowing him to more deeply draw in her freshly washed scent. Just as disconcerting was the warmth of her hip brushing his ribs.

"We shall begin with your eyes," she said, her lean indicating she reached to the bedside table.

A bag was opened—canvas, he knew from its fibrous, oiled scent.

A flask uncapped—alcohol, as told by its powerful, stinging scent.

A pot unstoppered—a salve of many herbs, as revealed by a scent so soothing he nearly closed his eyes.

The lady turned toward him, and when her hip settled firmly against his side, he jerked.

"Forgive me." She scooted away. "I did not know you were sore. Do you think your ribs bruised or broken?"

"Bruised," he said, then to calm his body, asked, "How many years have you, Lady? Two score? Three?"

Her soft laughter smelled of mint. "I am little more than a score."

He was not truly surprised. It was good she was young since she would be more impressionable, but bad in that he was too responsive. He needed to move her without himself being moved.

"As I sound a frog due to a throat malady from which I am mostly recovered," she said, "I do not take offense at being thought a woman of greater age." She tapped the underside of his chin. "Now your eyes."

He tilted his head back and drew a long breath of her. "You bathed in lavender water—and recently, as told by damp hair."

He was pleased to hear her tongue come off her palate, though not as much as he would be had something in him not answered something in her.

Still, I move her more than she moves me, he assured himself.

"You have a good sense of smell," she said warily.

"Nearly as good as my sight." It was a response of little thought, but much thought and bitterness once spoken. Tautly, he asked, "When does the physician believe it will be restored?"

Her hesitation made him tense further. "He told me naught."

Fairly certain she lied, he put between his teeth, "Naught

because he would give no answer? Or naught because you, who are to care for me, did not ask?"

"I...did not ask."

Hands aching to become fists, he said, "Interpretation of his silence and yours on the matter does not bode well."

He heard her moisten her lips. "I am sure it is too soon to know. Though he will visit again later this day, if you tell me what you are able to see—light or movement or both—I shall carry word to him so better he knows what to expect when he comes."

"I see white light of the thickest fog, the only other color dark grey when something passes through that light or draws very near."

"That sounds a good thing."

"Compared to being entirely in the black," he snapped, and hating the desperation in his voice, once more assured himself of God's favor.

"I think it must be poison to the body and soul to abandon hope long ere it abandons you, Sir Theriot," the lady said softly. "Pray, hold to hope, even if only for the sake of your family."

Her words jolted, not because they sounded of one far beyond her years, because they revealed her awareness of the lapse of faith that made him sound self-pitying. And that was not who he was. He was a D'Argent the same as the brother he had challenged to rise above destructive wretchedness following the loss of an arm at the Battle of Hastings. And that Dougray had done, as would Theriot if—

Not if, he told himself lest once more he rage against the walls of the body in which he was trapped. *My eyes will heal.*

A hand on his shoulder returned him to the woman who believed she knew him better than ever she would. "Close your lids so I may clean the scratches around your eyes, Theriot."

"*Sir* Theriot," he corrected as he ought not were he to bring her to his side. But then, it would rouse suspicion if he entirely suppressed these feelings.

"Sir Theriot," she acceded.

The alcohol stung, the salve soothed, and the cloth she unfastened from around his neck angered. "Do not cover my eyes."

"But it will keep the salve from—"

"Non!" Not only did binding them make him feel more helpless, but it offended the cloth that had long served as a reminder of God's favor was transformed into something that testified to a loss of favor.

Thankfully, the woman let it be and asked him to turn his head. "The swelling has lessened," she said after gently probing the back, then exclaimed, "Your wrists!"

They were sore, the flesh abraded when, finding himself blind and bound, he dumped the bed on its side and attempted to snap the posts.

"Once the food arrives to break our fast, I shall have the men unbind you so I can salve and bandage them," she said. "It should not be much longer." She shifted, then fell into the silence of looking close upon one believed unaware he was observed.

Feeling soft breaths among the whiskers of his jaw, sensing her gaze moving over his face, he set his eyes upon hers and awaited her reaction to his own observance, albeit his was of the smudge of her.

She turned further toward him, and her exhale swept down his throat and ceased to be felt as if she scrutinized him to his feet. When her breath returned to his face, she said, "We must attend to your ablutions and the laundering of your garments. If you are well with it, I shall arrange for a bath—if not this day, the morrow."

"Only if done by my hand."

"Of course."

When a knock sounded, she stood. "Come!"

The door opened, and the lad who entered bearing a rattling platter respectfully acknowledged the lady in the accent of the Scots, then hastened forward with the step of one less than half Theriot's weight.

Another padded in after him on four feet, and Theriot remembered when earlier he had caught the smell of fur. This dog had been here with the lady last eve.

When the boy set the platter on the bedside table, the hound ceased its padding and Theriot heard it sniff at his knee. It was not a dog of immense size, but were it, he would not be overly concerned. He knew animals well, even those with whom he was barely acquainted. This one was curious and, possibly, friendly—providing Theriot presented no threat to one it held dear.

"Merci," the lady thanked the lad and, as he retreated, called for the guards to enter and said something that caused the hound to draw back.

Theriot was unbound, then while Marguerite tended his wrists, the guards began feeding wood to what remained of last eve's fire. When flames were roused, their light was so intense he had to turn his eyes opposite.

The lady unbent. "Now food and..." She trailed off.

He knew the reason, having set his mind on what lay ahead to distract himself from fingertips moving across skin overly sensitive to her touch. Whether beneath the eyes of her and her men he fumbled over cup and platter or her eyes alone and with her aid, his thirst and hunger would be satisfied—and the opportunity to win her to his side exploited.

"Bind me," he said.

When it was done, the guards withdrew.

"The name of your dog?" Theriot asked.

"For the color of her fur, she is called Dubh."

"A Gaelic word?"

"Oui, it means blackness or darkness."

Hearing the catch of her breath, he knew her thoughts collided with his own—that Dubh and he had something in common. Lest anger was roused again, he said, "My horse is named *Ciel* for the color of his eyes."

"Sky," she translated, then said disbelievingly, *"Blue* eyes?"

"Pale blue, like a sunlit sky."

"I have not heard of such."

Confirmation Ciel had not accompanied him to Scotland. A good thing. Even were the horse not sighted by those who came looking for the king's scout, in addition to this chevalier of silvered dark hair being described to those questioned, mention would be made of the rare beast. And people would talk.

"I am hungry, Lady."

She lowered beside him and reached to the platter.

When last had a woman carried drink and food to his mouth? he wondered as, between her own sips and nibbles, she raised and lowered the cup of ale and put pieces of bread and cheese to his lips.

Three years of age and done by his mother, he was certain. And each time Lady Marguerite's fingertips brushed his mouth, more he wished she was the age of that fine woman.

Thus, he was grateful when his formerly dry mouth and empty belly agreed they were content. Though the throb behind his eyes had eased, of a sudden he wanted sleep. "I will rest now."

The lady moved to the foot of the bed, tugged the blankets from beneath his legs and spread them over him. "I shall go to the physician and tell of your sight. Should I arrange for a bath?"

"Non." He lowered his lids and, finding comfort in that dark with which he was longer intimate than that of milky white and grey smudges, murmured, "The morrow."

CHAPTER SEVEN

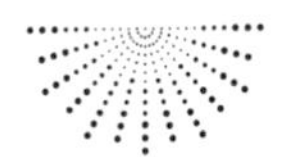

She had hoped to find only the physician and Hendrie in the sick room at the rear of the palace, but another was present and not merely visiting. It was her Saxon escort who had taken a blade to the shoulder during the brief encounter with Normans two days after departing Derbyshire, to which Stephen had put an end.

Now seeing how flushed and moist the man's face where he stretched on the bed opposite Hendrie's, here was confirmation that, as feared, infection had set in.

"It does not look good, Lady," the physician said in Gaelic as he rose from a bench behind the table upon which were arrayed pots and instruments. "Still, I believe his arm can be saved providing healing is given its due."

She understood. Though the Saxons were to pass a sennight here before journeying home, now it could be weeks—even months—ere they departed. The other two would not like it, but they would wait on their companion, it safest to travel in groups amid the harrying.

Marguerite crossed to the man. When he raised his lids, she

said, "We will see you healed, and you will go home to England and your family."

He gave a barely perceptible nod and closed his eyes.

"How fare thee, Hendrie?" she asked, turning to the Scotsman who sat against a pillow.

"Better than he who stuck me. Our king tells I must be satisfied with that. The Norman recovers?"

"That is why I am here—to discuss his injuries with Colban." She lowered beside Hendrie and noted the bandage around his waist showed no crimson. "It appears you heal well."

"Better now I am home."

She glanced up as the physician drew alongside and glimpsed in his eyes what she had seen before going south to bring her mother home—admiration of the courting sort. She had not been averse to it, but now... Though he was of good disposition and fair looks, it was less welcome.

"Lady?" he prompted.

After reporting Sir Theriot was fully conscious and what he had revealed of his vision, she asked, "Will he recover his sight?"

He shrugged. "The eyes are among the body's greatest mysteries. Though I have seen vision restored following similar damage, most often not—at least in full. And with Sir Theriot, there is also the blow to the back of the head which decreases his chances."

"The swelling has lessened."

"A good sign, but..." He shook his head. "The Lord knows better than I."

"Will you come to him again soon?"

His hesitation bothered, resentment likely the cause. By Malcolm's decree, just as it was the duty of the guards to watch over her while she tended Theriot, it was the physician's duty to care for the Norman who had nearly slain Hendrie.

"For you, Lady, soon," Colban said.

She thanked him, departed, and called for Dubh when she entered the hall.

The dog rose from beneath a table where other hounds stretched, but rather than reluctantly plod forward as often done when denied the company of fellow canines, it loped across the rushes.

She patted its head. "Very fine, Dubh," she said, and as the porter opened the door, felt a prickle in her nose. Sniffing deeply, she stepped outside.

HE HAD SLEPT the day away. Now, amid the dark, he awakened. "Marguerite?"

She was only drifting, having earlier been roused by the chill slipping beneath the door that prompted her to move her pallet to the fire pit. Untucking her chin from her blankets, she hesitated over the sight of Dubh alongside the bed, then rasped, "Theriot?"

Just as she did not remind him of her title, neither did he remind her of his when he rumbled, "My need is great."

She understood, having worried over that bodily function when he had not roused once following her visit to the physician—even when Colban entered, examined him, and confirmed his earlier diagnosis. "I shall call the men inside."

Though it was warmer at the pit, she shivered when she came out from beneath the blankets and knew the chevalier's need to relieve himself was not the only thing he required.

She snatched up one of her blankets and wrapped it around her, then with Dubh at her side, exited the hut and hastened to the guards huddled by their fire. When she asked the two to unbind Theriot to allow him a man's privacy and build up the fire inside, the men who were younger than those of the day's guards agreed without complaint. A quarter hour later, they exited, and once more Marguerite and Dubh closed themselves in with the chevalier.

The fire lent much light, allowing her to look upon Theriot over whom covers had been drawn—and the hound who returned to the place made for herself alongside the bed.

"I thank you," the chevalier said, light glancing off unearthly eyes before he narrowed their lids.

It once more appearing he looked upon her, she considered his vision might not be as impaired as reported, and for that he would not allow his eyes to be covered.

Was it a ploy to ease the guard over him so he might escape? Possible. And she hoped it more than possible, even if he recognized her as the woman who made herself bait.

"Have you drink?" he asked.

She hastened to the bedside table. Letting the blanket slide from her shoulders, she lifted the pitcher, filled a cup, and lowered beside Theriot.

He raised his head, and when she set the rim to his lips, drank every drop.

"More?" she asked.

"Non."

"Bread?" She reached to the piece wrapped in cloth following her solitary evening meal.

"Non," he said again, and she felt him quake.

The room warmed, but not enough for one who had gulped down cold water and whose bed was distant from the fire.

Marguerite retrieved her blanket from the ground and spread it atop the others covering him. It would help, but more so were his arms beneath.

Though tempted to unbind him, she did not dare. Even if his vision was better than told and he escaped, he stood little chance of avoiding recapture in the wilds of a foreign country. And Malcolm was unlikely to indulge her a second time.

Determining on the morrow she would request fur blankets lest the bitter cold persisted, she straightened.

"Again, I thank you," he said, then asked, "The physician?"

She tensed. "He came after the nooning hour."

"And?"

"He says it is a good sign the injury to your head heals well, but it is too soon to know what shall come of your sight."

"To *know*. What of his guess?"

Here another truth halved since she did not believe this the time to tell him sight was rarely restored following such damage, and even less likely with a head injury. "All he said was the Lord knows better than he what is to be."

His nostrils flared. "I do not know if more I feel or smell your lie."

So greatly perceiving his anger it was as if hands moved toward her throat, she crossed to her pallet and cast over her shoulder, "Since only a few hours remain ere morn, let us return to our rest."

As she settled and huddled into the one blanket remaining to her, she was flushed with gratitude that what had been embers were now flames.

"Who are you, Lady?"

His question jolted, less for who she was in truth than who she was to one rendered sightless. She considered feigning sleep, but it would not be believed, and from his tone his anger seemed mostly resolved.

She rolled to her side and thought how striking he was with firelight tracing the silver in his hair and playing across his face. However, so narrow were his lids, barely a glimmer reflected in his eyes. Likely, the light pained him.

"As well you know, I am Lady Marguerite of the Scots."

"But not entirely of the Scots."

"Not entirely."

"Then?"

"It is very late, Sir Theriot. The sooner to heal, you should sleep."

"I am fully awake now. As I dread the long hours of boredom, would you not indulge me?"

Though she feared yielding lest fatigue cause her to reveal what she dare not, it occurred she might gain more from him than he from her were he as receptive to giving as taking. "I am curious about you as well. So answer me a question, and I shall do my best to answer yours."

He grunted. "Not only do you seek a trade, but one in which you shall do your *best?*"

"Some things are more easily answered than others, but I shall expect no more from you than I can give."

"Then ask."

Surprised she was to go first, it took a moment to decide how to proceed. "I know you are of an honorable family—especially compared to most Normans."

"I am a D'Argent, and though the English have good cause to name the majority of my countrymen foul, it is not so. Now your question."

"Though Hendrie believes you were among the Normans who burned the village, Princess Margaret expressed doubt. Is she correct, or were you one of those who carried flame while pursuing the Aetheling?"

"I did not carry flame."

She believed him. However, recalling Hendrie's words that were he a scout and had he set the contingent after the Aetheling, he was as responsible for the fires, she said, "How did you come to be in the village so soon thereafter?"

"Now my question, Lady. Who are you?"

She drew in her feet beneath the chemise in which she usually slept and the gown in which she did not sleep unless cold or modesty demanded it. "I am Scots the side of my sire, Diarmad the Mad, and—"

"The Mad?"

She smiled. "Mostly of the axe, though perhaps a little of the head. He was a great warrior who stood the side of Malcolm when our liege came of age and returned to Scotland to take the throne from the one who stole his birthright."

"Macbeth whom Malcolm slew," Theriot said.

"Oui, and also the stepson who succeeded Macbeth. Ever my sire was at Malcolm's side, averting blades and shafts, hammers and fists. For it, when the rightful king was crowned, he renamed his faithful man Diarmad the Shield. Though my sire answered to that which was meant to honor him, still he preferred Diarmad the Mad, and not even the king ceased naming him that whilst my sire lived." The last a whisper, she nearly pressed a hand to her chest.

"I am sorry for your loss, Lady."

She nodded, then recalling he could not see, said, "I thank you."

He gave her some moments, then asked, "Was your mother Norman?"

That pain greater for how recent the loss, she determined to leave the second part of his probing unanswered the same as he had done hers. "The question is mine again. How is it you were in the village so soon after Edgar's pursuers attacked?"

"From a distance, I saw the fire and determined to give aid."

She frowned. "A lone Norman helping English set upon by his countrymen?"

"With much caution, of course."

She did not believe he lied, only that he also told half truths. "I am thinking the question asked of you is one of those less easily answered, Sir Theriot."

"It is."

Glad he did not deny it, she said, "Were you able to help anyone?"

"Once more, the question is mine."

Recalling what she had yet to answer, she said, "Oui, my mother was of your people. Long ere your duke determined he would be king and populate England with those of Normandy, her family crossed the channel with the exiled Edward who was summoned home to accept the crown his family had lost to the Danes. Now my question."

He started to shift onto his side, but his restraints were too taut. "I found the village deserted except for what sounded a child at the farthest reach."

Though Marguerite's escort who searched those homes had reported hearing no further cries from the one greatly aflame and told the other two were empty, still she had feared a child was quieted by smoke and fire.

"Was it a child?" she prompted.

"It was not." As silently she praised the Lord, he added, "A cat was the beginning of my downfall, and hardly had it sprung out the window than my fate was sealed by a woman."

He spoke of Edgar's boast the trap she had set to prevent a Norman from harming a child was of his own doing. Though Marguerite did not wish to further pursue the events of that night, lest her lack of curiosity rouse suspicion, she said, "The Aetheling told he made it appear a village woman was pursued by your fellow Normans to draw you out."

"That she did, and I fell into his trap."

My trap, she thought. "You sought to aid her?"

He frowned, and she expected he would remind her the next question was his, but said, "I did. Do you believe I meant her no harm?"

In the hope of more deeply burying her involvement in his loss, she was tempted to remind him she knew his family only by way of Princess Margaret, but she chose another half truth over a lie. "As I am inclined to believe your family honorable, I think you speak true."

And I think you deceit wrapped in something sweet, Theriot silently pronounced over her evasion to which he might have been deaf as well as blind had she not hastily retreated from talk of the physician's diagnosis. To keep anger from overwhelming his remaining senses, he had thrust that emotion deep and dropped a door over it, but the simmer was coming to a boil again, causing heat to escape the seams.

Cool thyself, he counseled that which could impede what was needed to gain his freedom.

"It is your question now," she said.

Having forgotten their bartering, he sought to look closer at the dark of her against firelight, but there was no face to be seen nor a good rendering of her shape. Feeling the door to his anger shudder, he decided he was done with this trade...game... whatever it was.

"I am cured of sleeplessness, Lady Marguerite."

"Oh," she said with obvious disappointment.

I have her attention, he congratulated himself as he turned his head opposite, *and I shall make something useful of it.*

He heard her settle, and before long her deepening breaths between the hound's soft snores.

Far from cured of sleeplessness but warm at last, out of habit more than an attempt to go inside himself, he lowered his lids. And was drawn to that door. He knew it would be hot, and it was. He knew it could prove hot enough to blister, but though it seemed evil on the other side, it intrigued for the insight offered he had not realized he lacked.

What he felt must be akin to what Dougray had experienced over the loss of an arm, Maël over a disfigured face, and Guarin over captivity by Saxon rebels. He had known their suffering was great, but this was a different kind of knowing. Despite the intrigue of something unfamiliar becoming familiar, it was painful. And if, like his kin who could not regain what was lost, neither could he, more painful it would be.

Prayer, he told himself. *With much prayer, God will continue to favor me.*

"Lord, let my will be Your will," he whispered and began praying the night away.

CHAPTER EIGHT

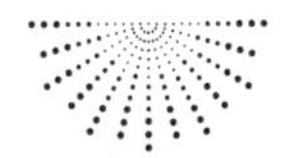

Though Marguerite was more favorably disposed toward Princess Margaret than when first they met, the same could not be said of the lady's mother and sister.

The older woman having become more confident of her place at court, she was haughtier in manner and speech. Marguerite was spared none of it, though it was expressed less in words than what Agatha exuded through scrutiny of the king's favorite—from Marguerite's head down to her toes.

Cristina was said to be as devout as her older sister, but from the beginning she had been disdainful of her accommodations, letting it be known Malcolm's palace was crude compared to Westminster. But now there was something else about her that bothered. Her resentment was more keenly felt when she believed herself unobserved as she looked upon the future queen. Jealousy or not, possibly here further proof that just as she was not as beautiful as her sister on the outside, her insides were lacking.

Thus, Marguerite was grateful Malcolm's betrothed asked her mother and sister to withdraw to allow her visitor privacy in which to complete her ablutions. Also of relief was the dismissal of the princess's maid who had begun to flutter around Marguerite. But then the one who insisted on being called *Meg* to avoid confusion in informal situations, began aiding one of far less import than she.

"You have lovely hair," she said.

Marguerite looked from her own reflection in the mirror on the dressing table to that of the woman who stood behind loosely braiding this lady's brown tresses. "I thank you, Princess, but I must confess envy. Only upon you have I seen hair as flaxen and thick from crown to ends."

"You are kind."

"Is it kindness when it is truth without question?"

A smile moved her mouth. "You sound like my Malcolm."

My Malcolm. " Heart warming, Marguerite said, "Now *you* sound like him."

She laughed. "Aye, he and I are fond of laying claim to each other as if already we are wed."

"I am glad. The princess I first met was not light of heart."

"That was a lady in exile who believed her desire to do God's work from inside the walls of an abbey was to be further delayed. This is a lady who shall willingly do God's work in a different manner and place."

"Do you love my king?"

The princess's brow grooved. "In the beginning, he seemed so uncivilized I did not think I could care for him in any great measure, but once I uncovered his heart..." She nodded. "I name it love, though I have told him it is not as great as what he feels for me and shall never be. I will be his wife and, God willing, mother of his children, but ever the Lord shall have first claim on me."

"You sound determined."

She paused, put her head to the side. "It is not determination. 'Tis truth of the state of my heart as it should be for all—love of the Lord above others and possessions."

Though Marguerite was less gullible than once she had been, she was inclined to believe this woman who made no attempt to ply her with professions of overwhelming love for Malcolm. "You make me ashamed."

"'Tis not my intent," the princess said. "I but tell how it is with me. Aye, it should be thus with you, and one day it shall be if you aspire to it, but I know you have not the advantage with which I was blessed." When Marguerite looked up, she continued, "The greatest portion of my education was received at the feet of the saintly King Edward who loved the Lord as no other I have known. Thus, so long I have breathed in God that He is and shall ever be my first and last breath no matter what—or who—comes in between."

Oh, to be so devoted, Marguerite thought. *Surely then one can face the ills of the world without closing eyes and ears and mouth.*

"You are not to be ashamed," the princess asserted and resumed work on the braid.

Marguerite smiled. "I am glad marriage is not being pressed on you, and that for all your love of the Lord, still you have some for the king. A love match is a rare thing."

"So speaks the child of one."

Mention of Marguerite's parents brought to mind the graveyard where she must go to honor them, as well as Cannie and the escort felled by her kin. But not yet. She cleared her throat. "I am thinking during my absence King Malcolm told tales of Diarmad the Mad who became Diarmad the Shield."

"He did, but as they are among his favorites, I knew some ere you departed Dunfermline, it being Malcolm's means of reciprocating for my readings to him from the Gospels."

Marguerite was struck by remembrance of the evening past when she had traded answers with Theriot. "You bartered?"

The princess wrinkled her nose. "Though he who shall take me to wife may consider it that, never would I require payment for sharing and discussing the Lord's word." She chuckled.

"Though I must admit had I sought payment, I would have been satisfied. Much Malcolm loved Diarmad and esteemed your parents—so much he tells his love for me is as great as your sire's for your mother, and he aspires to grow my love for him as great as your mother's for your sire."

"They were very special," Marguerite said. "Though not without their difficulties and griefs, they shared them and grew closer and stronger."

"So I understand. As for the tales told me following your departure, those were mostly an unburdening of Malcolm's grief over your mother's demise and what he believed yours. He has healed these months, but not as much as he did upon your return. I am glad you came home to us."

To us. Marguerite savored the words.

The princess did not speak again until she secured the braid with a ribbon. Then she came around. "You are well bathed and prettily groomed, even if few shall look upon you."

Certainly not Theriot, Marguerite thought. *But he will know my scent.*

"I thank you for your aid, Princess."

"Meg is what I would be to you, dear lady."

"Meg," Marguerite corrected.

Of a sudden, the princess dropped to her knees. "There is something of which we should speak."

Marguerite blinked. "Sir Theriot?"

She shook her head. "I believe I have told all I know of his family, and I can tell naught specific about the youngest brother. I would talk of your mother."

Marguerite caught her breath.

The princess grasped her hands. "As I am sure you wish to visit her grave alongside your sire's, I would offer to accompany you."

Marguerite knew where to find her mother's resting place—the sanctified ground of the small church on the side of the glen opposite the palace, near enough the river for the rippling and rushing water to be heard but not so near there was danger of flooding. "I shall visit, but not this day—when it is warmer so I may linger." She nodded. "I will think on your offer."

"As you wish. May I pray for you?"

Marguerite stared at this one of royalty kneeling so humbly before her it seemed wrong she herself remained seated.

"I believe I have God's ear," the princess prompted. "Allow me to bend it toward you."

Marguerite slid off the stool onto her knees.

Meg closed her eyes. "Lord Almighty, the Maker and Keeper of all, the Breath in our nostrils, Light in our eyes, and Voice in our ears and hearts, your servant speaks unto You. Here, my friend of much sorrow and loss, uncertainty and questioning. I beseech You, comfort and strengthen Lady Marguerite so she accepts all behind to better embrace the good and withstand the ill of all ahead. Keep this lady wise and safe as she does her tender work with Sir Theriot, and give her the confidence to be honest about the loss of his sight and the part she played."

Marguerite opened her eyes. On the day she returned to Dunfermline and was granted an audience with the king, she had revealed the necessity of keeping her identity hidden from the chevalier and felt the princess's disapproval, and even greater that disapproval when Malcolm agreed it was for the best. Now here it was again. It was not ill-founded, but Theriot would reject her aid if he knew the truth.

"And Lord," the princess continued, "just as Marguerite wishes the chevalier's swift healing and restoration of his sight, I add my prayers to hers. If 'tis Your will he see the world again as before, return form and color to his eyes." She drew breath. "As for the guilt burdening this lady over the death of her escort and the injury done Hendrie and Sir Theriot, I pray You ease it by encouraging others to show her grace and her to accept it."

Emotion shot up Marguerite's throat, the sob she swallowed

hurting all the way back down.

Meg squeezed her hands. "We bow before You, Heavenly Father. Amen." She sat back.

"Much gratitude," Marguerite finally found her voice. "I know what I did was not sinful, but I hurt for what I wrought."

"None of us are perfect," the princess said. "We can only hope others show us grace as we should show them."

Marguerite's thoughts went to Theriot. "Still, how is it you pray so sincerely for the chevalier though the brother you love wishes the opposite—and worse?"

She sighed. "Because of what Edgar wants, 'tis more imperative I pray for Sir Theriot—and my brother who is much changed from the sweet boy I carried on my hip. Great my sorrow he who should be king is not and may never be. Great my understanding that though my marriage benefits him, it pinches I who should never be queen shall sit alongside a king."

"His losses and disappointments are many," Marguerite acceded, "but he is yet young."

"Barely nine and ten, and even with Malcolm's aid, I fear Edgar's hope for the crown is only that. Methinks he fears it as well, and for that is bitter." She stood and, as she assisted Marguerite to her feet, said, "We must place our hope in God that all will come as right as possible for Edgar, England, and Scotland."

"When might that be?" Marguerite asked.

"If God chooses, it could happen this moment, a month hence, a year, even a thousand or more. But as it is His timing alone, we cannot know what He will do above with what we do below. And we must accept that is as it should be lest we live only as far as the eye and heart can reach."

I could come to love her, Marguerite thought. *I believe Malcolm is right—we shall become good friends.*

"I am grateful for our time together, Meg. Now I ought to return to my patient."

The princess touched Marguerite's arm. "Lady, pray on setting aright the deception worked on him. Not only is it the godly thing to do, but worse it will be if he learns the truth from another."

Marguerite did fear someone would reveal she had led the chevalier into the trap. Though Malcolm had ordered that none speak of it, she might be revealed, whether by a tongue loosened with drink or one stiff with spite.

"I will pray on it."

The princess inclined her head. "Do I not see you at supper, I will see you on the morrow when once more you make use of my chamber."

Marguerite knew she should attend one of the meals, but for now preferred the company of Theriot D'Argent. "On the morrow," she said.

"One more thing, Lady Marguerite. When my family and I arrived at Dunfermline and your king asked you to perform, I did not adequately express appreciation for your willingness to share the gift the Lord gave you. Pray, know I could not have been better welcomed to this foreign country than to have Malcolm's sparrow sing me into it."

"As it was an honor to perform for a princess of England, it shall be an honor to perform for the Queen of Scotland," Marguerite said and, moments later, began her descent of stone steps which Princess Cristina proclaimed were too rough to grace the inside of a palace. Not only did the burred edges and surfaces snag the lady's dainty slippers but the hems of her fine gowns.

The steps could not be set aright, interlocked and mortared as they were in the space between the tower's inner and outer walls, but during Marguerite's absence much had been done to accommodate Malcolm's royal guests. If not for the king's love of the princess, all would have been as when Marguerite left—or worse—regardless of whose senses were offended.

As evidenced by the royal chambers and interiors of other rooms she glimpsed during each spiraling ascent and descent, the accommodations had been improved with new and repaired furnishings and fresh paint.

Never before had the hall she stepped into been so presentable, the tables, benches, tapestries, and wall sconces either repaired or replaced. The usually sparse, heavily fouled rushes were fresh, thickly strewn, and herb-scented, and the fire pit was regularly tended rather than left to burn and smoke at will.

"Lady Marguerite!"

Having thought she passed through unnoticed by servants at work and retainers at ease, she swung around. "I did not hear you," she said in the same Anglo-Saxon with which Colban addressed her.

He halted. "Forgive me. As I have been in conversation with Princess Cristina, your appearance was too good an opportunity to let pass."

Then this the reason he did not speak in his native Gaelic. Marguerite looked beyond him to the young woman who stood outside an alcove watching them. "Too good to let pass?"

"Though the lass professes to dislike our rough countrymen, at times I feel hunted."

"Perhaps she has decided to eschew holy vows the same as her sister."

He harrumphed. "Best she eschew them for someone else."

"You do not think to wed again?"

"I do," he reverted to Gaelic and ran his gaze down Marguerite. "And to choose better this time."

He referred to his first wife wed four years past when Malcolm brought the physician down out of the Highlands. The woman had been unfaithful while pregnant with their first child, the blood of whom surely he would have questioned had the babe survived its birthing as its mother had not.

Feeling hunted herself, she said, "I am sure you shall. You will visit our Norman patient this day?"

Annoyance rumpled his brow. "As I doubt much has changed, I shall come again on the morrow or after that."

Deciding delivery of his opinion to Theriot regarding recovery of his sight was best delayed, she was disappointed in his answer only because it seemed retaliation. "I shall see you then," she said.

Feeling watched out of sight, she departed the tower and was surprised Dubh awaited her on the steps, having bounded from her side when they exited the hut the sooner to join other dogs roaming the bailey.

"Good, Dubh," she said. Upon reaching the bottom of the steps, she paused to look close on the palace as she had not done since her return home.

The outside was as altered as the inside, the tower whitewashed and shutters that had barely clung to window frames now supplanted by new ones capable of subduing light, cold, and heat. The clutter within the bailey and stacked against the tower's base had been cleared and organized, and the scattered buildings servicing the palace—including the kitchen and wash house—were repaired and all but the stable given new roofs.

"A far better fit for a king," Marguerite murmured.

As she moved her gaze from the sizable structure that was kept better than other buildings for the valuable horses it housed, she caught movement. Returning her regard to the stable, she saw Edgar duck inside. Had he been watching her? Of greater concern, had he been observing the hut inside which Theriot was bound?

Grateful for the Scotsmen guarding the king's prisoner, Marguerite turned her attention to meeting the chevalier's immediate needs, beginning with the keeper of the linens and ending with the cook.

CHAPTER NINE

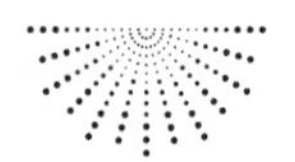

The men had grumbled, but when Marguerite and Dubh returned two hours following their departure, it appeared all was done as directed.

As evidenced by Theriot who wore clean garments where he sat with his back to her on a bench beside a generous fire, he had tended to his ablutions with the basins of water, soap, towels, tunic, and chausses delivered this morn.

The bed had been moved close to the pit, but not so close if overturned again he would find himself amid ashes or flames. On the near side of the bed, a metal loop had been fixed into the rail through which one end of the rope was threaded and drawn beneath the mattress to the opposite rail and its loop.

Henceforth, when he must be bound, his arms would be out to the sides, allowing for the cover of blankets and loose enough to permit him to turn side to side without reaching for what he ought not reach, nor drawing his hands together to make greater weapons of them.

Marguerite could not own to that cleverness, having learned it from her sire who was forced to secure his wife following the loss of their third son days after his birth, her grief so great it was feared too much movement would tear the stitches holding her together.

Recalling when she hugged the doorframe as her father knelt like a gentle monk beside the bed and wiped away his wife's tears, spoke words of love, and sung songs of Scotland's fierce beauty he said was matched only by hers, Marguerite thought, *Would that I could have a love like theirs, my heart in another's, another's heart in mine.*

As if she had spoken aloud, Theriot's head came around. Beneath recently washed hair drying on his brow, his ravaged eyes settled on hers as if clearly he saw her where she stood in the doorway.

I hope you do, she thought, and gasped when the hound pushed past. If not that Dubh had taken a liking to the prisoner, Marguerite would have snatched hold of her collar. As she and the guards on the opposite side of the fire watched, the hound passed near enough Theriot its tail brushed him. Then it came around and, just out of reach, lowered to its haunches as if to converse with the prisoner.

Wishing it was less accepting of him in the presence of guards who might alert the king this precaution appeared ineffective, Marguerite sidestepped and motioned forward a girl bearing viands better suited to feeding a hungry warrior than the bread and cheese with which he had broken his fast. Behind her came a boy with fur blankets.

Acquiring one fur from the keeper of the linens had not been difficult, but not so a second for the Norman who had wounded Hendrie. The usually kind woman having insisted winter was on the wane, only when Marguerite told she herself could endure and was grateful her patient would not suffer was she given another fur.

"The platter on the bedside table, furs on the bed," she directed as she stepped past Theriot. Turning alongside Dubh to face the chevalier, she saw his garments fit poorly. The tunic's seams strained and the hems of the chausses rose up his lower calves, but they would do until his own were laundered.

When Marguerite had inquired about the garments earlier delivered to the wash house, the head laundress, also averse to making Malcolm's prisoner comfortable, had said, *The morrow, the morrow after, or the morrow next.*

The morrow, Marguerite had insisted and scooped up the pile and given them to a younger woman with instructions they go in the tub immediately.

Though she understood their anger toward Theriot, it made her ache further, certain it was not due this Norman.

"You stare, Lady Marguerite," Theriot said.

So she did. When the girl and boy departed and closed the door against the cold, she said in Norman-French, "You appear much improved."

"Do I?"

Was that innocently spoken or a reminder that what her eyes could see his could not? "You do. Are you satisfied with the greater comfort provided you?"

He set his head to the side. "Since there is but an alteration in how I am bound, I assume I remain a prisoner."

He had been neither pleasant nor unpleasant this morn, speaking few words before she departed, but now his tone revealed he leaned toward unpleasantness. Had something happened that should not have?

She looked around the confines and at the Scotsmen. Just as there were no signs of an altercation, neither did she glimpse anger on their faces to indicate one had occurred. As usual, they but looked resentful their warrior skills were wasted.

"You remain in the power of the King of Scots who suspends judgment until you are recovered," she said.

The chevalier's nostrils flared, but he did not confront her over judgment he did not believe due him nor what could be the devastating limits of his recovery. "As these men prefer to be elsewhere, I am ready to be bound."

"Would you like to eat first? The viands are from the king's own table."

"I am well with you aiding me." He stood. There was confidence in his first stride as he stepped past her, but his next faltered as if he remembered his new limitations. She half-expected him to reach hands before him to ensure the way was clear, but he shortened his steps to negotiate the narrow space between pit and bed.

"Stay, Dubh," she said, and as she followed Theriot, noted the back of his hair, unlike the front and top, was dull down to its matted ends. Had there not been enough water to rinse out all the soap?

As he lowered to the mattress, she looked to the sideboard against the left wall where items for his ablutions were set. There were three basins, two filled with water—one for the body, the other the hair—and an empty one over which he would have bent to allow it to capture what was used to wet his hair in preparation for soap, then to rinse the soap from it. She had been certain there was enough water, especially since his hair was relatively short, but...

There—the dark of heavily moistened ground before the sideboard. Had he spilled water? Or had the guards?

Guessing the latter, anger stirred, but she reasoned had he been set upon, he would have retaliated and it would show. Thus, his inability to see must have caused him to shame himself. And here further proof his sight was as damaged as told.

As the guards bound him both sides, Marguerite realized moving the bed nearer the center of the room had eliminated the ability to prop him against pillows supported by a wall. Might she secure a headboard? Considering how difficult it had been to gain a second fur, impossible without the king's intervention. And best she not seek it since the longer Theriot remained out of Malcolm's sight, the better.

When the Scotsmen departed, she asked, "Would you like me to draw the covers over you? Perhaps a fur?"

"Non."

"I saw you were unable to remove all the soap from your hair. I..." She hesitated. "I could rinse it with drinking water."

"As if I am an invalid," he muttered and turned his face to her. "Though the guards did not speak of what happened, I believe you know, meaning you are observant."

"There is moisture on the ground before the sideboard."

"So now the question—did this D'Argent cause himself to suffer shame, or was it his jailers?"

"You."

"How do you know that?"

"There are no signs of an altercation here nor about your person, and I believe had the guards disobeyed their king, you would have retaliated and it would show."

"It would, though still I would be here, invalid and prisoner."

"I believe that a temporary state, that you—"

"Temporary, Lady?" Despite crimson bleeding across the whites of his eyes and clouded irises that could see only dark against light, still he was able to speak with them. And their depths revealed anger, perhaps even self-loathing.

She moistened her lips. "With greatest certainty I refer to your captivity, but I have hope your sight will be restored, for which both Princess Margaret and I pray."

Once more he gave her his profile. "Prayer," he murmured.

Though she caught no scorn about that word, she heard uncertainty as if he questioned the power of prayer to raise him up out of his present darkness. But perhaps there was more to it. Might he doubt the Lord, even reject Him? If the latter, was it only now because he felt helpless and abandoned, or had he never believed? Some professed faith only for the acceptance and protection it afforded.

"Do you worry over my soul, Lady?"

She startled.

"Do not. It remains faithful inside this shell and is less concerned than this flesh over what has become of its eyes upon the world."

Though she wanted to probe further and offer assurances the Lord was with him, she feared her trespass would be too great. "Ere we eat, will you allow me to rinse your hair?"

"As it feels stiff, my scalp itches, and I am bound, I will."

Just as she had known how to more comfortably secure him to the bed, she knew how to do this from aiding her sire with her mother. As she crossed to the sideboard, she said, "Lie down and shift upward until your neck is on the edge." When she turned back with a basin and towel, he was correctly positioned to prevent the mattress from being soaked.

Seeing Dubh had moved to the bed, her nose near the prisoner's hand, she said, "You do not fear my hound."

"She gives me no cause, being as certain I will not harm her as I am certain she will not harm me—providing I do not threaten you."

Marguerite gave a huff of disbelief.

"Believe it," he said as she set the basin on the floor beneath his head. "She may not show great affection, but she knows what is due you."

Marguerite lifted the water pitcher and paused to look at the hound who continued to familiarize herself with Theriot's scent. "I hope you are right, else I suffer watering eyes and sniffles for naught."

"I believe it is worth the discomfort, Lady."

After filling a cup full should Theriot prefer water over ale, Marguerite took the pitcher and lowered to her knees behind his head. "As the water was recently drawn, it will be cold."

He closed his lids, and once more she scrutinized his face.

Having met his eldest brother not long after first she encountered Theriot, she had noted though this D'Argent was of a leaner build and a bit shorter than Guarin, they shared so great a resemblance it was not necessary to stand them alongside each other to confirm they were related. However, since being reunited with this man, differences beyond build and height were apparent.

Theriot's eyes were more deeply set, lower lip less full, and barely visible beneath lengthening whiskers were dimples. Too, despite fewer years than his brother, he had more silver in what might become a full beard were a blade not soon taken to it.

Not, she hoped. Though he was handsome clean-shaven and she would like to see the depth of his dimples if ever again he smiled broadly, better she liked a bearded man to which she was more accustomed.

Catching up with her thoughts and feelings, which once more sought to make more of their relationship than there could be, inwardly she groaned.

"If you have had your fill of my face, my neck begins to ache, Lady."

Face warming, she was tempted to deny that was what she did, but she had told enough half-truths without adding lies in full. Deciding the best cover for her fluster was to make light of what she did, she said, "But you have such a fine face, it is not easy to gain one's fill, Theriot."

His eyebrows rose, mouth nearly smiled, and dimples deepened slightly. Though it was but one brief moment after another, her own lips turned.

"Would I could say the same of a face that remains unknown to me," he said, though not darkly.

Not unknown to you, she thought. Merely, he was unaware he had looked upon her months ago when she peered down at him from atop her mount, and less than a sennight past when she tried to save him from Hendrie. But since both times shadows had abounded, he could not possibly have had his fill of her face.

"I hope one day you shall look well upon me," she said, then silently added, *And forgive me.*

Ensuring the basin was centered before her knees, she reminded herself to have a care for the tender flesh where Hendrie's blade had failed to cleave his opponent's skull and began trickling water down one side of his head. Relieved he did not appear discomfited by cold, with her other hand she guided the moisture down to the roots and scalp and in to his nape.

Just as her sire had lovingly done her mother.

CHAPTER TEN

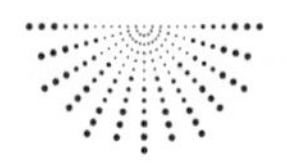

When Theriot had awakened well past dawn and found he was no more sighted despite hours of prayer, he had believed himself in control.

Determined to maintain his composure amid the indignity of performing his ablutions beneath the watch of the guard, he had memorized the placement of items on the sideboard and been frustratingly precise with movements that should be almost involuntary. But as he had finished setting himself aright, he erred in retrieving the rinse basin. Had not instinct for its path of travel and good reflexes allowed him to catch hold of it and sidestep, his garments would have been soaked and the contents entirely lost.

As if the spillage of half the water was not humiliation enough, the Scotsmen had spared him only in not laughing outright, their amused grunts and murmurings tempting him to an altercation of which this lady would have found much evidence.

To ensure he did not lose the advantage of this prison that could become a cell in which he was fit with chains rather than ropes, while he and the guard awaited the lady's return, he had continued to press hard on the door of his anger to hold inside that which made him long to pound flesh and bone. And more he had ached to strike someone when this woman entered and he became intensely aware of how impotent this warrior appeared—and how much he cared.

He had known that in seeking to win her to his side there would be a price to pay for shifting thoughts and emotions from helplessness and humiliation to the gentle ministrations and attraction of this lady. However, now as her hands worked water down to his scalp, causing his skin to warm as if a fur were drawn over him and his heart to beat so hard he feared she felt it, he knew the price would be higher than expected.

Imagine her a much older woman as first believed, he told himself. *Imagine no firm curves about her, hair more silvered than your own, and gnarled fingers against your scalp. Oui, older than your mother. No longing to have your fill of her face nor attentions.*

Lies, and yet heart and breath began to calm—until in an appealingly husky voice, she said, "Your hair comes clean, so much the silver turned grey is bright again, Theriot."

As she tipped more water down one side, defensively he said, "*Sir* Theriot."

She faltered, then her fingers resumed their strokes and tugs. "Forgive me. In Scotland, we are somewhat lax with titles, especially in close company."

"This captive is considered close company?"

She turned his head to the side, and he closed his lids against the fire whose flames yet pained. As she trickled water onto his hair, she said, "Certes, close company to this lady who shares this dwelling with you, gains her rest near enough to attend to your night travels, and ministers thus."

As she urged his head opposite, he said, "You imply I speak aloud my dreams."

"Fear not." Her breath fanned his brow. "Only as I awakened

this morn did I hear you, and as I could make no sense of what you spoke, your secrets remain your own."

What secrets? he wondered, but he did not have to deeply search his conscience. Like his brother who had scouted for the king, he had aspired to root out rebellion in the hope of sooner healing the country. Still, the service performed for William had troubled him before his encounter with Edgar, and more his conscience was battered that a village which had escaped the harrying had fallen to it. True, its people lived, but their lives would be harder now.

"I think it is done," the lady said. "After I towel your hair, you may shift down."

She was as gentle and thorough with the towel as she had been rinsing out the soap. When she drew back, his hair was barely damp.

He sat up. Glad his restraints were slack enough to permit him to turn toward her, he did so and saw the smudge of her lower to the mattress as if he could not one-handedly seize her and do harm before the dog at the fire pit was upon him and the guards inside.

"Is it that too much you trust me, Lady, or do you forget yourself?"

"I do not forget myself, nor what I know of you—by way of Princess Margaret. As you are aware, the guards and bindings are required by my king if I am to tend you here rather than in a cell where many go to die as you ought not."

"Not yet."

"I pray never, and more confident I am because of the princess's influence on the king. When first she came to court, I doubted the depth of her faith, but now that I meet her again, I—"

"Again?" he interrupted, knowing Malcolm had granted sanctuary to the Aetheling and his family last year. "You have been absent from court?"

"For a time," she said dismissively and began picking over the platter's contents. "I believe you have enough slack that if I place food in your hand, with a bit of lean you can feed yourself. Do you prefer that?"

He did. Not only would he feel less helpless, but having her place food to his lips was uncomfortably intimate. "I prefer it."

And yet when she set meat in his hand, the mere brush of her fingers also seemed an intimate thing—and further he was disturbed by the loosening of a memory of when she affirmed the dawn came soon. It had not, but that night when he took hold of a hand that felt familiar, he had been reassured. Now he knew better.

Lowering his head, he fed himself and was grateful for the distraction of how ravenous he was for food of substance. The lady hungered as well, only speaking between bites to ask which viand he would like and if he wished her to carry drink to his lips—until there came the sound of men riding on the tower, raised voices, and the rumble of the gate granting admittance.

"Likely the king returning from a hunt," she said.

He did not believe it, though not because his unnatural sense told him so. That which was mostly heard revealed urgency about the riders of few number unlike those of greater number returning from a hunt.

Assuring himself there was no reason to be alarmed the extra sense that gathered close and strengthened his other senses was not more present, Theriot asked, "Malcolm hunts with only two or three?"

"Non, it think it more than that."

"Two or three," he said firmly.

"Then mayhap it is tidings of import delivered my king. If so, we shall know soon."

Though they resumed eating, he remained attentive to what went beyond the hut while seeking to fully engage his extra sense.

When their appetites were satisfied, the lady said, "You should rest."

Confident of her position from the smudge of her and warmth of her body, he gripped her arm as she began to rise.

She startled, and a growl sounded from the fire, but just as the dog did not set itself at the prisoner, neither did the woman try to pull free. "Sir Theriot?"

"You make tolerable what is barely tolerable, Marguerite," he said, and though he spoke with self-serving intention, he had not meant to eschew her title. But it served. "I am grateful."

"I am pleased to be of aid. Now—"

"Do not tell me to rest. I am not tired." It was a lie. Having prayed away much of the night, he had slept little and was further fatigued by the effort to control anger that better allowed him to understand the struggles overcome by his brothers and cousin—and further acknowledge his life had been easier than theirs even before the losses they suffered at Hastings.

Having mostly fought in the front ranks of that bloody battle, Theriot knew it was not only God's favor and his skill that protected him. It was his kin who were determined the youngest depart the battlefield whole of body even if they could not. Thus, it turned his stomach to find himself in these circumstances and more helpless than any of them had been, and greater that shame should they suffer more losses in seeking to recover him.

Prayer, he determined as he had on the night past when he assured himself come the new day the Lord would give proof His will remained in accord with the one ever shown favor. Morn had come, and unanswered prayer had rendered him incapable of completing the simple task of rinsing soap from his hair. For that humiliation, he had allowed this woman a glimpse of the doubt rising on all sides of him. But as told, she need not worry over his soul.

Like his sire who believed God was given to interceding when called upon, unlike his uncle who had been certain the Divine was but an observer, Theriot would continue—*must* continue—to believe he would be raised up out of this darkness. It might be gradual, but God would not abandon him. And when next the physician came, the man would confirm patience was all that was required.

"...more tired than you think," the lady returned him to her presence.

He frowned. "What say you?"

"I said since twice I have asked what you wish to do rather than sleep, it appears you are, indeed, tired."

"My thoughts drift, that is all. If you are willing, I would pass the time with talk since"—he tugged on his ropes—"my options are few."

"Very well."

Feeling her settle in, he released her. "Tell me more about yourself."

"Are we to barter again?"

"If that is how it must be."

"It is fair, and more so this time that you pose the first question."

He nearly smiled. "How was your sire of Scotland joined with a Norman of Southern England?"

"Not all those who followed Edward across the channel settled in the South. To protect his country's farthest reaches, the new king awarded to his friends lands bordering Scotland. So it was with my mother's sire."

"Your grandfather was friendly with the Scots?"

Her laughter was both scornful and sorrowful. "He was not. Thus, from a distance my sire fell in love with my mother, and since her father would not allow a Scotsman to take her to wife, he took her."

Theriot raised his eyebrows. "You speak of abduction? Or was your mother willing?"

"Abduction. Believing he stole her only because she appealed to the eye, she told him she would sooner wed a blind man who thought her voice beautiful than—"

Theriot did not know if her words broke off because she realized how inappropriate they were for him or she felt him stiffen.

"Forgive me," she said. "And now surely you prefer the boredom of rest over my chattering."

He did, but since the reminder of his loss was unintentional, he said, "Did your sire force her to wed?"

"Non. He brought her home to Dunfermline, gave her into his aunt's care, and vowed that if after two months she had no love for him, he would return her to her family yet a maiden. Only days before he was to honor his word, he was walking with her in the glen to make memory of the time that remained and..." She paused.

"What?" Theriot prompted.

"My sire closed his eyes and said that more than the beauty of her face he loved the touch of her hands, the sound of her voice, and the smell of her hair. But most of all, he loved her heart and soul. So on the day they were to begin the journey that would return her to her family, they wed." She sighed. "That is the tale told me."

"A pretty story."

"But not all pretty."

"You speak of her family."

"Oui. They learned who had taken her, and when I was in her womb, her sire and brother stole into Dunfermline and took her back though she told she was happily wed."

"Diarmad the Mad came for her again."

"He did, and with many men. However, to prevent harm to his wife's kin, at great risk he entered the walls alone to bring her out. Unfortunately, ere they could reach my father's men, my grandfather and his garrison surrounded them. My mother clung to her husband, trying to shield him though time and again he set her aside to challenge her sire, but certain it would be no fair fight, she would not leave him be. Had my father's men of greater number not appeared, possibly both would have died. At the beseeching of my grandmother who feared she would lose not only a daughter but her husband, my grandfather withdrew. As he did so, he called on the Lord to punish my parents, gifting no boy child to Diarmad the Mad lest his blood further taint Norman blood."

Sensing great sorrow, Theriot asked, "Have you brothers?"

"Three came after me—one stillborn, one aged a sennight ere sickness took him, one aged only days when he did not awaken from a night's sleep. Then my mother could not bear to birth again and precautions were taken to ensure no more babes."

"Did your parents believe the Lord heeded your grandfather?"

"Not Diarmad the Mad of more faith than his wife—surprising for a man who abducted a bride, I think you would agree." At Theriot's slight smile, she continued, "My father said the Lord would not be made a weapon of vengeance for one so ungodly. Though my mother spoke little of it, methinks she believed her inability to give her husband a male heir was because of the curse called down upon them."

When Marguerite turned silent, Theriot said, "I am glad to know how you came to be accomplished in my language, but now I am curious about your Gaelic. Though you must be more fluent in your father's language, why do you speak no word of it to the men who tend me though it is best known to them?"

Marguerite stared, relieved he could not see her dismay, then cleared her throat. "It is out of consideration to you I speak

Norman-French," she half lied. Or was that three-quarters of a lie?

"I am proficient in the language of the Saxons," he said, "and have learned the guards speak a form of it which they prefer over my language when we converse. Do you know it as well?"

"Since many are the languages spoken at court, I am conversant."

"Then unless you wish to tell something you would not have them understand, I am well speaking that which makes it less difficult for them."

Did he suspect? she wondered. Were memories that stood between him and her secret surfacing?

Tell him, her conscience sided with the princess. *Now before he remembers or someone reveals you.*

"Providing you are comfortable speaking the Saxon language," he prompted.

Promising herself later she would delve her conscience, she said, "I am well with it," then moved their conversation elsewhere. "Not only was my answer exceedingly long and complete, but other questions were answered without trade. Will you afford me the same?"

"Speak, Lady."

What she wanted was confirmation of the belief that just as he was not among those who pursued Edgar through the village and set it afire, neither had he sent the contingent after the Aetheling. However, as he had eased her into revealing more than bartered, she would attempt the same.

Wishing it was not necessary to deepen her deception with feigned ignorance, she said, "Would you enlarge the tale of the D'Argents beyond what the princess knows?"

His mouth curved. "I am one of four brothers and have one sister and one cousin. Except for Nicola, I am the youngest."

That she knew. "The men are all warriors?"

"We are and crossed the channel together and fought with

William on the meadow of Senlac until King Harold fell to my duke."

"And stole his country," she said with little thought.

The bit of light about him beginning to darken, he inclined his head. "It did not seem so at the time, many of us certain a change of rule would bring needed reform to the Church of England. However, I am in accord with the rest of my family who now believe England was stolen rather than saved." He paused, then added, "Still, forget not King Harold first stole it from the Aetheling as I believe Edgar would attest."

"He would, though were he honest, he would agree it was better that a seasoned warrior who commanded the hearts and loyalties of most be the one to rule and defend the country ahead of one who was only ten and four when old King Edward passed. And no good argument is it that, in the end, Harold could not hold England against your William. Most agree if the country had not first been attacked by Norwegians, exhausting England's forces, Harold would have ended the duke's bid for the throne."

"Or had Harold refused to be provoked into battle before his forces recovered and numbers were replenished," Theriot added solemnly.

She nodded, then remembering he could not see, rushed to words. "Had he waited, perhaps instead of the slaughter of him and his forces..." She trailed off.

"Then the slaughter of William and his forces," he finished what she did not. "And I would not be here with you now."

"I would not want that!" Once again speaking ahead of thought, she corrected, "That is, I would not wish you to have fallen."

"Why would you not wish this Norman who aided in stealing England not to fall?"

Though likely she would regret answering, she said, "It is just that... It feels I knew you before I met you."

As if to ponder that, he went very still, then he smiled amid whiskers, allowing a glimpse of even white teeth. It was no sizable smile, and there seemed uncertainty about it, but it made her heart beat faster.

"Do you get your fill of my face again?" he asked, voice deeper yet.

Though embarrassed, again she suppressed denial. "As told and well you know, it is a fine face."

"And as well you know, great the advantage you have over me."

She moistened her lips, and when he moved his clouded gaze to them, her breath turned shallow—and ceased when his hand rose as if to explore the face blindness denied him. However, his bindings were too taut.

As if the tug on his wrist returned him to his wits, he lowered his hand. "I did not expect you to be so learned and opinionated about the conquering of England. Are these topics of conversation at King Malcolm's court?"

She swallowed. "Oui, and quite often." Then leaving unsaid that further she had become intimate with them during her time with the Rebels of the Pale, she asked, "Would you tell me of your home in Normandy?"

He considered that, said, "It is many years since I was—" He broke off and shifted his damaged eyes up to the side just as Dubh began rumbling.

"Theriot?"

"Men come, Marguerite."

She strained to hear footsteps, but the sounds outside the hut were indistinct. "It is mostly quiet out there. How do you know someone comes?"

"Ere the riders, there was pattern and volume to what goes beyond—of the guards outside the door and those who patrol and work the bailey. When the riders came, there was the sound of horses and shouted voices. Afterward, a return to what was before. Now there is the still of attending to something of interest." He returned his sightless gaze to her. "Oui, Lady, they come, and your dog knows it as well."

"It is likely the king," she said.

But it was not Malcolm, and it boded worse the voices of those who approached were Saxon, and when they were answered by the Scottish guard, their volume increased.

"Cut my bindings," Theriot commanded.

Having turned toward the door before which Dubh paced, Marguerite snapped her head around.

"I know you must have a dagger on you, Lady. Trust this D'Argent and free me."

She hesitated, but upon hearing Saxons demand entrance and throatier growls from Dubh, she took the dagger from beneath her skirt. As she sawed the blade through the rope binding his right wrist, threats were made on the other side of the door, then came the sound of struggle.

When the rope fell to the floor, she reached to free the other wrist, but Theriot so quickly relieved her of the dagger she thought it possible his sight was restored.

Dropping his feet to the floor on the opposite side of the bed, he whipped the rope free of the loop set in the rail. That corner of the room at his back, Dubh now barking ferociously, he yelled, "Get behind me, Lady!"

She stared at the man whose urgent eyes were clearly damaged.

"Behind me!" he repeated, the shouts growing louder and answered by others more distant. Then came the meeting of blades.

Marguerite hastened around the bed.

Hardly was she at Theriot's back than something landed against the door, causing the planks to shudder.

"Call your dog to you," he commanded.

"Dubh!"

Almost immediately, the hound was between her and Theriot.

"When they enter, tell what you see, Lady!"

Lord, he is truly blind, she silently bemoaned. *How can he think to defend himself, let alone me?*

And yet he looked capable despite eyes that saw but light and shadow and that his only bodily protection was poor fitting garments. His was a warrior's stance, legs braced apart, back foot weighted in readiness to launch himself forward, in one hand the dagger, in the other the rope still affixed to that wrist.

Marguerite yelped when the next assault on the door tore its hinges and dropped it and the Scotsman thrown against it to the dirt floor.

"What do you see?" Theriot demanded as a burst of cool air vied with the fire's heat.

With so many men clambering to enter amid barking, it was difficult to make sense of it, but she reported what was most immediate.

"One of the guard on the floor atop the door. He has lost his sword…is rising…drawing his dagger. Four Saxons entering, one face down outside. Dear Lord, their swords come before them."

"What else?"

"Three Saxons now. The guard outside has dragged the fourth back and the guard within is nearly on his feet and—"

"Oui, three Saxons." His muscles bunched as if he saw the same and prepared to attack those of bared teeth and blades of longer reach than his own.

Recognizing one of Theriot's assailants as being among the sacrificial group sent from the village to lead the Aetheling's pursuers distant, Marguerite gasped.

Here were the men who urgently rode on the palace—likely the only survivors of an encounter with Normans who discovered Edgar was not among them. And what these Saxons did now was vengeance possible only because someone had named Theriot responsible for the deaths of their countrymen and told where to find him.

You did this, Edgar, she thought. *Anger due you averted, and now this D'Argent may die.*

"Stay where you are, Lady," he said, then lunged at those who had slowed their advance as if questioning whether their prey would be as easy to put down as they were led to believe.

Regardless, it would prove an impossible fight for the sightless, ill-armed Norman. Even though the guard outside kept the fourth Saxon engaged at swords, and the guard within was moving toward the nearest of the three, what hope had Theriot against two whose blades he could not see?

"He is the king's prisoner! Leave him be!" Marguerite cried and sprang toward Theriot, believing the Saxons would regain their wits when Malcolm's ward came to notice.

She did not get far, Dubh placing herself in her mistress's path.

As if guided by God, Theriot ducked beneath the swing of a blade. Coming upright and shouting for her to stay back, he sliced his opponent's arm with her dagger, causing crimson to blossom through the Saxon's sleeve. Then the whip made of Theriot's rope struck the man's cheek, snapping his head to the side and causing his body to follow.

However, the second Saxon who had sidestepped to give his countryman space in which to complete the swing, lunged and arced his sword to deliver a backhanded blow.

Once more, Marguerite acted, going wide around Dubh as well as Theriot who bellowed for her to fall back. Then she and the baying dog were between the two men.

Sunlight slanting through a partially unshuttered window and the doorway ahead met upon the Saxon's blade which could have taken her life had not the man whose chest slammed against her back flung an arm around her and swept her to the side.

The second Saxon's momentum carried the warrior past, but though he corrected his footing, Dubh sprang at him. Blessed that, for still there was no relief given by the Scotsmen who could only keep the other Saxons occupied, surely due to their advanced years compared to the night guard.

"I am not your father, and you are not your mother!" Theriot snarled and thrust Marguerite to the side.

Her shoulder struck the wall, and as she dropped to a knee, she understood. He believed her attempt to protect him was inspired by what her mother had done to keep the man she loved from being slain. Though Marguerite had not consciously done the same, he scorned her for it, doubtless feeling unmanned at being shielded by a woman.

Now seeing the well-armed Saxons closing in on a sightless warrior who had only a dagger and length of rope with which to defend himself, realizing the dog was absent from the fray, she cried, "Dubh!"

Slowly, the hound rose from against the far wall.

Hoping she was only stunned, Marguerite thrust upright. Then once more placing herself between prey and predators, she threw her arms wide. "Cease! Pray, cease!"

As if to heed what they had not before, the Saxons began to quiet and still. But her pleading was not responsible she realized when what was likely a second roar sounded just outside the hut. And at the end of it, silence—until Theriot barked, "You!"

CHAPTER ELEVEN

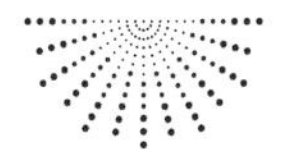

Malcolm, King of Scots, had come.

Theriot had never seen nor heard him, but he knew it was he whose bellow ended attempts to end this Norman's life.

It should be of greatest event that the one who held Theriot's fate in his hands was here—a hulking shadow which rivaled that of Vitalis, leader of the Rebels of the Pale—but more this blinded D'Argent's mind was on the lady. And who she was to him not in recent days but before he awoke on this side of the border.

When she had pleaded with the Saxons in their language to cease their attack, his mind had yanked him back to the burning village and those words cried in a voice he now recalled had been of an accent between Scottish and Norman-French—no different from that of the woman now standing before him seeking to protect him as it seemed she had tried to do then, though he could not unravel why she would after agreeing to be Edgar's bait. And how was it this lady of Dunfermline had been in the village though he had never seen a woman among the Aetheling's entourage?

Almighty! he sent heavenward. *If only I could give form to the smoke of other memories from that night—could see again her face and figure as I must have.*

"Your Grace," she said in Norman-French, returning Theriot to Dunfermline and making him aware of the dog passing near.

"To me, Marguerite!" the king commanded in the same language far different from that of his men arriving outside the hut.

"It is not as it appears," she said. "These Saxons attacked—"

"A Norman who is unbound as he ought not be, in possession of a dagger as he ought not be, and of danger to you as he ought not be. Come to me, Marguerite!"

Theriot heard the scrape of her slippers, but rather than the smudge of her decrease in size, defiance of Malcolm enlarged it.

Still she seeks to shield me! he silently raged. *If she knew my mind is now open to her deception, she would not dare.*

"Forgive me, my king," she said, further confirming she had drawn near enough Theriot could have the blade at her neck before Malcolm could stop him. "But until Sir Theriot's guard tell what transpired that forced me to release him and lend my dagger in defense of his life, I shall remain here."

Theriot heard the king draw a sharp breath, then he said, "Who injured your hound?"

"One of the Saxons when she sought to protect me."

"Dubh!" Malcolm commanded, and the dog padded forward. "She suffers no blood or broken bones, only a tender front leg," he pronounced shortly, then spoke words incomprehensible to one unfamiliar with Gaelic.

Answers were given by the guard, and Marguerite's attempts to add to what was told was silenced with harsh words that gradually softened with the telling of the events.

When Malcolm switched to the Saxon language to question those who had forced their way into the hut, Theriot's belief was confirmed that they were some of the Aetheling's men sent ahead to draw the Norman contingent away from the village. And once more Malcolm's words were harsh, and more so when the four answering what the fifth could not, refused to reveal the means by which they had learned Theriot was taken prisoner.

They sought to protect their liege, but it was futile. Just as Theriot knew Edgar had sent them to extract payment for their losses, so did Malcolm.

After the king warned if they tried again to relieve him of his right to dispense justice he would cast them across the border trussed and in the path of Normans, he commanded them from his sight.

With their departure, he addressed the guards in Gaelic. When they also withdrew, Malcolm said in Norman-French, "Lady Marguerite, I know I am not wrong in stating this warrior loathes you standing as his protector. Come away."

Thinking she might refuse, Theriot's anger quickened against one who was as responsible for his blinding as Edgar and Hendrie, and who had furthered her deceit by not revealing she accompanied him on that nearly senseless journey from England, doubtless tending him throughout. For this her scent had been familiar when first he awakened here.

She stepped forward. "Your Grace, do not punish Sir Theriot—"

"Neither do I believe he would have you beg mercy for him, Marguerite."

Her shadow parted from his and moved to the side, then the king strode forward. "I would have you yield Lady Marguerite's dagger, Sir Theriot, not because I fear you as you must know I do not. Because it bodes better for whatever comes of our acquaintance."

Since there was nothing to be gained in keeping hold of a short-bladed weapon that afforded minimal protection, Theriot had no reason to refuse. And yet, angered by Marguerite's deceit, the longing to more intimately know her face, and the inability to properly defend himself, he was tempted to test the king's wrath. However, that was what one such as Edgar would do, and at the moment the only one Theriot disliked more than Marguerite was the Aetheling.

He reversed the dagger and extended it hilt first.

The king took it. "Return this to yer person, Marguerite, then place two chairs before the fire."

Theriot felt her gaze as she concealed the dagger beneath her skirt as told by its rustling.

When she turned aside and Dubh followed, Malcolm's breath swept Theriot's face. "Though I have greater matters to attend to than making order of another of Edgar's messes, I shall take some minutes to become familiar with my..." He paused. "As there is no prettier word for it, let us name you what you are—my prisoner. But better that than the Aetheling's, eh?"

Theriot shifted his cramped jaw. "I have yet to see the advantage."

Malcolm grunted. "Be assured, what happened this day will not again. Though I am to wed the sister, and for that I aid and tolerate the Aetheling's struggle toward manhood, it does not change that I rule Scotland. Now, as I would not offend by offering to lead one yet capable of doing injury to warriors, follow."

Small mercy, Theriot thought bitterly. Then attending to the shadow that cut a straight path to the fire whose flames burned higher in answer to air entering through the gaping doorway, he narrowed his eyes against the light and followed. And so deeply resented feeling like a dog at its master's heels that when the king dropped onto a chair, Theriot's senses failed him—rather, he failed them.

With little warning, Marguerite was at his side, a hand on his hand, words at his ear. "Here is your seat."

Before he could rebuke the one responsible for his need for guidance, she set his hand on the back of a chair and withdrew. Though his senses remained relatively dull, hers were keen enough to know it was best to distance herself, even if she did not realize he had uncovered her deceit.

When she drew alongside Malcolm, the king ordered her to sit on the bed as if he also sensed Theriot's anger, though surely he believed it merely due to the lady shielding a warrior.

Marguerite called Dubh to her, and as they moved away, Theriot angled his body to keep direct firelight from his eyes.

"Ye nearly slew my man, Hendrie," Malcolm said. "An eye for an eye?"

Theriot tensed further. "As he denied me breath, I sought to stop him by putting a blade in him. For it, he did injury to my eyes. Should I fully recover as I am told he shall, what happened between us could be considered an eye for an eye. Should I not, it is far from an eye for an eye, and further yet from an eye for *two* eyes."

All that could be heard of the king was his breathing, then he said, "You should have died this day—that is, providing you truly dwell in the dark. Do you?"

Calm, Theriot counseled. *You can make no friend of him, but make him no greater enemy.* "Not the dark. I see light and what passes before it, but only as shadow."

"Without color?"

"Shades of white and grey."

The king sighed. "An ill thing for any, but especially a warrior. Be assured, Princess Margaret is much at prayer for the restoration of your vision." When Theriot did not respond, he added, "My betrothed is nearly a saint. If the Lord does not give answer as she beseeches, I am convinced none can persuade Him."

Refusing to dwell on the peculiarity that this brutal warrior sounded beguiled, Theriot said, "Should my vision be restored, will it be of use to me?"

"Now the matter of what to do with one whom Hendrie believes the scout who set Normans after the Aetheling. How do ye respond to that charge? And do give answer with the integrity of which I hear your family is known."

Though Theriot had avoided answering the same posed by Marguerite, he saw no reason to do so now. "Your man is correct in believing I tracked the Aetheling."

The lady made a sound of distress.

"Several days I followed before meeting up with a Norman contingent and setting them after Edgar. Regardless of my motive, I am only innocent of being more responsible than he for what befell the village he rode through."

"Your motive?" the king asked.

As Theriot struggled with pride that demanded he offer no further defense and indifference bred by certainty the judgment to come would remain unchanged, he saw the great smudge of the man lean forward.

"Why a scout, Sir Theriot of a family of renowned warriors?" Malcolm rephrased his question, calling to mind the meeting with King William when this D'Argent told he would not lead men who laid waste to the people and lands of the North. "Even if there is dishonor in the truth, Chevalier, less that dishonor if one confesses it in defense of his person."

Pride kicked Theriot opposite as surely this man said to be moved more by brute strength than strength of mind sought to do. "It was not fear that led me to serve my king as a scout. As a true warrior does not put innocents to death, whether by drawing blood or depriving them of what is needed to sustain life, I declined to be the blade and fire loosed on the North. Instead, I served by rooting out what remains of the rebels to ensure their further acts of defiance do not consume England."

"Their acts," Malcolm drawled. "You are certain Saxon

resistance, rather than your king, is what threatens to consume all of England?"

"I know William bears great responsibility, but as all ought to have learned by now, his appetite can only be controlled if the resistance ceases to offer up tempting dishes. Thus, unless the Lord wills different from what He has allowed these four years, the rebellion must end."

"A good answer, D'Argent, though the Aetheling is unwilling to accept it—and may never."

"Yet you will permit him to continue using Scotland as a base from which to stir William's wrath that will bring that wrath down upon your country?"

"Already there is much ill between your king and me. What is a little more? And be assured, Edgar is only that—a little more."

Malcolm spoke true only in that what had happened to the village was naught compared to the King of Scotland's recent attack on Northern England. However, though that incursion had been savage and many commoners were taken captive, it was nearly tame compared to William's harrying. Though Malcolm was a worthy adversary boasting numerous men and resources, so had been King Harold who lost his country at the Battle at Hastings. The King of Scots might believe he was William's equal, but he was not.

"You underestimate the impact of that *little more* you name Edgar," Theriot said. "Do you not leash him, what happened in that English village could happen in your villages. And you will be as responsible as he."

The straightening of Malcolm's back enlarged his shadow. "Even does one not consider your current circumstances, you are too bold, Theriot D'Argent."

His threat elicited a gasp from the bed.

Having forgotten their audience, Theriot wished he could

blame the lapse on his loss of sight, but once more he failed the senses that remained to him.

Almighty, he sent heavenward, *Malcolm is not the only one who needs to fit a leash. Aid me in hooking one to the collar of this anger.*

"Your Grace," the lady ventured, "what Sir Theriot warns of the Aetheling is no different from what Hendrie—"

"Do not defend me, *Lady,*" Theriot snarled, and forgetting the need for a leash, narrowed his eyes on the king. "I accept responsibility for much of what happened to that village since I was certain he who thinks he will be a better king than William would act in the best interest of those he wishes to free from Norman rule. Just as done other rebels who refused to disband when I stirred up their hives, I set the contingent after Edgar and his entourage once they were distant from settlements to ensure no innocents suffered."

Now Theriot was the one leaning forward. "My mistake was believing your betrothed's brother would do the same as rebels who have sacrificed much to place him on the throne—that he would avoid settlements. But rather than go well around that village, he led his enemy straight through it. If ever he is fit to rule others, and much I doubt it, you will be an old man with more regrets than you have now. I say leash him, King Malcolm!"

Amid the weighty silence, Theriot felt the lady's fear.

For me, he thought and resented it. Then guessing Malcolm would take this Norman's life as his man, Hendrie, had failed to do and strangely unmoved, he sat back.

"More bold, more offensive, Sir Theriot," the king pronounced. "But I shall allow it. You know why? Because I believe you speak true of what happened in the village ere you were lured away from what was feared a child you sought to harm."

The momentum of Theriot's thoughts arrested, he reversed them to ponder what Malcolm added to what was known.

Though Theriot had told Marguerite he but tried to save a child, when Edgar had boasted of the trap that captured this Norman, he had not mentioned it was laid to protect a child. Merely overlooked?

He started to further turn that rock but was struck by the realization those responsible for what had been done him—Edgar, Hendrie, and Marguerite—believed they had reason to bait the trap and attack him. As the village had been set afire by Normans, they had also thought they heard a child and glimpsed the enemy moving that direction. Of course they believed he intended harm.

That eased his anger, though not in great measure. Perhaps in time.

"Commendable restraint," Malcolm said. "More evidence ye are a man of integrity."

"Who mistook a mewling cat for a child," Theriot said between his teeth. Though his eyes were tempted toward Marguerite, he kept them on her king. "As I do not believe it was the Aetheling who told you the truth of what happened in the village, who was it?"

"My man, Hendrie."

"Who else?"

A long pause, then he said, "It was confirmed by others there and, doubtless, shall be told by the Saxons who this day sought to avenge themselves on you."

"Who else?" Theriot persisted, and receiving no response said, "What of the village woman?"

He was not certain whether it was imagined or felt, but breath was held and glances exchanged. Before a lie could further the deception, he said, "I know Lady Marguerite's secret—that she is the one I believed pursued by my countrymen, that she led me into the trap that ended in my injury."

She sprang up from the bed. "Theriot—"

"*Sir* Theriot!"

"Sir Theriot, I wanted to tell you, and I would have—"

"As further it is confirmed what you are to me, Lady Marguerite, you can have naught to say that I wish to hear."

She halted between Malcolm and Theriot. "What am I to you?"

"What I thought before this day though I began to think I wronged you—deceit wrapped in something sweet." To which he had nearly succumbed, tempted by a mouth he could not see. And that desire had naught to do with bringing her to his side.

Marguerite stepped toward him. "Pray, listen—"

"So you may lead me further astray? Once more become an instrument of Edgar?"

Had she intended to draw nearer, his words halted her.

"Lady Marguerite, leave us," Malcolm said.

She hesitated then hastened past.

"As I no longer require your services," Theriot called, "do not come to me again."

Would she have slammed the door were it upright and hinged? he wondered as her footsteps and those of the dog receded.

"You are very harsh with my ward," Malcolm drawled.

"Though now I know what was done me can be justified and am grateful for enlightenment, still she deceived—"

"Would you have allowed her to continue tending you as done throughout the journey to Dunfermline had she told she was the bait that caused a warrior to be deprived of his sight?"

Theriot nearly demanded why she had wished to tend him at all, but he recalled the Aetheling's taunting and that he knew the one taken prisoner was a D'Argent. For his family's reputation, surely Marguerite had tended him en route—and continued to do so when the princess further vouched for his family. But there were other matters whose answers were mere guesses that did not satisfy.

Ignoring the question put to him, he said, "I believed the silver in my hair revealed me for a D'Argent, and for that I was taken prisoner rather than left for dead, but Edgar knew my Christian name. From whom?"

The shadow of Malcolm shrugged. "As told, this king has greater matters to attend to than the Aetheling."

Then for now Theriot must be satisfied with the guess one of the Norman contingent captured by Edgar's men had revealed the scout's name. "What of Marguerite? As I know that lady of Scotland was not among Edgar's entourage, how did she come to be in the village?"

"Since the day you arrived here was the same I returned from putting down trouble in the North, I cannot tell the reason she was there," Malcolm said, then added, "Of course, once the Norman side of her had family over the border."

Though she had revealed that to Theriot, here another curiosity. "Once?"

"A bad business that, but it is done—all dead."

"How?"

Malcolm stood. "As you wish naught else to do with the lady and my time wastes, let us make good use of these last minutes."

Hearing a blade exit its scabbard, Theriot tensed in anticipation of defending himself.

"Be not alarmed, Sir Theriot. Though I have yet to determine what to do with you, I believe your captivity requires alteration. Hold out your hands."

Not a lie, Theriot was certain, this man having no need to work deceit on a sightless, unarmed warrior. And since neither did Malcolm require the protection of a blade at this time, it seemed the prisoner was to be freed of the ropes about his wrists.

Theriot stood and extended his hands.

"From what I have witnessed," Malcolm said as he sliced through the short-ended rope Marguerite had cut, "no longer do you require a keeper." The rope fell away, then the flat of the blade was against the outside of Theriot's other wrist and that of which he had made a whip was also severed. "Henceforth, the guards keeping watch outside will give aid only when requested."

"I am to be trusted?"

"Within limits. What trust ye earned is in part due to your vision being incapacitated. In greater part is the guards' report that though Lady Marguerite loosed your bonds, you made no attempt to harm her to keep the Saxons from your throat nor gain your freedom. They said you sought to protect her ahead of her own attempt to protect you."

Malcolm paused as if to give Theriot an opportunity to confirm it, but it needed no confirmation.

"Of course, since now you are aware of what she withheld, I question if henceforth she is safe with you. For that, had ye not told her not to return, I would have."

This required a response. "Even were she without excuse for being the bait that led to my injury, I would not harm her. I would do as already done so I not further suffer her presence."

"Then the D'Argent integrity remains intact."

"Ever," Theriot said and silently added, *Even if only by the short nails of my bloodied fingers.*

The blade scraped the scabbard's throat as it was returned to its sheath. "Still, henceforth you shall remain distant from each other, and much that will please the physician."

Theriot frowned. "He did not approve of her tending me?"

"He did not, though his objection has naught to do with her competence since the lady is skilled with healing."

"Then?" Theriot said and, feeling closely watched, was certain that just as what would be told him was no comment made in passing, how he responded was of interest.

"He wishes to wed her."

Though that should be of little concern to this Norman who barely knew her, and of no concern now he knew her better by way of her deception, it bothered.

"Though ye were bound and guards were without," Malcolm continued, "he disapproved of her being here with you—as did I, but since my betrothed spoke well of your family and Marguerite argued few could be trusted with your care after what you did to Hendrie, I agreed providing she honor my conditions. And this another reason it is best she not return."

The release of the captive, which had likely saved his life. That reminder softened Theriot toward her though, again, to no great extent considering the man before him remained a shadow.

Malcolm sighed. "Ere I grant the physician permission to wed her, I shall speak with Marguerite."

It sounded as if she would have a choice. Was it a real one? No pressure to wed someone she did not want—no threats made to her nor those dear that would bend her to another's will as done often to gain concessions and form alliances?

Immediately, Theriot scorned his pondering. It mattered not what became of her. What mattered was regaining his eyesight were it possible and returning to England. Fortunately, the end result of this day's assault was a good beginning.

"I shall leave ye," the king said and, as he strode past, added, "The door will be repaired forthwith to ensure your comfort."

Then Theriot was alone. As was best for one who had succumbed to deceit wrapped in something sweet.

MARGUERITE AWAITED the king on the steps outside the palace. Though glad he had not come sooner, having needed to calm her emotions and cool the whites of eyes surely gone red, he was not fooled.

Sympathy lining his brow, voice gentle, better she understood the reason when he expressed knowledge of what she felt for Theriot that she ought not. "Ye will not tend him again, Sparrow. Not because he does not wish it, because I command it for the protection of your body as well as your heart."

Hating the heat in her cheeks and the fool she must seem, she protested, "Too little I know Sir Theriot for my heart to be in danger."

He tapped her breastbone. "Though you are much like your mother, ever I have believed yer heart more of Diarmad for how quick it recognizes the kindred in others. Many the beautiful women he desired ere he looked upon his Marguerite, but never did he want more than quick embraces nor think it love as he did with her. 'Twas as if his soul knew hers." He sighed. "Unfortunately, even does yours know Sir Theriot's, it cannot know the one his shall become when it is certain the warrior of him has been stolen—even did he not know you were the one who trapped him."

"And laid that trap, which must yet be told."

"Leave it be, Marguerite. No good can come of him resenting you more." He started past her.

"Your Grace, what is to be done with Sir Theriot now I no longer care for him?"

He looked around. "As I do not believe he is a danger to anyone at this time, he shall remain guarded in the hut and, unbound, attend to his own needs."

That surprised. At best she had expected Theriot would be tended by a servant, at next best moved to the physician's sick room, at worst tossed into a cell. "I thank you."

He inclined his head, patted Dubh, and ascended the steps with such vigor his plaid flapped against his back.

She knew she should follow, but though he had told her to leave the truth untold, she could not. Blessedly, she had an excuse to return to Theriot.

"Stay," she commanded the hound and hastened toward the wash house.

~

DEEMED by Theriot D'Argent to be as dispensable as she was deceitful, then discovering her instructions to the laundress had been ignored, Marguerite had been of a mood to wash the garments herself—and vigorously.

Now staring at them where they dried before the brazier in the loveliest chamber of the palace, she whispered, "Dispensable. Deceitful." Then she lowered to her back on the pallet the princess had ordered laid alongside her bed despite Marguerite's protest it was time she return to her home beyond the glen. It was in that pretty cottage she was born and raised and loved—that place Cannie and she had closed up last year expecting to return with her mother.

Now she lies with papa, Marguerite thought as she stared at the ceiling the brazier's glow painted orange. *Soon I must go to them and settle my soul as it will not be settled this eve.*

She had known the princess was right to encourage her to tell Theriot the truth of his blinding before another revealed it. And that, it seemed, Marguerite had done since the only sense she could make of Theriot's revelation was her attempt to end the assault on him had loosened memories of that night when she had also cried out during his clash with Hendrie.

Aye, she was the informant, and more undone she would be if he allowed her to tell what she wished she had revealed when he unmasked her as the village woman—that *she* had set the trap.

She rolled to her side, but as that shoulder ached from Theriot's rejection of her shielding that landed her against the wall, she returned to her back. Feeling very alone, she almost wished she made her bed in the hall with Dubh.

For another quarter hour, she suffered wakefulness, then sat up and peered at the princess whose fair head was turned opposite.

Meg had been kind when she learned what transpired. The only time that kindness slipped was when realization of what was not told regarding who sent the Saxons to Theriot became anger, and it was not directed at Marguerite.

"Edgar!" she had rasped. "That is not the refined silver of which godly kings are made." Then she had taken Marguerite to the small chamber Malcolm had transformed into a chapel for her.

For far longer than Marguerite had done at any one time, she had knelt before the altar while Meg prayed aloud. First the princess had beseeched guidance for her brother, next asked the Lord to have mercy on the English who continued to suffer the ravages of war, then prayed for the King of Scots, his people, and reformation of their church. Lastly, she had asked for the healing of those injured during the attack on Theriot.

Thinking they were done, Marguerite had opened her eyes. However, when she saw Meg remained at prayer, she had settled into her own prayers guided by those already spoken and lingered over ones for Theriot's recovery and his forgiveness.

When they emerged from the chapel to tidings the injuries dealt the Saxons and Scotsmen were minor, she was more persuaded the princess had God's ear.

Returning to the present, Marguerite considered the brazier before which chairs had been positioned to accommodate the garments draped over them. Then she cast off the blankets and crossed to the nearest.

As she tested the material of the mantle, she recalled her anger at finding it and Theriot's other clothes in a corner. Watched throughout as she herself cleaned them, she had been tempted to correct the head laundress's beliefs about the Norman prisoner. True, he was responsible for putting the Aetheling to flight and had nearly slain Hendrie, but just as it was not evil that led to his blinding, neither was it evil what he had done in the belief sooner England would heal nor in defending his person.

The front of his mantle now mostly dry, Marguerite turned its backside forward and did the same to the tunic and chausses draped over the second chair. Having told Theriot she would return his garments, that she would do as well as deliver a walking stick fashioned by the palace's woodworker. Though wary of how the latter would be received, it would be of use in finding his way, even if only around the hut. And then...

"Confession," she whispered.

As she started back toward her pallet, she glimpsed a cloth on the floor and swept up that which she had first used to cover Theriot's damaged eyes. Though the material was as fine as that of his tunic, it was so worn she had nearly discarded it. Now as clean as his garments, she drew it through her fingers as she crossed to her pallet.

When finally she drifted toward dreams, it was with that cloth pressed to her chest and imaginings it was not only her heart beating there but Theriot's.

CHAPTER TWELVE

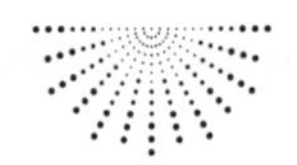

A few minutes was all she needed—providing he did not demand she depart and allowed her to speak without interruption.

In the light of dawn and with hope Malcom had not instructed the guards to refuse her entrance, Marguerite strode around the side of the hut with the confidence of one with a right to be there.

As expected, the younger guards of the night shift were before the warming fire. Having only heard what transpired here, hopefully they would be less wary.

"Lady?" said the taller as he advanced ahead of the other. "We were told you are no longer caregiver." He halted between her and the door, eyes glimmering with appreciation often cast at her.

She looked to her armful. "I return the prisoner's laundered garments." When he reached for them, she clasped them closer. "I thank you, but they are not heavy."

"I do not believe the king would be well with you entering, especially as your dog is not with you."

Though Dubh's leg injury was minor and the hound had

moved to accompany her from the hall, Marguerite had commanded her to remain.

"As King Malcolm entrusted me with the Norman's care," Marguerite said, "I do not believe he would forbid me to enter."

"Then you are unaware the prisoner is no longer bound?"

"I am aware and agree Sir Theriot is of no threat as proved when he protected me when it was feared those who attacked your fellow guards would do me harm."

The man looked to his companion who shrugged.

"Has he caused you trouble since being loosed?" she asked.

"He has not."

"Then though your concern is appreciated, I shall enter."

When he remained unmoving, she was tempted to further the argument, but as too much protest could lead him to consult Malcolm, she decided to prick his pride. "If it eases the burden of protecting me from a blind man, accompany me."

The second guard grunted. "Even were he sighted, no burden would it be, Lady. But as he is Norman and all know their blood runs yellow with deceit, we shall stand as shield between him and you."

Grateful they were less proficient in Norman-French than the older guards since what she wished to tell Malcolm's prisoner would have an audience, she said, "I shall follow."

When she entered, she saw Theriot faced them. Though he could have understood little of what they spoke in their language, he had to have recognized her voice. As evidenced by his tight mouth and narrowed eyes, he was not pleased she was here.

He hates me, she thought as she closed the door with her shoulder. *Woe to me that I care so much.*

She stepped between the guards. "I have brought your laundered garments," she said in Norman-French which the guards would better understand for knowing the reason she was here and that she spoke less rapidly than usual.

"I said you should not come again, Lady Marguerite."

"And I said I would return your clothing."

He jutted his chin. "The nearest chair to the left."

Certain between Malcolm's departure and her return he had become acquainted with the hut's every reach and content, she turned to the side and named each garment she set over the chair. "Cleaned, dried, and mended," she concluded and recalled the discomfort of being watched by the princess while putting needle and thread to Theriot's tunic.

"What of the cloth with which you bound my eyes?"

She had not thought he would concern himself with that small item, but lest her retrieval of it from beneath the neck of her bodice cause the guards to alert Theriot she wore it, she said, "I shall search it out. Is it of import?"

"I want it back," was his only answer.

Might it be a piece of a lady's gown given for remembrance? she wondered with a stir of jealousy. "It will be returned."

"Have another deliver it to me. Good day."

"There is another thing I brought," she said and, seeing the Scotsmen were nearly expressionless, whether because the conversation was dull or incomprehensible, drew it from beneath her belt and stepped toward him.

Immediately, the tall one gripped her arm. "Near enough, Lady."

Suppressing the impulse to pull free, she said, "It is a walking stick, Sir Theriot. Now that you are—"

"I do not require one." His darkening face was nearly as unrecognizable as his voice. "Now go."

She had been wary of offering it, but had to try. Lowering it to her side, she said, "Before I depart, I must tell what was left unsaid on the day past so truly we may be done with each other if still you wish it."

"We are done, nothing more to be said."

Go, she told herself, then snapped, "The wish to remain ignorant is unworthy of a D'Argent."

The certainty with which she spoke of his family as if she were acquainted with them causing interest to displace some of his anger, he said grudgingly, "Have done with it."

She moistened her lips. "I know the Aetheling boasted the trap laid for you was of his doing, but just as I was the bait, I laid the trap."

His nostrils flared.

"I heard the cry of what I thought a child and Edgar refused to answer it, so Hendrie and others accompanied me to give aid. When you were sighted and it was feared you meant the child harm, I determined to lead you away. Had I known then you were a D'Argent—"

Of a sudden, his sightless eyes swept past her.

Having learned on the day past to attend to what captured his attention, she pulled free of the guard and turned to await the appearance of one whose footsteps she heard now.

Heavenly Father, let it not be Malcolm, she silently appealed. *Nor another sent by Edgar to harm Theriot. Let it be but a lad bearing viands.*

The first two prayers were answered as she wished, but not the third.

The physician entered. "What do you here, Lady Marguerite?" he demanded in Gaelic.

Though the guards might not tell Malcolm she had come, this man would, and she resented it—and his disapproval. "As promised Sir Theriot, I have returned his laundered garments," she said in Saxon, there no longer a need to keep that language from her tongue in Theriot's presence and Colban being better versed in it than Norman-French.

The physician frowned, doubtless over her keeping the chevalier apprised of their exchange, then shifted to that language. "Even so, the king will be displeased you are here."

She stood taller. "He would not have allowed Sir Theriot to be unfettered were he a danger to me. And as you can see, I am not without chaperone."

He stepped farther inside. "Though this blind man is not to be bound, it was made known to me you shall no longer keep company with him."

Offended he thoughtlessly named Theriot blind, she snapped, "I do not keep company with him. I—"

"Leave!" Colban stepped to the side to clear the doorway.

As evenly as possible, she said, "There is a small matter I must discuss with the chevalier. Pray, go outside. I will not be long."

"Lady, the king gave me command over these guards. As it would make a bad beginning to relations between you and me, I prefer not to give threat, but if necessary I shall order these men to remove you."

Even more he offended, but she could not sling words for the turning of her mind over what he told without clearly speaking it. "A bad beginning to what relations between us?"

His smile was tolerant. "We shall discuss it later. Perhaps a walk in the glen?"

Before she could refuse, Theriot said, "I have no further need of you, Lady Marguerite. Do as your betrothed commands and be gone."

She caught her breath. Did he only guess the same as she? Or…? Recalling Malcolm's words she no longer tend the Norman to ensure the safety of her heart, it was possible he had warned the chevalier away by revealing she was promised to another.

Heart beating hard, she said, "If the physician believes he and I have relations beyond what I require of his services, he is as wrong as you, Sir Theriot. Now I go, not because it is commanded, because I am done here."

As she crossed to the door, ache in her hand reminded her of what she gripped hard, and she veered toward the chair upon which she had laid his garments. "The walking stick is here. Do with it as you will."

"I have no need of it."

"I believe you do," she said and departed. Though she had intended to reveal having briefly met him before he was blinded and that she had become acquainted with some of his family, now that he knew the worst of her and was as done with her as she with him, it did not matter.

Her insides tossing as she crossed the bailey in the brighter light of a sun now showing its face, she was surprised at being struck by the beauty of a day that promised spring.

Beauty he may not see again, her conscience prodded.

"I am done with him," she insisted, though not entirely true. She must persuade Malcolm to return him to his family.

And there was another thing of which he must be persuaded —that a match between her and the physician was not welcome. Even if she must remind him of what was owed Diarmad the *Shield,* she would to ensure she wed no man save one she wanted at the least, loved at the very best—a man whose heart was in hers as hers was in his.

THE PHYSICIAN'S intentions toward the lady, albeit spoken between his words, had been obvious, the same as it was apparent she was ignorant of what was planned for her.

Now as Theriot sat on the chair with the healer examining the injury done the back of his head and the guards keeping watch, he felt regret. He had not been receptive to Marguerite's return to the hut, and less so when the sound of her voice outside caused sightless eyes to ache more for the inability to look upon her than anything else denied good form and color.

Though he had been glad she came once she revealed the

rest of her truth, it giving him more cause to have naught to do with her, now he regretted supporting the physician in forcing her departure ahead of learning what else she would have told.

Still he did not know how she came to be in the village, and though it could not matter, the traitor of him continued to mull the possibilities.

"It has healed well." Colban's fingers moved off Theriot's scalp and he came around. "Lift your face."

Theriot clamped his teeth to keep from demanding a diagnosis of his eyes ahead of examination. Already he knew it was believed his vision was lost and, until the man looked closer, that diagnosis could not be confirmed nor refuted.

Tilting his head back, he felt and smelled breath on his face and knew the man's morning meal was washed down with ale.

"The bruising and swelling lessen, the blood corrupting the whites begins to fade, and the cut and scraped skin shall cast off scabbing soon."

Theriot nearly growled with frustration over things he did not need to know.

When the physician ordered a guard to bring light near, there came the sound of shifting wood, greater crackling and flashes of fire, then the intensity of light increased with each footfall.

Feeling the heat of the torch held before his face, struggling against squeezing his eyes closed to block the light paining him, he seethed at having only the thin shadow of his extra sense to warn him should the torch be made an instrument of torture. And even were it sufficient to escape cruelty in the moment, the next moment could prove detrimental.

"Much damage," the physician said. "What color your eyes, Sir Theriot?"

Gripping his arms tighter against his sides to keep from driving a fist into the man's gut, he said, "What color do they appear?"

As if Colban also struggled to remain civil, he was slow to answer. "Not the pale nor bright of blue. Possibly green, more likely brown."

Green, Theriot silently pronounced, *like those of other D'Argents though many the shades.*

"As told, much damage, Chevalier. There is healing, and I believe the clouds at the center thin, but much I question if they will depart entirely."

"That is your diagnosis?" Theriot bit.

The man grunted. "Will you allow me to probe further? Certes, it will be so uncomfortable you may wish a dagger to stick me as you did Hendrie."

"Probe," Theriot snapped and heard the scrape of boots, the guards surely beckoned near lest these fists defy him.

The probing was beyond uncomfortable and did turn his thoughts to retaliation—so much he sought escape in memories of when last he had wielded a sword.

A cat leaping from a window.

A woman pursued by what he believed his countrymen.

An opponent with the sound of the Norman about him.

Theriot paused on that. What the dying man had spoken in diluted Norman-French was near in memory—and then gone. Something of import had been revealed. Assuring himself he would uncover it later, he moved his thoughts to what had come after he put down that opponent.

A scream had sounded again, distracting him from the Scotsman coming for him, and in moonlight he saw the woman he now knew was Marguerite approach from the direction she had fled—a slim figure as told by the mantle flying out behind her and hair that appeared dark. That scream had rendered him vulnerable to the blow aimed at his head.

When he made it onto his back to defend what remained of his life, he had looked nearer upon Marguerite, though he could not recall if it was before or after he stuck his blade in the

Scotsman. Though much about her was blurred as she pleaded for the assault to end and fought whoever held her back, he had thought her familiar. Had they met before? Unlikely since he did not think he had encountered a lady of Scotland, even one who spoke Norman-French. She must resemble someone he knew.

Leaving memories behind, again he regretted not allowing her to tell all she had come to reveal. Even if what remained had naught to do with her presence in the village, he could have brought the conversation around to that and satisfied this—

He jerked as pain stabbed his left eye well above the unhooding of that lid, evidencing the examination was exceedingly thorough. Then the pain eased and he heard the crack of a back long folded over.

"Though time and prayer will heal far more than my skills," the physician said, "I shall visit again to check on your progress."

"Speak plainly," Theriot bit.

Colban stepped back, the glaring light shifted to the side, and the torch made of firewood was tossed into the pit. "To your end days, I am fair certain memories alone will be clearly visible to you. Thus, rather than a sword, a cane—or if it is easier, call it a walking stick—shall define your life. Now as that is as plainly spoken as possible, I leave you."

Moments later, the door closed behind him and the guards. And Theriot began the struggle to contain anger hotter for hopelessness and more hopeless for finding himself in a godforsaken country with no ally.

Breathe ere you give them cause to bind you again or do worse, he counseled. *Breathe, brother of Guarin who suffered much abuse and imprisonment but is stronger for it.*

"Still he sees," he snarled. "Still he is a warrior." The weak of him grasping that excuse to lose control, he gave his head a shake. "You have God's favor!" he assured himself, but he quaked and the flames tossed back the door dropped over them, scorched his throat, and rushed past his lips.

Once more, he who had little reason to rage before there was Marguerite, raged. And this time in the absence of fetters, he made chaos of all that came to hand, starting with the accursed cane.

CHAPTER THIRTEEN

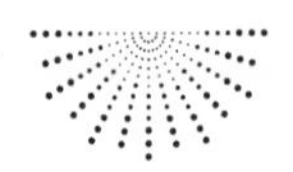

Confession granted her forgiveness, though likely sooner since the princess was present when Marguerite told Malcolm she had delivered Theriot his garments and revealed to him she was as much trap as bait.

The king was displeased, and more so when she said she would not wed the physician. What argument that would have led to could not be known since an instant later a bellow carried across the morning air, bent around the side of the palace, and leapt over the wall of the skeletal garden spring would soon resurrect.

Marguerite knew who it was and was more certain Theriot had been given no hope of restored sight than that he was under attack, but she sprang from Malcolm's side into his path. "Your Grace—"

Another bellow caused him to slice a hand through the air. As he listened, she noted greater silence had fallen as if all within the walls stilled to assess the danger of that Norman's roar. Then another bellow.

Malcolm lowered his hand, glanced at his wide-eyed

betrothed, and settled his gaze on his ward. In answer to the fear she could not disguise, he said, "'Tis understandable."

"What know you of it?" she asked amid Theriot's raging.

"What I *guess* is the physician has been more forthcoming regarding the chevalier's vision than instructed, and now the warrior mourns one no longer a warrior."

"Is it not too soon to say he will be blind evermore?" asked Meg.

Before the king's betrothal to this Saxon princess, he had been a man of temperate smiles when sober and exuberant smiles when many a horn of drink was drained. Now the smile he bestowed was gentle like those Diarmad had shone upon his wife. "Too soon to know for certain, perhaps, but far greater the chance he shall not see again, My Pearl."

Meg stood taller. "If God wills it, he will be healed in full. Or do you not hold to the truth all is possible with the Divine?"

He looked discomfited. "I know you believe it, and I am more at prayer than ever seeking that same strength of faith, but I have not attained it." He moved his regard to Marguerite. "Fear not for him, Sparrow. Having anticipated he would not like whatever was revealed, I instructed the guards to leave him be providing he presents no danger."

That was of some relief. "Your Grace, allow me to—"

"Marguerite, though you are daughter of Diarmad, you cannot understand what Sir Theriot has lost, whether it proves temporary with the Lord's intercession or permanent in the absence of a miracle. This is what the chevalier needs, and we shall leave him to it." He pointed a finger near enough she saw every barb of his chewed straight nails. "And you will keep your distance."

When she nodded reluctantly, he raised his eyebrows. "Regarding the physician—"

"Pray, let us not regard him!" she exclaimed, then seeing

ridges rise on his brow as if drawing up battle lines, she added, "At least for now."

"For now, dear Malcolm," the princess encouraged.

He shifted breath between his cheeks. "Very well."

Marguerite thanked him, then he set his betrothed's hand atop his ward's. In the silence that followed Theriot's next round of raging, he said, "There are matters to which I must give ear and eye, likely amid more din than usual." He bowed curtly and strode to the palace's rear door.

"Do not fear for Sir Theriot," the princess said. "The Lord can make good of whatever comes."

"Can, but will He?" Marguerite said.

"Whether Sir Theriot is once more sighted or never again, if he allows God to work in him, the beginning of what is to be shall be better than what was."

Marguerite sighed. "Like my king, I have not your strength of faith to know and trust God so well."

The princess slid an arm through Marguerite's. As they resumed the walk Theriot had interrupted, which was first interrupted by Marguerite seeking out Malcolm, she who would be queen said, "Even in the midst of the impossible, the more you seek Him, the more He seeks you. Spreading that certainty and hope to the people of Scotland is the work the Lord has chosen for me by binding me to a man who can be more ungodly than godly."

That last made Marguerite tense and her companion squeeze her arm. "I know there is much good in him and his sins do not compare with the one who stole the throne from my brother, but Malcolm can and will be more worthy of the people the Lord has given him to rule."

"I see changes about him already."

She smiled. "I am pleased, but still much patience is needed. Years of loss and warring shaped him into the man I first thought would be among the last I would choose for a husband.

Heavily worn knees will be required to undo whatever can be undone, but he is willing. Mostly."

They fell into silence all the more welcome for that into which Theriot had also fallen. As their slippers whispered over stones laid between barren patches, Marguerite wondered what the chevalier did now. If Malcolm had not assured her the guards would leave him be, she would fear he was silent because harm was done him. Had he dropped exhausted onto the bed?

She longed to go to him, but not only was it forbidden, he would welcome her less than any other—indeed, might return to raging.

"Though you need not confide," the princess said, "concern for your well-being bids me ask the reason you wear Sir Theriot's cloth which you told was used to bandage his eyes during the journey to Dunfermline."

Marguerite kept her hand from flying to what ought to be tucked out of sight, but she was unable to correct the falter in her step. She turned to the princess. "Concern for me?"

"Malcolm worries you come to feel much for this D'Argent."

Annoyance flickered through Marguerite. "Now you worry as well for this lady you hardly know and disapprove that I should feel anything other than hatred for a Norman."

As if her words were a slap, the woman blinked.

They *were* a slap. And undeserved. "Forgive me, Princess. That was ill spoken. Not only have you shown me much kindness, you did speak on behalf of Sir Theriot."

Sympathy curved the woman's lips. "Mayhap more than you know, you feel for him—the same as I did for Malcolm before I yielded up the longing to be of the Church. I do disapprove for the seeming hopelessness of it, though I have no right since did I not just admonish my betrothed for having too little faith in what the Lord can do?" She sighed. "Be assured, I shall increase my prayers for Sir Theriot and you, and when the Lord does with my beseechings as He wills, you may call on me whether the Almighty turns you left or right."

Marguerite's throat tightened. She was not without friends. As Malcolm told, her heart was quick to recognize the kindred in others. However, this woman seemed something more. Might this closeness be the sort one feels for a sister?

She smiled. "I thank you, Princess."

"I am Meg to you." She kissed Marguerite's cheek. "Now is there any way I may be of service?"

The future Queen of Scotland of service to me, Marguerite thought and nearly declined. Remembering the cloth, she drew it from around her neck. "I do not know the import of this since Sir Theriot would not say, but he wished it returned."

The princess took it. "As but one edge is hemmed and two pieces of equal size seamed together, I think it the lower portion of a tunic. And see"—she plucked at the frayed ends—"once these edges were also seamed. Since this does not look to be cut from a lady's garment, much curiosity over why it is of such sentiment he carried it on his person and wishes it returned."

"You will see it into his hands?"

"I shall. Indeed, I may deliver it myself."

Marguerite caught her breath. "Malcolm would not approve, especially for how wrathful Sir Theriot is."

"Hence, he would have to accompany me."

"Which he may refuse to do."

Pretty teeth showing, the lower ones slightly overlapped, Meg said, "Refuse me the opportunity to minister to a man who is hurting and assure him I shall pray for him? I believe I can bring Malcolm around, but if not, the chevalier will have his cloth by way of another."

"I thank you. Now I shall visit Hendrie and my Saxon escort who is eager to return to Derbyshire."

The princess put the cloth in her purse. "You are brave, lady who balks at being matched with the physician."

Marguerite raised her eyebrows. "It does not excite to so soon be returned to Colban's presence, but it must be done—and perhaps I can dissuade him from pursuing me."

"If you are certain you prefer another man's pursuit," Meg said.

Letting that lie, Marguerite left the princess to the solitude with which she seemed exceedingly comfortable.

As she entered the palace by way of the door Malcolm had used, she lamented, *If only I could be as certain as she that I am heard when I bend the knee and spill my heart unto the Lord. And to trust Him when the answer is not what I wish.*

Pausing outside the sick room, she beseeched the Lord to straighten the crooked paths of those who traveled them with her and stepped inside.

When she departed a half hour later, she was relieved, fearful, and vexed. Relieved Hendrie was no longer bed-bound and would begin resuming his duties within a sennight, fearful for the Saxon who showed little improvement, and vexed by the physician whose eyes felt like hands upon her.

"He thinks I am to be his," she muttered as she made her way abovestairs. "I think not."

IT COULD BE no secret he was unable to keep inside what wanted—non, *needed*—out, that he could not leash it as he had told must be done Edgar and his ambitions. But just as Theriot had been prepared for the guards who entered hours after he raised himself from the corner into which he slammed himself, he was prepared for those who came next.

Likely more than they marveled over his appearance, they marveled over the state of the hut. He had thrown and overturned all that could be made to suffer even a small portion of what he endured, but to avoid being bound while the mess was cleaned, he had set it aright, rearranging all to allow him to negotiate his prison without reaching hands before him and groping walls and edges—and certainly not sweeping a cane as the physician believed would be his fate.

Other than the clay pitcher reduced to pieces, there should be no evidence of brokenness since he had cast all he destroyed atop the fire and it was a half hour since their scent stung his nostrils.

"Sir Theriot," Malcolm said, "I have with me—"

"Princess Margaret," he said, having heard the guards outside acknowledge her. "I may be unable to look upon the Aetheling's sister, but my ears yet serve me well." He pushed up out of the chair whose creak evidenced his earlier assault on it and straightened the tunic Marguerite had returned to him. Then shifting eyes from the king and down to the right where he was certain the lady stood, he bowed. "Princess."

"Sir Theriot," she answered in a voice that should not be so melodious for the offense this chevalier had dealt her brother. "I am gladdened—and surprised—at how well you appear."

Which he would not had he remained in the ill-fitting, abused garments and not dragged fingers through his hair. "The storm is past," he said, "and now to discover what can be made of the ship broken on the rocks before its pieces are swept out to sea."

"That is nearly poetic, Chevalier, and surely a sign your mind heals as well as your body."

It was good he had given anger its due and it had exhausted him. Otherwise, what was offensive, even if unintentional, would have caused him to sharply inform her his body could not be said to be healing well since its greatest injury was to his eyes.

Shifting them to the king, he said, "I did not expect you to come again—that whatever you wished done with your violent prisoner would be done by order."

"And you would have been right had not this godly woman made a good argument for delivering what Lady Marguerite said you wished returned."

Theriot did not have to think far on what that was. Though tempted to tell the princess to leave it on the stool near the door to sooner restore his privacy, he said, "What argument, that?"

"I told my betrothed it was an opportunity to pray with you, Sir Theriot," she said.

Here proof her faith was as deep as reported? Theriot wondered. "That is kind, but I am poor company and expect I shall be for a long while. If you will leave the cloth on the stool, I will take no more of your time."

No kinder could he be in seeking their departure, which was far kinder than he would have been a half hour earlier. Still, the shift in the air revealed Malcolm was offended with Theriot's rejection of the princess praying for him in his presence.

But before the king could rebuke him, the woman said, "Since you wish such a frayed piece returned, Lady Marguerite believes the cloth is of import."

She probed, if not to satisfy her curiosity, then that of the woman he did not wish to come again. "Once it was of import, now I but wish what belongs to me."

Her shadow parted from her betrothed, and when she rejoined Malcolm, she said, "The laundered cloth is on the stool."

Though he should have expected it was cleaned the same as his garments to remove the residue of salve, he had not.

"Is there anything else I may do for you?" the princess asked.

"There is something. As you must know, some of the items that make this place habitable no longer exist. If you will have them replaced, I give my word they will not share the fate of the others." When she did not immediately respond, he added, "A pitcher for water and basins for my ablutions."

"They shall be delivered this day."

"I thank you." He moved his eyes to the left. "There is something I would ask of you, King Malcolm."

"Though I doubt I shall be as accommodating, you may respectfully petition me."

"I am sure an escort will be required to ensure the safety of your people"—he knew that sounded derision, and it was—"but I request time outside these confines."

"Easily arranged," he said as if the matter was already decided. "And do you prove capable of good behavior now you come to terms with your injury, after a time I shall afford this prisoner of high rank the honor of sitting at table with me."

Beyond the offense of believing Theriot accepted the limitations of a world of dark given crude form only in the presence of light, a surprise. Despite how barbaric Theriot's own king was in subduing rebellion, William was mostly civil in dealing with nobles who threatened his rule. For that, the Aetheling and his family had been treated well enough they were able to escape and seek sanctuary in Scotland. It seemed the supposed savage who ruled this country was of a like mind.

Though Theriot had no desire to sit in Malcolm's great hall and blindly feed himself beneath the regard of his enemies, he said, "Henceforth, I shall strive to behave as fitting an unwilling guest of the King of Scots."

A chuckle sounded. "See, My Pearl, ye smooth my barbed places."

When the one likely responsible for the concessions murmured her approval, Theriot acknowledged the power of women to alter the nature of men—in a godly way where there was love such as what his parents and older brothers, Guarin and Cyr, knew. He had expected one day it would alter him as well should he find a woman who engaged both mind and heart and he could provide well for her and their children, but now...

Malcolm cleared his throat. "We shall leave you."

"Peace be with you," the princess said.

Following their departure, Theriot crossed the room. Before he reached the stool and felt a hand toward the cloth, he caught a scent more potent in the absence of other scents now it was clean. It could be that of the princess who delivered it, but when he raised it, he was certain it was of Marguerite. As if…

He drew another breath. The scent of lavender met with her scent penetrated the cloth as if not merely handled but worn—further proof his efforts to make an ally of her caused her to feel much for him.

He grunted. Now her truth was revealed, it did not matter. As for the cloth worn to remind him of Hastings when God's favor most greatly shone on him…

He considered tossing it on the fire as done the walking stick, but surely that would signify acceptance of the physician's diagnosis. And he did not accept it. Not yet. But neither could he once more fasten the cloth around his neck.

Theriot measured his steps to the bed, lifted the mattress, and set the cloth atop shards of clay pitcher. Between now and deciding the fate of that which had long been his companion, it would serve as one more layer between prying eyes and the only keen weapons available to him.

He dropped the mattress and touched his thigh where he had secured the strongest and sharpest shard with a strip torn from the waistband of the poor fitting chausses. Then he stretched out on the bed and turned his thoughts to what he would do with the bit of freedom Malcolm granted him.

As he would not have his family pay for his release, whether by ransom or risk to their lives, somehow he must make a way out of here.

For the first time since his injury, a sightless Saxon woman came to mind—she whose granddaughter had married one of Theriot's brothers. Unless one caught sight of her milky eyes, her debility was not obvious. With confidence and few missteps,

Bernia had moved about her village with no stick going before her.

Hope in that. Or was there? After all, since it was age that stole her sight, her adjustment had been gradual. Too, she had only to better learn the boundaries of a village already known to her. Far more would be required of Theriot.

Though escape seemed impossible without aid and having only light and shadows to guide him, he would seek to make it possible—and despite growing doubt, continue to embrace his sire's belief in God's willingness to intercede over his uncle's belief God was merely an observer.

After what seemed hours of praying for full recovery of his sight as well as his extra sense, it was natural to raise his lids. Or had been.

Thinking how wrong it was that, though he could no longer see, still his eyes moistened as if he were a little boy who needed someone to hold his hand to keep him upright and lead him about, he squeezed his eyes closed. And found some comfort amid darkness that was rightfully impenetrable regardless of the state of his vision.

CHAPTER FOURTEEN

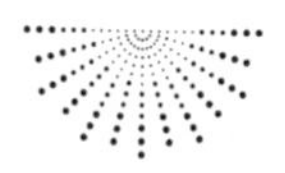

Mid-Spring, 1070

A month, and still she resided at the palace. Regret.

A month, and still she had not ventured to the graveyard. Regret.

A month, and still she saw Theriot only from afar when he was escorted outside the hut. No regret.

Nay, much regret. Despite how they had parted, and though in the end it would make her hurt more, she longed to speak with him, even if only to barter one curiosity answered for another, to look upon him, to touch—

Marguerite gasped. The needle having stuck her finger, she snatched her hand from beneath the material, pressed a thumb against the welling blood, and searched for crimson near the dark green leaves she had been embroidering around the edge of the veil Meg would wear for her nuptials.

"Do tell your wandering thoughts have not ruined it!" Princess Cristina entreated.

Marguerite looked up over the cloth at the young woman sitting opposite in light come through the unshuttered window.

As ever, this princess of less height than her sister and of brown rather than golden hair was mostly tense, and still she could not speak one kind thing without speaking an unkind thing by way of complaint or criticism.

The sisters' mother was not as vocal, but she had a similar air, and her glower spoke what her tongue usually withheld—though not now. "Well, Lady Marguerite?" Agatha prompted in an accent of her native country of Hungary rather than her adopted country of England. "Have you ruined it?"

"Of course she has not ruined it, Mama," Meg said where she sat beside Marguerite with whom she continued to share her sleeping quarters. "But had she bled onto it, the stain could be got out."

"Got out?" Cristina exclaimed. "That which covers your hair must be as pure as she who will be queen. The work would have to start again and—"

"Sister, 'tis not what covers me that concerns the Lord but that which is never covered to Him."

Cristina gave a huff. "Ever this Scottish lady is half outside her mind, especially while at prayer." Her eyes shot back to Marguerite. "You ought to be praying over that cloth as you ply needle, not thinking on that Norman who sought to deliver our brother into the hands of the evil one."

Tempted to speak what she ought not, Marguerite stood, draped the veil over the back of her chair, and started for the door.

"Ah, Cristina!" Meg chided, then followed her friend from the small sitting room where hours were given to needle and thread nearly every day.

As the princess closed the door behind her, Dubh rose from where she stretched in the corridor.

"Forgive me, Meg," Marguerite beseeched. "Your sister is right in saying my mind is not where it ought to be. I..." She sighed. "'Tis not only Sir Theriot, though he is often the cause. It is that I have not done what I should have a month past."

The princess set a hand on Marguerite's arm. "I would be pleased to accompany you across the glen."

It was not only visiting her family's graves that needed doing but returning to her own home. This day the former, she decided, soon the latter.

Though there would be some comfort having her friend with her, greater the comfort of being alone with those she had lost. "I thank you, but this I do myself."

"I understand, my friend. When you are down in the glen, ere you cross the water and go from sight, look up and you shall see me at the window entreating the Lord to breathe peace upon you."

"You bless me," Marguerite said, then trailed by Dubh, descended to the hall where servants arranged and prepared tables for the nooning meal.

Stepping into the shade outside the great doors, she considered returning abovestairs for her mantle to ward off the cool of a spring day, but since it would be warmer in the sun and the exercise of traversing the glen would shake off the chill, she descended the steps to the sound of men practicing arms beyond the wall.

As she and Dubh crossed the bailey toward the iron door in the outer wall that accessed the glen, she looked to Theriot's hut and was disappointed at catching no sight of him.

He had not recovered his vision, as reported by the physician who often sat with her during meals, but he was whole of body. Permitted to walk the bailey in early morning and late afternoon, likely he was acquainted with most of it, and at supper last eve, Colban had said the prisoner had sent word to Malcolm he would like to venture outside the wall.

Marguerite had nearly entreated the king to allow it. However, she had feared it would have the opposite effect since he would not like that she continued to concern herself over Theriot, especially as Malcolm believed she should be looking nearer upon the physician.

"Lady, is it to the glen ye go?" asked the man given watch over the iron door.

"It is."

He opened the door. "Then you may pass."

Of course she could. With the rare exception of when Dunfermline was under threat of attack, ever she moved about her home when she wished and as she wished. She nearly asked for an explanation, but realizing his concern was likely for her turning right rather than left, she commanded Dubh to stay behind to better ensure she was unseen when she did what she ought not.

Though the dog growled, it made no attempt to follow when she slipped past and went to the left as expected.

Since ever she had been welcome to watch the warriors at training and this day was not, the moment the door closed, she went right.

She followed the wall to its turning and, staying close, rounded the corner. It was a sight little different from others witnessed—three score warriors, some inside the fenced area trading blows, others outside it shouting encouragement and taunts.

The one who first captured her attention was Malcolm whose build several men aspired to match but could not. The second to catch her regard was the Aetheling with whom the king traded blows and shouted instruction. The third who should have been the first come to notice was Theriot, the sun at his back lighting the silver in his hair.

For this, the man-at-arms had confirmed the glen was her destination. Since likely the king had not anticipated the need to ensure Marguerite did not appear, to this situation the man had applied whatever order he and others were given that she remain distant from the prisoner.

Though she knew she should slip away before she drew attention, she stared at Theriot who stood outside the fence, a guard on either side. As ever, the walking stick she had given him was not present, whether because still he rejected it or he had destroyed it as done the wash basins and water pitcher. Likely both, she acceded for the dozenth time and moved her gaze to his eyes.

He was too distant for her to determine if they remained clouded, but the whites no longer appeared red and she could see the flesh around them was neither bruised nor abraded.

His hair was slightly longer, the ends brushing his neck, but greater change was in the lengthening and thickening of mustache and beard, the latter noticeably marked by silver. Wearing his fine belted tunic, chausses, and boots, he stood with arms crossed and legs apart, appearing a man watching a contest between a king and future king.

Was he watching? Though fairly certain a month past he could see no more than he told, it was possible he had recovered his vision and now feigned blindness.

"I pray it," she whispered, "that you have only to shift your eyes to see me, even if you hate this woman who never wished to make an enemy of you."

A shout of anger returning her attention to the king, she saw Edgar land on his rear near his fallen sword.

As if the others had half-heartedly engaged in their own contests to attend to this one, they ceased trading blows to look nearer upon what must have been a lesson. But not a planned one, she was certain.

The opponents were not garbed in the clothing of arms practice but what their high stations afforded as they moved among their lessers. Not that Malcolm dressed as extravagantly as the Aetheling, but there was nothing disposable about the king's tunic, chausses, and boots.

"That, Edgar, is how not to use anger to swing a sword." The king halted over the young man. "Now get up and make what you demanded of me a request, and forget not you are my guest."

The Aetheling thrust upright. "No mere guest—soon to be your kin, Malcolm."

Marguerite startled. Her king was free with his given name among intimates and even those less intimate during informal discussions, but these circumstances boasting an audience of liegemen did not qualify. Edgar was disrespectful, and still Malcolm exercised control, though likely not for much longer.

"Ask it of me, Edgar," he boomed, and Marguerite saw saliva fly in the light between their faces.

The young man should be frightened, but arrogance, self-righteous anger, and the confidence of being the Aetheling as well as brother to a woman greatly desired by the king, continued to make a fool of him.

Edgar turned his head to the side, raised his weaponless hand, and pointed at Theriot who stood as before though with more expression—eyes narrowed and lips curved as if this was of more interest than practice at arms. "It is ill enough my enemy is not chained and rotting in a cell, but that you allow him the reach of the bailey and now the training yard! What next, Malcolm? Am I to suffer that foul Norman at table?" He stepped nearer the king and looked smaller for being forced to tip his head further back. "Much that one's presence offends this royal person who can as easily withdraw his permission to wed a Saxon princess as grant it."

Lest Marguerite witness the landing of the king's fist, she nearly closed her eyes, but instead Malcolm's great hand gathered up the neck of Edgar's tunic and lifted him to his toes. "The betrothal will not be undone! And already much you have benefitted, though thus far you lay waste to all opportunities given you. I am king, your sister will be my queen, and I shall continue to aid in your quest to take the throne denied you—*if* you show respect and become worthy of that throne."

The Aetheling dangled, his boots brushing the dirt, mouth gaping, eyes squeezed shut as if in anticipation of worse.

Then Malcolm thrust him away. "Ask it of me, Edgar!"

The prince regained his balance and held up a hand. "I need a moment." As he tried to put order to his tunic, his gaze flicked over those who watched, even touching on Marguerite. She expected his eyes to sweep back, alerting Malcolm to her presence, but they did not, and she guessed his encounter with the king so rattled she was of no consequence.

She had little liking for him, but having spent a month in close company with his sister who had revealed much of his long, painful journey from a youth who should be king to a young man who was not, better she understood him.

He breathed deep. "Your Grace, as I would not have you grant such freedom to the Norman who ought to be dead for the trouble he brought down on me and my men, I request his removal from my presence."

Malcolm inclined his head. "Spoken like a prince who, in time, may make a good king. Now I shall give answer like a king who has earned his kingdom as ye must. Having given much thought to Sir Theriot and the circumstances of his captivity, I have determined he is of no threat to me or mine. Hence, until I decide whether to return him to his family or make use of him in negotiations with the conqueror, he will not be caged like an animal—"

"What? You intend to return him to his family?"

"Edgar! A prince does not interrupt a king. Listen! As long as the chevalier has a guard on him, he may go where he wishes. Within reason."

"I thank you," Marguerite whispered.

Edgar's throat convulsed as if he wanted to argue further, but he said, "As Your Grace wishes, though I believe you will regret it." Then he retrieved his sword and shoved it in its scabbard.

Marguerite looked one last time at Theriot and saw his stance was the same and expression nearly so. Still, he did not appear to indulge in satisfaction over Edgar's trounced pride but interest in what he could hear but not see.

Turning, she slipped around the corner. "He will leave us," she whispered. "Whether by Malcolm's decree or his own efforts, he will go. Blind or sighted, he has no reason to stay."

Not until she descended the glen by one of several footpaths and crossed the wooden bridge to the other side of the river did she recall the princess's instructions.

Turning, she saw a figure in an upper window. It was too distant to see Meg's expression, but Marguerite saw the hand raised in acknowledgment before the lady lowered her chin and began to pray.

"Aye, breathe peace upon me, Lord," Marguerite entreated and started up the side of the glen whose rise was more gradual than that upon which the palace was built.

THOUGH MALCOLM COULD BE violent and grasping like William, Theriot did not think he was the same as the conqueror beyond the formidable ability to take by force what he believed his due.

Indeed, one moment Scotland's ruler called to mind Theriot's uncle who had trained him into a warrior, the next his sire whose great debility allowed him only to supervise that training when he was not imparting tenets of faith.

I could come to like him, he thought as he measured his footfalls according to Malcolm's on his left and a guard's on his right—and hoped the ground before him was as unobstructed as theirs.

Since beginning his exploration of the bailey beneath the enemy's watch, humiliation over his limitations had become fairly common due to stumblings and encounters with the immovable. Though he did not believe it possible to grow accustomed to being an object of derision and much was required to control frustration and anger, still he could not bring himself to sweep a stick to ensure his path was clear. It would save him one sort of humiliation, but not that of a warrior made to look a helpless beggar.

Pride was a failing of his on which both sire and uncle had agreed though for different reasons. Godfroi had believed it exaltation of one's self above others to which he confessed having indulged as a younger man to his detriment and that of loved ones. Thus, he had advocated lessons in humility which Theriot had struggled to master since much in life came easy to him.

In contrast, Hugh had thought pride—even in excess—a good thing, but only in a seasoned warrior who boasted greater wins than losses. However, young Theriot's confidence in his unnaturally developed abilities was not the only thing that made him test his uncle who named him arrogant for believing he was favored by God. There was Hugh's resentment toward Dougray for bearing the family name of which he believed him unworthy due to his illegitimacy—a much loved brother whom Theriot did not believe needed the blood of D'Argents to be one of their own.

The skittering of pebbles returned him to the present in time to correct his footing and save him from one more lesson in humility of which Hugh would approve—and more he would approve for God having yet to restore the arrogant one to great favor despite much time at prayer.

Though there was improvement in Theriot's vision and

unnatural sense, neither was significant, but he pressed onward in search of opportunities to gain his freedom should all align.

Malcolm did not trust him entirely, especially after his prisoner's raging following the physician's diagnosis. However, the control Theriot had exhibited since had made the king receptive to requests such as the one that allowed him to venture outside the wall this day.

Now he knew the exact location of the iron door in the wall, that it was guarded by a single man-at-arms, the number of steps and turns required to reach it from his hut, and that its protesting hinges could reveal one lacking permission to use it. Further, he knew some of what lay outside the palace's eastern wall, most prominently the training yard. Unfortunately, there was more that must be known and greater patience required to learn it.

"Methinks you plot," Malcolm said when they were what Theriot believed a dozen strides from the iron door.

Mindful of loose earth beneath his boots, he turned his face to the king. "Without cease, Your Grace."

"I am glad you do not think me a fool," Malcolm said and chuckled. "Now that you have mapped more of my palace, would you like to map the glen?"

Having expected that concession would be difficult to gain, Theriot hesitated. Might this be a game of offering something only to refuse it? Immediately, he rejected the possibility, fairly certain the king was not that sort of man. "I would like it."

"Then we shall walk it." Malcolm halted near the door and ordered the guards to return to their posts.

From their delayed responses, they seemed as surprised as Theriot, but whatever passed between them and their liege did so outside of words. Then the hinges groaned, and as the men entered the bailey, something exited in a rush.

"Accursed dog," one of the guards muttered, and from its scent Theriot knew it was Dubh.

"Yer mistress left you behind, eh?" Malcolm said as the hound excitedly turned in front of him. "Most unkind to keep you from doing your work." Then as he conversed in his native language with the one who stood watch over the iron door, Marguerite's dog sniffed the prisoner.

"Oui, you know me," Theriot said when her snout began the return journey up his legs.

Dubh swiped her tongue over his hand.

As the door resettled in its frame, Malcolm said, "She is a fine judge of character. It bodes well she likes you."

"It is mutual," Theriot said and hoped he would not have to ask the question uppermost in his mind.

"I am told Lady Marguerite departed the palace," the king accommodated him. "She did not speak of her plans, but since she went alone, likely she visits her family's graves. Though we shall not go as far as that lest we disturb her, there is still much area to cover."

Theriot inclined his head.

"Lead on, Dubh!" Malcolm commanded, then said, "For now it is safe to continue side by side, but ere we begin our descent of the valley in earnest, you will have to take hold of me."

That stung, but in these circumstances, pride could be a terrible enemy. For this, had the king sent the guard away? "I shall, and I appreciate the consideration shown me."

"As I was also raised up into a warrior, D'Argent, I have only to imagine your suffering over a life so changed."

Loathing his pity, Theriot splayed hands at his sides to keep them from becoming fists.

"It is good you are determined not to lose control again," the king said.

Then he sensed—or saw—his prisoner's ire. "The more dangerous I am perceived, the less effective my plotting, Your Grace."

"Ha! I could come to like ye well, D'Argent."

Remembering he had recently thought the same of this man, Theriot nearly smiled.

"A pity you answer to William of Normandy who is… Well, it cannot be known exactly who he is, just as it cannot be known exactly who I am. Like your liege, much ill I have done and for it been condemned—though sometimes rightfully, more often wrongfully. When I returned from a raid of Northumbria with an abundance of Saxon slaves this past winter, my betrothed was horrified by the fate of her people. Doubtless, the same as your William, I explain myself to few, but I set her aright. Though oft I clash with those of her people over the border, I did not make chattel of them to fill my coffers. I provided them a chance to survive the harrying that would have seen them slain or starved. I did it for her, and now they settle in Scotland to begin putting their lives back together, which will be impossible in William's England for years to come." He sighed. "Does your king justify his actions the same?"

"When he justifies them at all. As you believe, he is not wont to explain himself."

They fell into what felt companionable silence, and Theriot used it to engage the senses available to him and create a map of the glen into which they had begun their descent amid birdsong.

So gradual was the decline, cut more sideways than downwards, it had to be a steep valley wall atop which the palace was raised. It was not without vegetation, the scents of winter replaced by those of budding spring. And the shadows of trees they traversed before the path's first turning provided proof groupings thrived here as well.

Narrowing lids against the sun's glare, Theriot turned his attention to what his hearing revealed. Many the woodland creatures here, but most prominently the coursing of water below. A stream, he was certain, though at other times possibly a raging river.

"It is a good-sized waterway," Malcolm said, "though this day it is little more than a stream and easily forded on foot."

Theriot's smile was genuine. "Might you seek to aid my plotting, Your Grace?"

"I do, in part making as level as possible a battlefield that cannot be leveled."

A battlefield across which a sighted warrior takes measure of an opponent lacking sight, Theriot thought. "The other part?" he asked.

"I do it for my betrothed and my ward. As neither approves of you being my prisoner, it feels more you are my guest. Of course, feeling and being are different things."

Silence returned, during which Theriot mostly attended to their footfalls and those of Dubh ahead.

"Here you must hold to me," Malcolm said.

The brush of an arm alerting him to where support could be found without the humiliation of being taken hold of, Theriot gripped it. That was enough humiliation, but more was to come. As they continued their descent, several times he nearly lost his footing, but he suppressed curses—until what felt firm ground became rolling rubble that caused Malcolm to halt and himself take hold of Theriot's arm to keep him upright.

Once they were moving again and the sound of water revealed they neared the bottom, the king said, "Such words, D'Argent! My betrothed would not approve."

Neither would my sire and mother, Theriot thought, his curses having been more foul for the fleeting wish to have Marguerite's walking stick to hand. "Now better I understand why you allow me to map the glen. Though I could negotiate it alone, it would be impossible to do so with the speed required of one pursued."

"That is as it stands now, but mayhap practice will make the impossible possible."

Theriot grunted. "I do not anticipate I will be at Dunfermline long enough to learn this glen. Do you?"

"Though I am of a mind to return you to your family, as the aftermath of the harrying is a poor time to do so, I shall take the weeks or months ahead to consider it well. And ere you ask, my decision will have some to do with my betrothed, her brother, and my ward." The king slowed. "We are at the bottom. I do not believe you require further aid."

Theriot released him and drew a deep breath of sweet, cool air that made him hate the thought of returning to his smoke-ridden hut.

"It is a beautiful place, though I did not fully appreciate it until I saw it through the eyes of Princess Margaret," Malcolm said. "Often we walk here, and ere we return to the palace, we sit and she reads scripture to me."

"It sounds the warrior king loves."

"He does. The marriage is of advantage to both, but our joining will be more than that."

"You are to be congratulated."

"I thank you." Malcolm moved away. "Ahead is the bridge. The hill on the other side is fairly gradual and atop it is my private chapel. If you would like to speak with the priest, we could go there."

"What of Lady Marguerite?"

"The graveyard is mostly out of sight of the chapel, and likely she will be there a long while. Thus, she will not know we are near."

Though Theriot preferred to better learn the lay of the land than seek the words and prayers of the priest, he said, "I would like to go to the chapel."

It should have been fairly easy to match Malcolm's footsteps and keep pace with him and the dog, but it was tiring, Theriot acknowledged after they crossed the bridge and were partway up the hill. He was not unfit, having subjected his body to strenuous exercises that warmed him better than any fire. The problem was that in the absence of good vision to mirror the other man's movements, it took much straining of senses that were now far from boundless to ensure he placed his feet well.

"Let us speak of Lady Marguerite," Malcolm said.

Theriot was not surprised.

"As a man can only grant grace as he sees fit, Chevalier, forcing it can make it impossible to truly forgive another. Thus, I worry over she who feels as responsible for your injury as you believe she is. It will be tragic should you not recover your sight, but had it happened to another, I believe you would concede that under the circumstances and in the absence of malice and recklessness, there is little to forgive."

Having given it much thought, Theriot knew that just as he was inadvertently responsible for the village being burned, so was she for his loss of sight. However, still there was her deception.

"I have watched her and see she is burdened," Malcolm continued, "and greater because it is more than guilt she feels for you. Thus, my efforts to match her with the physician are to no avail."

Theriot frowned. "She asked you to speak on her behalf?"

The king halted and, when Theriot ceased his own advance, said, "She did not, nor would she. For love of the daughter of my departed friend, I wish her to be at peace and make a good match with a worthy man."

"You believe my forgiveness will free her to accept your physician?"

"I do not, but I think it a good beginning."

Theriot nodded. "I concede the part the lady played in what was done me is forgivable, just as the one who dealt the injury is forgivable, but her deception… As you say, forgiveness cannot be forced."

"That is something, Sir Theriot. Let us continue on."

Hoping Marguerite would not further intrude on his mapping of the glen, Theriot followed in the footsteps of a king whom love had made malleable—worse, vulnerable.

May I never love like that, he thought, *especially now I am more vulnerable than ever thought possible.*

CHAPTER FIFTEEN

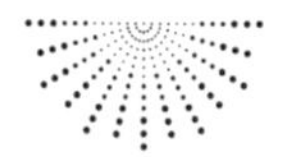

Once again, no warning given, though this was very different from being denied tidings of her mother's death.

Having halted the moment she saw something was amiss, gripping wildflowers barely ripe for the picking, tears trembling on her lashes, she stared at four headstones that ought to number five—one each for father, mother, and baby brothers.

This was not desecration, and yet the absence of the headstone most familiar to her felt that.

Enough, she rebuked. *Go forth and see how beautifully Malcolm honors your parents.*

She continued toward the stones of remembrance that would not forget her loved ones as long as they stood, and halted. By name, she acknowledged the little ones who appeared to have been buried at their father's feet though they were here first, then sank to her knees between her parents' graves.

Releasing the flowers to her lap, she moved her gaze over embellishments in each corner of a large headstone she had expected to be two smaller ones. Now, just as her mother and father had been one in life, they were one beneath a wide stone that had replaced that which remembered her sire alone.

"I am here," she said. "Forgive me for not coming sooner." Then she read words engraved in stone that were Malcolm's gift to those who were as far out of his reach as they were to the last of their line.

Here Diarmad the Mad, Diarmad the Shield,
husband of Lady Marguerite
Here Lady Marguerite, wife of Diarmad the Mad,
Diarmad the Shield
Here their tale—
Love seized Love
Love walked beside Love
Love rejoiced with Love
Love mourned with Love
Love healed by Love
Love parted from Love
Love reunited with Love
Love walks beside Love
Again

Marguerite tried to read it through again, but unable to see past her tears, lowered her head and began emptying emotions over all she had lost and what she had yet to lose—even though the latter was never truly hers.

SHE WEPT, and it pleased—as would the tears to come and greater pain than that of the heart.

"I could not ask for better," Pepin rasped and looked from the woman who had finally ventured to the graveyard, back to the men and hound ascending the hill. "You make me Your arm of vengeance, Lord."

Minutes earlier, he had been on the verge of leaving the cover of trees to seize his cousin who was as much his prey as Scotland's king, but one of the two mounted to his left had ordered him to wait.

He had nearly ignored the man who was no longer fit to command anything, but out of respect had paused to look where told. And quite the sight—the murderous king with only an aged, weaponless man accompanying him unlike the other times when an armed escort followed. Were this avenger alone, he would not challenge so great a warrior as Malcolm Canmore, but he was not alone.

We are six, four of us warriors whole of body, one of us half of body but dark of vengeance, and the other slippery as an eel, he assured himself. *That and surprise are enough.*

"There is something not right about Malcolm's companion," said the slippery foreigner regarding the one whose death would be mercifully quick unlike the king and lady. "He is too straight of shoulder and firm of stride to be as old as told by silvered hair. And yet mostly his head is up, eyes ahead without stray to the ground. Do you think him blind?"

Pepin looked nearer and noted the same and something else. The man's stride was nearly identical to the king's which, were the silvered one truly without sight, meant not only did he trust Malcolm to make a way for him, but he was accustomed to using other senses to move through the world one of a build and presence that would have made a formidable warrior of him.

"I think you are right," he said, then considered the mercenary hired to aid in this endeavor and jerked his head in the direction of the woman. Though he had thought to take her after dealing with Malcolm lest the priest at the chapel roused and rang the bell, he said, "With as little disturbance as possible, bring her to me."

As the man urged his horse opposite, Pepin nodded to himself. Though he had one less warrior whole of body to attack the king, considering what was known of Malcolm's companion, three would suffice.

He shifted his gaze to his father who was half of body and dark of vengeance, next the slippery one. "Keep watch over Sir Gerald. I believe already we have won, but should it go wrong, get him away."

The man smiled, revealing several teeth needed pulling.

"Make ready," Pepin said and drew his sword.

"D'ARGENT?" Malcolm rumbled.

Though Theriot knew the king had turned to search his prisoner's face, he continued to listen, smell and taste the air—more, engage that other sense of which he was in significantly greater possession than in all the days since the blinding.

Fairly certain of what was here that should not be, he took three short strides to Malcolm whose outline was less distinct with the hill rising at his back. "We are not alone, Your Grace."

"I begin to think that myself, as does Dubh, but best we resume our walk."

Clearly not best were he concerned only with his survival, but doubtless he considered Lady Marguerite and the priest—perhaps even his prisoner.

"Have you men patrolling the area?" Theriot asked, once more relying on the other man to forge a path and noting the dog did not advance as far ahead now its protective instincts were further engaged.

"Only a small number of men since we are mostly at peace with our own and distant enough from the border no army can cross without notice being received well in advance of their arrival."

"No army, but often of greater danger are the few unseen who slip in, slaughter, and slip out," Theriot said.

The king's grunt told he did not like being schooled.

"As they are mostly unmoving," Theriot said. "I cannot be certain, but methinks there are as many as half a dozen."

"How do ye come by that number?"

"The unnatural way, Your Grace."

Though he sensed Malcolm's curiosity, they continued what was to appear a leisurely ascent.

"It could be your family," the king said.

"It is not. I would feel them."

"Even if you speak true, I am to believe you would reveal them were they lurking in my wood?"

"They would not lurk."

The man sighed. "I have faced more than half a dozen at once, and still I am here, my swing as sure and blade as sharp as ever."

Theriot tried not to be offended the man believed he would be alone in what was to come. Though this D'Argent was not the warrior he had been, God willing the enemy would pay a good price to put him down.

"Woe to them I am eager to do some gutting," Malcolm said with what sounded a smile, which made Theriot's own lips curve. But whereas the king's was likely due to the excitement of a challenge he would not feel obliged to explain to his godly betrothed, for this D'Argent it was anticipation of an outlet for what roiled within—even if the inability to see beyond light and shadows rendered this his last day.

Though tempted to retrieve the shard strapped to his leg, he would leave it until needed so he not lose it to Malcolm should the watchers prove only that.

"I believe they will strike once we are out of sight of the

palace," the king said. "Though the exchange of blows will be heard, sooner sense will be made of what transpires if it is visible to my men, and sooner aid given."

"How long ere we go from sight?" Theriot asked.

"At this pace, a minute."

"How long will we be out of sight?"

"The trees form a skirt near the top of the hill on which the chapel sits. Unimpeded, a two-minute walk, providing cover under which to work evil." Malcolm grunted. "Now give ear. In these circumstances and on this day, we are allies. As I know you remain capable of inflicting damage, the moment they come at us, take the dagger from my belt and wield it as best you can. When possible, I will call out the direction of attacks on your person."

Then just as Theriot had taken measure of the king, Malcolm had assessed him, and not merely by way of the women who spoke on his behalf.

"In ten strides, we are in shadow, D'Argent. Be ready."

He was, and more so when it took another twenty strides before the riders commanded their horses forward absent fearsome shouts that would have sooner alerted the king's men to what transpired here. However, Dubh's ferocious barking should prove nearly as effective.

Though once more Theriot would be fighting for his life, and this time at great disadvantage, it felt good to hold a weapon that fit a warrior's hand.

"Dubh!" Malcolm shouted as he lunged left. "Marguerite! Go!"

Theriot approved of him sending the dog to the lady since it was possible one or more of the enemy sought to harm her as well. Too, Dubh's efforts on behalf of the king and himself would mostly be wasted, whether the animal was trampled or felled by a sword.

"Three ride on us, two remain distant!" Malcolm warned

where they stood five feet apart, then he laughed. "I have the honor of the biggest ones, and they do not mean to kill me—yet. Not so the one who sets himself at you. He arcs his right-handed sword back. When I give the command, go far right."

That would put Theriot in the path of the beast, but when he came out of it, he would have the opportunity to slice the rider's leg. Unfortunately, were his timing not nearly perfect, the horse could be cut. Though the result might prove the same, the animal's violent response unseating its rider, Theriot was not one to harm animals. However, being far from ready to die, he must take the chance.

"Go right!" Malcolm commanded, then bellowed ahead of the first meeting of swords.

Theriot did as instructed, trusting the blade coming for him was the other side and could not be brought over the mount's neck in time. When the horse swept past, Theriot spun and, with a roar that would reach the palace's walls moments after the king's, slashed at where he guessed the rider's leg gripped that side of his mount.

The horse screamed, and there was no benefit in that error as told by the animal being yanked to a halt and wheeled around.

From Malcolm's direction, an enemy cried out and cursed in Norman-French. That gave Theriot pause. But though at least one here was his countryman, if the D'Argents had sent these men to retrieve him, they would have identified themselves rather than attack Theriot as well as Malcolm.

The king's laughter burst across the wood, but his next breath was spent on the warning, "He charges again, D'Argent!"

Silently cursing his inability to see, Theriot assumed what he hoped was the proper stance.

"Backhanded swing!" Malcolm corrected, then once more steel met steel.

"Guide me, Lord!" Theriot entreated and altered his stance.

This time when the enemy's sword sought to part skin from bone, Theriot ducked and turned as he thrust upright. He was too near, but before his encounter with the animal knocked his feet out from under him, the blade he swept high found its target and it was the rider who screamed.

Having embedded the king's dagger in his opponent, Theriot landed hard on the ground.

It could not be known if Malcolm's next bout of laughter was for his ally's victory or his own, but Theriot heard the warrior he himself had stuck bring his horse around.

Snatching up the hem of his tunic, he retrieved his makeshift weapon, rolled to his feet, and strained his senses in preparation for the next assault.

"He is finished!" Malcolm shouted a moment ahead of the sound of a body dropping from a good height.

Trusting his opponent would not rise again, Theriot turned toward the king who continued to battle the other two. It was then he heard the shouts of men on the other side of the glen. They came, but not soon enough.

Though he could make little sense of the shadows convulsing amid those cast by trees, he ran forward. He was nearly upon the clashing warriors when Malcolm gave a triumphant shout and a second body dropped.

Swords met twice more, then a curse preceded the remaining Norman's retreat.

"Our fight is done for now," the king said above the pound of hooves that increased when the two who had hung back joined the one escaping the bloodletting. "As it was no attempt by your family to retrieve you, we ride, Sir Theriot."

Not to bring the enemy to ground, but to reach Marguerite and the priest lest they fought others, Theriot knew.

Were his vision not corrupted, he could as quickly mount the horse of the man he slew as Malcolm did that of the opponent he felled, but there was no time to make even a token effort.

"Come!" Malcolm said.

Theriot tossed aside the shard the king surely looked upon and swung up behind him.

"I did not know I was so near death before the attack," Malcolm said.

Theriot hooked an arm around him. "Only had *I* been near death, Your Grace."

The king chuckled and put heels to the horse.

CHAPTER SIXTEEN

Instinct urged Marguerite to seek the safety of the chapel, but remembrance of what the Aetheling had done turned her opposite lest the priest suffer like the Saxons when Edgar led the Normans through their village.

Had she not hesitated in trying to make sense of the one riding on the graveyard with sunlight glancing off chain mail and hair cropped in the style of the conquering Normans, she might have had time to find cover.

Armed with knowledge of the wooded hill opposite that which descended to the waterway, only when she committed to it did she catch the sound of a clash behind. Had she sooner, she would have risked fleeing there where Malcolm's men likely battled other trespassers.

Hoping to work her way around to that side, trying not to think on when last she was prey, Marguerite wove among the trees with raised skirts, turning sharply when the rider neared and loosing screams the king's men might hear. Each time her pursuer's mount slid on the sloped ground, he cursed her in Norman-French, and more vilely when the gullies to which she led him forced him to jump the horse to prevent it and its rider from being broken by the fall.

"Lord, give me strength!" she entreated as once more the Norman evaded her trap and she had to drop and slide down a slope to further distance herself. If she could reach the immense boulders climbing the hill's western face, she would be nearer the glen, and were that not deterrent enough, her pursuer would have to dismount to continue the chase. If he did so...

Though this time no Rebels of the Pale would come to her aid, the king's men were near.

As soon as the the boulders were in sight, she heard the baying of a dog. Praying its master was not the one chasing her since the animal's sure-footedness could take her down before she reached her destination, Marguerite glanced around.

Beyond the rider slowed by thickening trees that prevented his horse from running was a streak of black. "Be Dubh!" she gasped, then strained the reach of her legs and screamed again.

Did the barks turn more vicious? Or were they louder because the hound gained on the prey Marguerite might or might not be?

As she turned into dense trees the Norman would be forced to go around, he altered his course to negotiate the steep descent. When he was to the left and twenty feet beyond her, doubtless to cut short her flight once the trees thinned, she believed she had a chance of reaching the boulders ahead of him and turned back.

Though slowed by the ascent, it also affected the Norman who could not quickly come around without sending horse and rider crashing down the hill.

Above the barking, Marguerite heard a shout, then spraying dirt and skittering rocks as the man sought to arrest his advance.

Propelling herself upward, she reached the first moss-slicked boulders and, certain the hound should be nearly upon her, looked behind.

It was Dubh, and she sped toward the Norman urging his mount up the incline.

Fearing the dog would fall to the sword, Marguerite commanded it to her side, and when the hound ignored her, beseeched, "Lord, preserve her."

Then once more aware of sounds around the side of the hill, now only voices in the absence of steel on steel, she thrust the hem of her skirt beneath her girdle and began climbing toward the center of the boulders where best she would be protected should her pursuer dismount. A moment later, a howl of pain made her whimper.

Dubh had sacrificed something—perhaps all—to protect her mistress.

Tears wetting her lashes, the slick surfaces conspiring to bruise her knees and shins, she continued scrambling upward, all the while assuring herself her pursuer would not traverse the boulders, it being too great a risk to dismount with Malcolm's men soon to come. Or would they now they were no longer guided by Dubh's barking?

Marguerite peered over her shoulder. Refusing to look beyond the rider who neared, there being nothing she could do for the hound, she shouted, "I am here, king's men!"

She glimpsed indecision on the face of her pursuer who surely weighed whether completion of his task was worth risking his life. Then he bared his teeth, began to swing out of the saddle, and stilled. She also heard what made him search the hillside across which he had chased her. Though she could not see the horse pounding toward them, it came.

"Witch!" the man spat and dropped back in the saddle.

"King's men, I am here!" Marguerite cried again.

As the Norman descended the hill at a pace that could unseat him, she saw her hound struggling up the incline. Its fur was too dark to show crimson, but it glistened. Dubh was in pain—and in the path of the one responsible. Would the Norman put finish to her?

A moment later, the horse slipped, and Marguerite wondered if God had smacked its rump. It did not go down, but if the rider had intended Dubh further harm, he decided against wasting what could be the defining moment between escape and capture.

"Marguerite!"

She snapped her chin around. Though Malcolm was too distant to look well upon, his size and voice identified him.

"Praise, Lord!" she exclaimed and began descending the boulders.

More than the pain of her flight, she felt the injuries of her ascent. She would be scraped and bruised, but far better that than what had been planned for her.

When she came off the last boulder, she turned toward Malcolm and knew from the blood he wore he had slain one or more of her pursuer's companions. And saw he was not alone.

When Theriot swung off the rear of the saddle, the king commanded, "Remain with D'Argent, Sparrow," and turned in the direction of her assailant.

Throat tight, she stared at the man who appeared to stare at her. Clouds remained center of his eyes, but she thought she saw green.

As hope moved through her, he asked, "Are you injured?"

She shook her head, then lowering her gaze over him, wondered the same of him. Blood was on one hand and stained his sleeve's cuff, and there were sprays of crimson on the side of his tunic. Of further note were streaks of dirt and debris over his garments, evidencing he had not remained upright throughout his clash with a sighted opponent. And yet he was alive and well.

"Are you injured, Marguerite?" he repeated harshly.

Having shaken her head when first he asked, silently she rued, *Still, he cannot see.* "Not terribly, and it is of my own doing, but Dubh—"

"Where is she?"

Fearing the hound's silence, she looked to where last she had seen her protector. Head up, Dubh watched from where she had lowered beside a tree.

As Marguerite started past Theriot, she said, "Not far below. I do not know how badly she is hurt."

He stretched out a hand. "Lead me to her."

Though she wanted to protest for how steep this section, she took hold of him and, wishing the contact was no different from that of any other, asked, "How should we do this?"

"Side by side, my hand on your forearm so I can release you without taking you down should my feet go wrong. If you see something in my path, draw me away or give warning."

The strain in his voice revealing it cost much to instruct her in how to direct him, her eyes threatened to overflow.

As if he saw her tears, he growled, "Do not pity me."

"Forgive me," she whispered.

"I try."

Marguerite swallowed, moved his hand to her arm, and started forward. Despite the necessity of guiding him away from obstacles, they descended the hill at a good pace, and as they neared Dubh, the dog whimpered.

Theriot released Marguerite, dropped to his haunches, and moved his tucked hand toward Dubh's snout. "What hurts, girl?"

Frantically, the dog licked him knuckles to wrist.

"Her left shoulder," Marguerite said, and drawing in Dubh's scent as she lowered beside Theriot, felt a tickle in her nose. "The damp there is not perspiration, and the haunch that side is moist as well."

Fingers wide, he moved his hand between the dog's ears, then began probing down the neck and over that shoulder.

Dubh yelped and bared her teeth.

Cautiously, Theriot reached his other hand forward and set it atop her head. "I know it hurts, but we shall make it right."

The hound lowered quivering lips over sharp teeth.

"I do not think the blade went deep," Theriot said, stroking Dubh's head with one hand and exploring her bloodied fur with the other.

When he neared her haunch, she protested again, but did not show her teeth.

"Less blood here. Likely a single swipe of the sword cut her shoulder, skipped over her ribs, and caught her leg." He searched the opposite side. "Naught here. Providing infection does not set in, soon she will return to your side."

There being only concern on his face, Marguerite hurt over the other things she had seen there since his attempt to save a villager from ravishment made mince of his life.

It was too much for this guilt-ridden woman already shaken by her visit to the graveyard, the Norman's pursuit that immersed her in memories of when she fled her grandfather, and the aches of her flight.

"Marguerite?" Theriot prompted.

His awareness of her emotions making her shudder, she thrust to her feet and felt a tug on her skirt as she whirled away. When her forward motion caused him to lose hold of her, she rasped, "Pray, leave me." Then her knees gave, and she cried out as bruised flesh and jolted bone hit the ground.

Hearing Dubh whine and Theriot rise and move with more speed than was safe, she tried to crawl away. "I need a moment! Just a moment!"

A hand landed on the small of her back, and she jerked to the side and dropped onto her rear. "You are safe," he said, his hand that had been upon her now splayed as if entreating a frightened child to calm. "It is over."

"Over for me." Through tears, she peered up at him. "But what of you?"

"Me?"

"I cannot undo you—what I did to you! Had I recognized you that night, all would be different. Stephen would not have died, Hendrie would not have been injured, and you would have no cause to hate me."

Further he stiffened. "What do you mean had you recognized me?"

Now came the mess of her. Rather than spilled and swept up out of sight, it sought to be spilled and swept up in his presence. Dropping her chin, she drew up her knees and tucked into herself.

Theriot stared at Marguerite with eyes that could see only the smudge of her against the ground, then reluctantly relinquished curiosity over what she had spoken. He wanted to remain angry with her, but it was cruel, especially after compassion shown for the injured animal for whom he felt far less than this hurting woman.

Lowering beside her, he slid an arm around her back.

She jerked, and he thought she would resist, but she gripped his tunic and pressed her face to his chest. "I am sorry, Theriot. What I did was to save what I thought a child."

He knew how to hold a woman, many the kisses and caresses bestowed and received since reaching the age when relations with the fairer sex became nearly as desirable as the wielding of weapons, but this was different. Because he could not look upon her?

"All for naught—less than naught," she bemoaned.

He would not argue that, less than nothing gained in exchange for his eyesight. And it would be worse than nothing if what had befallen him was permanent. However, this day he had been gifted with evidence that once more he was in God's favor—not only the sharpening of his unnatural sense that aided in preserving his life but color.

Astride with Malcolm spurring toward the chapel, he had seen green when they emerged from the trees. The long grass trampled by hooves had been a blur but of a color beyond white and grey, and when he raised eyes heavenward, there was blue. Thus, greater hope for full restoration of his sight that would allow him to once more look upon even the smallest of stars.

He was tempted to reveal that hope to this woman to ease her pain, but he thought ahead. To ensure the loosening watch over him did not tighten, better he remain a blind man with little chance of escape than a warrior capable of making a way out of here.

When Marguerite's convulsions eased, she said, "Forgive my weakness. Even ere once more I became prey in a wood, the day was difficult."

He understood that last, Malcolm having revealed she visited the graveyard, but not the first since he did not believe she referred to the bait made of her in the burning village.

"You say once before you were prey in a wood, Marguerite?"

"Oui, and I wonder if…"

"What?"

"If it is the same predator."

"What predator?" When she did not answer, he prompted, "Malcolm and I were attacked while walking to the chapel."

She gasped. "I heard the meeting of blades."

"There were five men, likely all Normans. What of your pursuer?"

"Norman."

He nodded. "Two remained distant while two set themselves at your king and one at me. Malcolm did not believe they wished him dead, but my death *was* sought. Now who do you believe the predator?"

She drew back. "My kin. They…"

Theriot waited.

"It would not satisfy to quickly slay Malcolm and me. First, much suffering."

He frowned. "Malcolm told me your family over the border are dead."

She shuddered. "He saw to that and afterward set their home afire, but I am thinking not all died, that the one who made prey of me last year—"

Dubh whimpered.

"Ere she loses more blood, I must go for help," Marguerite said.

The voices of Malcolm's men revealing their search was in the direction of the chapel, Theriot released her. "I will carry her."

"But you—"

"I know I am sightless," he snapped, then breathed deep. "You have only to stay my side and give guidance when necessary. Can you do that?"

"I can."

It was difficult to get Dubh aloft, not because she was heavy, because each shift of her body made her yelp. If not for Marguerite's assuring words, those sharp teeth might have pierced Theriot's flesh.

Once the dog settled against his chest, the next challenge was to traverse the hillside around to the glen. Hopefully, they would be intercepted before a misstep further injured Dubh.

When Marguerite took hold of Theriot's forearm, he said, "Watch for what is below as well as ahead."

"I shall."

It struck him then her voice was changed from when he regained consciousness at Dunfermline. That which had been somewhere between hoarse and husky from what she told was a malady of the throat was now soft and melodious.

"Be my guide, Lady," he said tautly.

It took longer than expected to reach the side of the hill across from the palace, her instructions so precise it nearly annoyed. But more bothersome was his awareness of her. Thus, he was grateful when above the sound of coursing water men called to them from higher up the hill where two assailants had fallen to Theriot and Malcolm—doubtless, soldiers who kept watch while others searched the area.

"Two come," Marguerite said, then in Saxon called, "I am entrusted to the care of Sir Theriot so the king may give chase to the others. As my dog is injured, she must be tended."

They responded in Gaelic, which she translated, "One must remain here, but the other will carry Dubh across the glen."

Though Theriot would have no difficulty taking the dog the remainder of the way, he preferred to stay here to await the return of Malcolm and his men. But when one of the Scotsmen stepped near, Dubh snarled and snapped.

"Methinks you have made an ally of my dog," Marguerite said. "If you set her down—"

"Non, continue guiding me. I shall deliver her myself." Theriot turned his face to where the Scotsmen stood and asked in the Saxon language, "How fares the injured mount of the man I slew?"

Neither answered, and he guessed they struggled with being questioned by their king's prisoner.

Finally, one said, "Well enough one of our men uses it to search for the knaves who ran."

Theriot inclined his head. "Let us continue, Lady."

She adjusted her hold on him, but they did not venture forth alone. One of the Scots followed, and Theriot did not begrudge him the precaution. Regardless this prisoner had been entrusted to remain with the lady, regardless his arms were filled with a dog, it was wise to ensure ill that had not befallen Marguerite did not belatedly befall her.

As before, her efforts to direct him were without fault, but though the way forward was more certain once they crossed the bridge, he began to feel the strain of carrying Dubh uphill and knew his garments would need to be laundered to remove blood as well as perspiration.

Once they were through the iron door, the man who accompanied them exchanged words with its guard and turned back.

"What did they say?" Theriot asked as Marguerite guided him across a bailey rife with the tension of being on high alert.

"When the man who escorted us ordered the physician summoned to tend Dubh, he was informed Colban has departed for the monastery at Loch Leven where several suffer from fever. Thus, we shall have to care for Dubh ourselves."

Theriot inclined his head. "It is no longer necessary for you to hold to me. I am acquainted with this ground. You need only warn if something appears in my path."

Marguerite hated she felt a sense of loss when she dropped her hand from him, but was not surprised that more of the little bit of ground gained in distancing her heart from Theriot this past month was lost. Now she would have to begin again.

"All is clear?" he asked.

She nodded. "Other than those working the bailey, everything is in its place."

Beneath the gaze of those patrolling the walls and the castle folk, they continued to the hut and reached it without mishap. As Theriot entered sideways with Dubh, Marguerite said, "I will go for supplies," and hastened to the palace.

Though she was waylaid by many eager to learn of the attack on the king—among them Princess Cristina and Hendrie—she was not long in returning to Theriot. When she entered, he was beside the bed on which he had settled Dubh, a basin of water on the floor, a pink-stained cloth in hand.

"The shoulder may require stitches, but not her haunch," he said.

Marguerite swept her gaze around the room in search of a walking stick that was nowhere to be seen, then knelt beside him and opened the sack filled with clean cloths and medicines taken from the physician's room after a brief visit with her Saxon escort whose healing progressed slowly. Hopefully, he and his companions would return to Derbyshire before summer set in—and more safely now the harrying was over and most surviving Northumbrians had fled south.

"Salve," Theriot said, and she passed a pot whose unstoppering released an unpleasant odor.

Blessedly, among Colban's medicines she had found one that rendered a patient senseless. Had she not been quick to wipe fingers dipped in it over that lolling tongue, Dubh would have fought her. Now, lips drawn back, repeatedly the dog scraped her tongue over her palate.

As Marguerite cleaned her fingers on a cloth, Theriot said, "What have you done?"

Looking into clouded eyes that appeared to look into hers, she said, "Given her medicine that will allow me to stitch her without her suffering. She will sleep soon."

And so Dubh did.

It required many weavings of thread to close up the wound, then while Marguerite cleaned the mess they made, Theriot salved and bandaged the hound.

When he joined her at the cool fire pit, she said, "You like Dubh, and she likes you."

"I have an affinity with animals." He searched a hand behind and closed fingers over the chair's back.

Further proof of his sightlessness causing her throat to tighten, she watched him lower to the seat.

"There is more you have to tell me—more I would learn about you," he said. "Will you sit while we await your king?"

"I should go," she whispered, fearing she would weep again.

He nodded at the chair opposite. "Pray, sit."

"I—"

"I do not hate you, Marguerite."

She caught her breath.

"When I learned you were the one who set the trap, then of your deception, I thought it possible, but I do not feel that. I feel…" He shrugged. "To know that, I must understand you better. You told of how your father and mother found each other and her family's resistance to their union. Bad blood there, but so great your Norman kin wish you harm? So much harm that Malcolm slew them—though it seems not all?"

She did not swallow. She gulped.

"Were those who first made prey of you the reason you were in the village the night I was blinded? And what of your regret for not recognizing me sooner?"

"That is a long tale."

"Then begin. If we are interrupted, great the likelihood I will be here on the morrow."

Though she told herself it was not as if she was distant from those memories, it was hard to speak of them for how much she longed for her pallet and to pull a blanket over her head.

"Sit, Malcolm's sparrow," Theriot said. "Tell me your tale."

First her sire's sparrow, then that of the man who had done his best to fill his departed friend's place, but how she wished to be that to Theriot—albeit in no way fatherly.

That longing, which made her purse her lips in remembrance of when she had much over which to whistle, should have hastened her departure, but she lowered into the chair facing him.

"You are right. It is time you knew the rest—and therein how I recognized you that night."

CHAPTER SEVENTEEN

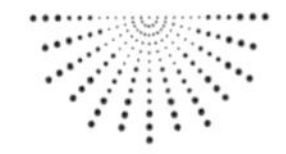

"Your uncle saved you."

"Though I do not know he would have were he not dying..." Marguerite's breath caught. "...he made escape possible."

Giving her space to calm emotions that several times nearly moved her to tears, Theriot considered what thus far she had revealed of the attempt to retrieve the mother she had not known had died. Here the reason Malcolm had put that family to the sword, though not all were she correct in believing one or more were among this day's assailants.

"That was the first time they made prey of me for being sired by Diarmad the Mad," Marguerite continued. "Knowing I would head for the border, they nearly overtook me, and I was forced to go opposite. Night fell. Albeit their numbers were fewer for dividing their efforts between north and south, still they came, carrying torches that burned away the dark I needed to..."

"Continue."

"They..." She muffled a sob.

Theriot cursed his impatience. Just as he had known the emotion to which she had earlier succumbed in the wood was not given its due, he knew some of this had much to do with him.

Stay, he told himself, then stood and reached for her shoulder. But it was her lowered head he set a hand upon, the silk of her hair beneath his fingers. "Do not cry, Marguerite," he entreated, as much for his sake as hers. She was too vulnerable and too great this longing to comfort her.

"Do not," he repeated, but when she quaked, lowered before her.

"I was so frightened," she gasped.

He should not have put his arms around her, but when she dropped to her knees before him, he did.

He should not have drawn her closer, but when she slid her hands around his neck, he did.

He should not have set his mouth on hers, but when she whispered, "And you… Truly, I am sorry, Theriot," he did.

He should not have made much of that kiss, but he did.

That was how the King of Scots found them. "He is a dead man!" Malcolm pronounced.

So I am, Theriot silently rued as the door tossed open bathed Marguerite and him in light.

Since what was seen could not be unseen, he held to the woman gone rigid in his arms, moved his mouth off hers, and set his gaze on the figure passing through the doorway.

The king broke stride. "What is this?" he barked.

Though it seemed his declaration of mortal fate had been for the Norman he pursued, that did not mean another declaration would not be forthcoming. And all because Theriot had been unaware someone approached as he would have been did he yet possess the breadth of the unnatural sense that aided him in the glen.

When Marguerite drew her hands from around his neck, he took her arm and raised her with him. "That was a kiss, Your Grace, nothing more," he said.

She drew a sharp breath. "It was I who—"

"Once more you defend a man who does not wish it, Marguerite. Now come to my side."

Theriot released her. "Go."

"But—"

"Go!"

She took a single step forward, then said in Theriot's language, "I am not a child to be ordered here and there, especially after all I have overcome without being told where to stand."

"Marguerite," Malcolm warned.

"I care not neither of you wish me to defend Sir Theriot. This is Marguerite, daughter of Diarmad the Mad, who is not a victim. Marguerite who once more kept wolves from her throat. Marguerite who cried though, had she a sword, she might have swung it as men do when they are overwhelmed. Marguerite who is not ashamed that Sir Theriot's offer of comfort led to a kiss." She drew breath. "I do not wish to wed Colban. If I want anything, it is nothing less than what my parents had."

Her next step forward likely startled Malcolm as much as Theriot who was only less her captive audience for having no sight with which to view her.

"Nothing less than what I believe you shall have with the princess," she said, then quieted as if to provide Malcolm space to respond, though how he could give answer to what merely sounded hysterics, Theriot did not know. Not only had she cause to be angry, but he had given her cause to justify her feelings.

"You braved much this past year, Sparrow, and now again," the king acceded. "It is natural to ease your suffering by searching out happiness, but you look the wrong direction in setting yerself at this chevalier. Though you are half Norman, you are of Scotland, whereas he is of Normandy and England

and shall return to one or the other. If you do not want Colban, I will find a more agreeable husband."

She was silent so long, Theriot wondered if she heard. And felt a surge of resentment at being unable to search her face.

"Do you not agree the lady wastes emotion on one who said it was nothing more than a kiss, Sir Theriot?" Malcolm asked.

Why did he hesitate even when she turned to him? Not to cruelly give hope before snatching it away though that was a better reason than the truth he was greatly moved by this woman he did not believe he had ever looked close upon though she recognized him at the village.

Regardless, Malcolm was right. She wasted emotion on him, and not only because her home was Scotland and the only way it would become his was if he died before failing to escape it. Because though he mostly forgave her knowing she had only sought to aid a child, if he did not fully regain his sight, it would be impossible to keep company with the one responsible for sentencing him to move cautiously and with stumbling through the remainder of his life. Such would require faith like that of his sire who, having fallen in battle and believed dead, had returned home a cripple and found his wife betrothed to another and a child in her belly.

Godfroi D'Argent had forgiven Robine, and when her misbegotten babe was born, claimed the boy as his third son. Then to the surprise of many who did not believe a man lacking the use of his legs could father children, a fourth son was born and named Theriot. Before long, a daughter followed.

Much grace granted Lady Robine and both told they loved each other better than before forgiveness was required to put their family back together. Now Theriot faced a debility that could end the warrior of him the same as his sire's injury put finish to the warrior of him, requiring him to hire men to protect his family and home and enlist his brother to train his sons into fighting men.

Though Theriot's legs remained firm beneath him, as they were of less use in the absence of sight to direct them, his injury would surely prove worse. But even had he his sire's great faith, still he could not imagine a life with Marguerite of Dunfermline —or any woman. If he could not protect his family, no wife nor children would suffer alongside him.

Determining it best to slay all hope, he said, "Your king speaks true, Lady Marguerite. You waste emotion on this warrior blinded by your misguided efforts. I have heart enough to feel for your plight and attraction enough to try the lips offered me, but that is all. If you wish a husband, your king will make a good match with one capable of providing for and protecting a family as is no longer possible for me."

Grateful her back was to Malcolm, Marguerite lowered her lids, shutting out the man whose hard eyes had been soft when they were so near she had seen more green in the thin amid the clouds. What had possessed her to reveal so much of her heart?

The mess of me who dares to love the mess I made of him, she silently answered, then opened her eyes. "Be assured, I shall waste no more emotion on you and only enough time to pray for your healing and return to your family."

She turned to Malcolm. "You said the one you pursued is dead. Dead now or after he is made to talk?"

He closed the distance between them. "Dead now, and though that sword for hire told little ere I put him out of his misery, it was enough to confirm this day was born of vendetta."

"My mother's family."

"Aye. Yer uncle, Gerald, lives and his son."

"Pepin," she named the one who had also been present when arrows slew her escort and Cannie.

"They must have been down a hole when I came for your grandfather. Though I would not know your uncle nor cousin by sight, I believe the former is the one who remained distant when Sir Theriot and I were attacked in the glen, the latter he who fled after we put down two of their men."

"We?" Marguerite snatched hold of that.

He jutted his chin. "Sir Theriot is far from defenseless."

Did she only imagine the stiffening of the man at her back who believed he could not protect a wife and children?

"With minimal direction, he can yet land a deadly blow."

It was surely wrong to be glad Theriot had taken a life, but had he not, likely he would be dead.

"They came for me as well as you, Marguerite," the king said.

"What of the second man who hung back with her uncle?" Theriot asked before she could question her kin's fate.

"An Irishman," Malcolm said.

"Dear Lord!" Marguerite exclaimed. "Was his name Patrick?"

"The man did not say, but likely it was the one to whom your grandfather would have given you had you not escaped."

"Did you find the three who fled Sir Theriot and you?" she asked.

"I did not. Thus, I have sent men to hunt them down. If your kin are wise, rather than make for the border they will go to ground a few days and one by one depart."

"*If* they depart."

"I believe they are not done with us, but I do not think they will strike soon since they were only six and now are three. More, they have lost the advantage of being thought dead."

She sighed. "Still, I will not be returning home, will I?"

"You will not. Ye shall remain here and go to the glen only with an escort." He looked to the bed. "Dubh?"

"She should recover."

"Good. I will have her brought to the tower. Now leave us. Sir Theriot and I have matters to discuss."

"What matters, Your Grace?"

His silence that of disapproval, she retrieved the physician's supplies. But she paused at the door. "The walking stick, Sir Theriot?"

Answer in the furrowing of his brow, she needed no more, but he said, "What was kind of you was ill of me, my only excuse that it was a dark day like too many come before. Much regret, Lady."

Without further word, she stepped outside and closed the door.

Wasted emotion, she reminded herself as she started for the tower. She had known it was so, but now greater the waste for the kiss shared with Theriot—a kiss unlike that of Michel Roche who had given her an escort home when she revealed her truth and apologized for being unable to heal a heart broken by another.

"Not at all like that kiss," she whispered. "This kiss…" Breathless one moment, all breath the next, then breathless again. Now better she understood Michel's disappointment when she declined to give him more time to grow her feelings for him. Now more she was sorry for the hurt dealt that baron.

"I ASSUME THERE ARE OTHER SHARDS."

"There are." Theriot jerked his head toward Dubh. "Beneath the mattress."

"I have been lax," Malcolm said.

Theriot settled his arms over his chest. "Certes, you provide more opportunities to strike and escape than the Saxon rebels provided my eldest brother during his captivity."

The King of Scots clicked his tongue. "Be assured, were you not without sight, a closer watch would be kept on you."

Theriot narrowed his eyes, and not for the first time wondered how long that instinctual habit of bettering his focus would persist. "Though this day I carried a weapon whilst in your company, it sounds you do not intend to increase the watch over me."

"I do not. I shall loosen it now I have further evidence of my betrothed's belief you are honorable. Like Marguerite, you will not depart the palace without an escort, but within these walls may go wherever you wish without a guard."

Theriot did not suppress his surprise.

"Even the tower, though not abovestairs. My men will know that is too far." Malcolm stepped nearer. "It is rare I am wrong about a man's character. For that and keeping close just enough doubt even for those I trust, I am alive and my kingship secure—likely the same as your William whose childhood was more dangerous than mine."

The two had much in common, both coming into their birthright as boys. But whereas William, younger than Malcolm had been, managed to keep hold of his dukedom despite attempts to end his life and make a puppet of him, Malcolm had been unable to take back the crown Macbeth claimed for himself until the dispossessed boy grew into a man. To overcome fearful uncertainty and suffering, both had become ruthless warriors and rulers, though there was much evidence the godly princess had wrought change in her betrothed.

"Be warned," Malcolm continued, "the wrath spared the Norman who nearly slew my man, Hendrie, will not be spared if you disappoint. As for the shards..." He blew out wine-scented breath. "As now you are more guest than prisoner, and outside my hall I would not deny a man what aids in defending his person, especially in the midst of those who hold grudges, I leave them to you."

"I am grateful, Your Grace, though more I would be were my sword and dagger returned."

Malcolm chuckled. "That would be overly generous and require I take from the Aetheling that in which he delights."

"As if he himself took the dagger from me," Theriot scorned.

"I know he did not, but as he causes my betrothed little grief at the moment, I indulge him. But be assured, providing you depart Scotland in good stead, you will do so with sword, dagger, and chain mail."

Theriot believed him as he would have been loath to believe King William. As this seemed an opening for that which would make the remainder of his time in Scotland more tolerable, he said, "I have a boon to ask of you."

"I have not done enough?" Malcolm said with just enough humor to temper offense.

"I could not hope for a more accommodating jailer, but I wish word sent to my family that I am held in Scotland, not only to ease fears I perished in the harrying but to end any rumors my disappearance was willful."

"Willful? If the D'Argents' reputation is true, why would any believe you deserted your king's service?"

"We are not without enemies. As you must know, envy is a powerful mover of men. Too, before and after the worst of the harrying, a good number of King William's followers determined they wanted naught else to do with the subjugation of England and took what coin they could get from him and returned to Normandy. As I scouted out what remained of the resistance rather than take sword and fire among innocents, already some think me weak—thus, more likely to desert than those who can pack away whatever conscience they possess."

"Hmm," the king murmured and crossed to the bed. There came the barely perceptible sound of a hand moving over coarse fur. "Good dog," he said and turned back. "I will not grant your boon. Until I determine how best you benefit me, you must remain missing. My days that run into nights are too demanding without keeping a pack of D'Argent wolves from my walls."

His words more expected than not, Theriot said, "Then I hope you will make use of me soon. I do not doubt your country has much to recommend it, but as you said, I am of Normandy and England."

"We are done here, Chevalier. I shall send a man for Dubh."

As Theriot watched the shadow of him—mostly grey with some blue—move away, what pecked at the back of his mind pecked forward, and he asked what he was to have learned this day. "Lady Marguerite tells she recognized me at the village. For that I was not slain nor left to the villagers who would have extracted payment for the destruction wrought by others."

The king turned. "That is so."

"How did she recognize me?"

Amusement rumbled from Malcolm. "Though ye kissed her, you remain unaware of how you were known to her?"

"She meant to tell me, but we were interrupted. Now I ask you to reveal it."

"Not my tale, Sir Theriot, though I will say there is more to the lady having seen you before and there are things about your family she knows that you do not."

Theriot felt as if sucked into a bog and thrown a rope that would free him only if he could swim to it. "Then I wish to speak with her again."

"Perhaps." Moments later, Malcolm closed the door behind him.

Further regretting the kiss for time better spent on enlightenment about her knowledge of him and his family, it was difficult to suppress anger. But not impossible. Lessons aplenty here to learn to control emotions that could undo a man.

"Control," he rasped. "You will control yourself, Theriot D'Argent."

CHAPTER EIGHTEEN

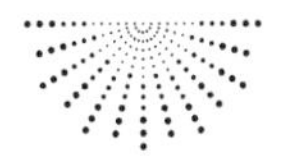

Late Spring, 1070

Once more Dubh turned traitor, and Marguerite did not mind. This past month, often the hound had gone missing though it did not lack for familiars in the great hall. The week after her injury was the first time her mistress discovered her absent. Marguerite had not had to venture far to find her, a man-at-arms reporting that twice in three days the hound had gone to the hut.

Then as now, Marguerite had waited for her to reappear. Not as then, but now more often, when the dog departed she did so in Theriot's company, trotting near as if herding him. And Marguerite believed that was what she did, making Malcolm's prisoner more a curiosity, so much he must be aware of his effect on those who paused to watch them.

While Theriot was accompanied by Dubh, and at a distance the clouds in his eyes could not be seen, his debility did not betray him any more than his stride, swing of arms, and turn of head in response to shifting shadows and sounds above the ordinary. In the hound's absence, one had only to watch a time to know he no longer moved through the world in a natural way for one his age and strength of body. He was tense, stride and swing of arms shorter, and response to shadows and sounds more abrupt.

Marguerite had not spoken with him since he agreed emotion was wasted on him, but from the little Meg told of her visits to pray for him, he fared well and wanted for naught—except to get word to his family. But at least the king's reasoning was mostly sound. He believed the D'Argents would come for their brother before he was prepared to negotiate the terms of Theriot's release that could benefit him where the King of England was concerned.

Not surprisingly, the tension between the two rulers had grown with the approach of Malcolm's marriage. Thus far unable to avert it, William surely felt the threat of the princess birthing sons with not only a claim to the throne of Scotland but England.

Marguerite had considered sending word to Theriot's family, but she could not defy her king. And even had she decided to risk his wrath, no longer was it possible by way of her Saxon escort, though they were ready to return to their liege.

Aware of Baron Roche's connection to the D'Argents, Malcolm had determined those men should continue to avail themselves of his hospitality and, for the second time, sent word to Michel that they were well and would return to Derbyshire before long. The Saxons were not prisoners, but nearly so since he would not grant safe passage and they were allowed their mounts only in the company of Malcolm's men.

Roche's vassals had expressed outrage to Marguerite, but just as the king would not relent on alerting Theriot's family to his fate, neither would he have those Saxons alert the D'Argents through Michel Roche. And the King of Scots' precautions to ensure his will was done did not end there. Not until after the nuptials would Edgar be permitted to venture beyond Dunfermline.

Malcolm was wise. The most effective means of preventing a marriage between him and the Saxon princess was capture of the Aetheling since threat to him would prevent Meg from speaking vows with the enemy of her enemy.

"My lady?"

Looking around, Marguerite saw Hendrie approached, his plaid tied around his waist.

He halted, jutted his chin at Theriot. "Just as Malcolm grants that Norman too much freedom, too much regard you show him—as does your dog."

It was not the first time since departing the sick room the aged warrior had spoken where he was not welcome, but since it was out of concern, she bore it.

Returning her gaze to Theriot and Dubh, she saw their destination was the stable where he visited the mount of the Norman he slew after the first blind swipe of the dagger found horse flesh rather than that of a warrior.

"Aye, too much regard you show the Norman," Hendrie muttered.

She startled. "Forgive me. I was late gaining my bed last eve."

He harrumphed. "Once one pries open the physician's lips, 'tis not easy to close them."

No truer words spoken, she mused. Though Colban was mostly likable, it was good she had decided better a life spent alone than as his wife. It was not only that once he began talking it was difficult to return him to silence, but that he preferred listeners to those who sought to converse. Last eve, several times she had tried to retreat abovestairs, but ever there was one more thing about which he wished to enlighten her.

"He is a good man," she said, "but he will never be more to me than that."

Hendrie sighed. "There are other Scots who could win your heart. Be patient, and our king will provide."

Doubtless, she was a topic of discussion between Malcolm and him, but they only wished her happiness and knew that did not lie in Theriot's direction. She knew it as well. Now if she could only forget their embrace. And that kiss.

She cleared her throat. "Have you resumed practice at arms?"

"Soon," Hendrie said, and his frown became hers when she followed his gaze to the Aetheling who strode from the smithy toward the stable, sunlight glancing off the jeweled hilt of the D'Argent dagger.

"Will the whelp's mind never grow into his body?" Hendrie muttered. "And why am I the one who must keep watch over him?"

Marguerite had not known Malcolm set him that task, though there was sound reason in doing so since he was acquainted with the Aetheling's machinations and not yet ready to take up arms again. Still, it had to offend that one much esteemed by his liege was reduced to this.

"You think he intends to trouble Sir Theriot?" she asked.

"I know he does. If he cannot harass William's men over the border, he will harass the one this side. And I will have to answer for any injuries done him."

It surprised more he was concerned over what might befall the prince than his blinded enemy. He did not like Theriot, but he respected him.

He cursed, then ran to overtake one so set on reaching the man in the stable he did not realize he was pursued. Within strides of the doorway, Hendrie snatched hold of Edgar, and as the young man swung around to face whoever dared set a hand on him, he was yanked to the side.

What Hendrie said beneath the regard of the castle folk could not be known, but a flush-faced Edgar wrenched free and stalked toward the iron door.

Hendrie looked back at Marguerite, rolled his eyes, and followed the Aetheling.

When one after the other passed through the door, Marguerite could not know whether they turned right toward the training yard or left to the glen, but after settling on the lowermost step to await Theriot's reappearance, she heard metal beating metal.

A good thing. Not only would it provide Hendrie practice, but allow Edgar to release some anger.

When Theriot exited the stable, once more Dubh was at his side. As they moved toward the hut, the hound's eyes landed on Marguerite, and she faltered as if caught doing something wrong.

Theriot halted. When he turned his head toward the tower, she looked upon a face framed by lengthening hair and a jaw covered by a fairly thick beard.

What did he see? Had there been improvement in his sight this past month? She pushed upright. Taking a step to the side, she watched for a change of expression or movement of the head to indicate he saw. If he did, it did not show.

He said something to Dubh, and the dog ran forward.

Then Theriot had seen her and commanded the hound to her mistress? Or did he merely send her back to the tower?

As he resumed his stride that was now less fluid, the dog stopped short of Marguerite, gave what sounded a joyful bark, and peered across her shoulder at the one whose company she preferred.

When Theriot disappeared around the side of the hut, Dubh looked to Marguerite like a child did its mother in the hope of being granted more play time.

She patted the scruffy head. "Go, Dubh. Give aid I cannot."

The hound loped opposite.

Not wasted emotion, Marguerite told herself. *Kindness and consideration due him.*

As she started up the steps, she was struck by a thought. Would Malcolm allow it? She smiled. Why not? He had to know Dubh spent more time in Theriot's company than hers. Hoping the king would grant her an audience, she hastened up the steps.

IT WAS TIME. This eve he would dine with a king not his own.

Though Theriot had declined every invitation, not the one delivered this day with tidings that until this prisoner departed Dunfermline, the hound known as Dubh would go where he went. It was worded to sound as if meant to ensure Theriot respected his boundaries, but it had to be of Marguerite's doing.

Though this past month there was only minor improvement in his vision, his unnatural sense continued to sharpen and this day alerted him he was watched in a way not merely of the curious nor hostile, though that he had also felt when he crossed to the stable.

It was not the first time he sensed Marguerite in the bailey, but previously he had ignored her. However, when Dubh reacted to what Theriot thought her presence, he had determined to verify it was her and commanded the dog to go to the one he named.

The black of Dubh had raced toward the figure near the tower, and the victorious bark told she had found her mistress.

Satisfied, Theriot had returned to the hut. Then came scratching at the door. Marguerite had sent Dubh back. Continuing to waver between offense at what he believed pity and gratitude for the hound's instinctual attentiveness that allowed him to move more easily through a world still far from seen, Theriot determined he would regard the lady's offering not as an insult but a gift.

Straightening the tunic earlier washed in a basin and dried before the fire, he turned from the sideboard. "We go."

Dubh bounded upright, but Theriot hesitated. Having earned the grudging respect of many of Malcolm's men for his seemingly impossible victory over one of the warriors who attacked him and the king in the glen, he should be fairly well received in the hall, but that would not save him from humiliation. He could make sense of the shapes and colors of food and had practiced eating with utensils to ensure he was not reduced to groping, but if light did not fall right on what was set before him...

He ground his teeth. It was loathsome he must be so mindful of feeding the body that protection afforded by closely attending to his surroundings was lost, but that was what he was reduced to. God willing, it would not always be thus, that just as prayers were being answered for his unnatural sense, more greatly they would be answered for his sight.

He lowered his lids. "Almighty, I thank You for giving me hope You will make all things right by daily strengthening the extra sense gifted me. But the days count higher, and still I am mostly blind. If You will make me whole again, I will be more faithful. I will—"

The words spoken aloud emphasizing how pitiful his attempt to strike a bargain, he opened eyes of little benefit to him. Holy men and his sire said God could not be cajoled into answering requests in a manner of which only the beseecher approved and that whatever answer was given, it would be best for all. But if Theriot's prayers were to be answered with a shake of the head rather than a nod, how would that benefit any but the enemy were he to move with much caution throughout the remainder of his life?

It was not the first time he pondered that, nor considered

were God unwilling to heal him it would be because of delayed punishment for the injustice of the conquest in which he had participated. And there was another thing to consider—that Hugh was right in believing God was not active in the lives of His creation, that ever Theriot was merely a recipient of good fortune now come to a painful end.

Feeling himself lean that direction as if preferable his prayers were unheard rather than denied, he moved his thoughts to the princess who occasionally visited. Despite the temptation to discuss his doubts with one of great faith, he had not. Thus, she had prayed for his eyes to be healed and asked that if God chose otherwise, He aid Theriot in remembering all his blessings and accepting his loss by finding good in it and making better of it.

Ever that last was received with resentment, but if that was to be his fate, even greater his need for God's aid.

Though the bell had rung to gather all for the evening meal, and further delay would make it impossible to slip into the hall among the masses, he crossed to the bed and lowered.

He thanked God for easing his anger, decreasing his sensitivity to light, returning shapes and colors to his eyes, and continuing to restore the unnatural sense that was his greatest hope of survival if functional vision were permanently lost.

"Pray not," he entreated. "Let it be Your will I see again, but if You deny me..." He breathed deep. "Help me accept it, find good in it, and make better of it." Then he added what the princess had not. "And let me burden none. Amen."

Beneath a sky darkened by night and clouds beginning to spit rain, he and Dubh began the short walk to the tower. Not until he was halfway up the treacherous steps did he realize he had left something behind.

The shard he should have secured to his leg remained on the sideboard where he had set it while tending to his ablutions. Were his sight not impaired, he would have seen it.

Loathing the necessity of being unduly conscious of where he placed items and remembering he had done so, he considered retrieving it, but already he came late. And too great the desire to turn back and forego what would surely be his most challenging exercise in humility. Thus far.

CHAPTER NINETEEN

Not until Princess Margaret of England agreed to become Queen of Scots had the blessing of the meal been of such duration. It frustrated many, especially warriors eager to ease their hunger, but Malcolm controlled grumbling by having drink flow beforehand and the meal delivered immediately following the blessing so it not grow cold.

As viands were carried through a side door, their scents vying with those of light rain come through windows and burning wood warming the hall, Marguerite glanced at Princess Cristina seated on one side of her and Colban the other.

Grateful the former remained at prayer, the latter engaged in conversation with an envoy of the Highlanders, she moved her regard to the western wall and stared at what had been concealed behind a tapestry upon her return to Dunfermline.

After her nearly disastrous visit to the graveyard, she had asked about her parents' headstone and been told the princess aided Malcolm in composing the words engraved there. Then the king had brought her here and removed a tapestry so worn it was a poor fit among the beautiful ones hung during Marguerite's absence. Seeing the original headstone was fixed to the wall with Diarmad the Mad's shield and crossed swords on either side of it, she had embraced Malcolm and wept.

Now, so intent was she on the tribute, she became aware of a shift in the air only when Colban said, "I did not think he would come. But then, neither did I expect the king to issue an invitation."

The envoy grunted. "The princess's influence over Malcolm is troublesome. Does she have her way, she will make a saint of him when it is a warrior king Scotland needs, and more than ever with William eyeing our country."

That last barely heard, Marguerite swept her gaze past diners whose interest was divided between the hunger of empty bellies and the starvation of dull minds. Theriot had come.

"Chevalier!" Malcolm called, causing Cristina to snap up her head and the chevalier and hound to halt in the aisle between crowded tables. "I began to think you changed your mind. Well come to my hall."

Theriot inclined his head. As he waited to be directed to his place, Meg leaned toward the king. When he nodded at whatever she said, the princess stood and descended the dais.

Not all present fell silent, but enough none had to strain to catch her words. "You shall sit at high table with us, Sir Theriot of the family D'Argent." Amid gasps and murmurings, she looped an arm through his and drew him forward.

As they neared the dais, Marguerite ceased breathing for fear he would place a foot wrong, but the princess said something as she and Dubh slowed and Theriot took the step up and strode past esteemed guests and retainers.

Many would think it unseemly a prisoner was afforded such honor, but none would protest in the king's hearing—perhaps not even Edgar were he present. Since being denied the reach of lands beyond Dunfermline, it was rare the prince dined here, but his men were in attendance. And then there was Hendrie.

Marguerite searched out the warrior who usually preferred

the company of the garrison at the lower tables. Having been relieved of his watch over Edgar, he was among them, eyes upon Theriot.

Just past Marguerite, Meg halted. "A place will be made for you between Princess Cristina and my betrothed's ward."

Marguerite's startle did not compare to that of the woman beside her. As if anticipating her sister's protest, Meg leaned near and whispered, "Christian charity."

Cristina huffed and shifted to the side the same as Marguerite.

"Intolerable," the envoy muttered as his future queen returned to Malcolm's side.

Marguerite expected Colban to agree. He did not, though surely he disapproved of Theriot sitting above others, and all the more since he had to know her feelings for this Norman were among the reasons she resisted his attentions.

"Princess Cristina, Lady Marguerite," Theriot acknowledged and stepped to the bench. His shin touched the edge as if gauging the height, then he lifted one leg over and the other.

As he settled, the brush of his arm caused Marguerite to catch her breath at the same moment Dubh jolted the bench in her haste to crawl beneath.

"Mercy!" Cristina hissed. "'Tis unseemly dogs of all breeds are allowed at table."

Marguerite looked past Theriot. From the woman's narrowed eyes, it was obvious her words were not directed at Dubh alone. Too, she had spoken in Norman-French which she detested. Did Theriot know she referred to one other than the animal between his and her mistress's calves?

Beneath the table, Theriot splayed his hands, above it ground his teeth. Though the princess offended, he would not give her the satisfaction of knowing he was aware she spoke of him, with which her brother would agree were he present.

Grateful to Malcolm's betrothed for mentioning Edgar was

unlikely to join them at meal, he decided to behave in a manner opposite what was expected of him.

Feeling Dubh's wet nose against his hand, determinedly ignoring Marguerite, he looked to one of brown hair and yellow gown. "You are kind to allow this Norman to dine with you, Princess," he said in her language to ensure she understood as she wished him to understand.

She turned her face to him. "Christian charity, even for the enemy."

"Much appreciated, though were you unable to extend it, I would understand."

"How?"

"As a vassal of the Duke of Normandy, I fought the side of he who dispossessed your family and is now King of England."

"King! That vile, misbegotten—" She bit back what he guessed ungodly words.

"Great the blessing your family not only found sanctuary in Scotland, but a home at Malcolm's court," Theriot said.

She harrumphed, then surprised by leaning near. "The price is my sister who did not wish to wed, and certainly not to a man as unrefined as her betrothed. As for this court, you must agree we live well below the standards to which our royal persons are accustomed—or you would if you could look upon it."

Theriot shifted his jaw. "It is a changed world for all. I am sorry for your discomfort."

"Sorry? Your people are the victors, mine..." She drew a sharp breath. "Much the Normans have ill-used us."

"So they have."

It felt she searched his face for something to give her cause to turn her back on him, then she said, "It is of credit to your blood you are not blind to our suffering, Sir Theriot."

This time he did not believe her choice of words deliberate and further proof was given when she touched his arm. It seemed still he possessed the skill of charming ladies, and more easy that since he had not needed to feign sincerity.

He cleared his throat. "One does not have to see well to know of the injustice done your people."

"I am tempted to thank you, Sir Theriot."

Then much progress made in a short time with one who equated him with a dog of poor breeding.

Movement alerting him to the approach of someone on the opposite side of the table, he watched the shadow halt before him, listened to liquid streaming into a vessel, smelled the mist of wine.

Pleased his thirst was not overlooked, he shifted his clouded gaze to where he would find his drink. When the servant departed, he saw a grey so uniform in length, he knew it for a cup rather than goblet.

Feigning ignorance, he said, "Tell, Princess Cristina, is my drink wine or ale?"

"Wine, regrettably of low quality. As told, we live below what is due us."

Setting a hand on the linen-covered top, once more he eschewed pride and requested what he need not, "Will you do me the kindness of moving the vessel to my fingers?"

On one side of him, he heard Marguerite catch her breath, on the other side sensed hesitation. Then the princess leaned near and slid the cup's base against his fingertips. "Kindness done."

"I thank you." He curved his hand around it and, though he thirsted, drank slowly to ensure no misplaced drop.

"Is it true all those of D'Argent blood and few years have black hair marked by silver?" she asked.

He lowered the cup. "Even the youngest of my siblings—my sister, Nicola."

Her groan was sympathetic. "I suppose it is attractive in a young man for how it draws the eye and piques curiosity, but a woman? Woe unto your sister she shall appear old long before her time."

"Not so, Princess. So much she resembles our lovely mother whom age naturally silvers, Nicola could be entirely silvered and still as comely as any woman half her age."

She laughed. "Careful lest you make me envious of her."

Could he see Cristina well, here would be the place to compliment her appearance. Though determined to learn more of her beyond her face and body, before he could move that direction, servants began delivering individual plates surely filled at sideboards.

Theriot was unaccustomed to eating in this manner, but though denied the opportunity to choose what appealed, there was advantage in not fumbling over the passing of platters.

Might Malcolm's betrothed have arranged it for him? Possible if not for the absence of expressions of surprise. Likely this was how it was done here.

When a plate was set before the princess, next him, he was pleased torch and candlelight made known the shapes and some colors of the viands.

Cristina leaned in again and pushed the rim of his plate against his thumb near the cup. "By your left hand is bread, on the right chunks of cheese, at the top a very small apple sure to be tart." She shuddered. "And at the bottom sliced venison."

Glad to know exactly what he was seeing—more, that all were acceptable to carry to the lips without spoon or knife, he turned to her as a low rumble of thunder sounded across the heavens. "You are kind."

"Christian charity," she said, slightly breathless.

A short while later, he became aware of a shift in conversations and the lowering of voices. Something of note had happened, and from the tension Marguerite exuded, knew it bothered her as much as Cristina. "What is it, Princess?"

For answer, she scooted nearer the person on her other side.

"He did not linger," mused a Scotsman several places beyond Marguerite.

Someone snorted. "Methinks none informed him who would be sitting at high table. First, she who is to be queen betrays, now she who is to be a nun."

They spoke of Edgar. Though he was not expected in the hall, he had come. And gone.

Theriot settled into his meal. He could have cleared his plate quickly, but he was loath to reveal how improved his vision, pitiful though it was compared to what it should be.

As rain began falling enthusiastically, its mist entering through open windows, his awareness of Marguerite increased when she began feeding Dubh beneath the table.

Theriot turned to her. "You are without appetite?"

"My hunger is satisfied. I but pass the remains to my hound."

He inclined his head. "I believe I have you to thank for the use of Dubh."

"Since she prefers your company and appears to be of aid, the king agreed she should stay your side until you depart."

"Generous." As he picked the apple from his plate, he saw her reach and the shape of the goblet she raised to her mouth.

Amid the din of those succumbing to the pleasure of drink and food, was this an opportunity to learn what she had yet to reveal of herself and what she knew of his family? "Lady, I would understand—"

"Sir Theriot." Princess Cristina curled fingers over his arm.

Because he had moved his attention elsewhere? "Princess?"

"I am thinking you prefer your apple sliced the same as I. Have you need of a meat dagger, you may use mine." He heard its blade slide across the wood of his plate and wondered how quickly someone would correct her for offering a weapon. Though Malcolm allowed his prisoner much freedom, it was unseemly to provide him a blade, especially in close proximity to one of the royals.

He touched the handle. "Peeled. I find the skin unappetizing."

"Then remove it. That is…I mean…"

That she who had been intent on offending now hesitated, roused sympathy for one who must be bereft of attention to so soon set aside anger and prejudice. It could not be easy dwelling in the shadow of a brother who was to have been king and a sister who was to be queen. Too, though it was said she was pretty, the older sister's beauty was lauded.

Pricked by guilt over so closely attending to her, he said, "I appreciate your concern and belief I can be trusted with a dagger, but even in the absence of sight, I remain capable of peeling an apple."

"I would like to see that." It was said with enthusiasm as if she wished a trick performed. And it was something of a trick. Though the boy of him had perfected the technique, absent sight it would be more challenge than amusement.

He moved his right hand to the plate, slid fingers over the rim, and turned them around a handle so smooth he knew it was fashioned of bone.

Within sight of any who looked their way—and for certain Marguerite watched—he verified the blade's upper edge was dull, moved his grip higher, and raised the apple in his other hand. Angling the dagger's point upward, he placed its keen lower edge near the stem, set the thumb of the dagger-wielding hand on the smooth surface to guide the way forward, and began turning the apple. Providing he did not err, the skin would come away in what would be a narrow ribbon without break.

The apple was nearly shed of its clothing when Cristina exclaimed, "Were your chin not up, I would question if 'tis true you cannot see."

It amused she was easily impressed, but embittered it was not the swing of a sword that gained her admiration.

Coming to the bottom of the apple, he twisted the blade to sever the last of the peel, dropped the spiraling length atop his plate, and turned the dagger's handle toward Cristina. "I thank you."

Wishing her touch disturbed the same as Marguerite's, he took a bite of what was barely ripe and flicked a thumb across his lower lip to wipe away juice intent on wetting his whiskered chin. Once more sinking his teeth into the apple, he returned his thoughts to what remained unanswered about Marguerite.

"I begin to understand why my sister expends prayer on you," Cristina said, "though so great a regard is inappropriate for a lady betrothed to another."

Though he understood what she alluded to and thought it bred of jealousy, he asked, "Inappropriate?"

"She visits you at the hut."

"With her betrothed's consent and many an escort."

She shifted on the bench. "Even so, our mother concurs better her time spent beseeching the Lord's blessings on her marriage to a man who is... Well, outside of battle, even your William is more civilized."

As told by the gasp on his other side, she had not sufficiently lowered her voice. Unfortunately, Marguerite rose from the table.

"You are unwell?" the physician asked.

She stepped over the bench. "My appetite is satisfied and I am weary. Good eve."

As she moved away, Cristina made a sound of disgust. "Also inappropriate is how much interest that lady shows her king."

Despite annoyance with the princess, Theriot mulled what he knew of Marguerite's relationship with Malcolm, but not for long. He sympathized with Cristina, but she could stir much trouble at court.

"Once your sister weds Malcolm, will you remain with her?" he asked.

She hesitated. "As she is not to give herself to the Church, 'tis for me to do. Though I know not when I shall take the veil, that is my fate."

"You sound displeased."

Breath whistled through her nose. "I believed it possible one day I would wed and bear children. I was not sure I wished it, but there was comfort in knowing I might choose life with a man over life in service to God. But what I want..." She sighed. "My mother says all must do their duty."

Though he sensed she wished him to disagree, he said, "So we must. Thus, I am where I do not wish to be, just as you may find yourself where you prefer not to be."

"Oh, pity us, Sir Theriot! If only our lives were our own."

Realizing she who denied him the opportunity to learn more about Marguerite might supply the answers, he said, "And pity Lady Marguerite. For all her kind regard for the king, he seems bent on wedding her to one of his choosing."

She *tsked.* "Her departed sire was highly regarded. Thus, she is spoiled for the blood in her veins."

So speaks one spoiled for the blood in hers, Theriot thought of the woman who scorned life at Malcolm's court, believing more was due her than what was given rather than earned.

He judged her, he knew, though not as harshly as he would if he did not acknowledge he had been spoiled with his claim to the D'Argent name. For it, what he now faced that he might to his end days would make it more difficult to accept.

"Colban is fine looking, learned, and more civilized than most men at court," she continued. "If she accepts him, a good husband he will be, though why he wants such a lady I do not know."

"I assumed she is lovely. Is she not?"

"For the sake of one who should have wed years past and out of kindness for the king's ward, I am tempted to mislead you, but I will not. As you must have noted, the lady has a youthful voice, but there is little to recommend her to a man such as yourself with an eye toward beauty."

An assumption, Theriot thought, though he was drawn to women of comely face and lovely figure ahead of what lay beyond what was seen. He liked those sharp of mind and kind of heart, but rarely did he delve what was invisible to the eye, there being little need since it was all flirtation, marriage for this D'Argent a distant possibility.

The only time he had seriously considered joining his life with another's was during the short time he served as keeper of one of his brother's castles and it was thought possible it would become a permanent position. But then King William removed that castle and its lands from his brother's holdings. Once more a warrior earning his living by the sword, Theriot had settled back into that life thinking it likely his until he was an old man telling stories to the offspring of a landed brother. Now even that might prove impossible.

"Not that she is unsightly," the princess said.

Though Theriot doubted he would learn the truth of Marguerite's appearance from her, it was the door through which he might pass to discover the rest of that lady's tale that intersected with his.

"Whereas my hair is a vibrant brown, hers is… Oh, this sounds cruel, but it is nearly the color of dried mud."

He kept his face impassive. Shades of brown were known to him, and Marguerite's was rich and deep—more so than Cristina's and far from the grey-brown of thirsting dirt.

"And whereas I am little more than a score aged, she is quite beyond that."

That he did not believe, but he asked, "How much beyond?"

She mewled as if giving it thought. "I think near ten and twenty. As for her figure… Well, if she does not better control her appetite, her gowns will have to be altered further."

He shifted his jaw. Not only had Marguerite fed more to her

dog than herself this eve, but when he had held her after the attack in the wood and later kissed her, he had learned that where she curved, she curved prettily.

Moving the conversation toward what he hoped would not be answered with further jealousy-induced exaggeration, he said, "It is understandable the king indulges the daughter of one loyal to him, but that he does so to the extent it endangers her? That surprises."

"Endangers?" The princess gasped. "Ah, you speak of her going to the glen, which no lady should do without escort."

He did not speak of that, though he concurred Marguerite should have an escort, especially after what happened. "It seems an unnecessary risk," he said, "though it hardly compares to her presence in the village over the border."

Though he hoped Cristina was too intent on belittling Marguerite to recall the reason he had also been there, she went silent. Then she blew out breath. "You who meant my brother harm make it easy to forget we are enemies."

"I did not wish him harm, only to sooner end what ails England."

"And you think what ails it is Edgar rather than your king?" she snapped.

"I am sorry for your brother's loss, but that is what it is—a loss, which I believe he must accept the same as it is required of you to accept your loss of a choice between becoming a bride of man, a bride of Christ, or no bride at all."

And you shall have to accept the loss of sight if that is to be your fate, reminded a voice within.

She returned to silence, but after a time said, "It pains me to hear such, but I shall forgive you since I believe it told without malice. And you may be right—just as I must accept my life is for others to command, Edgar may have to accept the crown of England is another's." She touched his arm. "Much to the Lord's displeasure, I am a jealous creature. It is just painfully difficult to be moving in an agreeable direction, then turn a corner that forces one to go a different way. You cannot know—"

"I believe I do," he tempered resentment as best he could.

"So it seems," she said, then asked, "I see the clouds upon your eyes, but is it certain you will not see again?"

Containing his roiling, he said, "Not certain, but increasingly likely."

"Then when you depart Scotland, you shall enter the Church the same as I?"

As he did not care to speak there, and believing better she turn from him than he from her, once more he ventured where he was not welcome. "It is bothersome to discuss what may or may not be. Would you not tell what was?"

"What was?"

"The reason Lady Marguerite was in the English village the night Hendrie and I fought."

She harrumphed. "You take too much interest in that lady."

"She is a curiosity."

"I know not why you do not ask her yourself, but I shall answer. Shortly after our family came to Scotland, the lady was given an escort to retrieve her mother from her Norman family's demesne across the border."

That he knew. And more.

"When she did not return, it was believed she was slain the same as her escort. Not until many months later did she begin the journey home. On the night my brother and his men fled those you set upon them, en route she stopped at the village they passed through."

Theriot nodded. "So now the question of where she was all that time. And why she did not return sooner."

"My mother and I would like to know as well, but it is between the lady, the king, and my sister."

Six months or more gone from Scotland, Theriot reckoned. Plenty of time for their paths to cross, enabling her to look upon him even if he had not seen her, thereby allowing her to recognize him the night she feigned pursuit by Normans.

"Regrettably, what is left untold of her tale you shall have to gain from her or another, Sir Theriot. And share with me."

He inclined his head. She might take it as agreement, but it was only acknowledgement. Though he continued conversing with her when prompted, in between he searched his memory for when he might have had an opportunity to first come to the notice of the woman he should not have kissed.

CHAPTER TWENTY

It was time to depart, and easier that amid the many so he not be on display again.

Taking the apple core and peel from where he had set them on the right side of his plate, he said, "I thank you for the company, Princess."

She stood. "Allow me to be your guide."

Dubh having come out from beneath the table, he nearly declined, but he stamped down pride. "Much appreciated, though I shall prevail only as far as the doors."

"Since it would be unseemly for me to venture further without escort, agreed." She chuckled. "You will find me more proper than Lady Marguerite." When he did not comment, she set a hand on his arm and they traversed the dais behind others whose figures were so near he could differentiate one from the other only by the color of their garments. Though many were of similar browns and greens, at least they were no longer smudges of grey.

"Why the peel and core, Sir Theriot?" the princess asked.

"It is for the horse I injured when the king and I were set upon in the glen."

"It has not recovered?"

"It has, but still I visit."

Halfway across the hall, feeling curiosity which was surely greater for Cristina's accompaniment, Theriot caught a voice not heard since its owner kicked him in the head en route to Dunfermline. Hendrie conversed with others near the hearth as revealed by heat emanating from that direction and the crackle and pop of burning wood.

"Sir Theriot?" Cristina said.

Realizing he had halted, he said, "Forgive me," and continued forward.

"I have angered you?"

"You have not."

"Then who? And do not say you were not roused. Such darkness rose on your face, I nearly looked up to see what clouds gathered."

Seeing no reason not to be truthful, he said, "I heard Malcolm's man. Though Hendrie did what he believed necessary to preserve his life, as long as darkness is as much my day as my night, I can have no good regard for him."

"Understandable," she said, then, "Here are the doors. I shall ask a man-at-arms to guide you to your hut."

Though barely acquainted with the steps whose descent would be more dangerous than ascent, especially now they were slick, he said, "Not necessary. I know the way."

She loosed him, and the porter opened a door, letting in the breath of rain once more falling softly.

"Chevalier," Cristina said, "if you would welcome my prayers as you do my sister's, mayhap I shall gain an escort and visit you."

Though her interest in him might prove of benefit, he pitied her for grasping at whatever attention this former enemy might provide. "I would be honored."

"Then we shall meet again soon."

Theriot continued forward, trading the light of the hall for the dark of night and rain that torchlight around the walls struggled to defy.

As expected, descent of the steps was more challenging. Just as earlier he had bumped the toe of a boot against the vertical support of the next step up to ensure his footing, now he bumped the heel of a boot against the support of each step down while Dubh stayed his side—and not for the first time wished a walking stick in hand. But as always, his stomach turned at thoughts of how pitiful and weak he would look with one guiding him forward.

And how will you look if you tumble down the steps? demanded an inner voice. *If not dead, then a prideful fool, and more they will laugh no matter how quickly you gain your feet.*

Feeling watched by those about the bailey, great his relief when he came off the steps. That success tempted him to eschew the stable lest between here and there he give them something over which to laugh, but he turned toward that building.

Occasionally, the hound nudged him as if to correct his course. In this instance, Theriot did not require aid, the torch on the wall beyond the stable allowing him to see the building's silhouette, but he would not discourage her, so fascinated was he by instincts that seemed almost as natural to her as breathing. Regardless of the state of his sight, when he departed Dunfermline, he would regret leaving her behind.

Thoughts moving to the woman from whom he would also be parted, he shook them off, opened the stable door, and entered an interior dimly lit by a single lantern hooked on the back wall.

No sooner did Dubh and he cross the threshold than a feral cry sounded and a body low to the ground shot past, causing the hound to whip around and give chase.

As with each time Theriot encountered a cat since his

blinding, he tensed. They abounded in the bailey, serving the palace inhabitants by controlling the rodents. Many made the stable their home, ascending to the loft and rafters when Theriot was accompanied by Dubh. This time one was caught unawares, and the hound had every intention of making it pay for not better attending to its senses.

Leaving the door ajar for her return, Theriot strode toward the light between the stalls and caught movement left and right as the great beasts stuck their heads above the gates and nickered.

Theriot murmured greetings and touched their muzzles as he passed, and when he reached the farthest, the stallion he had named Grendel fully extended his head. "I am returned," he said, setting a hand on its great jaw.

The animal huffed.

"Oui, I have brought you something." After feeding him the peel and core, Theriot slid his hand over the muscular neck and past its shoulder to the ridge that attested to this warrior's inability to differentiate between horse flesh and that of its rider. As told the princess, the wound was healed, and soon the Norman's mount would belong to an esteemed Scotsman.

As with each time Theriot visited the stable, he wondered who had claimed his blue-eyed destrier left outside the village and if he might regain Ciel. If that fine animal had not been sold, he would be—else one of the D'Argents would retrieve Ciel when they came looking for his owner. Had they yet? Would they soon?

Though the warrior of Theriot wished to gain his own release, increasingly he accepted that remained more vanity than ability. "Heavenly Father," he rasped, "be merciful in allowing me to once more see the unseen so I alone govern my days and nights."

He felt a nudge and thought it imagined until something deep told otherwise. Someone was here, and it was not Dubh.

Danger. Though not yet in full possession of his unnatural sense, it stretched, allowing him to feel the new arrival's presence—and that of others, though he was fairly certain the latter remained outside the stable, likely to keep watch.

Guessing night and the absence of Dubh emboldened the one who stole inside, and that just as Edgar was responsible for the attack in the hut, he was responsible for the one to come against this Norman who further offended in gaining Cristina's attention, Theriot kept his face in profile.

The horses also felt something, now more inclined to snorting than nickering, including Grendel whose muscles firmed beneath the hand upon him.

Lacking sight as well as weapons—not even an accursed shard!—Theriot felt a prick of helplessness that returned him to Normandy.

After being relieved of every weapon and dropped with a backhand that caused him to toss up his hands in surrender, his uncle, Hugh, had spat, *Never accept all is lost. Never give your opponent that satisfaction. Ever there is something you can do to make his existence more miserable even should you meet your end before he meets his. Now you who believe yourself favored by God, use those boundless senses of which you are unworthy, the anger of shame which is your due, and the skills I have gifted you. Honor your name, Theriot D'Argent!*

That youth had done as commanded, breaking a lofty nose never before broken so terribly as to be permanently bent.

Now as the one who sought to assail him drew nearer, Theriot took inventory of all that could be made into weapons, including fists and feet. But the best weapon was his extra sense that would permit him to make better use of the others were the one coming for him also sightless.

The lantern on the wall to the right was five feet away. His assailant was fifty feet distant, not yet near enough for Theriot to take full advantage of the sudden pall of blackness. Twenty feet would serve, giving the man's eyes little time to adjust.

Theriot eased back, reversing the slide of his hand and once more setting it on the horse's jaw. "This should not take long," he murmured.

The other horses grew restless and some stamped their hooves, but Grendel was still as if he trusted what was told him.

Theriot closed his lids, blotting out the dim to allow his own eyes to sooner adjust to the coming black.

The man was thirty feet distant now as revealed as much by what was heard as felt. Either he was not well-versed in stealth or overly confident in his ability to best one whose sight was impaired.

Twenty-five feet distant. Expecting if his opponent had not yet brought a blade to hand, soon he would, Theriot breathed in, and when twenty-five feet became twenty, swung to the side.

Guided by lantern's light seen through his lids, he reached with his left hand to preserve the right should he reach wrong. And grasped the hot translucent panes of horn enclosing flame. Gnashing his teeth, he transferred his grip to the leather-wrapped handle set on a hook and lifted the lantern down. Fairly certain the man had halted, he extinguished the flame.

Darkness complete but for torchlight squeezing through the stable's planks and knot holes, Theriot raised his lids, set the lantern on the floor, and sprang to the stalls opposite.

"If we are not well-matched now, knave who attacks downwind," he said in the language Edgar's followers best understood, "that shall prove your failing, not mine."

A threat there, and as he waited to learn how it would be answered, he used the dark and cover of shifting horses to draw nearer the man who remained unmoving on the opposite side, likely stunned by the discovery what he believed easy was to be a challenge.

Though Theriot discerned he was of decent height, he could not be certain of the man's build. Regardless, providing he drew near enough to surprise his opponent who would have one or more blades at the ready, he should be able to best him. The greatest threat was lightning. Whereas several times it had flashed through the hall's windows, only once had it done so since he departed the tower. So bright were those flashes, they could reveal him better than torchlight come through the stable's small openings.

As he started toward the doors to get behind the man and corner him before he ran or summoned those outside, he heard barking. Dubh had returned and found her way barred.

Lest harm was done her, Theriot moved faster than intended while holding his gaze to the shadow of the one here with him. And saw the moment the man decided to stalk another day when he turned toward the doors and torchlight slipping between planks flashed on his blade.

Ahead of him now, Theriot caught a scent very different from horses and rain—that of fear. No matter the warrior, all but those ill of mind exuded it when warranted. However, this being greater than it should be for a man not only seasoned but armed, Theriot knew who had followed him inside.

Moved by revenge—and likely the desperation of being unable to entice another to do his bidding—the Aetheling had found courage in his enemy's sightlessness to do this himself. As for steel briefly come to light, likely the D'Argent dagger.

Gripped by his own desire for vengeance, Theriot almost wished he did not know the identity of his opponent lest he inflict greater damage than he would otherwise.

As he bent lower and shot diagonally toward the first stall, words he had heard spoken to his brother, Dougray, who beat two of his peers for taunts over his illegitimacy returned to Theriot.

Let not vengeance persuade you what is wrong is right, my son, their sire had counseled. *Exercising control, giving godliness and good judgment their due, better serves a warrior. A* worthy *warrior.*

Theriot did not want to apply the lesson he would not have believed applicable in this instance, but the qualifier of *worthy* dug into him, and more deeply when he made it around the side of the stall into the area before the doors just before lightning flashed again.

Was it of the Lord? A test to see if Theriot would apply that lesson? he wondered as Dubh continued to protest. Though certain whoever held the hound had yet to quiet her because she belonged to the king's ward, lest she was harmed to prevent her continued agitation from causing Malcolm's men to investigate, this needed to end. Now.

When the hunched one hastened past, Theriot sidestepped, came up behind him, and hooked an arm around his neck. "Bonsoir, Edgar."

CHAPTER TWENTY-ONE

The prince gurgled against the pressure on his throat, then proving he was of a muscular build and not entirely deficient in self defense, displaced air by arcing his hand back over the opposite shoulder.

It was a good move, the keen point of his blade seeking his assailant's neck, but Hugh had impressed on Theriot the deadly error of underestimating an opponent. Thus, he was prepared for that and a backward kick. A clamp on Edgar's wrist and slam of booted foot rendered the dagger harmless and dropped the prince to his knees.

Struggling to honor Godfroi's lesson, Theriot kept his forearm against the throat straining to keep its airway open and squeezed the wrist beneath his fingers.

When pain and fear of broken bones caused the young man to drop the dagger, Theriot bent near. "As all *honorable* men know, that is no way to return a friendly greeting. I would have expected King Edward, God rest his soul, to have ensured his nephew possessed manners befitting one who might succeed him."

The smell of fear sharpened, covering the scent of Edgar's

rain-dampened hair and tunic, and when lightning once more entered as quickly as it departed, Theriot glimpsed his trembling as well as felt it. Though anger tempted him to scorn Edgar for one who would never be king, he bit back the words. That this blind warrior had bettered him must be enough, especially to ensure no harm befell Dubh.

"Tell those outside to come inside," he commanded.

The prince shook his head, but it was a hesitant thing, as if he wavered between fear over death and fear over being seen shamefully subdued.

"I lose patience, Edgar, and an impatient D'Argent you will like even less." Though before the injury that sought to entirely undo the warrior of Theriot, that threat would have been more exaggeration than truth, less so now he struggled against yielding to vengeance. "Do it!"

"Judd!" Edgar shouted. "Enter!"

Dubh ceased barking when she was allowed to advance ahead of the man who let in the dim of the bailey to illuminate those inside the stable.

Against that light, Theriot could see there were two others besides the one who surely held the hound's collar in such a way Dubh could not get her head around to bite him.

An instant later, all halted, doubtless at seeing Edgar on his knees, his opponent gripping his neck from behind.

"Once more, he who longs for a crown proves unworthy of bearing the weight of its responsibilities and privileges," Theriot said. "Now as it would be ill of me to injure the king's guest, release the dog and I shall send this pup to you."

"Prince?" one of the men asked in Saxon.

"Do as he says," Edgar rasped.

There was movement about Dubh, a shout and curse likely due to a bite, then the hound leapt forward.

Theriot wrenched the prince upright, but as he released him, caught the sound of others approaching that prompted the Saxons to swing around.

Ahead of the hound reaching him, Theriot thrust Edgar forward, then bent and swept a hand over the dirt and retrieved a dagger known to him.

Despite the return of that keen weapon and a panting Dubh drawing so near her rain-moistened fur was felt through Theriot's chausses, it could go poorly for this Norman if those who came to investigate the commotion sided with Edgar.

Very poorly, Theriot amended when he recognized the voice of the other against whom he longed to work vengeance.

"What goes?" Hendrie demanded as he and others entered, the one bringing up the rear carrying a torch that showed the prince was here. Then surprisingly, the Scotsman said with disgust, "Now what have you done, Edgar?"

"He—"

"Aye, he took back his dagger. And how might that have happened, eh?"

As the prince spluttered, Hendrie ordered someone to summon the king.

More spluttering, across which the Scotsman said, "You came for him again, and just as ye defied Malcolm's command to leave him be, I wager though you sought to do the deed yerself, you did not face him like a man."

"You cannot speak to me like that!"

"Yet I do. Yer sister will be my queen, but never will you be my prince."

Keeping the dagger before him, Theriot heard Edgar's draws of breath, then the young man said, "I leave the Norman to you," and ordered the Saxons who had kept watch to follow.

"Nay, boy," Hendrie said, causing the men who had accompanied him to move toward those seeking to depart. "You shall await the king." A crunch of dirt beneath boots sounded as he started forward with a hitch. "And ye, Norman, yield that dagger right quick."

Above Dubh's rumble, Theriot said, "As I took it from one who wrongfully claimed it and sought to turn it on me, I shall hold to it while we await Malcolm—unless you wish to challenge me for that with which twice I stuck you."

Hendrie halted, after some moments, said, "I cannot like you, but you have the courage and resolve of the Scots."

"You err. What I have is of the D'Argents."

The man grunted. "Could be the same."

Shortly, Malcolm entered ahead of others as evidenced by his height and breadth. "Edgar!" he barked, but continued past the prince to his man. "Hendrie."

"I believe you can guess what went here, Your Grace."

"I can." Malcolm took a step toward Theriot. "I would ask if you are injured, but methinks better I ask that of the prince who lives though I would not be surprised if injury to him or death could be... Well, punishable, but justified."

"Justified?" Edgar erupted. "First he seeks the attentions of my eldest sister who is your betrothed, now my younger sister who is soon for the Church."

"Enough, Edgar! You are spared greater wrath only because I share the blame for this, having too much hope you would keep faith with me when I should have exercised caution. But do you test me further..." He left the threat hanging.

"Nothing went here other than a game of hide and find, Your Grace," Theriot said, aware the insult to Edgar would be deeply felt.

"I see that, just as I see the prince brought a dagger to the game as is against the rules."

Knowing he would be required to relinquish it, and there was only humiliation in resisting, Theriot eased his stance and extended the weapon. "As it offends my dagger is in the possession of one incapable of earning the right to wield it, I ask you to keep this until I depart your country."

"Hmm," Malcolm murmured, then said, "Come to me, Edgar."

Angry strides carried him forward, and when he halted, the king said, "Give me the belt upon which the scabbard of D'Argent's dagger hangs."

Edgar's resentment was so keenly felt, Theriot would not have been surprised had he tossed the belt at the king's feet, but he did as bid.

"Even if never you wear a crown, we have much work to do to make you throne worthy," Malcolm said, "and we are not done this night. So we might add to what Sir Theriot has taught you, ye will go to my betrothed and tell what you did and beseech her to pray the night through with you."

"I will not."

"You will, even if you must be made to do it. And one more thing."

"What?"

"Nay, two things." Malcolm stepped forward, murmured to Dubh, "Good girl," and took the dagger Theriot extended. Its return to the sheath sounding a sigh, he said, "I had hoped ye would not require this, Chevalier, but as I am no more willing to cage you than I am the princess's brother, and once more you prove trustworthy, I return it."

Theriot frowned. Did he understand right?

"Your Grace!" Hendrie exclaimed.

Before Malcolm could respond, Edgar cried, "'Tis unseemly a prisoner possess a lethal—"

"Lethal, indeed," the king said as Theriot's seeking hand closed around the belt. "And yet not turned against you, though blood would be upon my boots were you relieved of it by any other prisoner."

"You detest the Aetheling!" The crack in Edgar's voice

portended tears. "For that, you provide him the means of slaying me without staining your own hands."

Malcolm heaved a sigh. "Do you hear any voice other than yer own? Do you see and accept anything that does not fit you in the moment? Aye, this Norman sought to deliver you into his liege's hands as was his duty, but no attempt was made on your life as twice now you have done his."

He did not respond. Because he *was* hearing a voice other than his own?

"Think on that. And know this, Edgar—if you defy me again, more greatly I shall restrict your movements and those of your men." Malcolm let that settle. "Now that other thing. Apologize to Baron Roche's men for drawing them into your quest for vengeance."

Theriot's hands fastening the belt faltered. He was familiar with that baron's name—had been for nearly as many years as he could remember—and now it returned him to where last he heard it. The elusive words of the Norman he slew at the burning village before the encounter with Hendrie had been, *Forgive me for failing you, Baron Roche.* What had he failed to do for that man? And why had he been so far north amid the harrying?

Before Theriot could drag other memories to the surface, one of those who had stood watch for Edgar said, "Since we required little enticement, we need no apology, Your Grace."

"Judd?" Malcolm prompted.

As that one stepped forward, it occurred these men had to know Theriot was the brother of their lord's illegitimate son. And yet they had aided Edgar. Did the connection with Dougray not matter because they were Saxon—albeit they served a Norman?

"Too much drink," Judd said, "your refusal to allow us to return home, and anger over this Norman slaying our fellow warrior moved us far more than the Aetheling could have had he offered coin."

Then for this it mattered not he was Dougray's brother, Theriot thought, and did not have to search far for the reason Malcolm did not allow them to depart. They would report to Roche the name of he who slew one of their number and that he had been transported over the border. As the King of Scots was not ready to let this roll of the dice land lest it deliver to him Normans he preferred remain in England until he determined what to do with Theriot, he would not risk Roche alerting the D'Argents of where their youngest brother was held.

"Your Grace," the man continued, "as we did our duty in delivering Lady Marguerite to you, the weather is good, and we are unafraid of traveling harried lands, it is past time we return to Derbyshire. Pray, grant us our leave."

Only distantly did Theriot hear what was spoken beyond Marguerite's name, memories once more transporting him, this time to the D'Argent camp beyond the battlefield of Stafford when the defeated rebel leader, Vitalis, risked all to deliver the injured Em to Dougray.

Beneath moonlight, Saxons had faced Normans, and Theriot's half-brother who hated the conquered for the loss of an arm had proven there was at least one he did not loath when he agreed to seek a physician to save Em's life and keep the slave-turned-rebel out of the hands of her Norman master. Entrusting her care to Dougray, Vitalis had insisted she be accompanied by a rebel named Margaret.

Margaret...Marguerite, he mulled.

He had aided the mute woman in mounting a horse and, strangely drawn to one unseen, had sought to make her seen. It had been dark and her hood caused shadows to shift across her face as he peered up at her, but his sharp gaze had permitted him to see much of that lovely visage.

Was it possible he had looked upon Marguerite of

Dunfermline? That he did know her face? That she was the one who looked back as she departed camp, moving him to raise a hand to let her know he looked upon her as well?

It would be a stretch he might not consider if not that weeks later Dougray had returned to William's service at York and revealed to Theriot he found a physician for Em at the castle of Stavestone. There, for the first time, he had met his sire, Michel Roche, whose indiscretion had made a misbegotten child on their mother.

Many the trials Dougray had faced to save Em from her pursuers. All were of great interest, and yet—strangely—Theriot had been nearly as interested in the mute healer's fate. His brother's expression evidencing he thought it strange as well, he had told it was necessary to leave the one called Margaret in Roche's care to sooner deliver Em to Wulfen in the hope of sending her across the channel where slavery was outlawed.

Margaret...Marguerite, Theriot considered again. It would explain how she knew Theriot by sight in that burning village and the reason what he had glimpsed of her there seemed familiar. But what of Marguerite playing a mute? He frowned. For that had hoarseness said to be a malady of the throat been only prolonged disuse?

"As told, in *my* time, not yours," Malcolm said sharply. "Now go. And have Colban tend your hand, Judd. A dog's bite is a dangerous thing." As four figures moved toward the door, the king called, "Do not defy me, Edgar. Seek my betrothed for a prayer vigil."

When they went into the night, Hendrie said, "I should return the chevalier to his hut?"

As Theriot tensed again, causing Dubh to press more heavily against his leg, Malcolm said, "May I further trust you not to stick my man again, Chevalier?"

Let not vengeance persuade you what is wrong is right, my son, Theriot once more heard and cleared his throat. "If you trust

Hendrie not to further injure me, you may trust my dagger will remain sheathed."

"Done." The king turned and took with him those who had accompanied Hendrie.

Thus, it was the man Theriot had nearly slain to whom he put his question when they departed the stable. "How long was Lady Marguerite gone from Dunfermline?"

Silence, but when they came around the hut whose eaves dripped rain, Hendrie said, "End of summer last, she departed to retrieve her mother from her family's Norman lands."

This Marguerite had told Theriot and that not only had she discovered her mother had passed but her escort was slain and prey made of her. What befell her afterward he did not know since Malcolm's arrival had interrupted the tale, but he had assumed she escaped back across the border.

"When she did not return, we feared her dead though we did not find her among her murdered escort. Then months later we happened on her in that village."

Since she had been in England all that time, she could have been the one who accompanied Em following the Battle of Stafford, Theriot considered again.

"Her accursed grandfather deserved what was done him," Hendrie growled. "Ever he hated Diarmad for loving his daughter. For it, he lost all and is dead." He halted. "Here your door."

Curiosity over Marguerite's sire once more roused, Theriot said, "Diarmad the Mad was your friend?"

"He was. And ere you ask, it was not jest nor taunting that he was mad."

"You say he was not right of mind?"

"Not when those he loved were threatened. But neither was he of two minds as said some who could not reconcile the berserker with one of great intellect and faith who, outside of battle, was fair and kind—firmly, rather than cruelly, correcting those who offended."

"Then you believe he was but moved by bloodlust."

"Bloodlust such as you have never seen. But though there were times I thought he might be ill of mind, methinks he was merely able to leave what needed leaving behind when threats were past—enjoying and praising the good out from beneath the dark of what had been. He knew to watch for danger, but he did not live backward. He lived forward."

"I thank you for enlightening me," Theriot said and opened the door.

"I do not understand why you did not slay Edgar," Hendrie gave him pause. "It would serve as well as delivering him to your king."

"Since William does not wish the death of so noble an enemy, it would not serve as well as ensuring Edgar lives out his days in such a way he no longer threatens my liege's rule. As you saw this eve, the prince but requires subduing."

"This eve, but a third attempt could prove your death."

"If it is necessary to preserve my life, I shall finish him, but only then."

"Ye are not like other Normans."

Theriot hesitated at the realization they conversed as if one had not twice put a blade in the other and the other had not blinded this one. "That sounds a compliment, one I would like better if it did not reflect poorly on those of my countrymen who have caused untold suffering."

Hendrie grunted. "Caused and continue to cause, but Normans are not alone in sowing pain." In answer to Theriot's frown, he said, "There is a difference between surrender and doing what is best for all, and I believe English acceptance of Norman rule will do more good than bad." He sighed. "Edgar and those who believe he can do what he cannot must abandon hope."

"Your king supports his bid for the throne," Theriot reminded him.

"So it *appears.*"

Emphasis on that last further confirmed Malcolm did what needed doing to ensure he gained the wife he wanted.

"Untold suffering," Hendrie mused. "We are hopeful beings, believing once we are past this current upheaval our world will find its center again—as if ever it had a center to return to. Unfortunately, it is but relative calm between the waves."

"You surprise," Theriot said.

"When you have far more years behind you than ahead, D'Argent, more you will accept what we suffer in this life is but a different version of what others endured before us and others shall endure when we are gone."

Theriot narrowed his lids and more clearly saw the colors of the plaid draping the man's brown tunic, as well as long hair and beard of deep red. "Had I not suffered much at your hands, I might think you a priest, Hendrie."

The Scotsman chuckled. "Better I like the company of fellow soldiers and swing of blades than the ranks of priests and recitation of scripture. And revelry…"

Also a weakness of Theriot, though since crossing the channel, his responsibilities had been too great to indulge as often as once he had.

Realizing the desire for vengeance against this man lessened, Theriot guessed for this his sire had said, *Know your enemy.* His uncle had said it as well but assigned the words a different meaning. Whereas Hugh taught his pupils the necessity of learning as much as possible about one's opponent to more easily defeat him in battle, Godfroi had impressed on his sons and nephew the possibility of averting battle if they sought to know their opponent first as a man whose motivations might prove the same as their own.

"Chevalier," the Scotsman said, "I did what I had to do to live."

Was that an apology for the damage done eyes that had yet to recover sight though Hendrie had recovered from the blade dealt him? It sounded one.

"As did I," Theriot said and closed the door.

FRENZIED KNOCKING BROUGHT Marguerite to sitting. The candles left burning for Meg's return from the chapel continuing to light the chamber, she saw the door shudder as knocks sounded again.

"Margaret!"

She sprang off her pallet, donned her robe, and opened the door.

Edgar pushed past her. "Where is my sister?"

"At prayer in the chapel. Is something amiss?"

He halted before the bed and stood unmoving as if certain Meg would appear there. Then his shoulders slumped and chin dropped so suddenly Marguerite was struck by the morbid thought if William of Normandy removed the threat of this young man by beheading, it would be as quickly as that.

"All is amiss!" he groaned and wrapped his arms around his head.

She stepped forward. "Sit while I go for your sister."

He dropped his arms, turned to her. "I am lost, Lady. Just as all fail me, I fail myself, again and again earning the scorn of my lessers—worse, my enemies."

She gestured at the chair. "I will not be long—"

"I weary of my sister's prayers. They go nowhere! And I am sick unto death of Malcolm who thinks himself my sire." His voice cracked, then he began to weep.

Marguerite took his arm and drew him to a chair near the

brazier. Elbows atop knees, head in hands, brokenly he revealed exactly what was amiss.

Fearing Theriot might have been injured since Dubh had not been allowed to aid him, Marguerite dropped to her knees beside him, but before she could demand assurance the chevalier was well, he said bitterly, "Bested by a blind man who is still a better warrior than I. And further Malcolm punishes me by returning the D'Argent dagger to that Norman."

She gasped. "The king allows him a weapon?"

He jerked his chin. "You see! He who is to become my brother—not my father!—treats me even less his equal."

Because he was nowhere near Malcolm's equal, Marguerite thought, and he would not be even if all aligned to place England's crown on his head.

"Oh, Lady, I tire of this life! Sometimes I think better I was not born, other times it occurs there is a solution to that."

It took her a moment to accept that was what it sounded, then fearing Edgar would take his life, she set a hand atop the one on his knee. "That is no solution. You have far more courage than that. Had you not, you would not have escaped William to deliver your mother and sisters to Scotland, and likely all those who remain of your line would be locked away until death. Now your sister is much loved, will soon be queen, and should the Lord bless her and Malcolm with children, they will have a claim to the English throne. All because of you."

His moist eyes searched hers as if to confirm she spoke true. And mostly she did. Though he gave her little reason to defend him, she could not refuse what he needed in this moment. Doubtless, it had been more in his interest than any other's he had approached Malcolm for aid, but it had presented greater risk to bring his womenfolk with him.

"Even if you cannot take back what was stolen, Prince Edgar, you have made it possible for future generations to right the wrong done your family."

His breath stirred the air between them. "I am grateful for your kindness, especially since I have given you little cause to grant such."

Hopeful she had moved him away from the ungodly and irreversible solution to his misery, she said, "As I am certain the Lord would like you to draw near Him, I think you ought to seek your sister in the chapel."

The sorrow in his eyes was a beautiful thing compared to the usual anger and bitterness, but something else entered there, and more fully when he lowered his gaze to her mouth.

Abruptly, Marguerite stood and crossed to the door.

He followed. "Were I that Norman, would I have been permitted to kiss you, Lady Marguerite?"

Though tempted to deny she would allow Theriot that intimacy, she turned and said, "Were you that chevalier, very possible."

His jaw convulsed. "He should have slain me."

"And would have were he not honorable."

He nodded slowly. "A rare thing for a Norman."

And a prince, she longed to say of one who had sought to steal upon a blind man. "Methinks no more rare than for a Scotsman or Englishman," she said, then before he could take offense, added, "I believe a friend made of Sir Theriot would better serve than an enemy."

His jaw convulsed. "Were it so, 'tis too late now."

"Perhaps not. If you—"

Footsteps on the stairs quieted her and quickly moved him onto the landing.

No sooner did Malcolm appear than he halted. "Why are you not at prayer with your sister, Edgar?"

"I go to her now," the Aetheling said and squeezed past.

When he was gone, Malcolm continued forward. "The price I pay for My Pearl," he grumbled. "Edgar is fortunate no price is too high."

Marguerite's heart swelled over how happy Meg made one who deserved something pure and beautiful.

"I had hoped you still awake so I might tell what transpired this eve," he said when he halted before her.

"Edgar confessed."

His eyebrows rose. "Unexpected."

"'Tis. Now tell me how Sir Theriot fares. And is it true you returned his dagger?"

"He is without injury, having once more proven his superior training and conducted himself better than I would have had Edgar played that deadly game with me. And, aye, as he took the dagger from the prince and did not retaliate as few would fault him for doing, I allowed him to keep it." He sighed. "It is the least owed one whose protection I can ensure only if I put him under lock and key."

"I believe him worthy of your trust."

"Better than many a man." He frowned. "Including Baron Roche's men. Did Edgar tell they kept watch for him?"

She gasped. "If he did, I could not know it for how broken his words once he fell to weeping."

Malcolm's head bobbed. "He wept?"

"He did. Though he is mostly unlikable, as you know, it is hard to fall from a life of great privilege and the expectation of greater privilege—and more so for having been little more than a boy when circumstances required a man challenge the one who toppled him."

"I do know, and how long, arduous, and bloody the climb back up. But if Edgar is to have a good future now he no longer has the excuse of being a boy, either he must yield to wise counsel or adjust his expectations."

She nodded.

"Ye ought know, Marguerite, not only did Roche's men aid Edgar, but their excuse for doing so—the wish to return to their liege and revenge for the one Sir Theriot slew—led to the revelation it was that baron who returned you to Scotland. Certes, Sir Theriot knew the name."

Wishing she had made a greater effort to reveal the rest of her tale that would explain how she had recognized Theriot and inform him of events regarding his family, Marguerite determined that on the morrow she would reveal whatever he had not unearthed.

"I know you care for Sir Theriot, but of what depth are your feelings?" Malcolm asked.

She blinked. "Of a depth I wish they were not."

"For that, you reject Colban."

"A year past, I believe I would have been satisfied to be his wife, but it seems very wrong to accept him whilst feelings for another are so present."

"Mayhap you just need more time, Sparrow."

Deciding to move the conversation elsewhere, she said, "I think you must return Baron Roche's men."

"I agree. Once I determine what to do with Sir Theriot—and I will soon—I shall send them back across the border." He kissed her brow. "Return to yer rest."

They parted, and when she resettled on her pallet, she began rehearsing what she would tell Theriot.

CHAPTER TWENTY-TWO

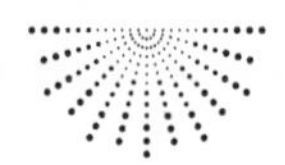

The only thing normal about this day was functional restoration of his vision remained elusive. Still, it was a better day, even if only for the return of the D'Argent dagger.

Answering King Malcolm's invitation to join him at the training yard, Theriot lengthened his stride as he moved toward the iron door, morning's light allowing him to make sense of shapes and colors and Dubh at his side occasionally nudging him to aid in avoiding the unseen.

"Sir Theriot!"

He turned.

The shape of the woman was immediately apparent for the color of her gown. "Princess Cristina," he said when she halted before him.

Since there had been no rebuke in her voice, he guessed either she was unaware of the encounter with her brother last eve, or her need for attention outweighed what otherwise would be deemed an affront.

"I came to pray with you," she said.

Narrowing his lids, he was pleased her blue gown sharpened

further and he could make some sense of a face more round than oval. "Your brother is well with that?"

She made a sound of distress. "He does not know, though I understand you give him more cause to disapprove."

"I but defended myself."

"So my sister says, though our mother… Well, Edgar is her favorite, is he not?"

It did not surprise. Most often an aged parent's fate rested in the hands of sons who were better able to govern their lives compared to females dependent on the good graces of male kin.

"Sir Theriot!" she exclaimed. "What happened to your hand?"

He flexed what should have blistered but had not. Though it pained less than last eve, he had rewrapped it this morn. "Miscalculating the placement of a lit lantern, I took hold of its panes. Now as I am for the training yard, perhaps we can pray later."

"Oh," she breathed, then said, "Though gently born, I confess to curiosity over a warrior's training. If you give your word you will not reveal me to my mother, I shall join you."

As Dubh pressed her head up beneath Theriot's hand as if to ease his tension, he said, "Then come."

Shortly, he settled his arms on the top rail of the training yard's fence and, turning his face from the woman whose accompaniment had set many to murmuring, made a count of those preparing to practice at arms. A score at least.

"It seems," Malcolm said low on Theriot's other side, "my betrothed's sister is even less keen on entering the Church than on the day past. Might you consider a bride of royal blood, Chevalier?"

Lest this unwelcome exchange was overheard by Cristina, Theriot did not scorn the suggestion but said, "My path is different from yours, Your Grace."

"I am glad to hear it." Malcolm cleared his throat. "Today's practice is with the two-handed sword. You are acquainted with it?"

"More I am versed with the single-handed, but I can swing both with deadly accuracy."

Rather, I could, he silently corrected.

When the king did not comment, Theriot guessed his thoughts had gone the same direction. If they did, it was not for long.

After commanding the contests to begin, Malcolm said, "Despite injury to your eyes, your skills are impressive, Sir Theriot. Not only do I marvel over the keen senses demonstrated in the glen, but your facility with stealth in besting Edgar last eve. I wonder at your training."

Seeing no reason not to enlighten him, Theriot said, "It was taught me by my uncle whose lessons were as often in the day as the night. He impressed on me that stealth is not merely hiding among and negotiating shadows, making it an instrument of defense, but using those shadows to transform it into an instrument of offense."

"This I know, as do all warriors of worth."

"Aye, it is obvious, but difficult in practice. As one's natural inclination is to make it defensive first, offensive second, most are more concerned with remaining hidden than using the advantages of nature and the presence or absence of light to advance more quickly on their targets."

"Continue, Sir Theriot."

"Great stealth is attending to what is felt beneath one's feet to sooner be aware of the approach of enemies on foot and astride, attending to scents and the direction the air moves to ensure one's own scents do not carry, learning the calls of creatures to use them as cover and communicate with others across the distance—and discern when the enemy does the same." He paused. "That is what my uncle taught me and what my keen senses allowed me to better."

He sensed the turning of the king's mind, but when Malcolm spoke no more, shifted his attention to what he could make of the clashes from what was barely seen and what others told by way of words and shouts.

~

SHE HAD MORE than slept the night through, and she was not alone in doing so. Meg remained curled beneath her coverlet when Marguerite departed the chamber past the hour of breaking fast. What time the princess and Edgar finished beseeching God's guidance she did not know, but the candles had consumed their wicks when the princess returned, her fumbling having awakened Marguerite.

Now, hunger satisfied, courage fortified with further practice at what she would say to Theriot, Marguerite was disappointed to find his hut empty. If he had ventured to the training yard whence came the sound of steel on steel, no privacy would be had there. Had he gone to the glen, little privacy there since both required an escort.

She considered awaiting him in the hut, but impatience had her moving among the castle folk and ascending the wall overlooking the training yard.

Theriot was below, Dubh on one side, Cristina the other.

Jealousy rippled through Marguerite and flowed when the princess touched his arm and nodded at two opponents wielding swords of such size few men could long swing them without the support of their second hand. Not so Malcolm who was one of those Theriot appeared to watch, slight movements of his head matching the dance of opponents. Here evidence his vision had improved?

Cristina leaned nearer, and more animatedly than Marguerite had believed possible, spoke as if describing what he could not see.

"Cease this jealousy!" Marguerite rebuked herself, and when her words caused a man-at-arms patrolling the wall to look around, apologetically shook her head. When she returned her regard to those below, she saw Theriot nod in response to something Cristina said. And was that annoyance flitting across his face?

It was wrong to hope that, but the jealous side of her wished it, and she was glad Cristina departed a quarter hour later.

Marguerite remained atop the wall until Theriot, joined by Malcolm whose garments were fouled, also withdrew.

They looked friends, Dubh trotting between them. And she wished it so, that Theriot would stay and—

"Enough," she whispered, and as they neared the iron gate, leaned forward to keep them in sight. It was then she noticed Theriot's left hand was wrapped though Malcolm had assured her he was uninjured last eve. Also of note was he used the cloth returned to him.

When they passed through the iron door, she began her descent of the wall.

Their long strides carrying them a dozen feet beyond the steps before she reached the bottom, Malcolm's words made her falter. "As you know, you gained my respect when we were in the glen and you knew we were watched ere I did, and when you slew one of our attackers—"

"With your aid," Theriot interrupted.

"I but called out instructions," Malcolm said, then continued, "You have gained the respect of many of my men, and now having bested Edgar who was armed as you were not..." He clicked his tongue. "Though some of my Scots, perhaps a few of my Normans, would resist your instruction in stealth, I believe most would be receptive."

Theriot halted, then Dubh, followed by Marguerite behind and Malcolm ahead. When the latter turned back, Theriot said, "It sounds you suggest this prisoner train your men."

"So I do, to my benefit as well as yours."

"Mine?"

"Methinks it would ease your longing to be no mere onlooker in the games of warriors. As for being my prisoner, you must agree other than not being permitted to depart, you are that in name only."

Theriot was slow to respond as if considering the proposal. "Though I am grateful to be accorded much freedom and a measure of trust, there are three problems with what you suggest. The first is that as long as William has my oath, he would consider it treasonous were I to aid in bettering skills that might one day be used against Normans. The second is I would think it treasonous."

Malcolm grunted. "The third problem?"

"As earlier told, the training I received was excellent, but much of what you perceive to be superior to what is already available to your men is likely due to my keen senses."

"Much, but not all, Chevalier. As we both know, instincts that are lacking can be sharpened. My thinking is—who better to sharpen the dull ones than a man whose own are very sharp?"

"Even so, the first two problems persist."

"Would they persist if I agreed to release you in two months' time?"

Theriot stiffened. "I will not strike such a bargain with you."

Fearing the king's anger, Marguerite tensed, but Malcolm said, "I am not surprised you hold close your oath to William. Though I am not pleased, I respect your integrity."

Theriot inclined his head. "I thank you. Now I would ask how much longer ere you decide what is to be done with me."

"There the question, but also this—what do you feel for my ward?"

Grateful the bustle about the bailey masked her gasp, Marguerite waited.

"What should I feel for the woman responsible for my loss of sight?" Theriot said. And now she almost wished him as unheard as she, but better she was left in no doubt about his feelings.

"I sought to match her with my physician," Malcolm said, "but I believe she is in love with you."

Marguerite nearly groaned aloud.

"Then I am sorry for her, and would advise she accept your choice of a husband and forget this Norman who but bides his time until he can return to his family and the company of women of his own kind."

"As ye know, she is as Norman as she is Scottish."

"King Malcolm, if your delay in deciding my fate has anything to do with her, you waste time, and again I ask that if you will not permit me to return to England, you send word to my family."

The king sighed. "Good day, Chevalier," he said and strode opposite.

Theriot remained unmoving as if he watched Malcolm, and when the smithy proved the king's destination, resumed his stride with Dubh at his side.

Of course he cannot entirely forgive me, Marguerite lamented as he walked a path mostly unobstructed though more castle folk were about their duties now. *Of course he can have no great feeling for me.* She touched lips his had touched. *But he does not hate me. I must be content with that. And all the sooner I will be once I persuade Malcolm to allow me to return home.*

Though certain the only way to gain his permission was to agree to the accompaniment of guards lest her kin yet sought to harm her, it was more acceptable than remaining at the palace. But before her departure that she hoped would sooner see Theriot released, she would reveal what he deserved to know.

CHAPTER TWENTY-THREE

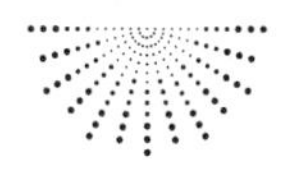

She was here. And he knew it ahead of Dubh.

Theriot dropped the cloth unwound from his hand and turned from the sideboard. "Enter!" he called a moment ahead of her knock.

She opened the door and was greeted by Dubh.

As Marguerite leaned down to pet the hound, Theriot strove to make sense of her, and as was increasingly apparent, better that was done with the right eye. Her gown was dark orange woven of threads whose sheen made it appear many shades of that color, and the rich brown draping her shoulders looked more a short mantle than loose hair.

"It is Marguerite."

"This I know." Still unwilling to alert any to his improved sight that was too little to give much hope of full restoration, but enough he had some hope further improvement could aid in escaping Dunfermline, he said, "Had it been any other than you or the king, Dubh would not have welcomed you in that manner." He followed the dog's languid return to the fire pit. "She has good senses."

"She does." There was disappointment in her voice. "I just wish..."

"What? My sight restored?"

"Much I pray for that." She took a step forward. "I did not know your hand was injured last eve."

No surprise she had been told what happened. What surprised was she saw the injury he would not think obvious absent the binding. Had she seen it ahead of his return to the hut? While he was at the training yard?

Having been once more reduced to less than an observer of those who wielded arms, the struggle to control his frustration could have distracted him from the sensation of being watched by one other than those among whom he stood.

If Marguerite had been on the wall, was she there when he departed? He could not know, the activity in the bailey and Malcolm's proposal that Theriot give training in stealth having caused him to neglect keeping the fingers of his unnatural sense stretched long and spread wide.

Had she been near, she would have heard her king question what Theriot felt for her and the answer meant to end such talk —as well as Malcolm's suggestion Marguerite loved his prisoner and Theriot's rejection of her. Hopefully, she had not been present since he did not wish her to—

What? he silently demanded. *If she does feel deeply for you and believes your greatest regard for her is attraction, more easily she will forget you. Hence, what is cruel now is kind later.*

"How were you injured?" she asked.

Returning the colors and shape of her to focus, he rotated his palm outward. "When I reached to put out the lamp to render Edgar as sightless as I, what I thought the handle were hot panes. Not badly burned, but sore."

She hesitated, said, "Though I am sorry for what he did, I am glad it led to the return of your dagger."

"And I am glad you came."

"You are?"

Hearing hope in her voice, he said, "I learned the Saxons who kept watch for Edgar outside the stable serve Michel Roche and that baron entrusted them to deliver you to Dunfermline."

"As Malcolm warned me," she said. "Now you know how I recognized you in the village."

"I do—that Marguerite of Dunfermline, who has a lovely voice when not coarse from disuse, was the mute Margaret of the Rebels of the Pale." He turned to the sideboard. "After I tend my hand, I would know what you have yet to tell." As he rubbed salve into his palm, he heard the door close, the rasp of her slippers, and creak of the chair.

Theriot moved to the seat across from hers and dropped into it. As he rebandaged his hand, the hound stretched out beside him.

"That is the same cloth I returned to you," Marguerite said.

"It is, though your scent is long gone."

Hearing her breath catch, he reminded himself, *Cruel now, kind later,* and tucked the end of the strip beneath the crossings. "I imagined you wore it around your neck the same as I, though now I make a bandage of it just as you did for my eyes."

He did not need to see her face to know it brightened, nor was he surprised when she averted by asking, "Of what import that ragged cloth?"

He sat back. "Are we to trade answers again? If so, you should know I have fewer to give than you."

She cleared her throat. "Since much is owed you, no trade is necessary."

"Then begin."

"Already I told what happened when I sought to return my mother to Dunfermline. What was left unsaid is that after I fled my grandfather's home, I was overtaken. If not for the aid of Saxons who believed me one of their own set upon by

Normans, my kin would have avenged themselves on this half-breed, giving me to Patrick of Ireland who would have acted on his desire for me, perhaps even sold me into slavery."

The ache in Theriot's burned palm alerting him to the fist he made, he said, "Continue."

"You know the Saxons who saved me as the ones who later risked all to enter the D'Argent camp following their loss at Stafford—Vitalis, Zedekiah, and Em. I did not fear them as much as I did those of my blood, but since there is the Norman about my voice as well as the Scots who raid into England, I thought it safest they believe me mute. Though I wished to return to Scotland, as I was distant from the border and all about were Normans of greater danger than Saxons, I remained under Vitalis's protection and used my healing skills to aid the rebels."

"That was before the resistance took the city of York from my king's men, was it not?"

"It was, and I believed that undertaking which caused the Aetheling to depart Malcolm's court and join his forces with Saxon rebels and Danes was the opportunity needed to put England behind me. But despite the resistance's victory, many were injured. As I was needed, I assured myself there was time aplenty to show myself to Edgar." She sighed. "There was not, his victory short-lived. Had York not been so ravaged by fire it could offer no protection for the resistance, perhaps the Danes would not have withdrawn their support and the Aetheling would not have fled with his men ahead of William's armies."

"So you remained with the rebels, accompanying them to Stafford where they sought to take another stand."

"And failed," she whispered. "As you know, many Rebels of the Pale died in challenging William on that battlefield, and not only was Em injured, she was seen by the Norman whose bonds of slavery she had escaped."

"Sir Raymond Campagnon," Theriot named the man.

"Evil," she said. "Do you recall assisting me into the saddle ere I departed camp with Sir Dougray to find a physician distant from your countrymen?"

Too well, he thought and said, "I do. Thus, the face I believed I might never know *is* known to me."

"Is it?" Her voice pitched higher. "It was dark, and I was hooded."

"Still I saw you. My eyes are..." His jaw nearly locked. "Once they were very sharp."

She swallowed loudly. "I looked back when we left camp and you raised a hand as if you knew I looked upon you. Do you remember that as well?"

Though he wanted to feign ignorance, he nodded. "I do."

"I told you it felt as if I knew you before I met you. That was the first time I felt that, and though I named myself foolish and fanciful, often I thought on you." She went silent, and he knew he was expected to respond to her confession, but he did not know what to say.

What seemed minutes passed, then she said, "We found a physician for Em in Derbyshire at Stavestone Castle. Its lord, Baron Roche—"

"This part of the tale I know," he interrupted. "That at last my half-brother met the man who sired him, hardly was Em recovered than he had to take her from Stavestone to keep her from Campagnon, and it was necessary to entrust your safekeeping to Roche."

"How do you know all that?" she exclaimed.

"After Dougray delivered Em to our oldest brother so arrangements could be made to send her to Normandy where slavery is outlawed, he returned to our king's service at York. He told me what transpired, and I saw he was changed from the vengeful warrior who hated Saxons—all for love of a rebel."

"And her love for him," Marguerite said.

That gave Theriot pause. Might he rise above his own loss

the same as Dougray whom he had encouraged to leave the past behind? Might love prove as great a healer for him as—?

My circumstances are different, he reminded himself. *The woman responsible for my loss is not—can never be—the remedy.*

"Continue," she prompted.

"William summoned Dougray and revealed Campagnon had petitioned him to aid in the recovery of the slave he believed hidden at Wulfen Castle. Despite my king's unwillingness to abolish slavery in England for the revenue that funds armies, he finds the practice abhorrent. Thus, he told he would accompany Campagnon south to see the miscreant's property returned to him, and that warning gave Dougray time to get Em away. What I do not know is what followed."

"Then I will tell you. After Baron Roche delivered me to Wulfen Castle, Dougray returned and Em refused to flee across the sea."

Theriot jerked. "Then both were present when William arrived?"

"They were, and your king gave Dougray the opportunity to best Campagnon at arms to gain Em's freedom."

Theriot would have been confident of his brother's victory if not for the loss of his arm. "I listen, Lady."

"Your brother was victorious."

He breathed out relief.

"But before he could put finish to Campagnon, one of the knave's men attacked him. Though Dougray bled out that one's life, it gave Campagnon time to recover. I cannot know if your brother would have himself recovered in time to preserve his life, but I think it possible."

Theriot frowned. "What say you?"

"Baron Roche took no chance on losing his only child. Much to William's displeasure, he slew Campagnon."

The love of a father—rather, fathers, Theriot amended. Though Dougray had wrestled with his illegitimacy despite acceptance by their mother's husband, good had come of it. "What of the king, Marguerite?"

"He allowed your brother to wed Em."

Theriot nearly smiled. His three brothers had taken Saxon wives as it was possible he would have done one day if not for... He shifted his jaw. "And Michel Roche?"

"William pardoned him."

Theriot nodded. "How is it Dougray's sire was the one who provided you an escort to Dunfermline—and not for many months thereafter?"

He heard her draw breath. "Feelings had grown between us. Though still I wished to return home, when he offered the position of keeper of his household so we might determine the way forward, I agreed."

Though Theriot told himself he had no cause for jealousy, he felt it.

"Not only did I wish to discover if what we felt could be more than attraction, but Stavestone was nearer Scotland. However, hardly had we returned than the harrying began, making it unsafe to travel north and providing more time for us to become better acquainted." She replenished her breath. "Though my attraction for him grew and kisses were exchanged, I did not feel love as he was moving toward. Not wishing to break again a heart first broken by your mother, I revealed my truth to him."

"His response?"

"He was understanding and promised to return me to Scotland once the harrying was done. He kept his word, ensuring my safety by including among my escort a Norman long in England the same as he—Stephen, the one you slew."

"The night Edgar fled through the village." Unable to keep anger from his voice, Theriot lowered his lids, shook his head. "Had I not sent the contingent after him—"

"You could not know he would risk harming his people,

Theriot. As for Stephen, Edgar and I are more responsible for his death than you who but defended your life, just as we would be responsible for your death if…"

Theriot understood. "The Aetheling would have left me to the villagers who would have killed me for being a Norman. It is good you recognized me."

"I am glad you think it so."

She was remembering what Hendrie had wrought. "If my sight does not recover, I do not know how I shall live without it, but I am thankful I yet breathe."

"As am I."

He hesitated to return to what she felt for him, but perhaps as much for him as for her, reminded himself what was cruel now would be kind later. "Malcolm believes you are in love with me."

Abruptly, she stood. "What needed telling is told. Now this half-Norman lady who would fare better to look to another for a husband has other matters to attend to."

Then she *had* been present when Malcolm pried at Theriot's feelings.

She was at the door before he overtook her with speed that could have shamed him were he not well-acquainted with the hut—and that he stayed ahead of the hound who followed. Closing a hand over Marguerite's shoulder, he turned her and set her against the door.

"Release me," she said above the whine of the dog uncertain as to whom it should side with.

Theriot wanted to restate it was impossible to feel greatly for her and let that be the end of this, but he could not.

Lord, he sent heavenward, *surely I ought to be able to choose whom I love.*

"Release me," she repeated.

Peering into her nearly featureless face, he said, "You were on the wall when Malcolm and I returned to the bailey. You overheard our conversation."

Breath expanded her chest against his. "I did and was horrified my king suggested I love you."

"Then you do not?"

"I...wish I did not." That answer was enough, those words and her tone making it sound as if her heart was breaking as she had feared breaking Michel Roche's.

"Certes, you ought not."

"This I know, that you could never—" She gasped when the hand he had pressed to the door filled its palm and fingers with the curve of her face. "What do you, Theriot?"

Sensing an easing of tension about Dubh, he said, "I wish to know how well I saw the face beneath the hood that night in the wood. Will you allow it?"

"If...you will not regret it."

He would, but he slid his thumb atop the smooth skin of her heated cheek, then to the outer corner of her eye. When she lowered her lids, he discovered the lashes were very long and fine and great their reach.

"Your eyes are larger than glimpsed the night I assisted you into the saddle. What color are they?"

"Green," she whispered.

"The same shade as mine?"

"I..."

Her apprehension a reminder the damage was not only to his vision but the appearance of eyes over which clouds gathered, he said, "You have met my brother, Guarin."

"I have, and great your resemblance to each other."

"The green of my eyes is darker than his."

"Then I believe yours and mine are a good match."

Throat tightening, he traced the lines of her nose. "This fits what I recall," he murmured, then moved to her mouth with which he was most familiar both by what was seen in the night and felt beneath his own. He traced the dip between the arches, followed the curve to one corner, and continued down and around her lower lip.

"It is fuller than thought," he said, then intensely aware his breathing matched hers, moved to her chin. "Some stubborn here, Marguerite of Dunfermline."

"You do not sound surprised."

He was not, nor by the longing to kiss her again—and thoroughly. He knew he should end this, but it was as if he was bound to her as once he had been to the posts of the bed.

He slid his fingers up the side of her face and over her eyebrows. "There is more to them than seen, and your brow is very smooth—except for this." He traced something near her hairline. "A scar."

Marguerite suppressed a shudder. Before Theriot, she had not believed her skin so sensitive. To a feathering touch—aye—but not one so perceptible. *"Is* it a scar?" she whispered, then fingers brushing his, explored it. "As I do not recall its getting, I must have been quite young."

"It does not compare to those on my face," he said.

Which numbered four as seen when she tended him whilst he was unconscious. Despite the shadow now between them, enough light tumbled through the window to allow her to study his visage. "Still, yours are not unsightly. Do you remember how they were got?"

"I remember."

When she set a finger on his jaw, he jerked. Finding a ridge beneath the many silvered whiskers of his beard, she followed its course past the dimple to his ear. "This one?" she asked.

"The slash of a dagger. I was ten and eight—yet a squire—when I stole to a tavern and challenged a chevalier for the attentions of a serving woman. He prevailed and afterward bought me a tankard of ale." A smile flitted across his mouth. "I thought it fair compensation—until I had to explain to my sire and uncle how I came by that cut."

"Was your punishment harsh?"

"It was, but not so much I did not repeat that adventure."

"You were rebellious," Marguerite said and thought how strange they conversed of such things standing in an attitude more appropriate for kissing—as if both knew they should distance themselves but could not.

"My uncle, Hugh, would agree since it was his wrath I most often stirred. Though his instruction shaped me into a warrior, and I am grateful for what it cost him in time and patience, it was not possible to like him for more than hours at a time."

"Why?"

"He was a hard man. Beyond his training, the only thing to recommend him was the great care he had for my sire. If he loved his wife and son, it was barely evident, and he left none in doubt of his dislike of my half-brother."

"He did not train Dougray?"

"He trained him—for my sire who insisted on giving his wife's son their surname."

Marguerite moved her finger to a ragged-edged scar near his left temple. "This one?"

"A rock thrown by the brother of a boy I knocked senseless when he besmirched my mother's reputation."

"How so?"

A muscle in his jaw convulsed. "The least of what he named her was wanton."

"Then that was the least of what he deserved." She touched the crescent-shaped scar bracketing his right eye. "This one?"

"A hawk won in a game of dice when I was twenty. I should not have unhooded the bird amid the revelry of drunken men. It is good its vicious beak did not..."

His words trailed off, and Marguerite was certain he had

nearly expressed gratitude the hawk had not taken his eye. "I am sorry," she said what could not be said enough.

Now he would draw away, as told by the narrowing of clouded eyes and the curve gone from his lips, but he rasped, "Marguerite." Then his fingers were in her hair—pushing deep, pressing against her scalp, tilting her face toward his.

She could have pushed him away, but she could no more resist this than could he whose resolve ought to be stronger than hers.

Pray, Lord, not only attraction, she silently beseeched as his head descended. *Despite what he has lost, let him feel more for me than desire. Let him stay in my Scotland. Let it become* our *Scotland. Much more I could love him if he would let me.*

"Theriot," she whispered.

As if that was the permission he awaited, he covered her mouth with his. It began as a gentle kiss, but when he angled his head, it became more.

The first time they had shared this intimacy, she had believed it could not be done better. She had been wrong. Determined to quench her own thirst lest this end too soon, she wrapped her arms around his neck.

He groaned, drew his hands from her hair, and cupped her face.

Marguerite heard their breathing, indistinguishable one from the other until he moved his lips to her cheek, then her ear.

Clearly, she heard her breath.

Clearly, she heard his.

Distantly, she heard herself say, "Stay, Theriot."

Distantly, she heard him say, "Your face is mostly as remembered."

Those words in her ear making her shiver, she turned her mouth toward his, but he released her and stepped back.

Why? she wondered. *Because he fears it could become more than a kiss?*

"Regardless of whether my vision returns, this is all there is for us," he said.

She raised her lids. "I do not understand."

"I am attracted to you, even moved to affection, but it is not love as you profess to feel. Thus, just as you did not wish to break Michel's heart, I would not break yours."

Too late, she thought. Hating the weak of her knees, she straightened from the door. "Is this revenge?"

His gaze flickered. "It is kindness clothed in cruelty. Like Michel, you want what you ought not, and better this is done now than later."

"Of course it is," she breathed.

As she turned to the door, Dubh rose and looked between her and Theriot. The hound did not like what was felt between them and likely questioned her place that must seem less assured than moments earlier.

"Stay," Marguerite commanded and slipped outside. "Now I go home," she whispered and went in search of Malcolm.

CHAPTER TWENTY-FOUR

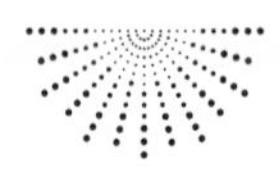

It had been the right thing to do—and for both, as evidenced by his reluctance to reject Marguerite's feelings when he followed her to the door, his willingness to acquaint her with his past, and another kiss.

Now with his back pressed to the floor, hands clasped behind his neck, Theriot eased burning abdominal muscles on a long exhale.

Once more, Dubh growled where she sat beside the door from which she had not moved since Marguerite's departure. As if displeased with what was told her mistress, she refused to draw near.

"Oui, I lied," Theriot rasped. The thought of becoming a burden to the woman whose heart sought to hold his was weighty, but it would be unbearable if frustration and anger at being unable to be a man in full, providing for and protecting her, caused him to break her heart in ways worse than denying he returned her love.

"It is a lie, but for the best. When I depart, sooner she will let go of what she should not have taken hold of."

As I shall let go of her, he assured himself. But when he closed his eyes, an itch at his temple drew a hand to the scar whose getting he had not fully explained to Marguerite. The youth who had spoken against his mother had done more than name her wanton. He had called her a harlot.

Those privy to the love of Theriot's parents had marveled over the depth of their devotion, not only because of that act of indiscretion but loss of the use of Godfroi's legs in battle that should have made it impossible for their relationship to be more than one in which they tolerated each other.

More impossible than your own debility? he questioned. *More impossible than Marguerite being responsible for it?*

"How was it possible, sire?" he breathed.

Three, my son, Godfroi answered from afar. *Only three needed to make it possible—God, your mother, and me.*

Before he could further ponder that, Dubh thrust upright and began barking.

Her agitation of a strength that reminded Theriot of when the Aetheling sent Saxons here, he rebuked himself for so deeply delving his thoughts he was not the first to sense someone's approach. However, as he crossed the hut with the dagger in hand, he perceived what the hound did not—the one outside exuded no aggression.

A second knock sounded. "It is Prince Edgar."

Then further Dubh bettered him, sensing aggression he did not.

Theriot tossed open the door.

Surely seeing the D'Argent dagger, the Aetheling lurched back. "I come alone."

"For what?"

"As you are aware, King Malcolm believed a prayer vigil with my sister would be of benefit."

Angered he could not read a face that might reveal aggression the young man still did not exude, Theriot said, "And?"

"I come to ask for forgiveness of my trespasses."

"By order of the princess?"

Hesitation, then, "We draw attention. May I enter?"

"Armed?"

"Well...you are armed."

"I have cause to be."

The prince grunted. "As I am persuaded you are a Norman of integrity, I shall leave my weapons outside."

His discomfort was felt—and fear—but that was all. Determined not to lower his guard, Theriot said, "You may keep them on your person."

The rasp of a buckle went silent and Edgar entered.

Theriot closed the door. Pleased the prince halted amid the light come through the window, rendering his figure exceedingly visible though his tunic and mantle lost much of their color, he said, "Your sister ordered you to seek my forgiveness."

"She did not. Though she encouraged me to make it right with you, prayer brings me here. Whilst on my knees—Almighty, hers must be bruised!—over and again I beseeched the Lord to calm the storm and guide me to the shore." He pivoted, immediately came back around. "It remains distant, but I know I have wronged you. What you do not know is how much I have been—" He groaned. "Nay, I will not make excuses for my behavior."

Admirable if he remained true to himself, Theriot thought.

"Not that I need to, the indignity and losses I have suffered at the hands of Normans are surely obvious to all."

Theriot waited.

"In asking for your forgiveness, I give my word I will not unjustly pursue recompense from you. What say you?"

His trespasses too recent, Theriot was not of a mind to agree, but as the Aetheling sounded sincere, he said, "If that is truly in your heart, I shall begin moving toward forgiveness."

"Moving?" Edgar clipped.

"That is honesty, Prince, which is all I will give you."

The young man shifted his stance. "'Tis enough, though I hope for more in future."

"As do I. Now I thank you for coming and—"

"There is something else I would discuss. Ere prayer last eve, I spoke briefly with Lady Marguerite about what happened in the stable."

Theriot wished the mere speaking of her name did not cause his chest to constrict.

"She said better a friend made of you than an enemy."

"We are far from friendship," Theriot growled.

"This I know, but... As you have a care for my sisters, mayhap for their sakes you will give aid in better protecting them."

Theriot frowned. "How am I to do that?"

"As I think you know, I came late to warring. Had I received Wulfrith training or that of the D'Argents—"

"Edgar, if you suggest I train you, you are as unseeing as I—and forgetful. This injury was dealt me because you led a Norman contingent through a Saxon village."

"Which would not have happened had you not set them after me!"

"This I know, and that I am also responsible for what happened to the homes of those people—your people."

Edgar muttered something, then said, "As told, I came late to warring."

It being useless to point out that consideration of the welfare of one's people was not learned in a training yard, Theriot said, "I cannot aid you."

"Not in traditional warring, but what you did in the stable..."

Stealth training, just as Malcolm wished for his warriors. Though Theriot had been tempted to agree so his efforts might give one whom he increasingly admired a better chance of keeping his country from being devoured by William once he finished digesting England, his oath forbade him then. And now.

Even were he inclined to impart knowledge and skills he did not believe would gain Edgar a crown though they might enable him to stay ahead of his enemies without sacrificing others, he could not without forswearing his oath, which could prove of detriment to his family.

Prepared for the young man who came seeking forgiveness to forget his good intentions, Theriot shifted his grip on the dagger at his side. "To remain a Norman of integrity, I must keep the oath given my liege. Though I care for your sisters, I cannot aid you."

Edgar breathed in, Edgar breathed out. "I had to ask," he said and strode forward.

Theriot opened the door.

The prince paused on the threshold. "If now you question my sincerity in seeking absolution for my offenses, know it stands. Good day."

Then despite his refusal to give aid, there might be civility between them whilst Theriot remained at Dunfermline. A good thing, perhaps even answered prayer.

THOUGH IT WAS NOT REQUIRED THERIOT ANSWER the princess's summons, he had come. What *was* required was he yield his dagger upon entering the garden. He did not begrudge Malcolm the precaution. As with all things precious, one must guard what others might take whether by way of harm or theft.

Halting before the queen-to-be who wore a gown of pink where she perched on a bench, he dipped his head. "Princess."

"Take your ease beside me, Sir Theriot."

Keeping a reach between them that should satisfy the guards

around a garden of greater size than the one inside the palace's walls, he lowered.

"Though once more I wish to beseech the Lord on your behalf, first I would speak of Marguerite," she said.

As suspected, just as he thought possible his meeting with her brother would be discussed. "What of the lady?"

"With Malcolm's leave and accompanied by guards who shall remain with her, she has departed for her home in the village of Widden."

A good thing, he told himself.

"She has become dear to me, Sir Theriot."

"She is worthy of your friendship, as you are worthy of hers, Princess."

"Allow me to return the compliment by saying you are worthy of the same," she said, then groaned. "It is dishonest to name what she feels for you mere friendship."

Then Marguerite had confessed love for him? Or was this woman merely perceptive?

"Indeed, I would say what she feels is at least as great as what I feel for the king. And I do not believe her feelings are misplaced. Though they may not be returned in equal measure, I think there is mutual longing, meaning if—"

"If," he said sharply, causing her guards to tense. Drawing a deep breath, he heard again the answer come across the sea —*Only three needed to make it possible. God, your mother, and me.* Theriot wanted to believe the Almighty was a bridge between great division, but once again doubt.

"Chevalier?"

"If is a long reach." He hesitated, then decided to let her in. "And impossibly long should prayers for my healing remain unanswered."

"Unanswered?" she said with disbelief warranted only had he fully recovered his sight.

"Aye, as may be the fate of most prayers cast heavenward."

She gasped. "I am thinking even ere clouds came unto your eyes, you did not see well, Sir Theriot!"

Though her words offended, he regretted discomposing her. "Be assured, I know of my good fortune, Princess."

"Fortune? It is not—" She sighed. "Forgive me for speaking ere ensuring my words are pleasing to the Lord."

"I am the one who should seek forgiveness."

"Then we are both forgiven. Now walk with me amid this garden whose beauty can be known well beyond sight."

They rose. Though the guards surely disapproved of her taking his arm, Theriot knew she sought to ensure his ease of movement in this unfamiliar place. He did not as greatly fear the humiliation of stumbling since in sunlight he could make sense of paths running between beds of flowers, trees, and hedges, but still he believed it best not to reveal the world before him was no longer only dark amid light.

They walked in silence, during which he learned the garden's arrangement, location of guards, and boundaries that on one side was wall, two sides grass sloping away from the palace, and one side mostly dirt and rocks descending to the glen.

The princess halted. "God has been here...*is* here." She released him and swept a hand over a bush of lustrous green and blooms of purple. "Just as I believe every prayer is heard, from the unspoken to the shouted and ranted, I believe all are answered, even when one does not feel God's presence nor attend to His response. Hence, I submit what you think unanswered prayer for it failing to yield what you wish is God saying, *That is not My plan for you,* rather than, *Go your own way though it is distant from Mine.* It is Him saying, *That is not right for you now,* rather than, *Do what is right for you in this moment though it is wrong in the next."*

She replenished her breath. "Like others of my family, I struggle to accept not being given that for which beseechings have pained knees and cried eyes dry, but ever I cling to it being a better thing to endure the ache of what is denied than the disease of rejecting my heavenly Father's guidance."

Though her words squeezed into places made resistant these past months, not only did Theriot consider his own disappointment over prayers for the remedy of his loss but her people's disappointment over prayers for their losses.

"Alas, I thought the faith of the man for whom I pray daily was of good strength despite being shaken," the princess misinterpreted his silence. "I believed you, a Norman born into an honorable family of privilege, a warrior who survived Hastings without great injury or deformity, and a conqueror free of the oppression of the conquered, would embrace much evidence of answered prayer. Are you truly of the faith?"

"I believe in God." Though he intended to say no more, her extraordinary faith made him yield. "My parents' beliefs were passed to me and embraced—likely too easily for the many blessings I attributed to favor shown me by the Lord. Now..."

He lifted his face to the sky and thought how blue it was distant from where the sun hung. "Of late, much I ponder my uncle's beliefs. Though he acknowledged God's existence, he said only the deceived and desperate believe the Creator does more than look down upon His creation—that even if one committed every beat of his heart to prayer, God would not intervene. He told what people name blessings are the result of great effort, the kindness of others, chance, and good fortune, and he pointed out that if God is present and just, people of ill intent would not prevail over good."

"I have heard that argument," she said. "Still you pray, do you not?"

"In the hope God will intervene, showing Himself capable and willing to restore my vision, I continue to go to Him."

"Then He who ought not serve is made to serve as mere

reinforcement, the same as soldiers held in reserve lest those doing battle begin to fall."

That struck Theriot as very wrong—at first because she believed his regard for the Lord was so conditional, then because he gave her much cause.

"I fear you suffer from what afflicts Edgar," she said, reminding him of his meeting with her brother of which she might or might not be aware. "Whilst we dwelt at the court of King Edward, our every need and desire met and good futures assured, little was expected of us. And that was especially true of Edgar due to his age and that the king, being a poor administrator and no warrior, asked even less of his great nephew. For that, warring came to my brother only slightly better than faith which more often seems a shrug upon his shoulders than a mantle clasped close."

It was as the prince had told and of which there was much evidence, though his shortcomings were not the same as this D'Argent's. "Little may have been expected of your brother," Theriot said, "but that is not true of me."

"I know none should question the warrior of you, and I believe your faith stronger than my brother's though you entertain doubt, but as you told, much in your life came easy. For that, methinks you are afflicted the same as Edgar. Just as he was not seriously tested in his younger years, neither were you in such a way you had to look beyond yourself and others to rise above life's struggles—that previous to your terrible loss, the fires from which you emerged merely singed."

Theriot could not argue that.

"I do not believe it necessary for all to face life-changing adversity to grow faith of a strength that neither fails them nor the Lord, but others..." Her shoulders rose and fell. "It is arrogance to believe the bright of one's life a result of things beyond God's abilities and desires. And ungrateful to believe when bad things happen to the good it is proof God either does not heed prayer or does not exist. I think—nay, I *know*—the many blessings preceding the pain and the blessings yet to come are further proof of His existence and work in our lives."

Theriot curled fingers into the cloth cut from his tunic. Was she right? Though God had not prevented him from being blinded and might not restore his sight, previously had He kept all manner of weapons from slaying this warrior at Hastings and in the battles and encounters since—if not in answer to Theriot's prayers then those of his family?

As if the princess waded amid his thoughts, she said, "We may never learn why He shields us from one thing and not another, but He does answer prayer—in His way, in His time."

He wanted to believe it, to clasp his faith closer, but his thoughts returned to the multitude whose prayers had not been answered as hoped. "Would you speak the same to the people you left behind in England, Princess? Saxon prayers for a good outcome at Hastings had to be more impassioned than those of Normans who had all to gain from opponents with all to lose. In the years since, even greater the suffering of your people, especially innocents. How much more suffering before God answers them well? Or will He not, their conquering punishment for sins as my king claims?"

"It could be punishment. Much ungodliness in Saxon-ruled England, much ungodliness in Norman-ruled Normandy, much ungodliness in all the world. Regardless, though we may not agree with how God sets things right, we must trust in Him. Thus, were I given the opportunity to stand before my people, that I would tell them even were it received no better than my brother receives it."

That last inclining him to believe she was unaware he had met with Edgar, he started to reveal it, but she set a hand on his arm. "You question if your loss of sight is punishment?" she asked.

"I have, if not the blinding, then the absence of healing."

He saw her nod. "Only God knows, though perhaps in time you will as well if you look back with all honesty at the trail of months—even years—that lead from now to then."

"Perhaps."

"I am glad to know more of you, Sir Theriot. Now better I may go to the Lord on your behalf and that of Marguerite."

It having come back around to that lady, he said, "I will leave you to your prayers."

"Ere you go, allow me to give you one more thing to think on. When I arrived in Scotland with my family, I had little hope of making a life far from all I knew and loved, and yet God made a way for me by opening my eyes to the beauty of this country and the love others have to offer me. Though your eyes may never see what mine see, I believe your heart will—if you allow it."

Theriot stared at the golden-haired exile who wished him to remain in Scotland, trusting that God, Marguerite, and he could make it possible as God, Robine, and Godfroi had made their love possible, then started to turn away. However, recalling he had yet to tell what might encourage her as she sought to encourage him, he said, "Your brother came to me this day."

She gasped.

"He asked for forgiveness and told though you urged him to seek it, prayer at your side was what moved him."

"Merciful Father, I thought him barely present. Did you think him sincere?"

"More I believed him than not."

She sniffed. "Prayer not yet answered as I hope the Lord will answer it, but nearer. I thank you."

He inclined his head. "Good day, Princess."

CHAPTER TWENTY-FIVE

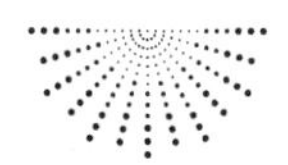

Widden, Dunfermline
Early Summer, 1070

Malcolm had not wanted to let her go, but tears evidencing her love for Theriot had moved him and, as expected, it was not alone she returned to her village.

Her sire having built his home on a hill that permitted him to keep watch on his liege's residence when Diarmad was absent, easily he had stayed apprised of those who came and went. In the rare instance he was needed, a spurring of his mount had quickly delivered him to Malcolm's side.

Hence, being so near the palace and far from isolated with neighbors a short walk away, four men-at-arms were not warranted to protect her. Still, she had not argued with Malcolm, being too grateful to distance herself from Theriot. But this day, three weeks following her departure, she would see him again.

He was still there, she was fairly certain since the guards who lodged in the barn were relieved by others once a week and she never heard talk of Malcolm sending the silvered chevalier back to England.

Standing taller, Marguerite told herself she must avoid Theriot for five days only. Once her king and Meg were wed and the celebration came to a close, she would leave again.

"Five days," she spoke aloud to the garden which had required much toiling to return it to life. It was too late in the season to yield much, but it would be plenty for one woman.

Two had Cannie not been slain, the thought slipped in nearly as often as thoughts of her parents.

"Lady!" a man-at-arms called.

She raised her skirts and, stepping stone to stone on the path laid by her father, hastened to the front of the cottage where a guard aided her in mounting.

After confirming all her packs were secured to the saddle, she looked out across summer-swept hills to the tower of Malcolm Canmore and wedding guests traveling the road before it, then nodded at those eager to end their monotonous guard over her.

Before they rode out of sight, she could not help looking around to ensure she returned to the cottage, just as done when last she departed to bring her mother home. Recalling it was Cannie who had encouraged her to always shine love back at that to which she wished to return, and that the older woman had also looked around, a sound of distress escaped Marguerite.

But I shall return, she told herself and determinedly imagined a time when another would be at her side and also look back.

When the cracks in this heart seal themselves, she thought, *I shall find someone else to love.*

"WHAT IS to be your answered prayer this day, Sir Theriot?"

Though often since Marguerite's departure the princess

asked it of him, and he revealed prayers mostly of little consequence beyond full restoration of his sight as well as his unnatural sense whose strength still was not what it had been, this day was different. This day Marguerite returned.

"It is for the burden of Lady Marguerite's feelings for me to be lifted," he said, "allowing her to give her heart to another."

The princess's disappointment felt, she halted center of the hall.

Theriot ceased his advance toward the doors that were his destination following the simple meal that would be the last of its kind until after the wedding celebration. When he and Dubh turned to her, once more he had to acknowledge how little his eyesight had changed since Marguerite's departure. Though previously the return of form and color had been gradual, it had been steady enough to give him some hope of full recovery. Not so these past weeks.

"We shall see what Marguerite and God think of that prayer," the princess said, "no matter you would have it answered one way and I would have it another."

Theriot inclined his head. "I thank you for the conversation at table. Now as promised your sister, I shall accompany her to the glen."

She sighed. "Further preparations for the wedding. It makes me wish a handfasting with a few witnesses were acceptable. But vows spoken with much ceremony it must be."

And more elaborate for the marriage of a king, Theriot knew from all the commotion. "Soon it will be past, then the English princess who lost all will gain more as Scotland's queen," he said, "and even more her new people will gain."

"So the king says. Just as I am grateful for his confidence, I am grateful for yours."

He bowed, then Dubh and he departed the palace that was now absent three of its long-term guests, Malcolm having granted Michel Roche's men safe passage home after deciding to do the same for his Norman prisoner.

Though Theriot had declined to impart techniques of stealth to the king's warriors, Malcolm had informed him of his pending release and that no ransom would be required. After the wedding celebration, he would be escorted to Wulfenshire.

It was a quarter hour before Cristina descended to a bailey teeming with castle folk receiving those who came from near and far to witness their king's marriage. Having gone abovestairs to exchange her veil for a lighter one whose pale blue fluttered about her dark hair, she and her escort halted before Theriot. "If you are ready, Chevalier, I am ready."

He smiled. These weeks had peeled away enough of her resentment, pride, and sorrow for him to like her in some measure. Too, though her prayers for him lacked the depth of her sister's, they seemed heartfelt—perhaps more so in a way they ought not for one destined for the Church.

Though he believed he made it clear he considered her a friendly acquaintance, still her touches lingered. They would have to speak of it, and soon since the same as he did not wish to hurt Marguerite, he did not wish to hurt her.

Not the same, he corrected. The same end—that each turn her heart toward another—but even less he wished to hurt Marguerite for how much more she felt for him and he for her.

When he started to remove his dagger, Hendrie who he had not realized was among Cristina's escort, said, "As the king tells you are no longer his prisoner but his special guest, you may keep it on your person."

"I am honored," Theriot said.

The princess set a hand on his arm, and they started across the bailey with her escort. Doubtless, the accompaniment of Hendrie and the others was mostly for propriety's sake since the patrol around Dunfermline had been reinforced to prevent attempts to interfere with the wedding, whether from Scotsmen who did not wish a queen of English blood, William's Normans who sought to extinguish the threat to his throne, or Marguerite's vengeful kin.

Though Theriot was now conversant with the glen, from the palace one side of it to the chapel the other, he allowed Cristina to warn of turns and other obstacles though, just as done Malcolm, he had recently revealed to her his ability to see forms and colors.

Upon reaching the top of the glen opposite the palace, the plodding Dubh stirred to life.

The princess halted and clipped, "Malcolm's pet has returned."

Theriot knew she felt his reaction to the tidings, and that it was magnified by frustration at being unable to catch movement that would reveal Marguerite's location.

"I do not see her escort," Hendrie said. "Likely they are overly confident of the patrol and eager to take their ease in the hall. Malcolm will hear of this."

The princess *tsked.* "No doubt she encouraged them."

Dubh turning more restless, Theriot said, "Where is the lady, Princess?"

"She leads her mount toward the graveyard."

Hendrie cleared his throat. "As two escort will serve you, Princess, I shall watch over the lady."

"As you will."

Theriot remained at Cristina's side until they reached the chapel that she was to confirm had been adorned as directed. "As I can be of no aid within and there is a matter I wish to discuss with Lady Marguerite," he said, "I shall leave you to your duties."

The princess caught her breath. "What is of such import you abandon me?"

Certain this was jealousy, he said firmly, "That is between the lady and me."

Though they were watched by her escort, she stepped very near. "How is it you have more regard for her than me?"

He bent his head, said low, "I am grateful for your prayers and enjoy your company, but if you believe I can be your savior, with regret I must tell I cannot be that to you."

After a long moment, she whispered, "To me. But what of Lady Marguerite?"

He raised his eyebrows. "What of her?"

She gave a huff of disgust. "If you cannot have feelings for me, at least be honest in acknowledging you *are* capable of devotion to a woman. Are you?"

Though tempted to lie for her sake, he said, "I am capable."

She breathed deep. "It is good you feel for her rather than me. Otherwise, I would suffer guilt for giving you hope of being able to wed as well as Malcolm shall. Since I am for the Church, the only way I might be persuaded to yield my calling is if I were presented with an offer of marriage to one of highest nobility and of great advantage to my family."

Prideful words, albeit true, Theriot thought. "As ever I have known not to cast hope beyond friendship, I am grateful for what you have given me, Princess."

She stepped back. "It *is* much, especially for a Norman, but the Lord works in this vessel, and I trust He knows you better than I." She swept an arm in the direction of Marguerite. "Though you depart Scotland soon, she ought to know of your devotion, even though naught can come of it."

Something could come of it—further hurt. Thus, having prayed and been prompted by Malcolm's betrothed, this day he would unburden Marguerite. And that was all.

Accompanied by Dubh, he strode toward the graveyard whose perimeter he knew from having walked it with Cristina's sister. Drawing nearer, eyes that had become less sensitive to sunlight picked out the shape and movement of three figures against the landscape.

Well back from the graveyard, standing alongside Marguerite's horse, Hendrie watched over the lady who was likely unaware of his presence where she stood amid headstones.

Theriot nodded at him, then passed between low stone walls. As noted before, the resting places of the bodies of those lost were neatly arranged to allow visitors to move easily between them without trampling greenery and flowers.

He was still a good distance from Marguerite when she lowered before graves he knew must be those of her family.

It only then occurring this was not the place for them to speak, he questioned how he could be so thoughtless. Not liking the answer—that he thirsted and Marguerite was a cool drink—he halted.

Had not Dubh lost patience, her temporary master might have departed unnoticed.

A BARK BROUGHT Marguerite's head around. Seeing Dubh running at her and Theriot following, she straightened and turned—and observed the latter traversed the path as if it were known to him. Was it? Or had his sight returned? That was all she could ponder before the dog forced her back to her knees to avoid being toppled.

Denied the opportunity to leap at her mistress, Dubh halted. Tail whipping, she licked a cheek, dropped to her haunches, and thrust her nose against her lady's hand.

"Have you been so mistreated you are pleased to see me?" Marguerite asked and wondered how she came by humor in this place of sorrow.

Rubbing her prickling nose, she set her other hand on Dubh's neck and looked to the man who continued forward. Noting the cloth last seen around his hand was tucked into the neck of his tunic, she raised her eyes higher over a shortened beard bordered by silvered hair brushing his shoulders.

Though there were yet clouds upon his eyes, might they be smaller? Thinner? If so, could he see through them?

Two strides distant, he halted and, appearing to look down upon her, said, "You are returned."

"I would not miss my king's wedding." She nipped her lip. "I regret still you are where you do not wish to be, but I am glad you appear well and..." She frowned. "You are permitted to depart the palace unescorted?"

"Malcolm has agreed to return me to England."

Her heart leapt—with joy, she told herself though more it felt a leap to its death.

Theriot nodded over his shoulder. "According to Hendrie, I have been raised to the rank of *special* guest."

She glanced at the Scotsman alongside her mount. Returning to Theriot, she thought how good it was to look upon him again, and further betrayed herself by opening the door to memories of their shared intimacies. She swallowed. "It gladdens me Hendrie and you are at peace and you shall soon return to your family."

"I am pleased as well."

Though she longed to ask after his sight, she said, "For what are you here?"

"Princess Cristina asked me to accompany her to the chapel to confirm all has been made ready for the wedding."

She nodded, then remembering the gesture was lost on him, said, "Two days and Scotland and Malcolm will be blessed."

"I think it a good match for all."

"Except your king."

"For that, Dunfermline is more heavily patrolled."

"So I saw." She frowned. "As you sought to aid your king in capturing the Aetheling, would you prevent the wedding if you could?"

"I would not. William is my liege, but just as I would not bury my conscience by leading men in harrying the countryside, once more I heed it."

Mouth dry for being so near him, she said, "Ere you rejoin the princess, answer me one thing."

"You would know of my sight."

"As you make your way forward better than ere I left, I have hope your vision returns."

"What I told none ere your departure, though all know now, is I see color and forms. Though often it is impossible to identify what is distant, when the light falls right, whether by sun or flame, I can see what is directly before me and often make sense of it."

Hope surged. "Then you—"

"My sight is better, but not enough to reclaim the warrior, and since improvement wanes, it may never be enough." A muscle in his jaw jerked. "It is not easy, but I seek to accept what Malcolm's betrothed tells—the Lord shall answer prayers for the restoration of my sight according to His will, not mine."

He was not at peace but no longer seemed greatly astir. "I shall continue to pray for His answer, Theriot."

"And my acceptance of it."

She inclined her head, asked, "Could you see my nod?"

"Since we are near, aye."

"Were we nearer, what could you see?" Immediately, she regretted how that sounded. "What I mean is…"

He stepped forward. "Here I can see the brown of your hair, shape of your face, and width of your shoulders."

Staring at the green ringing the clouded centers of his eyes, she said, "I am pleased."

His next step delivered him so close she felt the warmth of his body. "And here I see something of your eyes, nose, and mouth."

"Can you…?"

His eyebrows rose.

"Can you see the color of my eyes?"

"Even if I drew very near, I do not think I would glimpse the green you say is similar to mine." He stepped back. "Since soon I depart, I wished to tell you of my changed circumstances in the hope of easing your guilt."

She blinked. "How so?"

"I have been angry, breeding bitterness that found satisfaction in blaming you for the loss of my sight."

"I did cause it."

"Not willfully, as ever I have known, just as I know it was the result of wrong turns made by myself and others—that I set a Norman contingent after the Aetheling, Edgar rode through the village, I tried to save a child from a burning home, you tried to save a child from a murderous Norman, Hendrie and others sought to save you from what appeared an enemy who meant a woman harm."

Now she stepped closer. "You are saying you forgive me?"

"Nay." That word stabbed, but then he said, "That would mean I believe you so greatly trespassed you require forgiveness. As told, I do not feel that. What is true is that in doing my liege's bidding I am the one in need of forgiveness, as is the contingent for destroying the homes of innocents. Thus, it is I who seek forgiveness."

Though it was not possible for him to separate his loss from her, there was relief in knowing he cared enough to try. "Whatever forgiveness is needed is granted, Theriot."

As he continued to peer into her face, she was tempted to draw very near to test his belief it was not possible to see the green of her eyes.

"I will leave you to your privacy," he said and turned, causing Dubh to lift her head from her paws.

"I would not mind your company a while longer," Marguerite said with more longing than thought.

He came around. "You do not wish to be alone?"

"I thought I did, but of a sudden I weary of solitude."

"I was told you went to your family's cottage."

She nodded. "'Tis a lovely home with more beautiful memories than painful ones, but at times that makes the quiet… very loud. Does that make sense?"

"More sense than it would have before I found myself in Scotland."

Having not considered his impaired vision must magnify the silence, as well as the din, she winced. Then hoping he would remain, she lowered beside the graves. "Here are my infant brothers at the feet of their sire where they should have been in life to learn all the gentle and good of him ahead of the fierce and hard that allowed him to defend well those he loved." She looked up. "Just as your father was for you one side, your uncle the other." She gestured at the monument honoring her parents. "Here my parents."

"One headstone," he said, proving he could see its shape.

"Aye, when Malcolm returned my mother's body to Scotland, he replaced my sire's headstone with one of greater size to cover both. With the aid of the princess, he composed the words carved into it."

He stepped around her and went to his haunches beside the headstone. Setting a hand on it, he slid a thumb around the embellishment in the upper corner.

So near him their shoulders would brush if she filled her lungs full, Marguerite said, "That is a circular knot representing beautiful things without end."

He moved his thumb inward. Finding letters center of the circle, he began exploring the grooves cut deep to ensure they did not weather away. "M…" he said. "O…S…H…" He continued over the others, then turned his face to her. "Gaelic."

"Aye. *Mo shíorghrá,* meaning my eternal love."

"Beautiful, not only in meaning but pronunciation. The way

you speak it sounds almost a wind through the trees making tongues of leaves. That must be the sparrow of you."

The catch of her breath made his mouth curve. "It is as I have heard Malcolm name you. Since I know your voice is lovely now it no longer suffers from disuse, I have wondered if it is more so when you sing."

She shivered when his eyes flicked to her lips. "I sing well, but *sparrow* was given by my sire for my love of whistling. Though many think it unseemly a woman express joy in that manner, and even my mother feared ill would be thought of me, my father said I should whistle if so moved—except in formal situations when no invitation is forthcoming."

"Invitation?"

She smiled. "Many a dull winter night I have been asked to entertain at court, sometimes alone, both whistling and singing, other times accompanied by a harpist."

His brow furrowed. "I have neither heard you whistle nor sing."

"It has been a difficult year, not only of little joy, but much of it spent as a mute. Only in my garden these weeks have I indulged in birdsong."

Now he smiled. "Perhaps you will be invited to perform at the wedding feast."

She had not considered that. "Perhaps."

He slid his hand from the circular knot to the inscription and began tracing those grooves.

"Gaelic as well," Marguerite said. "Would you like me to translate what Malcolm and his princess composed?"

"I would."

She cleared her throat. "Here Diarmad the Mad, Diarmad the Shield, husband of Lady Marguerite. Here—"

"Where is the name of your namesake?" he asked, moving fingers over a word distant from the one he sought.

It disturbed he wished to know, and that the only way to answer was to guide him to it.

"This is not it," he said.

"That is the word for *shield.*" She leaned in and, shoulder pressed to his, curled her fingers over his.

Feeling breath gust her cheek, she moved his hand to the first instance of the name shared with her mother, set his fingertips on the peaks of the letter *M,* and released him. "That is where my mother's name begins." When he had traced every letter through to the last, she asked, "Should I continue?"

He lowered his hand. "Continue."

"Here Lady Marguerite, wife of Diarmad the Mad, Diarmad the Shield. Here their tale. Love seized Love. Love walked beside Love. Love rejoiced with Love. Love mourned with Love." She glanced at her brothers' graves. "Love healed by Love. Love parted from Love. Love reunited with Love. Love walks beside Love." She swallowed. "Again."

"Beautiful," Theriot said. "In those words I hear your king and she who will be queen."

"And my parents," she whispered. "It is as if…"

"As if?"

"Just as they were halves that could only be whole one with the other, I think it of Malcolm and Meg—that their union will be the blessed answer to many prayers."

"I think you are right."

His words drew her gaze to his mouth, and feeling the cessation of his breath as if he knew what she wished, she looked away. Eyes falling on what was visible beneath the neck of his tunic, she said, "Will you tell me the import of that cloth?"

He drew it from around his neck. "I cut it from the tunic I wore at Hastings."

"Why?"

"So I not forget the battle which made ruin of the garment without ruining me. That I remember how near death I came without suffering great loss like others of my family. That I remain grateful for God's favor, though..."

"Though?"

"As my sight remains corrupted despite beseechings by the godly princess, you, myself, and others, these months I have been moved to think myself merely the recipient of good fortune to have survived Hastings and other battles—that rather than act on prayers, God but watches what goes here below. But..."

Aching over the battle he waged, she said, "But?"

"I aspire to embrace the princess's belief the Lord is listening and doing, even if He will not do for me what I wish in my time rather than His."

"Meg is wise. I have known no one like her. Indeed, she seems nearer God than many a priest."

"The same is said of my sire, and yet both are of the world rather than the cloister."

"Perhaps that is why they are wise. Not only can they draw near God but come alongside those they counsel."

After some moments, he asked, "Do you believe as she does that all prayers are answered, that just because we do not like what comes does not mean the Lord is not listening nor acting? That His way, which may prove different from ours, is the better way?"

She considered the headstones. "It is hard, but I believe it. Even if I stray in the moment my faith is greatly tested, ever I remind myself of the blessings gifted me though it might cause another to hurt and think the Lord deaf to their prayers. No matter how bad something is, good can come of it, even if we blind ourselves to that good or do not live long enough to see it."

"That asks much of those left behind."

"It does, but I think the princess would say it is still far less than we ask of God and He gives."

"What good can come of my sight being impaired, Marguerite?"

She hesitated for what her answer would reveal of her, then said, "Do you not resist, mayhap it will hold you here so you may serve a king far better than William, so the worthy D'Argents of Normandy and now of England spread their influence and skills to Scotland, so you…" Unable to tell of her hope he would grow in love with her, she stood and said in Gaelic, "Tá mo chroí istigh ionat."

As she swung away, he rose. "Marguerite!"

Taking advantage of his poor eyesight, she hastened away.

"What does that mean?" he demanded.

"Nothing you wish to hear," she whispered.

"I will not remain in Scotland!"

Upon reaching her palfrey, she was grateful to discover Dubh had stayed behind. Evading Hendrie's gaze, she mounted.

"'Tis his loss, Sparrow," the Scotsman said as he passed the reins to her. "Soon he will be gone, and yer own loss will be small sorrow when you wed one of your own, and even smaller when ye have a babe in arms."

She nodded and spurred away. For the sake of her heart, she tried not to shine love back upon that to which she wished to return, but at the last moment, she looked around.

Theriot was where she had left him. Though she would see him again before he departed Scotland, it would not be—could never be—the same as coming home.

CHAPTER TWENTY-SIX

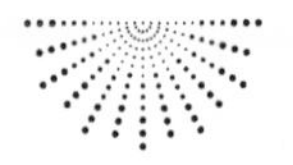

How she meddled!

Theriot had been grateful that to accommodate great lords from all over Scotland, Princess Margaret arranged for him to be seated at one of the lower tables placed perpendicular to the dais. He would not dine alongside Cristina during the feasts preceding the wedding, but neither would he find Marguerite on his other side.

He was right about the former since royalty sat at high table, but a short while later proved wrong about the latter.

Though Marguerite was the king's ward and well-loved, on such an occasion and with too few places of honor, her rank did not warrant dining among those who sat above others. No meddling that. The meddling was Malcolm's betrothed ensuring her friend shared a bench with this Norman as told by Marguerite's whispered protest and the one who escorted her informing her he followed the princess's instructions to adhere to the seating arrangements.

Godly though the queen-to-be was, she suffered few qualms seeking her own end instead of letting happen what would, whether by the actions of those directly involved or the Lord's intervention for which she professed much faith.

Thus, more difficult it would be for Theriot and Marguerite to go their separate ways. And already both made it exceedingly difficult by Marguerite wishing him to remain graveside with her and his yielding. Were that not enough, he had allowed empathy and curiosity to draw him nearer when he should have remained an observer.

Once he had lowered beside her, he had wanted more—and gained more when questions given too little thought were answered by her hand guiding his to the name shared with her mother. He was no youth, but the impulse to carry her fingers to his lips had been strong. And even lacking understanding of the Gaelic words with which she departed the graveyard, he did not doubt she continued to feel much for him. What he doubted was being able to leave her behind as easily as he had assured himself he could during her absence from court.

Now as she settled beside him, silently he repeated what he had cast at her like a boy determined to set out on a journey for which his parents refused permission—*I will not remain in Scotland!*

"Sir Theriot," she said, voice nearly drowned by the din.

He turned his face to her and saw she wore a cream-colored gown that contrasted well with dark hair fashioned into plaits, their ends secured with red ribbons.

Feeling Dubh move into the space between master and mistress, he said, "Lady Marguerite."

Though the light did not fall well enough to glimpse any of her expression, he knew she did not smile when she said, "I am sorry. I know you wish this no more than I."

He should agree, being cruel in the moment to be kind later, but he said, "With whom would you prefer to take meal?"

"I do not know, though I suppose I should not waste this

opportunity with so many here for the wedding, some of whom may be in want of a wife."

Jealousy kicked him, but he said, "I believe it would please Malcolm."

"It would, though methinks his betrothed would not be pleased. For all Meg must attend to, she keeps us in sight."

"She meddles," he muttered and set the flat of his right hand on the table and slid it forward until his fingers confirmed the base of his goblet was where the shifting light of torches told he would find it. Gripping the stem, he raised the vessel. By heft and what could be seen of drink dark against pewter, he gauged the level to ensure when he set the rim to his lips the tilt did not send wine streaming down his tunic.

"Oui, the princess meddles," Marguerite said, "but she means well."

That was the end of their exchange, the Saxon priest announcing it was time to bless the meal. And much he blessed it, doubtless causing guests to exchange sour expressions over the princess's influence over Malcolm that could do far more than delay the abatement of hunger.

She who would be queen meant to reform not only her coarse husband and his court but the worship and practices of Scotland's churches that were not in accord with Rome. Ultimately, religious reform might lead to bloodshed, but despite Theriot's annoyance with the princess, he believed her motive pure and this country and its people would be blessed when a daughter of England sat beside a son of Scotland. And if their union produced children, possibly those whose blood straddled the border between the two countries would wrought change in England—perhaps even the world.

Hours. Certain middle night approached, Marguerite peered out of the alcove into which she had slipped following a meal of many courses. The entertainment that followed was excellent, from jugglers to bards to beautifully costumed puppets prancing across a curtained stage to reenact the arrival of Princess Margaret and her family in Scotland.

Then came music and dancing that often moved her gaze to Theriot who stood on the opposite side of the hall among a gathering of Malcolm's Normans and Scotsmen with whom he seemed mostly at ease.

They had not spoken again following the priest's blessing, but once their hands had touched beneath the table when each sought to assure the whining Dubh who moved her head between their laps. Brief though the contact, it had made her heart beat so fast it hurt.

"Lady Marguerite?"

She blinked at a young lord of Perth who approached, a man she had met several times in years gone though she could not recall his name. "My lord?"

"Princess Margaret requests a performance to honor her upcoming nuptials."

Though there had been no time for the two women to speak before the feast, Marguerite had thought it possible she would be called upon. However, as night deepened, she had begun to think it would not be asked of her.

"However, she tells only if you feel of a mind and body, Lady."

In Theriot's presence, she interpreted that.

The young lord smiled in a way that reminded her of her talk of using this opportunity to seek out a man in want of a wife. "I pray you feel well enough, Lady. When last I was here, I was entranced."

Would Theriot be entranced? she wondered.

"Will you perform for the king and princess?"

She inclined her head. "How could I refuse my liege and his love?"

His eyes moved over her face as if seeking to discover some hidden land, then he offered his arm.

She allowed him to forge a path among the many toward the dais whose central table had been removed to form a raised stage that allowed not only the great nobility seated both sides a good view, but others in the hall.

Which song best serves in lyrics, tune, and mood? she pondered again those she had earlier considered. She had thought several appropriate, but as she neared the dais, deemed all unworthy of what she believed would grow into a great love—and too late wished she had composed something as deep of heart as what Malcolm and Meg had composed for her father and mother.

She caught her breath, smiled. "Aye, that will do well."

THE YOUTH STARED. Minutes earlier, he had accepted the only thing of import he would take from here was a conversation overheard after he entered the cavernous hall—that on the morrow King Malcolm would convey his betrothed across the estuary to Edinburgh to present a gift in advance of their wedding. But there was something of greater import.

As reported by the scout who weeks past observed a young man of silvered dark hair walking the outer garden with a lady—and now verified by the one entrusted with infiltrating King Malcolm's court—Sir Theriot was here. As not told by the scout, though surely suspected, this D'Argent was no captive.

Or so it appeared to Eberhard Wulfrith who had persuaded his adopted sire he could more easily enter the King of Scot's fortress than any of the baron's men. Not only was his youth an advantage, giving few cause to consider him a threat, but the length of his hair and facility with the Saxon language allowed him to pass as one of those Malcolm had herded out of the harried North to serve the Scots—a form of slavery but preferable to death by starvation, exposure to the elements, and barbaric Normans.

Sir Theriot was not well known to Eberhard who had labored in the kitchen alongside servants preparing the feast, ever keeping watch for an opening to steal away and search out the missing D'Argent. However, despite what could be seen of the man on the opposite side of the hall, it was hard to believe he had deserted King William's service and sent no word to his family to assure them he lived. The warrior whom Eberhard now claimed as an uncle boasted the same reputation as others of his family—as courageous in the face of enemies as he was honorable.

"Hear all!" boomed the bard whose performance a quarter hour past had nearly caused King Malcolm to topple his chair when he thrust upright to applaud. Once more standing center of the dais, the bard whose shoulders were draped in a plaid of bright colors repeated, "Hear all!"

More heeded him, but not everyone as he ought not expect since it was a rare performer who could enthrall all—and only then after a demonstration of the value of silence.

The lowering din proved of benefit to Eberhard who was finally able to make sense of a nearby conversation that had caught his attention when he heard the D'Argent name. It had been spoken by one of several Saxon nobles likely granted sanctuary with Prince Edgar.

"For one who professes to be our ally, little evidence of that with Malcolm continuing to hold that Norman prisoner when he ought to cut off his hands and feet as Le Bâtard does his enemies."

Eberhard glanced at Sir Theriot who stood in profile, appearing more an observer than participant in the celebration for how little he interacted with those around him—as if he were unseen. Surely these Saxons did not speak of the one who wore a D'Argent dagger?

"Prisoner?" another scoffed. "Does the miscreant who sought to deliver the Aetheling and his men to Le Bâtard look a prisoner to you?"

Eberhard breathed out relief. They did speak of his uncle who had most recently served as a scout to uproot the resistance, the greatest prey of which was Edgar. He had not deserted but been captured.

"These days he is even afforded a weapon," said the grizzled Saxon, "and as many have learned, the chevalier is not harmless despite—"

"And yet the Aetheling says Malcolm has decided against ransoming him," a younger Saxon interrupted.

The aged one growled. "D'Argent is dangerous, but mostly in close quarters. What think you his liege would pay for the return of a warrior no longer a warrior, eh?"

Trying to make sense of what did not fit his uncle who looked as much a man of arms as ever, Eberhard shifted his regard to him.

"Little he would pay," the old Saxon answered himself. "If anything."

The younger one gave a grunt of disgust. "Not until Malcolm exchanges D'Argent for ransom need it be revealed the chevalier is blind."

Eberhard jerked so hard the back of his head struck stone and his teeth snapped on his tongue. Tasting blood, he narrowed his gaze on his uncle who remained in profile among others and yet detached, but not as if unseen—as if he could not see despite raised lids and the appearance of staring at the distant dais. *Was* he blind? If so…

For this—having no means of escape—he was not caged? For

this he was trusted with a dagger among enemies? For this, a hound at his side to keep watch over him?

As Eberhard roiled over the blinding he imagined done to extract information, the bard bellowed, "I say, hear all!"

Further, the din lowered, among those who closed their mouths the Saxons who had revealed what was more unexpected than would have been the death of Sir Theriot. Though some of the guests continued to disregard the bard, an excess of wine rendering them either senseless or too bold, Malcolm did not call any to account. And Eberhard guessed his calm a result of words whispered in his ear by the princess whose brother, the Aetheling, sat on her other side.

Brow weighted, mouth pinched, the bard looked to his liege. Receiving a nod, he turned back. "In honor of our great overlord and his princess, the Sparrow of King Malcolm's court shall perform a song of love." He bowed and strode left.

The lady handed onto the stage by a nobleman was not as lovely as Princess Margaret, but there was something breathtaking about her. Greatly she resembled the healer who had been present at Wulfen Castle when Dougray D'Argent trounced his enemy to win the hand of the rebel, Em. Might she be the same?

He dismissed the possibility. That young woman had been mute, worn a commoner's garments, and as one of the Rebels of the Pale had to have been Saxon. Doubtless, were he able to draw near this lady who wore a fine gown, he would see she only bore a resemblance to the rebel who returned with Michel Roche to Derbyshire.

Now facing the royals, she said something in Gaelic, then in the language of the Saxons spoke what he guessed a translation. "My king...my queen...for you."

Her accent was peculiar. Though it sounded of the Scots, Eberhard heard Norman-French as well—further proof she and the mute could not be the same.

Malcolm nodded, then his sparrow turned forward. Drawing breath that raised her shoulders, her eyes flitted in the direction of Sir Theriot. Then instead of parting her lips to pour out song, she pursed them and softly…sweetly…began to whistle.

CHAPTER TWENTY-SEVEN

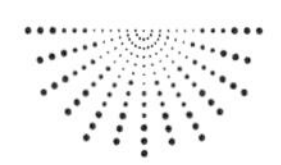

Theriot barely breathed, as seemed the same for all, even those who had continued to converse despite the bard's petition they honor a performance many in attendance surely expected to be like any other that passed the time and sought to make the unmerry merry. This was different, and surely the reason those who had the means to keep caged birds did so.

Marguerite was no tiny, feathered creature, but he would have believed it had he entered at the beginning of her performance, though only until her birdsong became something more—music both of the natural and unnatural that spread its wings and soared wider and higher through the great hall.

He whistled well and knew others more accomplished, but just as none were women, none compared to the lady who made her lips into a beautiful instrument. He could not see her beyond an indistinct shape center of the dais, but he closed his eyes to better hear and feel what was not quite bird, not quite human.

She trailed off, and her next replenishment of breath not only carried the tune but Gaelic words.

Theriot lifted his lids, and above the heads of others saw her turn toward those soon to wed. Then came the Saxon translation more softly sung like an echo.

"Here Scotland's son, defender of all"

The next verse was in Gaelic, then once more Saxon.

"Here England's daughter, the pearl of his heart"

And so it went, soaring in one language, drifting in the other as she made sentiments written by Malcolm and Margaret into song meant to bless the king and queen with a love like that of her parents.

"Here tale of their love told one hundred years
Here tale of their love told one thousand years
Oh, blessed this age, so blessed this age
When love seized love
Love walked beside love
Love rejoiced with love
Love mourned with love
Love healed by love
Love parted from love
Love reunited with love
Love walks beside love…"

A deep breath, the silence of anticipation so complete its sweet draw was heard around the hall.

"…again."

Then once more facing the guests, the tune first whistled

was whistled so softly it was as if the bird came down out of the rafters, lit upon her perch, and folded her wings to sing herself to sleep.

The last noted faded, and Theriot wondered if ever there had been so great a still in a place teeming with people. Was it because their hearts pounded as loudly as his? He could be moved by music, but this...

"Now you see the sparrow," Hendrie said low.

He did, though not as he would have before battling the Scotsman. And for that he could not stay no matter what he felt for Marguerite. "Beautiful," he rasped in the space before King Malcolm once more led his guests in showing appreciation for a performance.

Hendrie leaned near. "Methinks she could be yers," he said without sarcasm or taunting.

Theriot watched as, seemingly unassisted, she stepped from the dais and went from sight among those crowding the floor. "Better she is someone else's," he said.

"Better *for* someone else. But her?" The Scotsman shrugged. "I fear even in yer absence ever the sparrow will long for you as her sire would have longed for her mother had she not given him the chance to love her near rather than from afar."

"Marguerite's mother had much to offer Diarmad. You more than any know I am not what I was."

"And yet still a warrior as proven by the attack in the glen and the enemy who fell to your sword."

"Just as her sire needed to protect his family, so would I were I to take a wife."

"Certes, during times of threat your household would require more sword arms," Hendrie allowed, "but were ye to serve Malcolm, I am certain he would provide."

Theriot's thoughts moved to his sire whose household had been reinforced with trusted warriors to allow Godfroi to rule despite being unable to move about his fortress and demesne without being carried from one room to another and lifted into the saddle.

Hendrie sighed. "Men have wanted her, and she has declined in the hope of gaining what her parents had. If you take that hope with you by departing Scotland, she may yield to the attentions of one here who now covets the songbird he did not know flew about Malcolm's court."

As she herself had considered while at meal...

"That, or just as she is alone now, she shall remain—no husband nor children."

Theriot scowled. "For two who did great injury to each other, it is not natural there should be such civility between us."

"True, but all should aspire to be Diarmad the Mad, eh, Norman?"

Deciding there was naught for him here, Theriot started to turn away.

"What was it the lass said ere she left you in the graveyard?"

That Theriot also wished to know, though surely it was better he did not. "You did not hear her words?"

"She did not cast them as loud as you did in demanding to know their meaning. I am thinking they were Gaelic. If ye can repeat them, I shall translate."

"Tá mo chroí istigh ionat," Theriot said grudgingly.

Hendrie chuckled. "You listen well. I doubt there are many unfamiliar with our language who could almost flawlessly repeat such rare words."

"Though I understand little of Gaelic, I have become acquainted with its sounds and rhythm. Now the meaning."

"As I said, rare words. They profess even after you are long gone, the sparrow shall yearn for you—hence, that which you take of hers that you ought not."

"The meaning?" Theriot growled.

"My heart is in you." He nodded. "Where you go, her heart goes, leaving her empty here."

Pain in the center of him as if his own heart were being stolen—further confirmation this was love he felt—he said tautly, "I thank you, Hendrie. Now I am for bed."

"Ah, but will ye sleep?" the Scotsman called to his back. "I think not, Norman."

A door was opened for Theriot, and when it closed behind him, he lifted his face to the sky. It was entirely black, no silver and white twinklings to form images exceedingly still compared to those formed by clouds during the day.

He missed stars, he missed clouds. But more, when he left Scotland, he would miss the face of Marguerite he knew better by touch than sight.

"SIRE?"

Guarin, born a D'Argent and made a Wulfrith through marriage to a great Saxon lady, knew he should not resent Eberhard's prompting, but the tidings delivered across the estuary beneath an ink-black sky hours from sunrise felt a blow to heart and gut.

Theriot lived. Blessed tidings.

Theriot was no deserter. No tidings that.

Theriot was neither chained nor beaten as once Guarin had been and he moved among the enemy as if accorded respect. Blessed tidings, though only if he had not suffered greatly between capture and the feast of King Malcolm who may have been the one who blinded him. Blinded!

A hand touched his shoulder.

He swung around, arms trembling with the effort to keep his knuckles from bloodying the one who trespassed on...

What was this? Grieving? Of a sorts, for it could prove the death of a warrior even if Theriot survived as had their sire who had more to return to—a wife and children—than had his youngest son.

"Guarin!" Maël said with warning.

Bringing his cousin's scarred face into focus, Guarin knew from the expression delivered with the warning that though Maël might fail were blows exchanged, his opponent would be hurting as well.

Maël leaned near. "That he has lost his sight is terrible, but what happened cannot be changed. We can only control what happens next." He peered behind and Guarin followed his gaze to Dougray who stood to the left of the tent opening, the lantern's light causing his shadow to shift across the canvas. His face was as livid as his oldest brother's felt, his single arm at his side ending in a fist.

"My words are for you as well, Dougray, and they are not of my sire who trained us at arms but of Godfroi who imparted wisdom with which to wield those arms."

Even before Maël spoke them, Guarin knew the ones to which he referred.

"Battle threats of the moment by going into the past only to retrieve lessons learned," his cousin recited, "and into the future to make use of those lessons to better one's chances in the now."

Dougray's eyes, different from those of D'Argent blood, just as the gold of his hair was different, shifted to Guarin. Ever he who shared only a mother with the D'Argent siblings had been closest with Theriot. If he did not cool as Guarin must as well, mistakes would be made.

"Maël is right," Guarin said. "If we are to free Theriot without casualties, we must lean hard on the training of our uncle *and* our sire."

"No casualties our side," Dougray growled.

"Do we succumb to vengeance, Brother," Guarin said, "it

could blind us worse than Theriot." He strode to Eberhard, gripped the young man's arm, and was grateful for this son who was not of his body but loved as Guarin imagined his own sire loved the misbegotten Dougray. "You are worthy. Your mother will be as proud as I."

He started to turn to Sir Guy whom William had earlier sent across the border with a contingent, but Eberhard said, "There is more. At noon on the morrow—or I suppose it is this day now—Malcolm shall bring the princess to Edinburgh to present an early wedding gift."

Guarin swept his regard to Guy.

"Likely the chapel he raises," the chevalier said, "though it is far from finished despite fortification of the castle having ceased to allow the workers to labor solely on that House of God." He nodded. "One of my spies reported the grumblings of many who do not believe it should take precedence over defense of their country against William's ambitions." His smile was slight. "It is said the princess is very devout, not at all in the way of William's brother, Bishop Odo."

"True faith," Guarin said, and knew for this Guy wrestled with what was expected of him.

Before Eberhard's return, the D'Argents had conversed with the warrior who would surely become the captain of William's guard once Maël relinquished that position by disappearing from England to begin his life with the Saxon lady he had aided in escaping the conqueror. No matter the cost in Norman lives, Guy was to prevent the princess from becoming Queen of Scotland, preferably by way of abduction which would see her locked away for life, ensuring she birthed no children with a claim to William's throne.

Though Guy strove to serve his king well, he had confided it would be difficult, perhaps impossible, to deprive the godly woman of a good life after all she and her family had lost.

As this eve's tidings presented the chevalier a greater chance of stealing her away, he did not welcome them. Where he was concerned, the only good of this was the men under his command were ignorant of the opportunity Malcolm would present to fulfill their mission. More easily William would grant forgiveness for failing to abduct the princess were it believed Guy lacked the time to devise the means to do so.

It was the same for the D'Argents who would be expected to aid the chevalier though the king had granted them permission to retrieve Theriot—a rescue too long in coming.

Weeks past, efforts to locate their missing kin had led to the discovery of Theriot's horse of unusual color and eyes near Scotland's border. Not only had Guarin bought the stallion from a Saxon who claimed he had found it outside his village, but coin was given for tale of what happened the night the Aetheling led his men through its streets, followed by Normans who set much afire.

Further, the man had revealed the village physician had tended a seriously injured Norman and a Scotsman, and the prince took both north.

Immediately, Guarin had sent a scout into Scotland. When the man returned with tale of a silvered, dark-haired young man walking in the outer garden of Dunfermline's palace with a lady, Guarin and his kin had prepared to go in after him. And would have had not his wife sent tidings his sister was in danger.

They had no choice but to turn south, assuring themselves since it did not appear Theriot was ill-treated he could better protect himself than the reckless Nicola—Nicola who had recently wed the Saxon warrior who proved her savior, then she his when William sought to avenge himself on the leader of the Rebels of the Pale.

Would the Lord once more bless Guarin's family by turning tragedy into good? And was that even possible if Theriot's eyes were put out? Unfortunately, Eberhard had been unable to draw near enough to confirm or refute it following what he named the most beautiful performance by a woman said to resemble the mute friend of Dougray's wife, Em.

"First, in between, and in the end, we are D'Argents," Dougray returned Guarin to this moment. "We go for Theriot on the morrow, not the princess." He looked to Guy. "Until we have departed for Dunfermline, your men cannot know she and Malcolm come to Edinburgh. It will be no easy thing to steal inside the palace, but we will not be denied the opportunity to enter walls more easily breached in the absence of Malcolm and the sizable entourage he is sure to take with him. Oui, Sir Guy?"

The chevalier looked from one D'Argent to the other, inclined his head. "At this moment, I am fast asleep—have been for an hour, mayhap two."

"We thank you."

Guy smiled tautly, but as he turned to exit the tent to which he had been summoned upon Eberhard's return, Guarin called him back.

"Baron Wulfrith?"

"What comes after this?"

"You speak of when I fail to stop the marriage of Malcolm and Princess Margaret?" He shrugged. "Regardless of whether or not I become captain of the king's guard, methinks I go to the Isle of Ely. Unless Hereward and his rebels accept they have no chance of ousting William now the Danes have deserted them, by force that isle must be brought under Norman control. Once that is done… God willing, the unrest ends and the beautiful England made ugly by the conquering shall flower again." He dipped his head, pivoted, and ducked outside.

"God willing," Guarin said, then he and his kin began laying plans.

When finally they sought their rest, it was to little avail. One after another rose to walk the deep-cut valley where Guy had made camp on the recommendation of Normans long of these northern lands whom he paid well to ensure Malcolm's enemies moved unseen through his country. Though the two men were of the warrior class, an injury sustained by the oldest mercenary rendered him no longer capable of effectively wielding a blade. Just as it was possible Theriot would never again do.

CHAPTER TWENTY-EIGHT

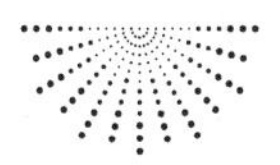

The clamor was too great and too sudden to be that of a new day through which awakening men and women trudged. Dubh knew it as well, having begun pacing the hut.

Theriot turned his face to the unshuttered window through which night air drifted. As expected, only the dim of torchlit dark was seen, no hint of dawn to reveal how many hours had passed since he gained his bed.

As he sat up, the shouting began. Though the voices lacked the urgency of men preparing to defend their lives, quickly he donned tunic, belt, and dagger and dragged on his boots.

Dubh was at his side when he stepped into a bailey rife with movement that converged on the stable whence the king's voice sounded.

"Guide me to Malcolm," Theriot said.

The hound fit herself to his side, but with so much bustle and flickering light, Theriot trampled pride and hooked fingers around her collar to guarantee his footing.

As if now she could better perform her duty, she increased her pace. It alarmed, making him feel off balance, but he yielded to her lead. Though sharply she corrected their course when someone anxious to do the king's bidding shot into their path, there were no mishaps.

"Sir Theriot!" Malcolm boomed. "A bad business this."

Theriot halted. "What has happened?"

"I was hardly abed when word was delivered that an outer wall of the chapel I shall present to My Pearl collapsed as the workers began returning home for the night."

Theriot wondered if it was of William's doing, but since it had transpired while the workers were present, likely not. "Faulty craftsmanship?"

Malcolm grunted. "It appears. Still, precautions will be taken. I go there now and not by ferry—the long way around to accommodate a sizable escort with the best horses at our disposal."

"I am sorry your plan is ruined, Your Grace."

"Not ruined—only inconvenient. Once I confirm all is as told, I shall have the damage repaired ahead of the princess's arrival at noon, even if the workers must sweat blood to see it done."

"Your betrothed will be disappointed you do not cross the estuary with her."

"It cannot be helped. I will not have her learn—" He broke off, shouted, "Boy, saddle Sir Theriot's horse!"

Theriot could not contain his surprise—one moment at the realization it was Grendel of whom he spoke, the next over the belief this Norman could sit a horse well and ride hard.

"I will not have My Pearl learn of the collapse lest she believe God is displeased with my gift," Malcolm said. "She sees His hand in everything, you know."

"I am surprised you wish me to accompany you, Your Grace."

"Only a bit sooner than the morrow."

With which Theriot had been uncomfortable enough for the

short ride to the dock, but now he was to go to Edinburgh by land, a long ride in the dark made more dangerous for its urgency.

"You question your ability," Malcolm said. "Were you a lone rider or one of a few, understandable. But that you will not be, and I am told the horse you won from your attacker is fond of you. Too, he ought to require little guidance beyond what is provided by the others running ahead of him."

It was true, though still a lead might be needed once the running was done, and imaginings of another guiding him was nearly as distasteful as sweeping a stick before him.

As if Malcolm knew his thoughts, he said, "Soon you return to England. Will you do so in a cart the same as you arrived at Dunfermline or astride?"

Theriot ground his teeth.

"Begin here, Chevalier, and I shall have my squire deliver your armor and sword."

This was even more unexpected than riding with warriors, but Malcolm was right. Better Theriot continue piecing himself together in Scotland, even if this piece landed him face down in the mud, than in England where he could not escape pity.

"I shall await your squire," he said. Once more holding to the hound who would not like being left behind, Theriot turned away.

PLANS GONE BAD—BLESSEDLY before the D'Argents and their dozen men were more than a league distant from camp. It was Sir Guy's squire who overtook them, revealing all had changed and telling they must return.

They followed and learned the collapse of one of the chapel's walls had altered Malcolm's own plan. Before expected, the King of Scots and a sizable retinue that included the Aetheling had arrived in Edinburgh to supervise repair of the wall ahead of the princess's arrival. But it was not that which necessitated an alteration of the D'Argents' plan. It was that Theriot accompanied Malcolm as reported by mercenaries who aided in keeping watch over that fortress.

Guarin jutted his chin at where the two hired warriors ate cold pottage. "They are certain Theriot is among Malcolm's entourage?"

"They are, and so tells one of the patrol who also witnessed the king's arrival. *A young man of silvered dark hair,* he said, *surely he whom the D'Argents have permission to retrieve.* Too, he told not only was your brother astride, his mount running at the rear, but he had a sword on his belt."

Greater the mystery of Theriot's captivity. A blind prisoner allowed to move among his captors with a dagger at his side and now the most esteemed weapon of a warrior? Was it possible the injury to his eyes was not serious, even feigned? God willing, it was so. But for what did Theriot accompany the king as if one of his men?

"He is no deserter," Dougray bit, then swung his gaze to Guy. "No matter what your man believes."

"Though he may think it, he made no accusations," Guy said. "However, he was surprised to learn Theriot is without sight."

Hopeful, Guarin said, "How did he learn that?"

Guy jutted his chin at the mercenaries. "The bent-backed one taunted him for his lack of observation. He said my man must be as blind as that D'Argent not to notice he does not look upon the world in a natural way."

Hope fading, Guarin said, "Eberhard told Theriot's sightlessness is not obvious, that it was apparent only after he overheard my brother was blinded and watched for signs."

"Perhaps in that situation, but riding could prove very different," Guy said.

Guarin considered the mercenaries, both of whom wore

blades and had bows and arrows fixed to their backs. "Swords for hire cannot be trusted, but instinct tells these two less so."

"I agree. Unfortunately, Scotland is so foreign and wild it is necessary to employ them to provide my men good range of movement with little risk of detection. And another thing—my own coin ensures they do my bidding without question."

Guarin understood. Were Guy given the chance to deliver Princess Margaret to his liege and chose not to, more easily his dissent could be kept from William if use was made of mercenaries rather than the king's men. But even that was a risk unless he slew his accomplices to prevent extortion, which Guarin believed Guy would not do. Hence, just like Maël must leave England to make a life with the woman he loved, Guy might have to do the same.

"So a new plan," Dougray said.

Though already one was forming, when Guy revealed the size of the force accompanying Malcolm to Edinburgh, Guarin rejected it. Were it possible to extract Theriot, which would be more difficult with his impairment, too many could die both sides—a great risk were the life of the youngest D'Argent brother in peril, an unconscionable one since he was treated well beyond whatever had stolen his sight.

"I see two possibilities." This from Maël who leaned against the tree before which they had gathered distant from the others.

"Tell," Guarin prompted.

"As it is best not to involve Sir Guy and his men since none of us wish the princess to fall into Willam's hands, the first possibility depends on how many armed men deliver her across the estuary and whether or not Malcolm sends others to escort her from the dock to Edinburgh. The second…" He thought on it, shook his head. "Less likely to work. Thus, we make a trade, which could also fail if our timing is wrong or we lose control of outside forces."

As well Maël knew, having recently lost his bid to trade the woman to whom he was now wed for Guarin's sister. Blessedly, all had shaken out better than expected for that D'Argent.

"Let us pray the men loyal to us are all we need to take back Theriot without bloodshed," Maël said.

"And pray for restraint," Guarin added. "No matter what was done him and how it was done, as testament to our faith and for the sake of our wives, we do only what we must. Hawisa awaits my return." He moved his gaze to Maël. "Mercia awaits yours." More heavily he set his eyes on Dougray. "And you have your beloved Em."

With less grudging than expected, his brother nodded.

Not for the first time marveling at the power of love to heal and change the broken, Guarin turned to Guy. "Now we need an excuse for you to withdraw your men so none carry tale to William."

"I SHOULD NOT ALLOW myself to be stirred to such excitement," Meg said. "We are to store up treasures in heaven, not on earth where moths and rust corrupt and thieves steal."

Marguerite longed to reassure her that though Malcolm's gift was here on earth, its fruits would reach to the heavens and bless thousands upon thousands, but what was unknown to the princess might become known, depriving the king of her genuine reaction to what a man made more godly by love had done to honor her great faith.

Feeling color in her cheeks roused by an unclouded summer sun, Marguerite lowered her chin and looked to the woman who sat on the bench beside her facing the shore toward which the ferry moved.

"I think it is good you are excited," Marguerite said and leaned forward to stroke the hound who remained disgruntled at being left behind when Theriot accompanied the king to Edinburgh. "Does not the Lord delight in our joy, Meg?"

"When 'tis not of the selfish, and I fear this is."

Sniffing down a sneeze, Marguerite withdrew her hand from Dubh. "No matter the nature of my king's gift, I have no doubt his queen shall share its goodness with as many as possible."

Meg raised an eyebrow. "You make it sound as if you do not know what that gift is." She raised a hand. "Not that I would have you tell."

Marguerite did know and that the princess would cherish it. "I am glad you do not wish me to say, for I would not break the word given your betrothed."

Meg nibbled her lower lip. "Aside from excitement, I am in the grip of worry over the change of plan that sees Malcolm at Edinburgh rather than here with me. He knows how much I dislike water travel."

"I know no more of his change of plans than you, Meg. What I know is that it is important the presentation of his wedding gift is flawless in your eyes."

The princess sighed. "Over and again, I pray he is not terribly disappointed I cannot put him ahead of my faith as he puts me ahead of his."

"I believe that is why he loves you so well. No purer wife could he have in word nor deed."

Meg turned thoughtful, and when the shoreline was more clearly in view, said, "I hope just as you so generously shared with all last eve, making hearts beat hard not with drink but awe and reverence of the gift with which you are blessed, so shall I, honoring the great commission given me by moving Scotland's people to greater love and respect for our Savior."

Marguerite laughed softly, but before she could offer further assurance, Meg entreated, "Tell me you do not think it funny for believing I can be a worthy representative of the Lord."

Far more familiar with the princess's confidence than lack of it, Marguerite set a hand atop hers. "It is not funny at all. It is inspiring, and for that I love you."

Meg's expression reflected gratitude, then with teasing, she said, "But more you love Sir Theriot."

Marguerite longed to deny it, but not only was this woman undeserving of falsity, she could not be fooled. "Three weeks was not enough to correct the lean of this heart, but I shall see it straight again."

"See there!" Cristina exclaimed from her bench near the bow.

Marguerite startled, not only because she had forgotten the other woman's presence, but for her enthusiasm. Unlike her mother and older sister, she was not averse to water travel—even appeared to enjoy it.

Cristina stood and pointed. "Our escort to Edinburgh. Look ere they go from sight."

As both women peered beyond the warriors accompanying them, they saw a half dozen riders on the road that followed a portion of the shoreline, the colors of their plaids barely visible. More visible were the riderless horses which would deliver the new arrivals to Edinburgh. At a leisurely trot, they descended the crest and went from sight.

"'Tis too distant to know if Malcolm is among them," Meg said.

Marguerite smiled. "Soon you shall see him. Then on the morrow, ever you shall be his queen."

THE NEW PLAN fell into place.

King William's Normans had broken camp and moved south when Guy announced their position was compromised with Malcolm's forces expanding their patrol to protect their ruler and the Aetheling. They did not know the princess was expected to join her betrothed, only that the D'Argents would retrieve Theriot regardless of the risk.

Now with minimal bloodshed, the six Scotsmen sent to escort the princesses and their guard to the great fortress had been subdued by sixteen, though not easily. Their leader, an older warrior, had fought so fiercely it was difficult to defeat him without landing a mortal blow.

Taken into the wood distant from the road, the Scotsmen had been bound and gagged and their horses tethered nearby. There they would remain until the trade was made—the princess for a prisoner.

Though Guarin knew the temperament of the King of Scots only by reputation, he did not doubt it would be no friendly exchange, but there *would* be an exchange. Hopefully, when the D'Argents and their men spurred away, the Scotsmen would clasp close their future queen rather than pursue those who had bettered them.

"It seems two princesses shall come into our hands," Dougray said, peering over the ridge where he lay between Guarin and his cousin. "Methinks the dark-haired lady of exceedingly fine gown is the younger sister."

"The one standing at the fore," Maël murmured. "I think you are right."

"Then even greater the enemy we could make of William if he learns what we held and set free," Guarin said and was pleased he had given much thought to which men accompanied him to Scotland—Saxons all and intensely loyal to his lady wife. More important in this moment, they were loyal to their Norman lord.

He peered over his shoulder at where his men and Eberhard were concealed in trees bordering the road upon which those crossing the estuary expected six of Malcolm's warriors would reappear.

When Eberhard showed himself and shook his head to indicate no other Scots approached, Guarin looked back at the ferry that neared the dock and moved his gaze from the princess at the bow to the women center of the vessel. The fair-haired one had to be Princess Margaret, but what of the other? Likely one of her ladies, her gown less fine.

"It is time," he said.

They raised themselves and, hunched, sped to the wood. There they added three Saxons of long hair and beards to their numbers to look the escort sent by Malcolm, drew around them plaid cloaks taken from the Scotsmen, and the two with silver in their hair covered their heads with mail coifs.

"Forget not my lady wife's code—mortal injuries only to protect our lives," Guarin instructed. Then to the ten who would remain in the wood, one of whom held the lead to a riderless horse, he said, "The moment the women have disembarked and are off the dock, make yourselves heard with battle cries. And ride hard. Our disguises will not hold long."

CHAPTER TWENTY-NINE

It should be incomprehensible so beautiful a day could go wrong, but since Marguerite's discovery her mother had passed, days like this had become more common.

Swiftly, the men who had accompanied the three women across the estuary surrounded them as the six no longer believed sent by Malcolm drew swords and descended the road in a far from leisurely manner that turned Dubh's barking vicious.

Whether they were disgruntled Scots, vengeful Saxons, or conquering Normans in disguise, it mattered not. Despite being greatly outnumbered, they meant to attack. Or so it seemed until ten more warriors bellowing Saxon battle cries came out of the wood behind them.

Fear of the six revised, it thought they but rode hard to offer further protection, not until they neared the places made for them among the princess's guard was the lie of their plaids confirmed—and possibly first by Marguerite who recognized one whose face so resembled that of his youngest brother she did not need to see the hair concealed beneath a coif.

Here Baron Guarin Wulfrith. Here his brother, Sir Dougray,

who had no cause to cover his golden hair. Here their cousin, Sir Maël of disfigured face who had been present in the D'Argent camp when the rebel, Em, and Marguerite were given into the care of the misbegotten D'Argent. And with them three others, doubtless Saxons of Wulfen Castle, the same as the ten coming behind.

Hoping she would be recognized, giving the D'Argents pause and her time to assure them Theriot was in no danger, Marguerite lunged from beside the stunned Meg and Cristina. As she and Dubh slipped between two guards, she cried in Gaelic, "Do not fear!"

"Lady!" one shouted but could not catch hold of her.

Fairly certain he and the others would not risk breaking the wall around the princesses, Marguerite called over her shoulder what she hoped would be heard above Dubh's barking, "They but come for their kin, Sir Theriot!"

She halted before horses being sharply reined in. Thrusting arms out to her sides as if to shield those behind, she was not surprised when Dubh lunged in front of her and assumed a muscle-quivering stance.

As both hound and mistress were sprayed with dirt flying from beneath hooves, Marguerite cried in Saxon for all to understand, "See me, Baron Wulfrith, Sir Dougray, Sir Maël. No one need die here!"

Amid the flash of swords and ring of chain mail covering the warriors shoulders to thighs, the six settled their mounts while the ten continued their advance.

The eldest D'Argent narrowed his eyes on her, then turned his mount sideways and raised an arm, causing those coming behind to slow.

Marguerite stepped alongside Dubh and set a hand on the hound's shoulder. "Quiet!" she commanded.

Dubh did not entirely obey, transforming howling into

growling and once more turning her body in front of her mistress.

"I speak true!" Marguerite called and looked between the three D'Argents whose faces reflected recognition, then glanced over the others that now included the ten come from the wood who had fanned out to enclose all. Returning her regard to the one at the fore, she said, "No one need die, Baron Wulfrith."

He dropped the coif down around his shoulders, revealing silvered dark hair longer than when last she was in his presence. "No one need die," he said in French-accented Saxon. "On that we agree…Margaret."

She moistened her lips. "There is only one Margaret here—my king's betrothed." She looked around at the princesses standing behind the shield made of their guard, then settled her gaze on Sir Dougray who knew her best. "I am Marguerite, once of the Rebels of the Pale and friend to your wife, Em."

She expected his expression to lighten since the only ill between them was when she aided Em in escaping him, but he remained grim. "So you are and have found your voice."

"The mute thought to be a Saxon is a lady of Scotland," Sir Maël said with what might be accusation.

She inclined her head. "I am. And you yet live, Chevalier Maël."

This D'Argent did smile. It was slight but seemed genuine. "Vitalis and I have made our peace—as he has done with King William."

She frowned. "Then…?"

"He has wed my cousin, Nicola, and returned to the service of Lady Hawisa."

Marguerite startled, both with surprise and joy for the mighty Saxon who had saved her life and the D'Argents' bold, vibrant sister who she prayed would come to love Vitalis well.

"And therein a tale ripe for the telling—were we not pressed to recover my cousin who is your king's prisoner," Sir Maël continued. His mouth flattened. "And blind, we are told."

Joy washed away by heartache, Marguerite said, "It is so, just as it is true the one who stands before you is at fault and no other should suffer for what was done him."

But for the hound's growling and the shifting of men ahead and behind, silence fell. Then Baron Wulfrith said, "No other shall suffer for it, Lady Marguerite, not even you if you are, indeed, responsible." He looked past her. "We are here, Princess Margaret, not to prevent your marriage to King Malcolm but to use the currency of you, your sister, and your guard to retrieve our kin. Unless there is resistance, no blood will be shed. You have my word."

"Stand firm, Cristina!" Meg commanded, and when Marguerite peered over her shoulder, she saw the younger sister clung to the older one's arm. "Just as you know Sir Theriot to be a Norman of integrity, you know he honors his family's reputation."

Though the crossing had put pink in Cristina's face, she had gone pale, making her eyes appear unusually large as she moved them over the D'Argents and their men.

"Stand firm," Meg repeated and pulled free and stepped in front of her sister. "Baron Wulfrith, Sir Dougray, Sir Maël," she acknowledged them. "Whilst in Dunfermline, Sir Theriot has been treated well and accorded the respect due a man of honor though he set a Norman contingent after England's rightful king who shall soon be kin to Scotland's king. It is true your brother suffered injury to his eyes while pursuing the Aetheling, and for that was tended by Lady Marguerite as well as King Malcolm's physician, also true that though some of his sight is restored, far more is not and may never be. As for the prisoner made of him, that he is no longer, my betrothed having decided to return him to his family without ransom." She raised her eyebrows. "So what you do is not only unnecessary but of great danger."

She was so beautifully spoken and persuasive, Marguerite believed herself convinced of that which she embraced already. However, when she looked back at the D'Argents, she saw the doubt of warriors whose survival depended more on actions being an indicator of truth than words in a world teeming with liars.

"I do not believe knowingly you speak false, Princess," Baron Wulfrith said, "but as I will not yield so great an advantage, it is King Malcolm who must make this right." He looked to Marguerite. "I require your assistance, Lady."

She blinked. "I will give aid however I can."

"Eberhard!" he called.

Marguerite knew the name and visage of his adopted son who urged his mount forward, in his hand the lead of the riderless horse.

He halted to the left of the baron. "I am pleased we meet again, Lady, and that you recovered your voice well enough to perform last eve."

She caught her breath.

"Aye, my son was there," Baron Wulfrith said. "It was he who learned of Theriot's blinding, his eyes and ears that determined our course, though it had to be altered when your king left early for Edinburgh and my brother accompanied him."

Wishing she could sound as fearless as Meg, Marguerite asked, "How would you have me aid you?"

"You shall ride to your king, assure him those sent to escort you to Edinburgh have merely been subdued, and give these instructions which, if followed, will ensure he weds the princess and no ill befalls her guard—he is to be accompanied by no more than four men and Sir Theriot. As soon as the dock is within sight, all weapons will be sheathed and his party will advance at a walk and halt on the road directly above the dock. He will send forth my brother, and when Theriot reaches middle ground, we shall withdraw and leave Scotland forthwith."

Lord, Malcolm will be angered, Marguerite sent heavenward. *Though he is well with releasing Theriot, greatly the D'Argents trespass in holding the princesses hostage. Pray, let him do as directed so none fall to the blade and this is over for Theriot so he may heal better.*

"Lady?" the baron prompted.

"I will deliver your terms." She started toward Eberhard, but Dubh snapped her head up and growled.

Then the eldest D'Argent said, "Though it appears safe for you to travel the road alone, especially with your hound running alongside, I will not chance it. Choose a warrior to accompany you, preferably one of lesser build since you shall share a horse."

She frowned. "Why do you not send only one of the guard to deliver your message?"

His mouth curved. "The release of the Lady Sparrow of Dunfermline shall serve as proof of my goodwill."

It would take some of the sting out of the offense dealt Malcolm, but enough? Marguerite turned to the warriors surrounding the princesses.

There was fire in their eyes as expected since they were trapped before the dock with no hope of returning their two remaining charges to the ferry without giving their backs to the enemy. All they could do was protect the princesses, and if a clash ensued, quite possibly sacrifice their lives to warriors of greater number who also had the advantage of being mounted.

Dubh at her side, she stepped before a Scotsman of medium build and looked to his sizable captain. "You are well with this?"

Grudgingly, he inclined his head.

Marguerite turned. Certain the hound would protest her

mounting the horse held by Eberhard, she called to the young man, "Send it forth."

The baron nodded at his son who released the beast and smacked its rump.

As the warrior she had chosen swung into the saddle, Marguerite looked to Meg. "You will remain safe. I am certain of it."

"As am I," Malcolm's betrothed said.

Still Dubh did not like her mistress going astride, and Marguerite half-expected the hound to clamp teeth on an ankle, but the Scotsman swung his charge up behind him. Moments later, with Marguerite holding to him and Dubh following, they went wide around the D'Argents and their men.

Once they reached the beaten path, the Scotsman said over his shoulder, "Hold tight, Lady. We ride as if the devil breathes down our necks."

That was how it felt, the spurring so jarring and the dust so dense that when she looked behind it was through a cloud that rendered indistinct the forces facing each other.

"Lord," she sent heavenward, "give them no cause to do more than that."

~

THERIOT HAD KNOWN Marguerite was to come to Edinburgh, just not like this.

One moment Malcolm had been pacing his horse before the city gates and grumbling over the chapel repair merely sufficing, the next he was spurring beyond the walls to meet those the sentry in the tower announced rode at great speed on a single horse—a Scots warrior and a lady accompanied by a hound.

A dozen of the king's guard had followed, their duty to protect Malcolm of greater import since earlier he had tossed off his chain mail to labor alongside the workers. And two others came after them—Theriot to whom Grendel had proved worthy during the journey from Dunfermline, and Edgar who announced he would not learn secondhand the reason the royal party was not on that road.

Now that the reason was given by Marguerite and the soldier surrounded by those come from the city, the storm of Malcolm gathered.

"Almighty, he dares!"

Sympathetic to his rider's angst, his steed snorted.

"He steals into my country! Threatens my betrothed and her guard! Sets terms for their release!"

"Your Grace," Marguerite beseeched, "Baron Wulfrith and his kin do no more than would you were your brother held in England."

"Donalbane? That—!" Theriot heard his teeth snap, doubtless on words of no credit to his sibling.

"Still, you would go for him, Your Grace," she said with what sounded less certainty. "And as told, until the princess informed the D'Argents you intended to release Sir Theriot, they believed him yet a prisoner and surely saw evidence of ill-treatment in his blinding."

"Evidence gained by sending a spy into my hall—trespassing on me and my guests!"

Hearing the jangle of spurs and seeing the blur of the King of Scots advance on him, Theriot straightened from where he had leaned down to stroke the hound who had come to his side.

Malcolm drew his horse near, then as if this D'Argent had trespassed, demanded, "What say you, Sir Theriot?"

"That the princesses are safe with my kin, the D'Argents will keep the terms set, and since already you agreed to release me, you have all to gain in adhering to Baron Wulfrith's terms—above all, a beautiful, godly wife on the morrow."

He heard the king breathe deep, then Malcolm chose four men to accompany him.

"They are my sisters," Edgar said. "I go as well."

"You are suggesting I replace one of my guard with you?" the king growled.

"I will not fail you, Your Grace, and especially not my sisters."

Theriot expected Malcolm to refuse, but he said, "Very well, I shall trust you to behave a man and warrior, ensuring 'tis a wedding I attend on the morrow, not a funeral."

They should have started for the dock, but Marguerite said, "I would like to accompany you."

"Marguerite!" Malcolm warned.

"Baron Wulfrith specified a guard of four," she rushed on as if fearing he would give her no time to persuade him. "I cannot be counted as one of them, nor do I believe he will mind if I return with you."

"The lady may ride with me," Theriot said and, amid the restlessness of men and horses eager to depart, heard her gasp. Too little thought he had given words birthed by the emptiness of knowing he would not see her again and that it gaped larger on this day that came earlier than expected, but he would regret them later.

"I am well with this," Malcolm said. "Now get astride, Sparrow. We ride!"

Though surely she expected to mount behind, when the Scotsman drew his horse close, Theriot extended a hand and said, "Before me, Marguerite."

She set her palm in his, then with a lean, a rustle of skirts, and a twist, she crossed from one horse to the other and settled across his thighs.

Curving an arm around her waist and cupping the soft span between ribs and hip, Theriot said low, "I will not hold you again, Malcolm's sparrow." It was honest, but when he felt her quake, he knew he should not have revealed this was more than kindness.

She turned her head, and he felt her searching gaze. "You would if you made me *your* sparrow."

Just as he should not have spoken, neither should he have shared his mount. Hoping to correct his error in some measure, he said, "That would require I make myself *your* burden."

That turned her forward and moved her to convulsive tears as he gave Grendel his heels and Dubh followed.

Cruel now, kind later, he excused what he did. But more than ever it rang false since he had created this situation.

Selfish, he silently rebuked and set his faulty gaze on movement and color that confirmed they brought up the rear.

PATIENCE WAS AN EXERCISE IN PAIN, this day the pain so great Pepin had come close to dishonoring his sire, a man increasingly more burden than help since his warrior's flame was extinguished when Marguerite passed through the sieve of her pursuers with the aid of the Rebels of the Pale.

Though Pepin's sire barely survived that encounter, he continued to command his son this way and that, and often the wrong way. For that offense, the need to avenge slain kin, the destruction of their home, and the loss of the slippery Patrick who determined the risk was too great to gain Marguerite, Pepin had nearly shouted at the shell that remained of his sire when Gerald ordered him to wait on letting death fly.

Had he yielded to impatience, he might have been heard by the opposing forces before the dock whose exchange was witnessed by these noblemen forced to turn mercenary. Then this vantage farther down the road from where the D'Argents and their men earlier concealed themselves would have been revealed.

Now as all came together with the appearance of half a dozen horses and riders on the road, Pepin was glad his sire had insisted they wait not only to see what came of Marguerite's flight to the city but use the time to gain leverage lest all go wrong. Much gratitude to the D'Argents for making that fairly effortless.

Pepin peered over his shoulder at the horses secured fifty feet distant. Though saddles and packs fit the backs of two, it was a bound and gagged warrior beyond his middling years who fit the third.

From among the Scotsmen the D'Argents had secured in the wood, this one was chosen for several reasons—that he was of some import and much culpability for having been at Malcolm's side when destruction was wreaked on the noblest of Norman families, and he was well enough past his middling years to be manageable. Unfortunately, that last proved illusion when a slam of the forehead nearly knocked Pepin's jaw out of joint and the only way to get the warrior over the horse's back was to render him unconscious. Now, should leverage be needed, father and son were not empty-handed, which greatly improved their chance of surviving what his grandfather had not.

Remembering the old man standing before the mass grave from which the bodies of those with arrows in their backs were removed, feeling those rheumy eyes on the wood where he had commanded his grandson to take Gerald who had yet to heal from injuries dealt by Saxon rebels, hearing again the barked order that if the old man did not escape the barbarian's wrath it was for Pepin and Gerald to avenge him, the youngest of his line ground his teeth—and harder when he recalled his grandfather toppling into a grave distant from holy ground and shared with commoners.

Suddenly aware of what sounded a panting dog, Pepin sealed his lips and so deeply drew breath through his nostrils the passages closed. His exhale opening them, once more he focused on those en route to the dock.

Though Marguerite whose back had earlier presented a fine target was now lost to revenge, not so the King of Scots who wore no chain mail and precisely followed instructions as if Baron Wulfrith had pierced his nose with a ring, hooked a finger through it, and wrenched him forward.

Or did he follow them precisely?

As Pepin shifted his gaze to the rider bringing up the rear who looked to be two, another among Malcolm's guard gave him pause. No Scotsman that.

"Prince Edgar," he rasped, then narrowed his eyes on the rider at the rear. Including the King of Scots, the Aetheling, and Sir Theriot, it was seven who came, and the woman sharing the latter's saddle had to be Marguerite. Further evidence of that was the trailing hound likely so fatigued it would be of little use in protecting her.

Pepin turned against the ancient tree that provided cover and shoved his lower face into the crook of an arm.

"What is it?" Gerald demanded.

Pepin wished the laughter he muffled was not joy of the morbid order, but since likely he would never again feel true joy, he indulged himself.

His sire gripped his shoulder. "Tell me!"

Pepin dropped his arm to his side. "Much gratitude to the D'Argents, though they know not what they do."

"What do they?"

"Fill this bucket of clear water with fish aplenty."

"Do not speak in riddles!" Gerald snapped.

His sire's sight being too poor to clearly see those approaching the dock, Pepin said, "Not only is Malcolm absent chain mail and Marguerite shares the saddle with the blind D'Argent, but the greatest threat to our king's throne is among those come from Edinburgh."

"Edgar," Gerald said. "Much reward if we put down that dog."

Providing we survive to collect it, Pepin thought. He did not excel in flying arrows, but was proficient enough he could loose several with good accuracy before he and his sire must regain their mounts to outrun those likely to give chase.

As if he had spoken aloud, Gerald said, "With greatest aim, my son—Malcolm first, Edgar second, and Marguerite have you time to let another fly."

As thought, though he did not have much chance of extending vengeance to his cousin since the Aetheling was to fall ahead of her. Possible if she rode behind, but she sat on the saddle's fore, making a small target—and even less a target if the blind D'Argent turned his horse when Malcolm and Edgar dropped. But since his sire accepted the possibility of that failure, Pepin was well with it.

As was required of him, he did not like Marguerite, but he saw enough through the thick of vengeance to know the King of Scots was more responsible for what befell his family than she who had overpowered their uncle, Claude—a man ever a weight around the necks of all.

"Malcolm, Edgar, then Marguerite," Pepin agreed.

"And ere the trade to ensure fewer pursuers."

Though Pepin need not be told that, certain when the arrows flew those guarding the princesses would close tighter around them and hold their positions, he echoed, "Ere the trade."

Then he drew arrows from his quiver, shoved the points of all but one in soft earth between the tree's roots, raised his bow, and nocked the first. Leaving the string lax, he turned and, keeping a shoulder to the tree, considered Malcolm's cautiously advancing party.

Just before they came off the road to begin their descent to where the D'Argents awaited them, they would be within range of a well-drawn arrow.

"It will land true," he rasped, then said over his shoulder, "Be ready to run for the horses. Once I put them to ground, the others will come for us."

CHAPTER THIRTY

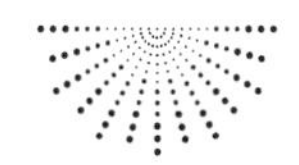

Even had Theriot not known what lay ahead, his senses would have been heightened by the unnatural one alerting him to blood spilled and yet to be spilled.

Oui, danger where the ferry docked this side of the estuary whose blue waters sparkled beneath a summer sun. Naught unusual there, danger inherent in enemy forces facing each other. However, it did not emanate from that direction alone. Senses of a strength not felt since before the Aetheling led his men through that northern village warned of greater danger to the left and farther ahead.

If not for the sudden sensation of being leagues distant from here, Theriot might have thought it more of Guarin's men among the trees. It was not. "It feels I am in the glen again."

"In the glen?" Marguerite alerted him he had spoken aloud.

It was habit to look down into the face she turned to him, but not fruitless, the sun angling across it allowing him to ascertain its shape. "Aye, the glen. Now be still so none guess what I tell and we lose the advantage of advance warning. I sense your kin here."

She gasped. "Where?"

"The wood opposite the dock is the only cover available. Methinks soon they will make their presence known."

"But with so many of Malcolm's and your brother's warriors here, their numbers would have to be great to present a threat. Likely they but keep watch, awaiting an opportunity—"

"This opportunity, Marguerite. Malcolm is here with fewer to watch his back than those who protect his future queen, you are here, and if they recognize Edgar, he could prove opportunity as well. I feel they are not many, but they are vengeful."

"But if they are not many—"

"How was your Scots escort slain when you sought to return your mother to Scotland?"

She shuddered.

"Oui, arrows," he said, gripped by so great a need to protect her it was difficult to think clearly about what was best for all. As if…

As if she is a D'Argent, he silently yielded. *First, in between, and in the end, a D'Argent.*

This must be how his brothers felt for those they wed—that they would as fiercely protect their wives as any whose veins ran with D'Argent blood. A different kind of love from what was felt for Dougray who also possessed only the family name, and yet the same, Theriot expected.

"I need you to tuck into me to make yourself smaller, Marguerite."

When her arms were around him, head pressed beneath his chin, he was struck by how different it felt to be held rather than to hold. And wished he did not want more of this.

Certain his kin would not move against Malcolm knowing this D'Argent was the one who disregarded their instructions, Theriot spurred Grendel toward Malcolm.

As Dubh gave a bark and leapt alongside, the king snapped

his head around. "What do you?" he demanded. "If ye think to—"

Theriot slowed. "No deception, Your Grace," he said only loud enough for the five here, certain the king's guard would move against him if he trespassed further. "I am the same man you have known these months, and you will have to trust me on that since there is no time to further prove myself."

"I am not of a mood—"

"The threat does not come from my family but Marguerite's." Then more for Edgar than any other, Theriot added, "Do not be obvious in looking for what you will not see, but methinks they are in the wood beyond the dock."

Amid the silence of consideration, Marguerite said, "You have trusted his senses before, my king, and he has earned trust beyond them. Pray, continue, else what happened to my escort and Cannie may happen here."

"You are certain of this, Sir Theriot?"

"Only certain I feel again what was felt when we were in the glen, though more anger and desperation now and I believe they are fewer. Thus, arrows."

"Almighty!" the Aetheling rasped.

"Silence, Edgar!" Malcolm commanded, then to Theriot, "Are we within range?"

"I do not know, though likely the D'Argents and their men are, perhaps even the princesses. Much depends on their exact location and bow skill. Regardless, they must remain unaware they are found out so they not act ahead of us."

"I shall slaughter them!"

That Theriot did not doubt—providing the King of Scots was not put through.

"Further I shall have to trust you, Sir Theriot, but I believe I know the man you are. Albeit instructed to halt on the road directly above the dock, we do so now though we shall be more distant in making the trade." He reined in, as did the others.

"Yer kin do not like this," he reported what Theriot could not see. "Let us assure them this is no trickery. For Marguerite's protection, I send you forth, and not by way of the road. Immediately turn off it, shielding her with your back, and ride at good speed while my men draw around Edgar and me. If arrows fly, we shall know whence they come. If they do not, inform your kin what goes and as recompense for the offense dealt me, command them to aid in bringing the miscreants to ground."

"They will require no incentive, Your Grace."

"Then go. And keep my sparrow safe."

Theriot shifted his regard to the shore and saw the forces arrayed there, the offensive in front of the defensive. Certain the figures at the fore and center were his family, he said, "Hold tight, Marguerite."

"Stay, Dubh!" Malcolm commanded, doubtless intending to make use of the hound who knew their attackers' scent from when last they trespassed.

Theriot urged his horse forward, and as soon as he was beyond the king, reined hard right and gave Grendel his heels. He did not know how Guarin and the others would interpret his sudden flight, but he was coming to them as whole as possible, and they would do naught to endanger him nor this woman.

Moments later, shouts sounded ahead and behind. Then just as Theriot heard great movement of those from whom he distanced himself, he saw movement of those he rode upon and the princesses' guard draw nearer their charges. Though he caught no sound of loosed arrows, he believed Marguerite's kin flew them and, regardless of whether they landed well, would fly more.

Was it of benefit he had no cause to heed the impulse to look behind and discover if the first arrows struck one or more targets? No sooner did he wonder that than he jerked with an impact just off center of his back.

It was like being struck hard with the sharp end of a pole that, blessedly, pierced little skin and no muscle nor bone—above all, no possibility of going through him into Marguerite. Likely, the one who flew it did not know his target wore chain mail. But had Theriot turned to the side to look around, Marguerite would have made a better mark.

"Theriot!" she exclaimed.

"Hold tight, Marguerite! My mail protects better than my tunic. 'Tis but a scratch."

Moments later, she said, "Guarin, Dougray, Maël, and Eberhard come."

"Their men?"

"Half. The others move nearer the princesses' guard."

To add to their protection, Theriot thought since they must realize this treachery was not of Malcolm.

"They are nearly upon us," Marguerite said.

As he could hear better than see.

She leaned to the side. "And Malcolm and his men go to the wood. It appears none are injured."

Then likely no more arrows, the only flight that of her kin running ahead of the king's vengeance.

Slowing Grendel, Theriot called, "Those were Norman arrows —a private vendetta against King Malcolm and Lady Marguerite."

Then his kin were dragging on their reins.

"Praise, it is good to see you!" Dougray said and came alongside and gripped his brother's arm. Then eyes that searched Theriot's were as felt as they should be seen. And not only Dougray's but those of his eldest brother and cousin.

"What Normans are they?" Guarin demanded.

"My uncle, Gerald," Marguerite answered, "my cousin, Pepin, and possibly others."

"Likely only those two," Maël said.

"How do you know?" she asked.

"That must wait," Theriot said and shifted his gaze from one figure to the other. "Be assured all is well with Malcolm and me. Now to ensure all is well between him and you, we must aid in ending this assault."

"We?" Dougray said. "But you—"

"I believed in you," Theriot said. "My injury is different from yours but I am not helpless." He turned his face to his nephew whose figure was slight compared to the three warriors. "Take Lady Marguerite onto your horse, Eberhard. We must ride."

Though Theriot felt her reluctance to be parted from him, she loosed her hold and moved onto the youth's horse.

After Guarin commanded the half of his men who accompanied him forward to return to the others, he said, "Lady Marguerite, you will speak for your king and me in assuring the princesses' guard that the ill between us is resolved and we give aid in bringing down those who loosed arrows."

"I will," she said, and Theriot knew she wished to speak something to him, but he turned aside.

"Take the lead, Dougray!" Guarin commanded the one whose ability to track was most exceptional.

Theriot disliked bringing up the rear, allowing those ahead to serve as shields and forge for him an unobstructed path through the wood, it once more making him feel the little brother too young to do for himself. But there was good in it, furthering his determination to adapt to his loss of vision should it not adequately improve. If when all that could be done was done and still he fell short of the warrior he had been, only then would he adjust his expectations of an altered life, perhaps a lonely life, but still...life.

"We are dead men."

We, Pepin mulled. *Not I—we.*

Though his own thoughts had gone that way and not for the first time, to hear it spoken and not be told to run and assured Gerald would draw them away from his son…

The same as his sire, Pepin had wanted to avenge his losses, and the possibility of death was acceptable to see Malcolm and Marguerite suffer, but three of the four arrows flown before he and his sire were forced to gain their saddles lacked the range needed to reach Malcolm and Edgar. And the fourth…

A perfect draw. A perfect release. A perfect landing made more perfect had the blind D'Argent not worn mail that prevented the arrow from piercing both riders.

"Naught to show for it," his sire said. "It feels God is their side, condoning what was done us as if they are the ones wronged."

His tone, sounding less of bitterness than wonder, brought Pepin's head around. Peering at Gerald amid the shadows of this dense wood bordering a ravine whose sides were mostly sheer rock, he waited. And heard the silence of the Scotsman bound over the back of his horse. Was it that of senselessness or listening?

"Do you think them more wronged than us?" his sire asked as Pepin considered once more bringing his dagger's hilt down on their hostage's head. "Or is God merely cruel, our lives but things sacrificed to entertain Himself ahead of protecting His children?"

Possible, Pepin thought. After all, little consideration did Gerald show *his* son. And much that tempted Pepin to abandon him to increase his own chance of survival.

"What think you, my boy?"

Pepin breathed deep. "Only the Lord knows."

After a time, Gerald said, "*We* are not dead men. I am." He set a hand on his son's arm. "As soon as Malcolm and his men pass out of sight, I will follow, and you will go opposite, neither thinking nor looking back."

Resentment born of desperation beginning to loosen the knots into which it tied him, Pepin exclaimed, "Father—"

"Non! My mother warned that my sire led their sons wrong, and as I would not accept it for fear of disappointing and angering him, I have led you wrong, pulling you down the ever-forking road that shall prove my end as it proved his. Though I have too little warning to prepare for death—no confession, no absolution—I will not deny you that. Honor my wishes and go from me, being done with this vengeance as I should have been long ago."

"Long ago?"

Momentarily, he closed his eyes. "Had I prevented your grandfather from slaying Marguerite's escort, heeding what my mother taught me, none would have died and still we would have our home. Oui, an angry old man in our midst, but when was he not angry?" He sighed. "You will go?"

Pepin swallowed hard. "You believe I could turn my back on you, knowing they will kill you?"

"Turn your back on me or not, I die this day, but be assured I will give none the satisfaction of putting me in the grave as done my father."

"Then—?"

"Do not ask." He gripped Pepin's arm. "Do as I say so you not die without warning."

The longing to agree caused bile to rise.

"Son?"

Pepin gulped, nodded.

"And no vengeance. It ends here, else you could lose your next wife not to childbirth but more of this."

If he wed again, and what chance of that now he was reduced to the life of a mercenary? "I understand, Sire."

"Not truly, but if you have children, one day you may—if you lead them better than you were led."

Only possible *if* any children born to him survived since the Lord seemed intent on extinguishing his line—no children born to the sickly Claude who had no reason to make a family, no children who survived the birthings that took Pepin's wife the second time she delivered a babe, and only Marguerite surviving her mother's birthings.

"It is decided, Pepin. Now pass me the—" Gerald's teeth snapped, then between them he said, "Malcolm comes. Pass me the Scotsman's reins, then thinking and looking ahead—never again behind—go."

CHAPTER THIRTY-ONE

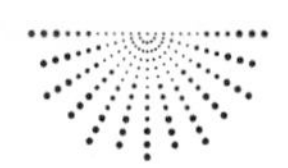

Dubh's barking indicated the direction the D'Argents should go to overtake the King of Scots and those hunted. And yet...

"Halt!" Theriot shouted, so abruptly reining in the dust of the narrow road billowed, stinging eyes and wending nostrils.

His kin came around, and when he revealed he sensed those pursued were nearer than Malcolm and his men, as ever they had considered his instincts, they considered them now—as though naught had changed.

Since this was not the time to indulge the D'Argent returned to them less than whole, was it habit? Or did they still have faith in his ability to sense things beyond their reach?

Amid hesitation, likely they also questioned it, but Dougray said, "Point the way."

When Theriot altered their southwestern course in favor of a southeastern one that took them into a dense wood, the others did not question him in any way perceptible.

Though perhaps they should, doubt squeezed in as once more he urged Grendel to follow those ahead.

They should not, he silently countered, and much proof he

had of that now a prayer often sent heavenward was answered as longed for—full restoration of his unnatural sense so in the event his sight was not entirely healed, he would have that to aid in moving through the world when he departed Scotland.

His extra sense weaving itself through the others, stitching all together and beautifully finishing their edges, reached out on all sides of him. However, it was not as familiar as once it had been. As if compensation for what was lost, it felt of greater strength.

Shortly, Dougray reined in and slowly moved his mount around the area. "It is as Theriot sensed," he said. "Three horses were here. When they departed, two went southwest in the same direction as King Malcolm, one southeast."

"Then we follow the latter," Guarin said. "Ride!"

When they came out of the wood, before them was an expanse of gently rolling hills with few trees, doubtless making it easy for those of good sight to see any who fled. Though Dubh could still be heard, only just.

"There—far right returning to the wood!" Dougray shouted. "He knows we follow."

No matter how Theriot strained to see past his clouds, the rider was too distant to pick him from the landscape. Thus, all he could do was follow his kin and match their pace.

"We have him!" Maël called. "If he reaches the wood, he will have too little time to draw it around him."

Shortly, Guarin announced their prey accepted the hopelessness of his flight. "He has his bow to hand and comes around—coifs up, spread out!"

Theriot dragged his mail hood over his head, and as they fanned out to put distance between themselves, used the figure of Dougray and his mount ahead to guide his flight.

Grendel surely sensed danger, but the steed did not falter, even when Dougray warned an arrow was loosed and Theriot heard it pass between him and his brother.

"He nocks again!" Maël warned.

"And flies!" Dougray shouted.

There was nothing straight about their ride, but the one who released the arrow either anticipated well their swiftly meandering approach, else luck landed it true, the impact knocking Guarin out of the saddle.

Certain he of little sight was of greatest use to his eldest brother, Theriot shouted, "I have him!" and jerked his reins left to circle back.

The other two remained true to their training that taught one injured or dead could fast become many when fear and compassion moved warriors to abandon their objective. And the objective here was to keep Marguerite's kin from doing worse than already they had done.

When the figure of Guarin quickly regained his feet, Theriot rasped, "Merciful God!"

"My shoulder shall be bruised and sore like your back, but no blood drawn," Guarin said when his brother came alongside. "Blessed chain mail."

Gripping Grendel harder with his thighs, Theriot reached to aid him in mounting behind. Then wasting no moment on retrieving Guarin's horse, he spurred toward those ahead.

"What do you see?" Theriot called over his shoulder.

"That we are not needed. The miscreant flees again, and I believe Maël intends to knock him off *his* horse."

Still Theriot urged Grendel to swiftly deliver them to the others, and they were near when Guarin once more reported what Theriot could make little sense of. "Maël has dismounted and taken the knave to ground. Go right so we not trample him."

Theriot did as told, and as he neared Dougray who also reined in, saw Maël sweep his blade toward the man at his feet.

It should be my blade, Theriot thought. *I should be the one to take him to ground for the ill he sought to do Marguerite and me.*

"Breathe too deeply, Pepin, and I shall consider it a request to die at my hands rather than King Malcolm's," Maël said. "Of course, if he is as barbaric as told, you may prefer I do the deed."

Guarin dismounted and strode to Maël. "A coward's arrow sought the back of my brother, a fleeing man's arrow sought my heart. Though it is our due to give answer to these offenses, I believe my cousin is right. Better Malcolm Canmore decide your fate."

"My slaughter," spat the Norman of diluted accent, "and that of my sire."

"The cost of treachery," Guarin said, then commanded, "Divest him of his weapons, bind him, and get him astride."

As Dougray swung out of the saddle to aid Maël, Guarin strode to Theriot. "Well done, Brother. As ever, you know what we cannot. Be assured, we shall exploit that God-gifted sense to see you made as right as possible."

As possible, Theriot thought, though with little bitterness and much gratitude his brother did not give false hope of returning him to the warrior he had been.

Guarin gripped his arm. "First, in between, and in the end, Theriot."

It was of comfort, but of less comfort than expected was that soon he would depart Scotland.

As is best, he reminded himself. *Cruel now, kind later, for both Marguerite* and *me.*

The return journey with their captive was nearly as swift as their departure, and it surprised when once more Dubh was heard, her barks sounding from the same direction as when Theriot's instincts caused the D'Argents to veer away. Surely by now Malcolm and his men ought to have captured or slain their prey and started back.

After passing through the wood and returning to the dirt road, they followed the hound's din to a clearing.

Dougray riding at Theriot's side told that Malcolm and his

men sat their saddles a hundred feet distant from Pepin's sire who stood at the edge of a ravine. "The miscreant has a Scotsman on his knees before him, a dagger at his throat."

"The hostage?" Theriot asked.

"Doubtless, the knaves were watching when we overwhelmed those who rode to escort the princesses from the dock and bound them in the wood. They took the leader."

The man Theriot no longer first thought of as the one who blinded him. "He is Hendrie."

No sooner said than Marguerite's uncle shouted above Dubh's barks, "This is not our bargain, Malcolm! You agreed my son would go free. Do you not release him, I will cut this dirty Scot's throat!"

"Hold, Gerald!" the king commanded. "The D'Argents and their prisoner will come to my side—no nearer—and we shall discuss these altered circumstances."

"He goes free else—!"

"If you draw one drop of my man's blood, I shall cut your whelp's throat—then yours."

That silenced him.

"We are summoned forth," Dougray informed Theriot.

As was Dubh who ceased barking when the king called her to his side.

Moments later, amid the curses of Pepin muffled by the cloth in his mouth, the D'Argents halted near Malcolm. From the tension, Theriot knew that just as the king's men were prepared to draw blood, so were the D'Argents if either side moved as they ought not.

"Baron Wulfrith, you are responsible for my man falling into the hands of your fellow Norman," the King of Scots said with just enough control his voice did not carry to the ravine. "If not for the attempt to put an arrow in your brother's back, I might think you conspire with them. Or perhaps you did conspire, unaware a personal vendetta would see them turn on you."

"King Malcolm, when we captured your warriors, it was with the intention of trading the princess and her entourage for my brother—naught else, though our king would see it as betrayal we sought our own end rather than prevent your wedding. We did not know we were observed by those who are fellow Normans only for being born in the country of our birth, having believed the men who posed as swords for hire to negotiate this foreign land had departed. I apologize that what we did to gain my brother's release allowed them to take one of your men hostage. But now we deliver his son to do with as you like."

"What I would like is to bleed him alongside his sire. Unfortunately, your capture of Pepin changes naught. It but prolongs the wait."

"The wait?"

"To preserve my man's life, not only did I give my word I will not pursue Gerald's son, but I was required to give proof by ensuring Pepin an hour's lead. That hour we were counting down when you arrived, and now we must begin anew. Accursed D'Argents! Did I not know your family's reputation and had not Sir Theriot earned my trust, this day would not end well for you."

Nor you, Theriot knew his brother was thinking.

"We came to retrieve Theriot," Guarin said, "and that we have done with no loss of life on either side."

The king grunted. "Admirable and testament to the good spoken of your family. Now let us—"

"What of our bargain, Malcolm?" Gerald called. "Does it stand?"

"Almighty, if only Hendrie were not almost a brother to me," the king muttered.

"As told, I am the one responsible for all," Pepin's father called with what sounded greater desperation. "Providing my son lives, this day the vendetta ends."

"The bargain stands, Gerald," Malcolm answered. "Your boy goes free, but know this—if an hour hence you do my man harm, no matter how far I must venture into Le Bâtard's kingdom, I will pursue Pepin and do worse to him. And if he returns to Scotland, he will be a dead man days—nay, weeks—ere I permit him to draw his last breath."

"Then release him so the hour may begin counting down again," Gerald shouted.

It was Maël who unbound Pepin, and the moment the gag was removed, the knave demanded, "What of my sire?"

"His end is here," Malcolm said. "Now that you know the terms, it is for you to decide whether to hold to them and live or break them and die."

"But—"

"Your son questions the terms, Gerald! I would not have my man die, but give me no choice and it will cost two Norman lives for one Scotsman's."

"Leave, Pepin! Now!"

Though Theriot could not see the emotions working Pepin's face, he felt them—and anguish amid anger.

Then Marguerite's cousin put heels to his horse. When the sound of his retreat faded, silence reigned beyond an occasional muttering from the Aetheling and Dubh's impatient whimpering as she paced between the king and Theriot.

It was Gerald who determined the passing of an hour. "That suffices! Now as I keep my word, King of Scots, keep yours and leave my son be."

"He has released Hendrie," Dougray said, and Theriot made out what appeared one figure becoming two, the forward one advancing with a slight hitch and the one behind...backing away.

"Gerald!" Malcolm bellowed.

"The terms are kept, barbarian! My end is here. And now." He took another step back and dropped into the ravine.

"Wretch!" Malcolm barked. "He denies me the satisfaction of —" His tirade ended abruptly, and he chuckled. "Better for both of us. He is no longer a threat, and I do not have to hide from My Pearl what I would have done to him. Now let us finish this, Baron Wulfrith. After you show me where you bound my other men, you will retrieve yours from the dock, take your brother, and leave my country. And I shall try to forget the ruin nearly made of this day."

"WHAT WAS your answered prayer *this* day?"

Theriot released the princess's hand he had drawn to his lips, and as he set his gaze in the vicinity of hers, felt the brush of Dubh settling alongside. "A prayer answered as hoped, Princess."

She put her head to the side. "And yet you are leaving us?" she said as if hopeful his prayer on the day past that Marguerite's feelings for him be lifted had been replaced by one in which he made a life with her in Scotland.

Theriot nearly shifted his regard past her to where that lady was among her countrymen who stood at attention though it was mostly formality now the D'Argents and their men prepared to depart.

Assured their conversation extended only as far as the princess and Malcolm at her side, Theriot said, "I praise the Lord for the answer given in accord with my prayer for full restoration of my unnatural sense. That was done this day. As for your prayer for a future for Marguerite and me, still I do not believe it can be answered well."

"Of course it can be—*you* can answer it well!" The force of her response reminded him of Hugh who snatched his seven-year-old nephew up out of the dirt and commanded that never again he claim only the Lord could do what was asked of this

D'Argent—that he do and do again until all that could be done was done.

Then Hugh had forced Theriot's fingers around the lance tossed aside and told if it took all day into night for him to prevail over the quintain whose sandbag continually knocked him out of the saddle, so be it. It took until dusk shadowed the training yard for the boy to defeat the quintain a dozen successive times, but he had done what he declared only the Lord could do.

"Forgive my passion," the princess said. "What I am saying and as I believe you know, is it is not enough to beseech Him to put this right so you can do that, put that right so you can do this. 'Tis not all for Him to do."

Unlike his uncle, her faith was great, and yet like Hugh she placed much value in doing for one's self. As taught Theriot, he did as well, but regaining sight was different from the relentless practice and teeth-grinding strategy required to effectively wield weapons—and exercising caution to protect the warrior as he had failed to do that night in the village, albeit for selfless reasons.

She set a hand on his arm. "Just as I am certain restoration of your keen sense was not all of the Lord, who I believe more delights in aiding His children than in heaping gifts on them, I am certain what yet eludes is within your grasp. Though ever your sight may be impaired, by way of acceptance you can make good of it—and better than most for the Lord preparing the way by long ago gifting you that extra sense."

It *was* as if the Almighty had known he would require it and made provision for him—that He was no mere observer. Though neither was He a granter of hopes and desires, there was comfort in knowing prayer was answered ahead of its need. Certes, lacking his unnatural sense, his blinding would be…

Possibly beyond redemption, he thought, and assured himself if sightlessness was to be his fate, in time he would accept his loss as his sire had accepted his own. But though with the aid of kin he would find ways to negotiate life with the least amount of assistance, that did not mean he would be fit for a future like those of his brothers. To be a burden to wife and children…to suffer the humiliation of being unable to properly provide for and defend them…

"Beware of pride," the princess said softly. "It can cost you things most precious."

Once more marveling over the insight and wisdom surely gifted her in preparation for the day she became Scotland's queen, he said, "I shall beware," and turned to Malcolm. "I thank you for the trust and privileges afforded me, and for Grendel."

Those high and broad shoulders shrugged. "He is Norman the same as you, and you won him."

Theriot inclined his head. "I regret I shall not attend your wedding, the occasion of which will surely be momentous. In my absence, know I wish you and your wife happiness, many a lusty babe in arms, and long lives."

"Much appreciated, Sir Theriot." The king paused. "And know this—ever you are welcome at my court, whether you but visit or remain a time."

"I am honored. Now with your leave, I shall speak with Lady Marguerite."

"I insist." Malcolm called her forward and drew his betrothed aside.

Marguerite did not come alone, on one side a warrior whose hitch revealed it was Hendrie, on the other side Cristina.

"I have enjoyed your company," the princess said and touched his hand as had become habit during their acquaintance.

Alerted to where he would find hers, he took it and kissed her knuckles. "As I have enjoyed yours, Princess Cristina."

"Godspeed," she said and moved toward Malcolm and her sister.

"I am well with you, Chevalier," Hendrie said. "Are ye well with me?"

"I am."

The Scotsman leaned in. "Do right by the lass," he rasped. "Even if she sees you not again, leave *yer* heart in her keeping as she leaves hers in yours."

The opposite of cruel now, kind later...

Hendrie clapped a hand to Theriot's arm. "Godspeed, Norman."

As the Scotsman followed Cristina toward his liege, Marguerite stepped near. "Though I wished this day soon come and gone, 'tis too soon. Like death around a corner one thought yet distant, there is too little warning to truly prepare for it. Is it too soon for you?"

Cruel now, kind later, he commanded himself. And disobeyed. "It is what I sought, but—oui—too soon."

She stepped nearer yet, causing Dubh's tail to wag so fiercely it knocked the backs of Theriot's knees, tilted her face higher, and whispered, "Tá mo chroí istigh ionat."

He closed his fingers into his palms, but what they should not touch, his words did, defying him as Hendrie would approve. "Tá mo chroí istigh ionat."

Marguerite stared at the man who gave back words pronounced perfectly as if practiced. "You..." She swallowed. "Do you know the meaning?"

"Hendrie told me."

Feeling as if she came up out of sleep to find herself someplace unexpected, she said, "Then you have a great care for me as I have for you?"

"I do, but still I go."

She moistened her lips. "But loving me, you will return?"

"Only if the warrior once capable of protecting and defending others is restored, and..."

Movement at his side drew her regard to Dubh who ran her

tongue over Theriot's hand. The same as the hound, Marguerite felt his turmoil. He did not believe he would be restored to the extent required of himself, and his next words confirmed it.

"Do not wait for me. Many will be the suitors of Malcolm's sparrow. Choose well and live well."

"Without a heart?"

"You have mine. Be kind to it as I shall be to yours."

Though aware of the audience made of her people and his on the estuary's shore, she moved so near her feet were between his.

"Marguerite?"

She set her hands on both sides of his face and pushed to her toes. "I am being kind to your heart—and mine," she said and pressed her lips to his.

At worst, she thought he would push her away, at best be unresponsive, but he put his arms around her and made her inexperienced kiss one of great experience. It did not last long, but she assured herself it and his profession of love were enough to hold dear for however long this was all she had of him—even if he did not return.

He set her back, and when she peered into his clouded eyes, the lips that had been on hers were pressed thin. "It is not enough that at this distance I can see the shape of your face. So I say again, do not wait for me."

Vision blurring, she lowered her gaze and saw an edge of the cloth tucked beneath the neck of his tunic. Impulsively, she drew the ends free.

"Marguerite?"

"You are much favored by God—and me," she said and knotted the cloth at the base of his throat so it was more felt. "Will you grant me a boon?" At his hesitation, she prompted, "It requires only a moment, but it would mean much to me."

"I will do it."

"Ere you go from my sight, look back as I looked back the

first time we met. Even though you may see naught of me, know I am here where you leave me, praying for your return."

"It is the same my mother asked of her sons when we rode to join Duke William in making England Norman." He nodded. "I will look back."

She was grateful he did not tell her again not to wait for him. But then, likely he thought it discouragement enough to reveal her request was no different from that of his mother to whom he had not returned these four years.

"Stay, Dubh!" he said and turned away.

Though Marguerite felt like hanging her head the same as the hound who closed the distance between what was wanted and what must be accepted, she kept her chin up and watched Theriot gain the saddle.

"Tá mo chroí istigh ionat," she whispered, and as she waited for him to look around, began praying him back to her.

SHE WAS where he had left her, though as she had known, he could not see her on the shore before the estuary's sparkling waters. Having looked back, he and his kin ought to resume their journey, but he remained unmoving atop Grendel.

"I thought if I saw the mute Margaret again, it would be in Derbyshire," Dougray said, drawing alongside, "and she would be wife to he who fathered me. It must have surprised you as well to learn she is Marguerite of Scotland who I understand sings more beautifully than a sparrow."

Movement on the shore indicating Malcolm prepared to deliver his betrothed to Edinburgh, Theriot held his gaze to where he believed Marguerite watched, Dubh at her side. "It did surprise, and much there is to that, Dougray."

"As told by your kiss." There was a smile in his brother's voice. "I look forward to learning all that transpired as likely you learned from Marguerite how I came to be husband to the rebel, Em."

Tugged toward memories of their time in the hut, Theriot murmured, "She told me."

"My brother loves."

He did, but this was not a conversation for now or the near future. "How did you learn I was Malcolm's prisoner?"

Dougray chuckled over the attempt to sweep away Marguerite who could not be swept away. "We shall save the details for later. For now, know it required persistence, discovery of a horse of unusual color and eyes who awaits his master's return, and patience when our plan to sooner bring you out of Scotland was thwarted by tidings Nicola required our aid."

It was on Theriot's tongue to tell he had hoped the steed would point the way to him, but fear for their sister brought his head around. "Nicola is well?"

"As there is much tale to what befell you, there is much to hers though, more often than not, Nicola befell Nicola. But be assured she is as well as our cousin, Maël, whose exploits are also worthy of hours before a campfire." He gripped Theriot's shoulder. "You have missed a great deal, but we shall enlighten you. And once we return to Wulfen Castle, it begins."

Hearing resolve in his voice, Theriot understood the meaning of that last, but he said, "What begins?"

"Just as you and Cyr demanded of me what was needed to begin reclaiming the warrior who lost an arm at Hastings, this one who no longer believes himself nameless shall be fearless, merciless—even heartless—in ensuring whatever is lost to you that can be restored is restored, whatever cannot be restored, replaced."

Theriot felt resentment that would surely go deeper when his brother sought to make good his vow, but he had to smile. "All that and reckless as well, Dougray?"

"Reckless?"

"Recall the fist I took to the face when you proved unreceptive to *my* efforts."

"I thought my knuckles broken." Dougray chuckled, then said, "Oui, if necessary, reckless. And when we are done, you must speak with our sire."

"As I find myself in similar circumstances, I think often on seeking his counsel." Theriot frowned. "Did you after losing your arm?"

"I did not, but seeing I was drowning in self pity, he ventured where he was not welcome, and I rejected what he shared. But as you are receptive, I believe the tale told me in full will be of use to you."

"The tale?"

"Of Godfroi and Robine—before the illegitimate Dougray and after." He sighed. "Now we should ride. The journey is long, and the sooner we complete whatever work must be done, the sooner you may venture beyond that kiss."

Theriot nearly rebuked him for seeing a future almost certainly lost to this D'Argent since he would not return to Marguerite unless the warrior was well enough restored. Instead, he looked to the shore and touched the cloth knotted at his throat. "Is she still there, Dougray?"

"She is, the hound at her side, and Hendrie leads a horse to her."

"I have told her not to wait for me."

"And yet I believe she will. But lest I am wrong, when you wish to strike Guarin or me, work harder, little brother."

Theriot grunted, then turned Grendel and rode out of sight of the one to whom he had given the keeping of his heart.

CHAPTER THIRTY-TWO

Castle D'Argent, France
Late Autumn, 1070

The King of England had released him from his service, underestimating him just as Theriot had underestimated himself when he feared he would not fully recover his sight, but that was as planned should it become feasible for this D'Argent to depart England—and not merely to journey to Normandy as done two days past.

During William's recent pause at Wulfen Castle, the conqueror had been given no reason to believe Theriot would be of further use to him. Though his esteemed warrior and scout had moved well about the great hall, it was with the aid of stick and hound, the former grudgingly wielded in poor light and unfamiliar surroundings, the latter less instinctual than Dubh but progressing well in guiding its master clear of obstacles.

Thus, as Theriot was now of little consequence to his liege, he would not be missed, unlike Maël who had disappeared shortly after he and his cousins departed Scotland. Also as planned, William believed ill had befallen his captain of the guard en route to returning to his service, unaware Maël had crossed to the continent to begin life with a woman whose threat to the conqueror's rule had necessitated it being made to appear she had died.

As Dougray told, quite the tale that, and one that rivaled Nicola's, though potentially more dangerous for the deception worked to escape the reach of one of the most powerful men in Christendom. But as the links of that deception had held these four months since Maël took his bride distant from Normandy, it seemed unlikely their welds would break.

As for Theriot's deception, he was fairly confident it would hold when William learned where this D'Argent made his home. It was not misfortune rumor had reached the king that during his scout's imprisonment he became entranced with his Scottish healer. William had pried at that while at Wulfen, unaware he himself had met her once. When all he gained was acknowledgement Lady Marguerite was winsome, he had pronounced it greater folly for a Norman to join with a barbaric Scot than a Saxon.

Before much longer, Theriot would give him cause to once more congratulate himself on being immune to the imprudence of mere mortals who could never be king. But no matter how it pricked one's pride, best William continue to believe in his superiority.

"Beloved Theriot," his mother said again, then lifted her face from his tear-dampened tunic. "We have held close your missives, praying over tidings of your training with Guarin, Dougray, and Nicola's husband. Now—" Her voice cracked. "At last you are home."

He kissed her cheek. "It has been too long."

When he released her, she turned to Dougray who had gone first into the arms of his wife who had expected him to collect her from her in-laws sooner than love for his brother allowed.

Just as Theriot would not remain long at Castle D'Argent, neither would Dougray who should have returned to England with Em months past to begin administering the lands to which Michel Roche had made him heir. The sooner they departed, the better since likely their unborn child had made its presence felt during their embrace.

"Well come, little brother," said Godfroi and Robine's second son as he stepped from his wife's side.

A growl sounding, Theriot set a hand on the hound's head. "Friend," he said, that one word all that was required to calm Liath who was named for the grey of his fur.

The brothers' embrace was fierce, and when they parted, Theriot knew Cyr searched his eyes for what could and could not be seen—unsurprisingly, without pity, which still had the power to offend.

The hugs of his sisters-in-law were more gentle, not only for being women but because Aelfled carried her son on her hip and Em a child in the cradle of her firm belly.

Lady Robine returned to Theriot. "Do you remember Aelfled's grandmother, Bernia, who now resides with us?"

Recalling the wily blind woman over whom he had marveled for her ability to move about her village as though sighted, he said, "I do."

"She would like to speak with you later."

Likely to impart advice. Months ago, Theriot would have been affronted, but no longer. "I look forward to meeting her again."

Robine slid an arm through his. "Your sire is eager for your return to heart and hearth. We have kept him waiting too long."

Liath's long body brushing his master's leg, they climbed the steps and entered the great hall where the light was good, permitting Theriot to locate the figure in the high seat.

"Stay, Liath," he commanded when they reached the dais and his mother released his arm.

Godfroi D'Argent could not rise to greet his son, but neither did he voice a greeting, and Theriot knew the reason before he dropped to a knee—much emotion, as further evidenced by the large, quaking hand that settled atop his head and the other that gripped his shoulder.

"A thousand prayers answered," Godfroi finally spoke. "Now rise and embrace your sire."

Theriot pushed upright and put his arms around the man whose upper body, in defiance of the lower, still felt as broad, muscular, and powerful as when he gave his sons his blessing to join the Duke of Normandy in asserting his claim to the English throne.

"I have missed you and mother," Theriot said.

Godfroi swallowed loudly. "Sit beside me. We have much to discuss." As Theriot lowered into his mother's chair, the baron called, "Dougray, my son!"

The third-born stepped from between his wife and Cyr and knelt. Godfroi set a hand on his head, and after praising the Lord for returning him to his family—above all Em and their child to come—they also embraced.

"This evening, we feast," Godfroi announced when Dougray returned to his wife. "For now, I would be alone with Theriot."

When all had withdrawn but Robine, she stepped onto the dais, took the hand her husband offered, and turned to her son who respectfully rose before her. "If you are blessed to love and be loved and allow God to stand all sides of you, ever you and your love will be whole to each other. What is in here and here" —she touched Theriot's brow and chest—"is what binds you even when tribulation tramples joy."

He set a hand on her forearm, drew it down over her palm, and kissed her fingers. "I thank you, Mother."

She touched her lips to his cheek, then left father, son, and the hound who crept onto the dais and stretched out beside the chair into which Theriot once more lowered.

Silence descended, but it was not uncomfortable, merely the silence of feeling the pulled seams on either side of the great time and distance between father and son move toward each other.

Then Godfroi adjusted the blanket draped over his legs and said, "The Lord is good, even when we think He is not and cast our grievances far and wide and ignore much evidence He has little care for us."

"Greatly I have questioned Him and still do," Theriot admitted, "but between the good and bad...the bad and good, I forge a path back to Him."

The baron inclined his head. "I believe what I wish to share will ease your journey."

Then as hoped, Theriot would receive what once Dougray had rejected. "Share it with me, Sire."

Godfroi settled back. "Though you know the story of your mother and me, there is more untold than told. Now attend, my son, and I will reveal what I believed you need never know—not only the beauty of our tale but the ugliness and suffering that required much faith to overcome. Attend."

Village of Widden
Dunfermline, Scotland

ANOTHER SUITOR?

"Pray not," Marguerite muttered, having thought she had seen the last of them a month past when Dubh took offense at a lord of middle years attempting to steal a kiss. In the Scot's haste to depart, he had left behind the torn plaid that provided no barrier between his calf and the hound's teeth.

Now, the strength and pitch of Dubh's barking different from when a villager called, Marguerite was tempted to swing open the door before which the hound paced, but she would deal with this herself.

Before Dubh realized her intent, she was out the rear door. Had she not slammed it, the hound would have made it through and bolted for the road.

Morning air nipping at her, Marguerite was grateful for the blanket she had dropped over her gown while kindling last eve's fire back to life. Drawing it closer, she stepped stones marking the path through a garden whose summer beauty had been lost to autumn.

As she neared the front of the cottage, she caught sounds that told it was not a single rider who approached. Where suitors were concerned, there was nothing unusual about that, several having been accompanied by retainers when her absence from court forced them to seek her here. What was unusual beyond a hound trotting alongside three riders was that two of her visitors had silver in the dark of their hair.

Halting, Marguerite fixed her gaze on the one center of the others. Were his eyes upon her? They must be, for he had said he would return only if…

She called his name, snatched up her skirts, and somewhere between the cottage and road shed the blanket.

Guarin and Eberhard halted their horses and the riderless one following on a lead, that stallion's eyes of such pale blue the color could be seen at a distance. A moment later, its owner reined in. Then he was out of the saddle and had only enough time to open his arms before she fell into them.

"You have returned to me!" Those strong arms closing around her, her heart soared higher and wider. "My prayer answered in full!"

Surely he did not stiffen? "Answered, but not in full, Marguerite."

She wished she did not feel nor hear him right, his tension

and tone a poor match for her joy. But then why had he welcomed her into his arms as if she might remain here?

He drew slightly back. "Look at me, Marguerite."

She raised her gaze over the cloth she had knotted around his neck, a short, well-groomed beard, and flared nostrils. She paused, then set her eyes upon his. Though she could see more green, they remained clouded.

"You see?" he said.

Heart beginning to break anew, she breathed, "Not answered in full." Meaning this was only a visit.

"I see you better, but still not well, Marguerite. More I saw you when first we met in the night and you were hooded."

She dropped her arms from around him and stepped back. "You should not have come."

His jaw shifted, and movement at his side drew her regard to that which made her nose prickle—a hound of grey slightly larger than Dubh who had resumed barking.

"Why should I not have come?"

Feeling the chill of morn that was all the colder for the chill of sorrow, she wished the blanket once more around her. "Because I thought you came for me. Now…" She drew a shaky breath. "When once again you leave, more I shall ache than when first I lost you."

"Did I not look back as you asked of me?"

Her breath caught. "You did."

"Thus, I have returned to you—to stay and serve your king."

"But you said…"

"That I would come only were my vision fully restored." He turned and removed a sword from a scabbard fastened to his saddle. Nay, not a sword.

"Theriot?"

"There is little hope I will see again as once I did," he said. "For that—this."

She stared at a cane wrought of oak and topped with an iron pommel.

"The second gifted me by Dougray. I was even less receptive to the first than I was yours." He smiled wryly. "So here I am and would have been sooner had I not journeyed to my sire to receive his counsel on how a broken warrior can make a better life than the one before."

Mouth very dry, she said, "What did he tell?"

"What he had told before and I had regarded as mostly sentimental. He said only three are needed—God, my mother, and him. Then he gifted me their tale in its entirety, which I am to share with you. Should I tell his parting words?"

"Pray, do," she whispered.

"He said even those greatly favored must be broken, and it is good to be halved so we might make a better whole as Robine and he did." He smiled. "Tá mo chroí istigh ionat, Marguerite."

Tears spilling, she set a hand on his chest and felt the powerful beat against her palm. "My heart is in you."

"I kept it safe."

She caught up his hand and pressed it between her breasts. "I kept yours safe."

As if counting the beats, he was still a long time, then he said, "You remember when you told me soon the dawn comes?"

She swallowed hard. "I remember."

"It is here, Marguerite. Now. Even were my sight fully restored, I could not see you better than this."

A sob slipped from her, then once more she was in his arms.

Their audience did not complain over the duration of their embrace, unlike the one whose barks became more ferocious.

Theriot lifted his head. "Do you think Dubh knows I am here?"

Marguerite smiled as if he could see every curve and line of her joy. "I do."

Now he smiled, and the dimples whose true depths were

previously denied her showed through his whiskers. "Take me to her. Once we are reacquainted and she and my hound are well with each other, we go to the glen."

"The glen?"

"Malcolm and his queen await us at the chapel."

Her heart leapt, then what she had earlier let slip past came back around. "Truly, you are to serve my king?"

"As William has released this blinded warrior from his service, I shall enter the service of he who shall be my king henceforth."

"Does William know?"

"He will learn of it, but methinks it will be of little more consequence than if I entered the cloister as he suggested."

She bit her lip. "You will assist Malcolm with stealth and night training?"

"With the aid of my kin these past months, strategies and techniques have been devised and honed to better enable me to move through my darkness as well as train the sighted to more effectively wield them as weapons—which will be of much use to the Scots if William decides England and Normandy are not enough for him."

"You think he will bring war to us?"

"It is possible, and all the more so for being unable to prevent the Aetheling's sister from one day giving Malcolm children with a claim to England's throne."

Marguerite looked to Guarin and Eberhard who sat easy in their saddles. "Though you shall stand different sides, your family is well with this?"

"It is not ideal, but we hold close that ever we are D'Argents first, whether born under that name or the name of Wulfrith. We cannot know what the ages will make of our descendants who may or may not stay true to our tenets, but by faith we know whom we are now and ought to be, and that we shall remain no matter whom we serve after God and family."

Marguerite leaned up and kissed him. "First Dubh, then the chapel," she said and, taking his arm, led him to the cottage where they would make their home as Diarmad and the first Marguerite had done.

~

MALCOLM HAD INSISTED. Theriot had insisted otherwise. Thus, the nuptial chamber was not in the great tower but the single room set apart from the rest of the cottage where husband and wife could be intimate with little chance of interruption—and certainly none this eve unless Dubh and Liath, who continued to walk wide around each other, determined to challenge the other for the best stretch of floor.

"I believe Dubh will prevail," Theriot said where he stood behind his wife in the doorway, hands on shoulders covered in a chemise gifted her by the queen that, for all its beauty, needed shedding so silk of a different kind was beneath his fingers.

Marguerite peered over her shoulder. "Dubh prides herself on being your first guide."

"And yet she is my third, the Lord my first and you my second."

She laughed softly, then looked back at the hounds on either side of the hearth. "Poor Liath. Faithfully he followed you to Scotland only to be thrice displaced."

"I am sure he will find his place here as I have found mine," Theriot said, then drew her back, closed the door, and led her to the candlelit bed.

There was much he wished to tell her of what passed while they were apart—the months of training so intense he had little time to dwell on her except in the night. Even then, he had not lingered over Marguerite, so exhausted had he been. But that was as he wished since the greater part of him needed to focus on exercises conducted in the training yard, the cellar, the underground passage from castle to wood, and the wood itself. His kin had been relentless, and he was not the only one to benefit.

By challenging and broadening Theriot's boundaries and abilities, training in both day and night stealth were improved and would be passed to those aspiring to knighthood at Wulfen as well as those in Scotland. Whenever conflict between the two countries caused its people to aggress against each other, at least on this front they would be well matched.

Theriot would reveal it to Marguerite as he had done the King of Scots when he, Guarin, and Eberhard gained an audience this morn, but this night was for them alone.

Halting at the foot of the bed, he turned Marguerite into him.

She tipped back her head. "How are we to do this?"

"Slowly. While I look well upon my wife with my hands, learning her every stretch and curve, I would have her look well upon me with both hands and eyes."

"Much I wish to be known and to know you, Theriot." She touched the cloth around his neck. "May I remove this?"

"Only you."

When she surprised by fastening it around her own neck, he brushed his mouth across hers, stepped back, and drew off his undertunic.

"Theriot," she breathed, then closed the space between them and slid her hands over his chest, shoulders, and arms. His heart raced, and pounded when she retreated and her silhouette against candlelight revealed she also cast off her garment. "Now further learn me, Husband, though not too slowly."

He chuckled, lifted her into his arms, and followed her down to the mattress. There was nothing slow about his kiss nor the one she returned, and when she wrapped her arms around him, he moved his lips to her ear.

"Tha gaol agam ort," he rasped the Gaelic profession of love received and given back when they had spoken vows in the presence of the King and Queen of Scots, Cristina, Hendrie, and his kin who would return to England on the morrow.

When once more he moved his mouth to hers, she said, "Is ceol mo chroí thú."

More words he must learn ahead of all others in making his life with her in Scotland. He raised his head, and though her face was denied him, felt her gaze and smile. "Tell me the meaning, beloved."

"You are the music of my heart."

Silently, he thanked the Lord for guiding him back to her, then repeated the words. She corrected his pronunciation, and when she assured him he spoke it well, he said, "You have much to teach me, Theriot's sparrow."

She sighed. "At last, I am that to you."

"At last."

She drew his head down. "Now will you teach me to be your wife in all ways?"

"If you will teach me to be your husband in all ways," he said, then added what Hendrie had translated for him following the wedding, "Mo ghaol."

Marguerite laughed softly. "It is good the night is long, mon amour."

Dear Reader,
Thank you for joining me in the age of castles, knights, ladies, destriers, and deep, dark woods. If you enjoyed the sixth Wulfrith origins tale, I would appreciate a review of BOUNDLESS at your online retailer—just a few sentences, more if you have time.

As for what's next in the AGE OF CONQUEST series... That's the long-awaited tale of Sir Guy who first appeared in LADY OF CONQUEST. Watch for the release of LAWLESS: Book VII in 2021 and enjoy the excerpt that follows.

Wishing you many more hours of inspiring, happily-ever-after reading. ~ Tamara

AUTHOR'S NOTE

Dear Readers,

I hope you enjoyed Sir Theriot and Lady Marguerite's love story as well as a look at the pious Princess Margaret's journey to becoming Queen of Scotland that led to her being canonized as Saint Margaret. What you may not know is that though her brother never regained the crown lost to William, Margaret and Malcolm's daughter—the Aetheling's niece—wed the conqueror's son, Henry I. Thus, in their children flowed not only the blood of Normans but Saxons, returning the latter to the English monarchy. The daughter of Henry I and Matilda of Scotland was the mother of Henry II, the king who often appears in my Age of Faith series. And so you see, the world keeps turning—or perhaps it's better said, *circling back.*

LAWLESS EXCERPT

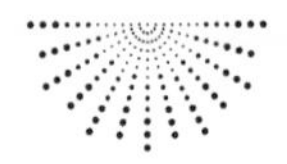

THE WULFRITHS. IT ALL BEGAN WITH A WOMAN

From USA Today Bestselling author Tamara Leigh, the seventh book in a new series set in the 11th century during the Norman Conquest of England, revealing the origins of the Wulfrith family of the AGE OF FAITH series. Releasing 2021.

PROLOGUE

The Fenlands, England
Late Spring, 1071

Could she stick a blade in a man? This time do what she had failed to do four years past? This time be the one who did not hesitate to take life? This time *not* be the one responsible for the death of a loved one?

Holding a whimper behind her lips, one hand convulsing on the dagger at her hip, the other gripping the rail of the boat alongside which she knelt in the mud, Vilda peered across the fairly level ground at the northernmost camp whose position remained known only by the glow of the Norman invaders' warming fires—as it ought not.

Though under attack, the bursts of fires all sides of the camp had yet to be seen and, she feared, were not forthcoming. More frightening, the foray was not to have lasted this long. As with most night raids, this one's goal was to harass the enemy by slipping past their patrol and putting down those who caught sight of rebels who excelled at playing ghosts, setting alight supplies, and disrupting the sleep of warriors already disheartened by the inhospitable fens.

But most frightening of all was that the defenders' shouts and cries she had been told to expect were punctuated by the clash of blades which evidenced some of the voices belonged to rebels who should be here now, putting oars in the water and sending the flat-bottomed boat gliding back across the river toward their refuge, the Isle of Ely.

Hand quaking on her dagger, Vilda beseeched the Lord to give strength and discernment to her countrymen, ensuring once more they prevailed over the forces of he who had crowned himself King of England—William the Conqueror, more aptly known to the conquered as *Le Bâtard.*

Whether or not in answer to prayer, there was a shift in the clash between Saxons and Normans. Though shouts continued to sweep across the night to where she shivered in water lapping at her waist, no longer were they accompanied by the clang of steel on steel.

Holding her breath, she searched for figures moving in her direction, which would have been more easily seen had her cousin and his men succeeded in setting their fires.

They had escaped the confrontation, she assured herself. Though likely some were injured, making it more difficult to negotiate the dark at a speed that allowed them to evade pursuers, they came toward her. Or did they?

In their desperation to escape, they might go wide of where they had disembarked, but if she—

Nay, you were given one task only—to stay with the boat, she reminded herself. *And you promised.*

"Pray, Hereward," she rasped, "come."

As she continued to watch for movement, wondering if as many minutes passed as it felt, once again she was tempted to leave the boat. She would go no farther than onto the bank where better she could see anyone moving toward the river and, if needed, alert them to her position.

Removing her hand from the dagger, she touched the mud her cousin had smeared on her face to hide the pale lest it catch an enemy eye—the same he and his men had done before the boat carried them from Ely—and discovered what had dried and made her skin itch had begun to crack and peel.

Having accompanied Hereward and his men to the dock where the youth who was to remain with the boat began coughing, Vilda had offered to go in his place lest his malady reveal the presence of rebels to those on vessels blockading the isle or patrolling the shore before which the Normans encamped. To avoid the delay of sending for another youth, which could have jeopardized the foray whose timing was imperative, her cousin had agreed.

"And you promised to do as told," she whispered even as she pushed the bow deeper into the mud to anchor the boat. Continuing to hold to the rail to leverage out of sludge sucking at her knees, she moved her bent legs up the bank and onto grass her weight flattened.

As she reached for more mud to ensure the pale of her face remained hidden, above the distant sound of angry Normans in disarray she heard movement—that of men running through grass slapping at legs and soft soil squelching beneath boots. Hopefully, they were the rebels, though likely some of the enemy came behind.

Frantically, Vilda searched the land. There—farther left than they ought to be—men moved at a good pace though not as rapidly as they would were they uninjured. Since they made for the shore, they had to be those she awaited.

"Lord, let them be my own," she breathed. Then lest seconds prove the difference between escape and capture, she determined it was more important she was seen than not, even if by pursuing Normans.

Lurching to her feet, hearing the skirts tied up around her thighs suck at water as they emerged, she dragged an arm across her face to expose more of the pale, thrust arms high, and waved.

If she must, she would add her voice to alerting the rebels to the need to alter their course. Blessedly, almost immediately they veered toward her. Eight, she counted. Only eight, meaning five had fallen to the enemy.

Nay, three, two others following at a distance—unless they were Normans.

She waved more vigorously, and when the rebels were near enough she was certain the stout one at the fore was her cousin, she swung around and thrust her weight against the boat's bow to get the craft off the mud. When it floated free, she sprang over the side, swept up a pole, and jabbed it down through the water into the mud to steady the boat for boarding.

Moments later, Hereward was there. Though the night was dim with little moon and his tunic dark of color, she knew he wore blood, hopefully the enemy's alone.

Sparing her no word, he thrust his sword in its scabbard, then splashed into the water, took hold of the boat to further steady it, and commanded the others aboard. As they clambered over both sides to prevent the vessel from capsizing, Vilda knew from their movements, groans, and curses which among them wore their own blood—and felt that stickiness across the back of a hand when one took the pole from her and told her to get low.

"Almighty, he is down!" Hereward snarled as she started to hunker between two benches, then he sprang onto the bank and ran to the man who had dropped to his hands and knees. But those figures bringing up the rear whom Vilda had hoped were two of the five missing rebels were not. As they drew dangerously near, she could hear the ring and rustle of chain mail and see bits of light glance off it.

Straightening, she stepped over a bench to the bow. When she saw the Norman running ahead of the other was too near for her cousin to heft his man onto his shoulder and get him to the boat before he arrived, she cried, "They come, Hereward!"

He turned from his injured comrade, once more brought his sword to hand, and ran forward.

"Non, Jacques!" shouted the Norman at the rear. "To me!"

But the one nearest Hereward, whom she guessed a very young man when his shout cracked as did those voices which had yet to attain the full breadth of a man's register, kept coming.

"To me, Jacques!" the command came again, and when Vilda looked the direction of the warrior whose accent was not as thick as some but voice deeper than most, she glimpsed more Normans beyond him. The only good of it was the latter were distant enough it was possible Hereward could put down both enemies here and be well off shore before the others arrived.

The young man gave another cracked battle cry, then swung his blade in an attempt to take her cousin's sword arm.

It did not surprise when Hereward evaded the attack by ducking, pivoting, and sweeping up his own blade, but still Vilda feared for him—and more so when he was the one to land a blow to that limb which meant all to a warrior. Though his victory caused Jacques to lose hold of his sword and grip his bleeding arm as he toppled onto his side, it gave her cousin little time to defend against the second Norman.

Pray, not too little, Lord, she silently pleaded as she looked between Hereward and the one who would surely prove formidable, being a man of good height and breadth and moving with ease despite the weight of much chain mail that evidenced the rigor and discipline to which he subjected his body.

When Hereward did not run at that warrior, she knew it was not for lack of courage. He wished to engage him at swords—to beat out frustration, anger, and hatred on yet another Norman—but he had to know if he did not soon get his injured comrade aboard, he would be overwhelmed by more of the enemy. And those who would not leave without him, including Vilda, would be captured as well.

Wrenching his injured opponent upright, her cousin hooked a tattooed arm around the neck of one who convulsed with silent tears as he cradled his sliced limb, then Hereward set his blade across the young man's abdomen. As surely hoped, the second Norman ceased his advance.

"What remains of me and mine are leaving here as whole as possible," her cousin announced in Norman-French to the one who faced him with one leg behind in preparation to push off it and sword drawn back the sooner to thrust it forward. "If you and this lad wish to do the same rather than be granted a warrior's death, you will take this Jacques before his arm bleeds out and innards spill, and I will take my man and go back to my isle."

The Norman whose mail hood was down around his neck, revealing enough of his face Vilda could see he was lightly bearded, glanced behind—to gauge how soon his fellow Normans would arrive, she thought as she glimpsed in profile dark hair upon a broad brow, a boldly straight nose, and a firm chin.

Following his gaze, she saw the other Normans would not arrive as soon as they would if the slam of blades yet guided them here.

Silently, she thanked the Lord. Though still the enemy headed this direction and they looked to be a half dozen, they were as far left as the rebels had been before she showed herself.

"You trust me to honor such a bargain?" the chevalier asked, not in Norman-French but the language of the Saxons, his accented tongue across her words and depth of his voice increasing the shivers coursing her head to toe.

Reverting to his own language, Hereward said, "As I know you to be one who is not as Norman as your countrymen, I trust you as much as it is possible to trust an enemy." He shifted sideways to cast more of the miserly light on the blade against the young man's abdomen that required a single slice to see yet another conqueror buried in the fens, though likely it would see these Saxons interred here as well. "Now ere I do what cannot be undone, decide if you wish to save your squire, Sir Guy Torquay."

Vilda startled. She knew his name for the necessity of avoiding the elite force he commanded. Though they numbered fewer than other forces, making their small camp seemingly the most vulnerable, that had been disproved several times to the detriment of rebels who slipped in to take lives and wreak havoc but could not slip out—at least without having something with which to bargain.

Torquay did not sacrifice his men, even if he must trade several rebels for the life of one Norman. Thus, Hereward was counting on him to value a lowly, foolish squire above the leader of the resistance and his men—and cousin, though that last Torquay could not know even had Vilda removed all the mud and there was adequate light to look well upon her where she leaned forward in the bow, one hand on the rail, the other gripping her dagger. And for a moment, she thought it possible he did look upon her, though likely it was the others toward whom he turned his face, those yet whole of body having drawn blades the same as she to let them fly were they provoked.

"Release Jacques and take your injured," the chevalier said, though his stance and sword remained at the ready. "And be quick about it, Hereward."

Hardly was that last spoken than the squire was thrust forward, staggered sideways, and fell to his knees before his lord.

"Does the Norman not turn deceitful, leave him be!" Hereward commanded his men, then hefted onto his shoulder the slack rebel who, God willing, had only lost consciousness.

He did not will it, as told by her cousin after passing the rebel to two of his men and heaving himself into the boat. "He is gone from us," he rumbled, causing Vilda to falter as she moved forward to give aid. "As soon as he was on my shoulder, I knew him for dead. Now pass me those oars."

Having turned from the bow which poles had pried from the mud, Vilda stared at the one laid between two benches. She knew him as she knew all the men here—and his kindness. He was ten years older than she and protective when men showed her attention ever unwelcome when it crossed the line between civility and flirtation. Had he intervened in hopes of gaining her attention for himself, it had never been obvious. Now he was dead like so many others these five years.

Do not yield to hatred, Vilda told herself. *Cover him, take his hand, and sit beside him as he passes over waters last traversed while yet he breathed.*

She resisted a moment longer, then turned back into the bow that shuddered as the boat moved through dense reeds that, though easier to negotiate than mud, could still prove their undoing.

Torquay had his squire in his arms, and as he turned toward the Normans nearly upon him, she threw her dagger. Anger made her do it despite awareness there was now too much distance between them for her to make her mark. Or perhaps that was why she did it—to prove to herself she could, indeed, stick a blade in a man, even if it was all a lie.

"Norman pig! Unworthy of Saxon slop!" she cried and nearly laughed bitterly at the realization how much *she* looked like a swine given to wallowing.

The chevalier had stilled, and though she caught the glitter of his eyes, she more felt than saw his gaze upon her.

She raised her chin. "Knave! Thief! Miscrea—!"

"Get here, V!" Hereward shouted. "Now!"

She did not want to get there. She wanted to berate Torquay over and again, but as night and the ever-widening water choked him down along with fellow Normans come to assist, she gave him her back.

Moments later, she dropped onto the bench facing her cousin. "I know. I do." She swallowed a lump in her throat. "I should not have broken my word." Another lump needed swallowing. "Forgive me, but I could not simply watch when I saw you and the others veering away. I had to…" A sob escaped, then she heard the oars he released thump the rings through which they were threaded and felt his hands on her shoulders.

"I thank you for breaking your word," he said gruffly, "but never again disobey me."

"I will try not to."

"V!"

She popped up her chin. "I can only try. Until the moment is upon us that is not as certain nor safe as the moment in which we agree to do one thing and not another, that is all we can do —try."

Unlike the eyes of Sir Guy, she could see enough of Hereward's to be certain he glared, but then he sighed heavily. "We must get past the blockade, which will not be easy with those on the nearest boats surely aware ill has befallen their fellow Normans. But once we are safely through, we shall put this night behind us so it is done and stays done."

His words not meant for her alone, he was heard by all. However, she was the only one to respond. "'Tis done," she said and hoped it was so.

But the night's ordeal was not done. Though they made it through the blockade, more ill befell them before reaching Ely, and this time it came from the enemy this side rather than the other side—several of the weary, desperate survivors who lost six of their friends proclaiming their cause hopeless and predicting soon Le Bâtard would sweep the rest of them off the playing board made of England.

Hereward was not of a mood.

Dear Reader,
I hope you enjoyed this excerpt of LAWLESS: Book Seven in the Age of Conquest series. *Watch for its release in 2021.*

For new releases and special promotions, subscribe to Tamara Leigh's mailing list: www.TamaraLeigh.com

AGE OF CONQUEST PRONUNCIATION GUIDE

Abelard: AA-buh-lahrd
Aelfled/Aelf: AYL-flehd
Aethelflaed: EH-thul-flehd
Aetheling: AA-thuh-leeng
Aiken: AY-kihn
Alditha: AHL-dee-thuh
Alfrith: AAL-frihth
Alvilda: ahl-VEEL-duh
Ardith: AHR-dihth
Asbjorn: AHS-bee-yohrn
Asketil: AAS-kuh-tihl
Balliol: BAY-lee-uhl
Bayard: BAY-ahr
Bernia: BUHR-nee-uh
Bjorn: BEE-yohrn
Boudica: BOO-dih-kuh
Boursier: BUUR-see-ay
Campagnon: KAHM-paan-yah
Canute: Kuh-NOOT
Chanson: SHAHN-sahn
Ciel: SEE-ehl
Colban: KOHL-buhn
Cyr: SEE-uhr
D'Argent: DAR-zhahnt
Daryl: DAA-rihl
Diarmad: DIHR-maad
Dougray: DOO-gray
Dubh: DOOV
Dunfermline: duhn-FUHRM-luhn
Ebbe: EH-buh
Eberhard: EH-buh-hahrt

Edelwine: EH-duhl-wihn
Ely: EE-lee
Em: EHM
Emma: EHM-uh
Estienne: EHs-tee-ihn
Fortier: FOHR-tee-ay
Fulbert: FOO-behr
Gerald: JEHR-uhld
Gloucester: GLAH-stuhr
Gloucestershire: GLAH-stuhr-shuhr
Godfroi: GAWD-frwah
Godwine: GAHD-wihn
Gospatric: GAHS-paa-trihk
Grandmesnil: GRAHN-may-neel
Guarin: GAA-rahn
Guy: Gee
Gwain: GWAYN
Gytha: JIY-thuh
Hawisa/Isa: HAH-wee-suh/EE-suh
Hendrie: HEHN-dree
Hereward: HEHR-uh-wuhrd
Hugh: HYOO
Ingvar: EENG-Vah
Is ceol mo chroí thú: Ihs kyohl muh kree hoo (you are the music of my heart)
Jaxon: JAAK-suhn
Lavonne: LUH-vahn
Leicestershire: LEH-stuhr-shuur
Liath: LEE-uh
Maël: MAY-luh
Maerleswein: MAYRL-swiyn
Marguerite: MAH-guh-reet
Mary Sarah: MAA-ree-SAA-ruh
Mercia: MUHR-see-uh

Merle: MUHRL-uh
Michel: MEE-shehl
Mo ghaol: muh gihl (my love)
Mo shíorghrá: muh HEER-grah (my eternal love)
Nicola: NEE-koh-luh
Ordric: OHR-drihk
Pepin: PEH-pihn
Pierre: PEE-ehr
Ravven: RAY-vihn
Raymond: RAY-mohnd
Richard: REE-shahrd
Rixende: RIHKS-ahnd
Robine: rah-BEEN
Roche: ROHSH
Roger: ROH-zheh
Sévère: SAY-vehr
Séverine: SAY-vuh-reen
Sigward: SEEG-wuhrd
Stephen: STAY-fahn
Stigand: STIY-guhnd
Sweyn: SVIHN
Tá mo chroí istigh ionat: Tah muh kree ihsh-tihg uhn aat (my heart is in you)
Tha gaol agam ort: Haa gihl ah kuhm ohrsht (I love you)
Theriot: TEH-ree-oh
Torquay: tohr-KEE
Turold: TOO-rohld
Vilda: VEEL-duh
Vitalis: VEE-tah-lihsWarenne: WOHR-ihn
Wulf: WUULF
Wulfrith: WUUL-frihth
Wynflaed: WIHN-flehd
Zedekiah: ZEH-duh-KIY-uh

PRONUNCIATION KEY

VOWELS

aa: arrow, castle
ay: chain, lady
ah: fought, sod
aw: flaw, paw
eh: bet, leg
ee: king, league
ih: hilt, missive
iy: knight, write
oh: coat, noble
oi: boy, coin
oo: fool, rule
ow: cow, brown
uh: sun, up
uu: book, hood
y: yearn, yield

CONSONANTS

b: bailey, club
ch: charge, trencher
d: dagger, hard
f: first, staff
g: gauntlet, stag
h: heart, hilt
j: jest, siege
k: coffer, pike
l: lance, vassal
m: moat, pommel
n: noble, postern
ng: ring, song
p: pike, lip
r: rain, far

s: spur, pass
sh: chivalry, shield
t: tame, moat
th: thistle, death
t~h: that, feather
v: vassal, missive
w: water, wife
wh: where, whisper
z: zip, haze
zh: treasure, vision

AGE OF CONQUEST GLOSSARY

ANDREDESWALD: forest that covered areas of Sussex and Surrey in England
ANGLO-SAXON: people of the Angles (Denmark) and Saxons (northern Germany) of which the population of 11th century England was mostly comprised
BLIAUT: medieval gown
BRAIES: men's underwear
CASTELLAN: commander of a castle
CHAUSSES: men's close-fitting leg coverings
CHEMISE: loose-fitting undergarment or nightdress
CHEVALIER: a knight of France
COIF: hood-shaped cap made of cloth or chain mail
DEMESNE: home and adjoining lands held by a lord
DONJON: tower at center of a castle serving as a lord's living area
DOTTER: meaning "daughter"; attached to a woman's name to identify her by whose daughter she is
EMBRASURE: opening in a wall often used by archers
FEALTY: tenant or vassal's sworn loyalty to a lord
FORTNIGHT: two weeks
FREE MAN: person not a slave or serf
GARDEROBE: enclosed toilet
GIRDLE: belt worn upon which purses or weaponry might be attached
HILT: grip or handle of a sword or dagger
HOUSECARLE: elite warrior who was a lord's personal bodyguard
KNAVE: dishonest or unprincipled man
LEAGUE: equivalent to approximately three miles
LIEGE: superior or lord

MAIL: garments of armor made of linked metal rings
MISCREANT: badly behaving person
MISSIVE: letter
MOAT: defensive ditch, dry or filled with water
MORROW: tomorrow; the next day
MOTTE: mound of earth
NITHING: derogatory term for someone without honor
NOBLE: one of high birth
NORMAN: people whose origins lay in Normandy on the continent
NORMANDY: principality of northern France founded in the early tenth century by the viking Rollo
PARCHMENT: treated animal skin used for writing
PELL: used for combat training, a vertical post set in the ground against which a sword was beat
PIKE: long wooden shaft with a sharp steel or iron head
POLTROON: utter coward
POMMEL: counterbalance weight at the end of a sword hilt or a knob located at the fore of a saddle
PORTCULLIS: metal or wood gate lowered to block a passage
POSTERN GATE: rear door in a wall, often concealed to allow occupants to arrive and depart inconspicuously
QUINTAIN: post used for lance training to which a dummy and sandbag are attached; the latter swings around and hits the unsuccessful tilter
SALLY PORT: small hidden entrance and exit in a fortification
SAXON: Germanic people, many of whom conquered and settled in England in the 5th and 6th centuries
SENNIGHT: one week
SHIRE: division of land; England was divided into earldoms, next shires, then hundreds
THANE: in Anglo-Saxon England, a member of the nobility or landed aristocracy who owed military and administrative duty

to an overlord, above all the king; owned at least five hides of land

TRENCHER: large piece of stale bread used as a bowl for food

VASSAL: one who holds land from a lord and owes fealty

ALSO BY TAMARA LEIGH

AVAILABLE IN EBOOK, PAPERBACK, AND AUDIOBOOK

~

INSPIRATIONAL HISTORICAL ROMANCE

AGE OF FAITH: A Medieval Romance Series

The Unveiling: Book One

The Yielding: Book Two

The Redeeming: Book Three

The Kindling: Book Four

The Longing: Book Five

The Vexing: Book Six

The Awakening: Book Seven

The Raveling: Book Eight

AGE OF CONQUEST: A Medieval Romance Series

Merciless: Book One

Fearless: Book Two

Nameless: Book Three

Heartless: Book Four

Reckless: Book Five

Boundless: Book Six

Lawless: Book Seven (Spring 2021)

Dauntless: Book Eight (Autumn 2021)

~

CLEAN READ HISTORICAL ROMANCE

THE FEUD: A Medieval Romance Series

Baron Of Godsmere: Book One

Baron Of Emberly: Book Two

Baron of Blackwood: Book Three

LADY: A Medieval Romance Series

Lady At Arms: Book One

Lady Of Eve: Book Two

BEYOND TIME: A Medieval Time Travel Romance Series

Dreamspell: Book One

Lady Ever After: Book Two

STAND-ALONE Medieval Romance Novels

Lady Of Fire

Lady Of Conquest

Lady Undaunted

Lady Betrayed

INSPIRATIONAL CONTEMPORARY ROMANCE

HEAD OVER HEELS: Stand-Alone Romance Collection

Stealing Adda

Perfecting Kate

Splitting Harriet

Faking Grace

SOUTHERN DISCOMFORT: A Contemporary Romance Series

Leaving Carolina: Book One

Nowhere, Carolina: Book Two

Restless in Carolina: Book Three

OUT-OF-PRINT GENERAL MARKET REWRITES

Warrior Bride 1994: Bantam Books (Lady At Arms)

*****Virgin Bride*** 1994: Bantam Books (Lady Of Eve)

Pagan Bride 1995: Bantam Books (Lady Of Fire)

Saxon Bride 1995: Bantam Books (Lady Of Conquest)

Misbegotten 1996: HarperCollins (Lady Undaunted)

Unforgotten 1997: HarperCollins (Lady Ever After)

Blackheart 2001: Dorchester Leisure (Lady Betrayed)

For new releases and special promotions, subscribe to Tamara Leigh's mailing list: www.TamaraLeigh.com

ABOUT THE AUTHOR

Tamara Leigh signed a 4-book contract with Bantam Books in 1993, her debut medieval romance was nominated for a RITA award, and successive books with Bantam, HarperCollins, and Dorchester earned awards and appeared on national bestseller lists.

In 2006, the first of Tamara's inspirational contemporary romances was published, followed by six more with Multnomah and RandomHouse. Perfecting Kate was optioned for a movie, Splitting Harriet won an ACFW Book of the Year award, and Faking Grace was nominated for a RITA award.

In 2012, Tamara returned to the historical romance genre with the release of Dreamspell and the bestselling Age of Faith and The Feud series. Among her #1 bestsellers are her general market romances rewritten as clean and inspirational reads, including Lady at Arms and Lady of Conquest. In late 2018, she released Merciless, the first book in the new AGE OF CONQUEST series, followed by Fearless, Nameless, Heartless, Reckless, and Boundless unveiling the origins of the Wulfrith family. Psst!—It all began with a woman. Watch for the seventh book in Spring 2021.

Tamara lives near Nashville with her husband, a German Shepherd who has never met a squeaky toy she can't destroy, and a feisty Morkie who keeps her company during long writing stints.

Connect with Tamara at her website www.tamaraleigh.com, Facebook, Twitter and tamaraleightenn@gmail.com.

For new releases and special promotions, subscribe to Tamara Leigh's mailing list: www.tamaraleigh.com

Made in the USA
Columbia, SC
19 January 2021

31255212R00248